Lying

Lying

wendy perriam

Peter Owen
London

PETER OWEN PUBLISHERS
73 Kenway Road, London SW5 0RE

Peter Owen books are distributed in the USA by Dufour Editions Inc.,
Chester Springs, PA 19425-0007

First published in Great Britain 2000
© Wendy Perriam 2000
Paperback edition 2001

ISBN 0 7206 1128 8

A catalogue record for this book is available from the British Library.

Printed in Great Britain by MPG Books Ltd, Bodmin, Cornwall

For Pauline Maria – Grandma's miracle!

All we have gained then by our unbelief
Is a life of doubt diversified by faith
For one of faith diversified by doubt:
We called the chess-board white – we call it black.
              – Robert Browning, 'Bishop Blougram's Apology'

If, like truth, the lie had but one face, we would be on better terms. For we would accept as certain the opposite of what the liar would say. But the reverse of truth has a hundred thousand faces and an infinite field.
              – Montaigne, *Essays*

I

1

'Alison! Where the hell have you got to?'

Alison put her head round the door of the office kitchen, where she'd been making her first coffee of the day. It was already half past two, but Christine disliked her 'wasting time'.

'I need you. Now. This instant.' Christine marched into her office, her face like granite, her long grey mackintosh dripping dark stains on the carpet.

Alison followed a pace behind. She had hoped her boss would be in a more mellow frame of mind after lunch with an old friend and fellow editor.

'That bastard Leo Marsh!' Christine wrenched off her mac, all but spitting out the words. 'I've just discovered he's auctioning a first novel by some young Brazilian prodigy and seems to have punted it out to everyone except us. He sent it to Vanessa a *fortnight* ago and she's putting in a big offer. Apparently he's already turned down a pre-emptive bid of a hundred and fifty thousand. Which means half of London's talking about a book I haven't even seen. So much for his promises of keeping us in the frame . . . Anyway, I rang him there and then, before we started lunch. And do you know what he had the nerve to say?' She tossed her mac on to the already precarious piles of manuscripts which took up half the floor space. 'That he didn't think I'd be interested. It wasn't my sort of thing. Meaning I'm too old to appreciate a love story written by a kid who's barely out of nappies.'

'Oh, I'm sure that's not what –'

'I told him I wanted it biked round straight away. The auction's on Monday, so I'll have the weekend to read it – or what's left of the weekend by the time I've traipsed over to Bromley to see my bloody mother. She's had another fall, would you believe.'

'I'm . . . sorry.' Alison hovered between the door and her desk, which was stationed just outside Christine's office in a sort of glorified cubby-hole. 'How is she?'

'As well as she'll ever be. Now, listen – get on to the post room and ask them to phone you the minute that manuscript arrives. It may even be there already if Leo's got his act together.'

'Yes, of course. I'll –'

'Are my letters done?'

Alison nodded. 'I put them on your desk with the messages. The phone's been ringing non-stop.'

Christine snatched the top sheet off one of the piles of papers and scanned it with a frown. 'And get the manuscript copied, will you?' she called. She rarely used the intercom since Alison was conveniently within shouting distance; both of them cut off from the hubbub of the main open-plan office. 'Well, jump to it! What are you waiting for?'

'Actually, I was wondering if I could nip out for a bite to eat, now you're back yourself?'

'I suppose so,' Christine said grudgingly. 'But don't be long. And find out about that manuscript first.'

As she dialled the post room, she could see Christine through the glass partition: pink spots of indignation coloured her usually pale cheeks as she sat at her desk, flicking through the letters and taking long drags on the inevitable cigarette.

'No luck yet, I'm afraid,' Alison reported via the intercom.

'Well, get off for your lunch then, but make it sharp. I want you back in half an hour.'

From the shelter of the portico Alison watched the rain pummelling down remorselessly, bouncing off cars and umbrellas alike. Turning up the collar of her jacket, she ventured out, giving her customary nod of acknowledgement to the brass plaque on the wall: Shaw Hilliard, Publishers. She had made it into publishing – and as PA to the editorial director, no less. Admittedly, typist and general dogsbody would be a more accurate description, and the editorial director in question would never be voted an award for charm. None the less, it was a definite advance on this time last year, when she'd been stuck at home playing husband to her mother and temping in a dreary council office. And she had worked out a career plan, with goals and dates to achieve them. All it needed was determination – and patience.

To escape the downpour she made straight for the covered market-place, where there were cafés in profusion. She never ceased to marvel at the quantity of eating places in London – hundreds in Covent Garden alone – and the range of foods they served. The sole culinary offering of their one shabby village pub at home was meat pies of dubious origin.

Today it would have to be a sandwich, and eaten on the hoof. Christine was a stickler for time and, given today's events, it would be unwise to be back even a couple of minutes late. But at least she had this brief respite from the hassle.

A sudden burst of applause drew her to a crowd of people in the centre of the covered square. Squeezing her way to the front, she saw a string quartet taking their bows – a bizarrely unconventional bunch: two men and two women, all about her age and dressed in clothes so badly creased they looked as if they'd been slept in. One of the players sported hair striped black and silver; another had a shaven head, while the cellist's hands were stained with rust-coloured paint.

Responding to the cries of 'Encore!' they launched into another piece, the female violinist laying aside her instrument and stepping forward to sing. Her scrawny frame (accentuated by ragged jeans which revealed patches of bare flesh) belied the strength and beauty of her voice. '*Softly awakes my heart . . .*' she sang, to an accompaniment of throbbing chords from the other three musicians.

Alison closed her eyes and let the melody pour over her like a stream of warm, dark, liquid chocolate.

> '*But say, O well-beloved,*
> *No more I'll be forsaken . . .*'

The girl was *living* the song; conjuring her unseen lover into existence through the very passion of the words. Such passion could be dangerous, Alison knew. She had experienced it as a child. Not for lovers, obviously; not for anything in particular – just shellbursts of emotion seizing her at unguarded moments, perhaps when she was dawdling along a country lane or staring out of the window at the trees. She had longed to share the feelings, but with whom? Her parents were so drably practical; her friends preoccupied with pocket money or Barbie dolls. She had learned early to dissemble, to acquiesce – outwardly, at least – to life's dull round of school, and homework, and shopping trips, and roast and two veg on Sundays. But now this girl's voluptuous voice was reawakening memories

13

of heights and depths she had no words to explain but which left her both unsettled and inspired.

The last note died away, followed by a few moments' silence before the audience again erupted into applause, showering coins into the open violin-case on the ground. Alison took a fiver from her purse – tribute to the potency of the music, which had swept her from the mundane to the sublime. Never mind that funds were low; an ice-cream would do for lunch. And in fact she still derived a certain satisfaction from defying her mother's strictures about 'sitting down to proper meals'. However, as her parents were a hundred miles away, there was no fear of comment on her choice of food and no warnings about the perils of dirty, dangerous London. For her, London meant the freedom to be whatever you chose – a paint-stained cellist; a virtuoso singer with her clothes in holes and a butterfly tattoo on her left wrist.

Emerging from the covered market into Covent Garden Piazza, she was surprised to see the rain had stopped. There were even glints of gold in the sky, as if the music had worked its magic on the weather, although it was still bitterly cold for mid-March.

She bought a strawberry cornet and wandered round the stalls, which sold everything from antique jewellery to herbal pills and potions. Whatever the season or the time of day, the market was always pulsing with life: portrait-painters and tarot-card readers vying with jugglers and guitarists to extract money from the crowds. A cascade of feather boas caught her eye. She tried on a brilliant purple one, then added more – scarlet, emerald, pink.

'They look great together!' The woman behind the stall handed her a mirror.

Yes, she thought, the different shades did clash rather deliciously and emphasized the darkness of her hair. Gorgeous, Jim called it, but then Jim was probably biased. True, it was her best feature – almost long enough to sit on and worth a mint, her father said, if she were to use her nous and sell it – but she tended to be more conscious of her deficiencies. She wasn't thin enough, for one thing, nor tall enough, and her eyebrows were a trial, in need of constant plucking.

Reluctantly she unwound the boas from her neck and put them back on the stall. Time to return to work.

In the foyer of Shaw Hilliard she glanced up at the clock – still five minutes in hand. She took the stairs two at a time, singing the odd phrase from 'Softly Awakes My Heart': '*Ah! Once again, do I implore thee . . . something, something, something . . . say you adore me . . .*'

'Alison! About time too,' Christine barked from her office. 'I'm still waiting for that damned manuscript. Ring Leo, will you, and check the courier's actually left. His secretary's quite useless. And make sure she's sent the right book. It's called *Lying* and it's by Francesca de Romero. The author's name should help – it sounds suitably exotic. Although I'm not sure I like the title.'

'*Lying*. Mm. I suppose it depends on –'

'And take my calls. I don't want to speak to anyone. I've got that report to finish. Say I've gone to Siberia. Say anything you like, as long as you get rid of them.' Christine disappeared into her office and slammed the door.

'*Jawohl, mein Führer,*' Alison muttered, picking up the phone.

Leo Marsh's secretary sounded anything but useless, although she did admit there was a delay with the courier. 'I've been trying to get a bike for the last hour – you know what it's like on a wet Friday afternoon. But they have promised me one in ten or fifteen minutes. I'll call you as soon as it's left.'

'Thanks,' said Alison sympathetically. The poor woman was probably as harassed as *she* was. It wasn't easy standing up to an overbearing boss. Many a time she was tempted to tell Christine that she hadn't gone into publishing to type letters all day and be shouted at, but invariably she bit back the retorts. *One* day, though, she'd . . .

Suddenly the phone rang. The bike, she prayed, on its way. 'Hello? Who? . . . Oh – Glyn . . .' Addressing a world-famous author by his Christian name seemed something of a cheek, but Glyn had insisted from the start and his notorious Welsh charm would brook no opposition. 'How are you?' she asked, despising the flirtatious note which had crept into her voice.

'I'm angry, Alison. Bloody angry.'

Oh no, she thought, not another one.

'Put me through to Christine.'

'I'm sorry, Glyn, she's, er, in a meeting.'

'Well, get her out of it.'

'I . . . I'm afraid the meeting isn't here, Glyn. It's in . . . Knightsbridge.'

'Shit! When d'you expect her back?'

'I'm not sure.'

'Well, you should be sure. Doesn't she *tell* you what her movements are? You publishing lot are incredibly inefficient.'

'She, er, probably won't be long.'

'She'd better not be! I've a few choice words to say to her about that moron of an editor who's mangled my book. The proof's just come back littered with idiotic corrections. I mean, "nigger" crossed out every time. This is nineteenth-century Tennessee we're talking about, not 1990s New York. The woman should be flayed alive – she's utterly devoid of historical sense. It's political correctness gone mad. Why Christine insists on using these witless freelances I simply can't imagine. And you can tell her from me that if she doesn't sort this mess out by the end of today I intend to find another publisher.'

'Wait, Glyn, I . . . I think I can hear her now.' Frantically she pressed the intercom. 'Christine, it's –'

'I've *told* you, Alison, I don't want to be disturbed.'

'I know, but it's Glyn Griffiths. He's going berserk, threatening to find another publisher and –'

'Put him through.'

The partition was thin and she could hear Christine's voice – ingratiating, deferential. And with reason. Glyn Griffiths was the biggest author on her list. His books sold by the million, and his recent historical trilogy had proved such a runaway success he had abandoned Wales to live as a tax exile in Jersey. If he did carry out his threat to leave Shaw Hilliard it was quite possible that Christine would be sacked. Yet it wasn't really her fault; as editorial director she hadn't time to edit every book herself and was forced to rely on freelances, whatever Glyn might think about the system. And she could never be accused of slacking: she was the first in the office every morning and often the last to leave at night. She held her back ramrod-straight and her lips were set in a thin line, as if she were permanently on the defensive. Alison felt sorry for her in some ways. Certainly she was saddled with a difficult mother – one of the few things they had in common, although Christine's mother was eighty, whereas hers was only forty-five: the same age as Christine herself.

Emerging from her office, Christine looked thoroughly defeated. Her hair hung limp and straight and her calf-length skirt (the colour of cold gravy) emphasized the gauntness of her hips. 'That's my weekend down the drain. I've got to go to Jersey tonight. Book me a ticket, will you? The last plane's at seven thirty.'

'Yes, certainly. Returning tomorrow?'

'No, Sunday. Glyn insists on going over the entire manuscript, and he reckons it'll take the whole weekend. That's bullshit, frankly, but I'm in no position to argue.' Christine lit a cigarette and flung the match in the waste bin. 'Bloody Anne-Marie! I told her a hundred times to *check* the freelance's work. Christ, she's in for an earful when she gets back on Monday morning! If she'd concentrated on her job instead of her bloody trip to Venice this fiasco would never have happened.' Christine snorted out a plume of smoke. 'By the way, has that manuscript arrived yet? I'll have to read it on the plane.'

Alison phoned Leo's secretary again, who said the bike had just set off and should be with them by five at the latest – well before Christine needed to leave, thank God. 'What about overnight stuff?' she asked. 'Have you time to go home and pack anything?'

'No, not a hope. Well,' – Christine shrugged – 'if Glyn expects me to rush off at a moment's notice, he can damn well lend me a toothbrush.'

'Would you like me to go out and buy you one? And a T-shirt or something, to sleep in?'

'Alison, you're a miracle! I really would appreciate it. And some aspirin, too. I've got a shit-awful headache.'

The shopping trip took longer than Alison intended, and by the time she got back to the office at two minutes to five the Friday exodus was already under way.

'No sign of the manuscript yet?' she asked Christine as she handed over the Jersey survival pack. She had hoped to get away at five and have time for a nice long soak before dinner with Jim.

'Fat chance! I should have sent a bike from *this* end. In fact I'm beginning to wonder if Leo isn't doing this on purpose. After all, he said the book wasn't right for me . . .'

'But his secretary told me distinctly the bike had left.'

17

'Well, go down to the post room and have a look, will you? I wouldn't be surprised if they've all buggered off and left the damned thing sitting there till Monday.'

Alison came back empty-handed, which entailed yet another phone-call to Mitchell Marsh Associates. Leo's secretary was beginning to sound tetchy.

'All I can say is the bike set off over an hour ago. I'm sorry, there's nothing else I can do.'

Alison glanced at her watch. Five twenty. There wouldn't be time to get the manuscript copied, even if by some miracle there was anyone left in the copying department. Tension curdled the air like the smoke from Christine's cigarettes – she had been chain-smoking all afternoon and was now frantically trying to finish her work between placatory phone-calls to her mother.

At five thirty-five she thrust the signed letters into Alison's hand. 'It's no good, I'll have to get someone else to read that manuscript. I can't afford to hang around any longer. The bike must have broken down. I just hope to God I can *find* another editor. I know Barbara's gone already and Alan said he had to . . .'

She hurried away, muttering to herself, but was back within a few minutes. 'I might have guessed. Not a soul around.' She stared intently at Alison, who shifted uneasily. What now? Another rocket?

'Well, Alison, this is your chance. *You'll* have to read the book. Stay here until it arrives and take it home.'

'*Me?*' Christine had never given her a manuscript to read, despite her numerous hints about wanting to do more editorial work.

'Yes, you. Why not? It sounds just up your street. You're the right age-group, and a torrid love affair's more your thing than mine.' Christine gave a humourless laugh. 'But I want a good detailed report, mind – no skimping. And I need it on my desk by eight o'clock Monday morning. Understood?'

'Yes, of course.'

'And don't get it wet. Have you a bag to put it in?'

Alison was too stunned to reply. She had been asked to report not on some questionable thing from the slush-pile but on a novel potentially worth thousands of pounds.

'Hang on. I'm sure I saw . . .' Christine was rummaging in a cupboard. 'Yes. Here we are.' She handed Alison a black briefcase. 'That should keep it dry. Now I must dash or I'll miss the plane.' She put an awkward hand on Alison's shoulder. 'Thank you. You've been marvellous. I don't thank you enough, do I? I'm very pleased with your work, you know, and if I seem to take you for granted, I . . . I . . .' For once she was at a loss for words, and Alison flushed, realizing that each was as embarrassed as the other.

'Now' – Christine's customary brusqueness returned – 'get on to that courier firm and give them hell, OK? You don't want to be waiting here all night. On my way out I'll tell security you're expecting a delivery and to phone you the minute it arrives. Goodbye. Good luck!'

Once alone, Alison went to the file where readers' reports were kept. On Christine's advice she often studied them in her lunch-hour, in order to learn the skill of condensing a book into a cogent thumbnail sketch – a skill she would need if she were to achieve her ambition of becoming an editor herself. But to start with such a major project was daunting in the extreme. The author's future was at stake, her own future, maybe even Christine's. In the past six months Christine had failed to attract a single new young writer and had remarked bitterly just last week that other, rival publishers seemed to have no trouble snapping them up.

She selected half-a-dozen reports and was soon absorbed in reading them. It must be dark outside by now, although the office had no windows so it was easy to lose track of time, enclosed by book-lined walls and a low polystyrene ceiling and working by artificial light all day. Only when she left the building would she become aware of trees and sky again; feel cool air on her face and be swept into the rumbustious roar of London.

The noise of the phone startled her. The package had arrived! She rushed downstairs, almost disappointed to be handed an ordinary brown Jiffy bag, no different from the dozens which found their way on to Christine's desk each week. The novel had expanded in her mind to such fantastical proportions she half expected to be handed a jewel-encrusted casket.

Upstairs again, she opened the bag to make sure it was the right book. Yes, *Lying*, said the title page. She scanned the agent's letter: 'Although barely twenty, Francesca de Romero writes with a passion and sophisti-

19

cation which mark her out as an exceptional talent. She understands relationships in all their pain and subtlety and brings a refreshingly new slant to the enduring theme of love . . .'

The author's biography was equally impressive. Born in Rio de Janeiro to a Brazilian father and an English mother, she was the youngest of seven children and had displayed a precocious talent from early childhood, writing poems, plays and stories. When the family moved to England, Francesca, now sixteen, had run away from home and travelled across three continents by camel-train and horseback. She had played in a rock band, worked as an artist's model and had been briefly married to a wealthy Polish count, whom she had left for a life of creative self-expression.

After the biographical details came a statement from Leo about the auction: date Monday 18 March; all offers to be in by ten o'clock that morning at the latest.

Alison sat staring at the letter. How colourless her own life was. She was three years older than Francesca, yet had seldom travelled abroad and, far from running away from home, had been practically tied to her mother's apron strings until only a year ago.

She slid the rest of the manuscript from the bag. She ought to get going or she'd be late for Jim, but she couldn't resist glancing at the first few paragraphs.

Twenty pages later she was hooked. Admittedly the style was over-rich in parts – adjectives and metaphors swarming like honey-drunk bees – but the pace was fast and the main character well drawn: an interesting blend of slattern and saint. In her bones she knew the book was good. It compelled you to read on and possessed that shining spark of originality editors spent their lives seeking but rarely found. If it lived up to its promise then Christine must definitely bid, which meant that she, too, would be involved for once in the excitement of an auction.

She devoured another chapter: the heroine had met a poet and fallen desperately in love with him. The romance was perhaps too sudden to be entirely credible: no sooner had Caterina laid eyes on Luis than she was swearing undying love. Indeed the plot in outline sounded like a corny boy-meets-girl story. What put it in a different league was the quality of the writing and its conviction and intensity, as if Luis and Caterina had reinvented love, releasing it from clichéd sentimentality.

Their passionate interchange was cut short by the office cleaner trundling a noisy industrial Hoover into the room.

'You still here, love? I hope they give you overtime!'

'I wish!' Alison returned the manuscript to its Jiffy bag, which she then put into the briefcase. For good measure she took the reports as well. She was half inclined to cancel dinner with Jim tonight, but that would be unfair and anyway she had the rest of the weekend to work. She would read the manuscript twice at least before even starting her report. As well as a précis of the story it must include an assessment of the book's potential niche in the market and how it compared with other contemporary novels. Well, that shouldn't be too difficult – she always had her nose in a book, as her mother used to complain.

'Have a nice weekend, love,' the cleaner said, as Alison manoeuvred her way round the Hoover.

'Thanks,' she smiled, hugging the briefcase to her chest. 'I intend to.'

2

Alison clutched the briefcase under her arm for safety as she was shoved and jostled from all sides. Much as she loved London she found the Underground horrendous, particularly the Friday evening rush-hour, when impossible numbers of people tried to cram themselves into each carriage: beleaguered rats fighting for space. And tonight there was more congestion than ever, although the rush-hour was usually over by now. A points failure at Waterloo had sent hordes of main-line passengers scurrying down to the tube instead, added to which there seemed to be a hold-up; she had been waiting fifteen minutes and there was still no sign of a train.

She could feel drops of water sliding off her hair down the back of her neck. Everyone else looked just as wet and uncomfortable, yet despite the crush all eye-contact was strenuously avoided. Alison was accustomed to the fact that strangers didn't speak to each other in London. Although just now she felt on such a high she would have gladly announced to the whole platform that she had been given her very first job as an editor and that her hyper-critical boss had, miracle of miracles, praised her work.

At last there was a distant rumble, which grew rapidly into a roar, and the yellow eye of a train appeared in the blackness of the tunnel mouth. Like a shoal of fish moving in formation the waiting crowd heaved and rippled forward on the platform, intent on pushing into the already jam-packed carriages. She had learned months ago that the capacity of a train to absorb passengers depended less on cubic feet than on dogged determination. The doors jerked open and she was swept along in the surge and found herself inside, trapped between a man with garlic breath and a youth with a backpack whose metal struts dug painfully into her shoulder.

As the train rattled on its way her thoughts returned to Francesca de Romero. She wondered if the novel was autobiographical; if Francesca, too, had had an affair with a moody Brazilian poet and, if so, what ensued. Tomorrow, she decided, she would get up really early and treat Saturday as a normal working day. However long it took, the report must do her justice.

At Waterloo more ill-tempered commuters bulldozed their way on board, and it was standing room only until Stockwell. Hers was the next stop, thank God – Clapham North. As the train juddered into the station it gave an unexpectedly violent lurch and she lurched with it, losing her balance, losing her grip on the briefcase. She scrambled to her feet, disoriented for a moment and clutching her knee in pain.

'Are you all right?'

She murmured an embarrassed thank-you to the anonymous inquirer, then saw with alarm that the doors were beginning to close. Grabbing her briefcase, she almost tumbled on to the platform, only to realize a split second later that it *wasn't* her briefcase. In panic she tried to prise the doors apart and hammered on the glass, but the train slid away, uncaring.

Paralysed with shock, she stood watching it gather speed and finally disappear into the tunnel, bearing the precious manuscript further and further away. Christine would never forgive her; she would lose her job, her future. The thought made her feel physically sick. People walked past with shuttered faces. Another train lumbered in. Impulsively she stepped on, dithered for a second, then got off again. What was the point of following the first train? Whoever had picked up her briefcase could alight at any of the stations between Clapham Common and the end of the line at Morden, and she had no way of knowing which one. But *they* would want their own briefcase back, just as much as she wanted hers. She must find out who it belonged to.

She limped over to a bench and laid it flat. Fortunately it wasn't locked, and the lid sprang open to reveal a copy of the *Financial Times*, a couple of magazines: *Accountancy Age* and *Accountancy*, a book on chess openings and several manila folders. With shaking hands she took out one of the folders. A loose paper fluttered to the ground. Appalled, she scrabbled for it under the bench. Heaven forbid she should lose any of the contents. Best to take it home and look at it there. She stuffed the paper back inside and, clasping the case tightly with both arms, made her way to the exit.

By the time she reached the house she was drenched by the rain and sobbing aloud. She dragged herself up the three flights of stairs to the flat.

'You're back late,' Linda called. 'I gather there was a delay on the . . . Hey, what's the matter?'

Once she'd heard the story Linda took charge. 'Now you sit down, while I have a ferret in here.' She handed Alison a wad of paper hankies, then removed the folders from the case and started riffling through them. 'Bingo! Look at this – a load of letters, signed James Egerton. Mm, interesting – he works for Garrard Ross.'

'Who's Garrard Ross?'

'A firm of accountants in the City. Very swish.'

Alison wiped her eyes and peered over Linda's shoulder. 'I've never heard of them.' All she knew about accountants was that they were staid, conservative and the butt of frequent jokes. 'Anyway, what's the good of his office address? Isn't there a home one?'

'Give us a chance.' Linda found a notebook tucked into the inside pocket, but its pages were blank. 'That seems to be the lot, I'm afraid. But try the office. You never know – someone might still be around.'

Relieved to be told what to do, Alison dialled the number. 'It's an answerphone,' she groaned. 'They're shut till Monday morning.'

'Wait! Here's something else.' Linda was brandishing a small printed postcard. 'It's from his dentist. About a check-up. That would be sent to his home address, wouldn't it? Which means we can get his phone number.'

'Brilliant! Where does he live? Do you think he's had time to get there yet?'

'Conyers Road, EC1. Mm, could be a problem. EC1's definitely north, not south. So if he was on the same train as you he can't have been on his way home.'

'Oh, *no*.' Alison sank down on the sofa.

'But don't forget *he*'s lost his briefcase, too. And judging by this lot, he'll probably be going ballistic. They're clients' files, marked Private and Confidential – tax assessments and stuff. He'll be frantic to get them back, so he may decide to go home after all.'

Alison looked dubious and sat shredding a paper hanky into fragments.

'Cheer up. Accountants are the soul of rectitude. Even if we can't contact him he's bound to contact *you*.'

'He can't, though. That's the trouble. It was Christine's briefcase, not mine. And if it's got her phone number inside I'm done for.'

'I thought you said she'd gone to Jersey.'

'Yes, but if he leaves a message on her answerphone . . .'

'Well, ring him first then. Even if he's not at home he might have a wife or kid or something.'

'But what if he's annoyed?'

'Don't be stupid. He'll fall on your neck in gratitude. Let's see . . .' Linda was looking in the phone book. 'Egen, Egerstedt, Egerton. Shit! There's only one J and he's John and lives in NW9. Mind you, this is five years old. We'll have to try Directory Enquiries.'

'I'll do it.' Alison needed to keep busy.

'OK, I'll put the kettle on. I'm sure you could do with a cup of tea.'

'I haven't time for tea.' Alison's voice was rising in distress. 'I'm supposed to be going out with Jim. Except I'm not. I can't! I can't go anywhere until I've got the manuscript back.' Jim would be arriving in half an hour and she couldn't think of anything but Christine's reaction when she found out what had happened. It wasn't only the book that had gone; there was also the file of readers' reports, some of which were not duplicated. They weren't meant to be taken out of the office, since other departments used them too. Everyone in the building would get to hear about it and she'd be utterly humiliated.

She grabbed the phone and rang Directory Enquiries. To her relief they had the number. As she dialled, she murmured, 'Please be there, oh *please* be there,' but seconds later she was close to tears again. 'Another answerphone,' she wailed.

'Well, leave a message – quick!'

She tried to keep the explanation brief but was soon floundering in irrelevant detail.

'Give your *number*,' Linda hissed.

She added it in a rush and then again, more coherently, with a plea for him to contact her: she'd be in all evening – all night – waiting for his call. She replaced the receiver and sat staring into space. There was no guarantee he would ring; no knowing even where he was.

'I reckon this calls for something a bit stronger than tea.' Linda was clattering bottles in the sideboard. 'Take your pick. It's either dregs of vodka or dregs of whisky.'

'Linda, I've just had an awful thought. I may have *his* bag, but it doesn't necessarily mean he has mine. Somebody else might have taken it.'

'Unlikely. He must have been standing very near for you to pick it up by mistake.'

Alison tried to recall her fellow passengers, but they'd been little more than a blur, except the young backpacker who had got out at Kennington. Anyway, he would hardly be the owner of a smart executive briefcase.

'I suppose we could try Lost Property,' Linda suggested.

Alison seized the phone again and was soon listening dispiritedly to yet another recorded message. 'They're closed the whole weekend,' she said. 'And they don't accept phone inquiries anyway.'

At that moment the phone rang. Alison pounced on it but it was Maeve, for Linda. She tried not to listen as they discussed some colleague at work. All *she* could do was imagine Christine's fury when she found that she couldn't bid in the auction. There would be no skilled, concise report – no manuscript, for heaven's sake.

Linda had hung up by now, and was sitting frowning over her drink. 'I've just remembered all those notices about unattended bags. They always say you should contact the police. Well, what if someone has? Let's ring the local nick.'

'OK.' Alison was willing to clutch at any straw, although the sergeant who came on the line was not encouraging. No, he said, nothing had been handed in, nor any suspicious packages reported, but he would inform her if anything turned up. 'Do you think it's likely?' she asked.

'I'm sorry, madam, I really couldn't say. And it might be a while in any case. All items have to be checked against the records.'

She took a mouthful of neat whisky, shuddering at its strength. The doorbell was ringing and she got up wearily to let Jim in. Trust him to be early. He greeted her with his customary grin, flinging off his jacket and shaking the rain from his shock of curly hair. Right now she almost resented his good humour. However, on hearing about the lost manuscript he was instantly sympathetic. He too worked in publishing, in the production department of a much bigger firm than Shaw Hilliard, so he knew what was at stake.

'Why don't I drive you to this James Egerton's place?' he offered. 'Even if he's not in, one of his neighbours might know where is. I admit it's a faint chance but better than sitting here doing damn-all.'

'Oh, *would* you?' Alison put an arm around him, ashamed of her ill-feeling. 'I'm terribly sorry about all this, Jim. *And* about dinner.'

'Don't worry. I understand. Conyers Road, did you say?' Jim had unearthed the A–Z and was flicking through the index. 'Yeah, found it. It's in Islington – well, Finsbury really. Off Myddelton Square. Mm, that's a pricey area.'

'Well, he *is* an accountant,' Linda put in. 'And by the looks of these files he specializes in tax. Not someone I'd care to meet, ta very much! You two get off and I'll stay here and nurse the phone.'

Alison squeezed her hand. 'Thanks, Linda. I just hope he's in by the time we get there – and that he has the briefcase. If so I'll buy you two a crate of champagne!'

Number seventeen Conyers Road stood in total darkness, a terraced Georgian house, four storeys high, with black railings in the front and matching wrought-iron balconies on the upper floors. Alison pressed the bell until her finger ached, but it was obvious that the place was empty. Although the rain had slackened off a little, deep puddles glistened coldly in the gutter and the streetlamps cast eerie shadows across the pavement.

'Let's try next door,' Jim suggested. 'There's a light on there at least.'

A wizened little fellow appeared. He seemed to have no English but was clearly cross at being disturbed. With an incomprehensible tirade of abuse he slammed the door. They rang the bell of the house the other side. After a few clickings and rattlings the door opened a crack and an elderly woman peered at them over the chain.

'No, I don't know anyone called Egerton. That's the Walwyns' house. They must have been there – oh, a good twenty years.'

'*What*'s their name?'

'Colonel and Mrs Walwyn. They're often away weekends, mind. They've got a place in the country.'

'It's hopeless,' Alison muttered, after the woman had bolted the door again.

'Well, it certainly doesn't make much sense.' Jim moved nearer to a lamp-post and peered at the dentist's card. 'This is dated only two days ago, and it's addressed here. I think you should leave him a note, in case he does come back.'

'I've already left a message. Anyway, what's the point if he doesn't live here? That answerphone might not even have been his voice. They didn't give a name.'

'Leave a note in any case. What harm can it do? Perhaps he's a friend of the Walwyns, staying with them or something.'

'Yeah, away for the weekend,' Alison said bitterly.

'I doubt it. He'll be desperate to get those letters back. He won't want his clients' private tax details going astray.'

'Jim, I've just thought – couldn't we *phone* one of his clients? They might know where he is.'

'Don't be stupid, darling. That would land him in it good and proper.'

'You sound sorrier for him than you are for me.'

'Well, we Jameses have to stick together!'

Irritated by this fatuous remark she turned and stalked off down the street. A car flashed by, its headlamps momentarily blinding her. She stood in the shadows, feeling horribly alone. It was all very well for Jim to joke; she was the one who had to face Christine on Monday. She'd probably be sacked on the spot.

Jim, a blurred figure, was approaching in the dark. She had no right to be so hostile to him when he had given up his evening – *and* his dinner – to come with her on this wild-goose chase. It would have been ten times worse on her own: by tube and then a long walk in the rain. She slipped her hands inside his jacket and drew him close. 'I'm sorry to be so ratty,' she whispered.

'That's OK.' He bent to kiss her, just as a large, cold drop of water plopped on his neck from the plane tree overhead. 'Let's get in the car,' he said. 'In fact, we can sit there for a while to see if he comes back to the house.'

They sat side by side staring into the dark. 'I feel like a detective on a stake-out,' Jim remarked. 'Waiting for a murderer to return to the scene of the crime.'

Alison shivered. *She* was the criminal, more like – guilty of gross negligence. She would never find another job, certainly not in the small, incestuous world of publishing, where a harsh word on the grapevine could finish a career.

She reached out for his hand, which closed warm and solid around her icy fingers. Despite the puny efforts of the heater a film of condensation was beginning to mist the windows. Jim leaned across to kiss her on the mouth, but she was unable to respond; all her normal feelings numbed by dread. They were sitting close, their mouths and bodies touching, yet he must feel as if he were kissing a corpse.

There was a movement outside, and she pulled away and peered out of the window. A man crossed the road in front of them, evidently making for the house opposite. She jumped out of the car. 'I'll ask him if he knows this Mr Egerton.'

She returned to Jim in slightly less despondent mood. 'He says he *has* seen someone new at number seventeen.'

'But surely that woman next door would have known.'

'Not necessarily. Londoners are notorious for keeping themselves to themselves. That guy hadn't even heard of the Walwyns. At home I know practically the entire life history of everyone in the village.'

'Yes, but that's the wilds of Leicestershire.' Jim rummaged for a cloth and wiped the windscreen. 'Anyway, it's a glimmer of hope, isn't it?'

'I suppose so. But there's no knowing whether he'll come back this weekend or even if it *is* our Mr Egerton.'

'How long do you want to stay then? You're freezing.'

'OK, let's push off now. If the Egerton bloke *does* live here and *does* come back, he'll get my phone message. And if he doesn't, we're wasting our time.'

'Leave him a note, though, anyway.'

Jim handed her a pencil and a scrap of paper, and she wrote laborious instructions to ring *her* and not Christine, underlining her phone number three times. She pushed the folded paper through the letter-box and, returning to the car, noticed Jim's profile silhouetted against the light: boyish pudgy cheeks, good-natured mouth, endearing little dimple in his chin. Thank heavens he was here; without him she would be a gibbering wreck. When they got back, she'd make it up to him . . .

But whatever happened, they must sleep on the sofa in the living-room. She had to stay within reach of the phone all night – all weekend, if need be.

3

Late on Sunday evening Alison was staring out at the whirling flakes of snow, frantic white against the darkness of the sky. Snow blocked roads and delayed trains, and could well prevent James Egerton, wherever he might be, from coming back to London. Planes, unfortunately, hadn't been affected by the weather. She had rung Heathrow, hoping against hope, only to learn that the eighteen-thirty flight from Jersey had landed safely. That was a couple of hours ago. Christine would be home by now and maybe at this very moment listening to an answering-machine message: her briefcase, containing a manuscript and a bundle of reports, had been found abandoned on the tube.

She wandered listlessly around the flat. The Sunday papers lay jumbled on the sofa where Linda had been reading them this afternoon. Odd phrases drifted into focus: Saddam and the Kurds; Norman Lamont's Budget speech on Tuesday. Tuesday, she thought – I'll be out of work by then.

For the umpteenth time the phone rang. She hadn't realized how many calls there were at weekends. Normally she enjoyed chatting to her friends, but today she had to keep the line free (even though she had virtually given up hope of James Egerton ever ringing). 'Hello?' she said tersely.

'It's Mum, dear. I thought you were going to phone this morning.'

'Oh, Mum, I'm sorry. I've been . . . busy.'

'Am I interrupting something?'

'N . . . no.'

'Well, can't we have a chat then?'

'It's a bit difficult at the moment. I'm expecting an important call.'

'Oh.' The short word conveyed both disappointment and displeasure. 'How are you, Mum? How's the leg?'

'Still giving me gyp. It wouldn't be so bad if I wasn't on my feet all day. It's time I found another job.'

'But I thought you liked the shop.'

'Not with that new woman. She's a right old battleaxe. Still, at least it gets me out of the house. I'm alone today, as usual. Dad's in Leeds. That's his story, anyway.'

'Mum – I'm sorry, honestly. I'd love to talk, but there's this . . . problem at work, you see.'

'Work, on a Sunday? They're taking advantage of you, Alison.'

'Look, can I ring you later?'

'That depends. I'm going to bed at ten.'

It was already half past nine. Alison knew that without looking, having spent all weekend clock-watching, a virtual prisoner in the flat. In less than twelve hours she would have to confront Christine, with or without the report. 'I'll ring you tomorrow, Mum, OK?' If she did get the sack there would be all damned day to phone home.

'All right, dear. But I don't like the way they treat you. You sound really down in the dumps.'

'I'm fine, Mum,' she lied, not entirely out of altruism. Her parents had never approved of her coming to live in London, and any hint of trouble on her part would provoke the inevitable 'I told you so'.

After ringing off she sat fiddling with the phone lead. It was hard to concentrate on anything. Reading was no good – books only reminded her of the one she'd lost. What she *had* read, several times, were James

Egerton's letters, in the hope they might provide a clue as to his whereabouts. One of them referred to a 10 a.m. meeting on Monday – tomorrow – in his office in London Wall. It was with a client from Geneva, and the senior partner would also be present. Surely he'd be back for that? She was beginning to hate this Mr Egerton – a pompous, rapacious accountant who probably bent the law to help wealthy businessmen avoid paying tax. All his things were obsessionally neat: the *Financial Times* perfectly folded; his signature on the letters in mincing copperplate. The briefcase, too, was impeccable – no scuffs or scratches, no debris in the bottom. She could almost see the wretched man, pedantic in his pin-stripes and old school tie, apoplectic with rage at her impertinence in tampering with his possessions.

She tried ringing him one final time, although even as she dialled she knew it was hopeless. The now familiar recording clicked on once again: the plummy voice whose every nuance grated on her. She slammed down the receiver and mooched into the kitchen. Well, at least she could wash up – a small return for Linda's moral support. She wouldn't be here at all if it hadn't been for Linda, who had come to London first, straight after university, and had shared the flat with an old friend. But when he moved elsewhere Linda was left with double the rent and an empty room to fill. 'London's where it's happening, Al,' Linda had insisted and finally talked her into leaving home. Although the flat was hardly a palace, this was the first time she'd lived independently, free of her parents' interference. And when, three months after moving in, she managed to get a job in publishing, the future looked bright. But London with no money would be a different matter entirely.

Suddenly decisive, she abandoned the washing-up, put on her thickest sweater over the old tracksuit she was wearing, and a padded jacket on top, then found a scarf and an ancient pair of boots. Shoving Mr Egerton's papers back into his briefcase she clicked it shut, clutched it under her arm and left the flat, heading for Conyers Road. A pointless exercise, no doubt, but anything was better than staying cooped up here alone.

Walking to the tube, she tried to convince herself that Mr Egerton *would* return for his Monday morning meeting – after all, it sounded as important to him as hers was with Christine. He might even be home already but had decided not to ring her for some reason. Or the phone was playing up. Or he was ill. Or drunk. Or deaf. Or just a pig. Whatever, she was determined to find out.

Number seventeen was still in darkness, its balconies now furred with white. The pavements were treacherous as slush froze into ice, and several times she had slipped and almost fallen. Her feet were numb, her ears ached with cold, and when she pressed the bell – a futile action clearly – her fingers felt as clumsy as wood. She stood, blinded by the snow, envying the lighted houses round about, where normal people were leading normal lives. Or perhaps the lighted windows were only façades, as on a film set; no one real behind them, no other person left in London.

She stamped her feet for warmth. The noise was reassuring in the oppressive snowbound silence. She took a few steps away from the house, only to turn back again, unwilling to accept that this second expedition was as fruitless as the first. She thought of Jim and Linda ensconced in the King's Head, probably glad to escape her foul mood. Linda was her best friend – they had met at college and hit it off immediately – but now she felt estranged from her and even from Jim, despite his protestations of love. Love for Jim meant sex. That was the only time he told her he loved her. She had felt so lonely last night, lying beside him and staring into the darkness while he went straight to sleep. Surely love meant sharing pain as well as pleasure.

Her arms ached from the briefcase, which she was holding under her jacket to protect it from the snow. It had become a monstrous burden, weighed down by her fury with Mr sodding Egerton. She imagined him smugly sipping claret at the Walwyns' country seat, without a thought for his poor clients. She was tempted to dump the briefcase on the doorstep – too bad if it was nicked. What a fool she was to have come out at this hour. Her boots leaked, her socks squelched, and she was exhausted from the effort of battling against the snow, which blew in spiteful flurries down her neck and into her eyes. She squinted at her watch. Twenty past eleven – decision time: either leave at once and catch the last tube home or stay all night and risk pneumonia, or worse.

Suddenly she heard footsteps approaching – running footsteps. Only a madman would run on such icy pavements. Instinctively she ducked down beside the railings as the urgent steps pounded closer. She crouched uncomfortably, trying to lose herself in the shadows and hardly daring to breathe.

The footsteps lurched to a stop only a few feet away. Through the falling snow she could make out a muffled shape: a man with something bulky concealed beneath his coat. A gun, she thought in terror.

But when he pushed open the gate of number seventeen and walked up to the front door, she dashed in pursuit, prepared even to brave a bullet for the sake of the lost manuscript. 'Please!' she blurted out. 'Does a Mr Egerton live here?'

He turned. 'Yes. That's me.'

She stared. The balding, pin-striped pedant had metamorphosed into a youngish man in a duffel coat and jeans. '*You're* Mr Egerton?'

'That's right.'

Wordlessly she took his briefcase out from under her coat. Also in silence he produced the 'gun' – *her* briefcase.

'Oh, I can't tell you how relieved I am,' she exclaimed.

'Me, too. But, look, come in. It's too cold to stand out here.' He unlocked the door and motioned her inside.

She hesitated. Now she had recovered the manuscript she ought to race home and start work. Christine's deadline was only eight hours away. 'I'm sorry,' she said, 'I have to get back to Clapham.'

'But you're soaked. Hadn't you better dry off first?'

'No, really. I'll miss the last tube.'

'You can't go by tube! Let me order you a cab. It's the least I can do when you've been kind enough to return my briefcase. Careful – don't trip. I'll put some lights on.'

Apprehensively she followed him into the hall. She was alone with a stranger in an otherwise empty house. And yet the thought of a taxi-ride home was too tempting to resist. And she was intrigued by his appearance, so unlike her expectations. His face was thin and almost sallow, with well-defined cheekbones; his hair dark, cropped short; his eyes intensely black. Beneath the duffel coat he was wearing a polo-necked sweater the colour of burnt toffee. His hands, too, were unusual: long, slender fingers suggesting more an artist than an accountant. However, the house itself looked prosperous enough, furnished in period style with gilt-framed paintings in the hall.

'I live at the top, so it's rather a trek,' he said, leading the way upstairs. 'I take it you're Anne-Marie, by the way.'

'No,' she said, confused.

'That was the name in your briefcase – Anne-Marie Cunningham. I've been ringing her the whole weekend, but there was no reply.'

Alison gave silent thanks. The briefcase wasn't Christine's after all; it belonged to her assistant editor, who was safely away in Venice till tomorrow.

'And I was going to try Francesca de Romero, but I couldn't find her number in the book.'

'No. She lives in Brazil!'

'And then I rang Mitchell Marsh Associates, and of course being after hours there was only an answering-machine. I should have tried harder to find you, but I'm afraid it's been one hell of a weekend.'

'Same here,' she said with feeling.

By the time they reached the top floor her nervousness had returned. Who would hear if she screamed? Yet his manner was courtesy itself as he ushered her into an austerely elegant room. The floor was polished wood, with a Persian rug in rich shades of green and gold. The furniture was sparse – a desk, a sofa, a bookcase – but each item had the look of an antique. There were several paintings on the wall, dark-toned swirly abstracts, quite different from the tranquil landscapes downstairs.

'Do take off your wet things.'

That would mean every stitch, she thought, aware that the damp had seeped right through to her underclothes. She stifled an urge to laugh. She felt elated, almost manic, like a long-term prisoner just released.

'I'll phone for a cab, and we can have a drink while we're waiting.'

She handed him her jacket, suddenly conscious of how appalling she must look. Her jersey was shapeless, the tracksuit trousers were baggy at the knees, and her hair was hanging in rats' tails down her back. He had taken off his own coat, revealing long lean legs. The sweater was a chunky knit, yet it couldn't disguise his whippet thinness. And he seemed to have an animal-like energy, moving with rapid grace as he drew the curtains, switched on a fan-heater and two brass lamps, and cleared some papers off the sofa for her to sit down. He then phoned several taxi firms, fortunately without first listening to his messages. How humiliating it would have been to hear her own panic-stricken voice gabbling on the tape.

'I'm afraid they're all terribly busy,' he reported. 'Even the quickest one can't get here for half an hour. Apparently we're lucky to get anything in this weather. I'm so sorry to delay you. I'd drive you back myself, but the only wheels I own belong to a rather rickety bike.'

A bike? She had imagined James Egerton at the wheel of a new Mercedes. 'That's OK,' she said, although inwardly chafing at the loss of yet more time.

'How about a brandy?' James suggested. 'I could certainly do with one.'

The fiery liquid burned her throat, but she took another sip. No use fretting: there was nothing she could do until she got back home. And she did find him rather fascinating. There was a raw vigour about him, somehow at odds with his gracious manner and well-modulated voice (not snobbish, as it had sounded on the phone). And she approved of his taste – the subtle olive-coloured walls, the absence of clutter and the dark glow of the antique furniture, which harmonized surprisingly well with the modern abstract paintings. *She* seemed to be the only jarring element; her purple sweater garish and her slush-spattered boots in danger of staining the rug. Yet he was at pains to make her welcome, fetching a towel for her to dry her hair and offering the loan of a sweater.

'No, honestly, I'm fine,' she said, cupping her hands round the brandy glass. 'I'm feeling more human by the minute.'

'Me too.' He sat opposite her at his desk, a mahogany affair with lion claw legs. 'I still don't know your name.'

'It's Alison. Alison Ward. Anne-Marie's my colleague. We work in publishing.'

'Yes, I realized that. In fact I planned to deliver your briefcase in person tomorrow.'

'I'm glad you didn't have to. I might have got the sack.'

'Oh dear! I've obviously put you through the mill. But I just couldn't get back earlier. My grandmother had a fall and cut her head very badly. She was taken to Intensive Care and only regained consciousness this evening.'

'Oh, I'm sorry. How awful. Is she going to be all right?'

He nodded. 'She's seventy-seven, so it was quite a shock, but she's out of danger now. Even so, I didn't like to leave her. We've always been tremendously close. I won't bore you with the story. Suffice it to say she saved my life before I was even born. And she still calls me her miracle baby!'

Alison glanced at him, intrigued. Babies were cute, pink, chubby, passive, smiley, and James was thin, sallow, solemn and coiled like a spring. She remembered that he'd been running to the house. Was he late, for something or someone, but too polite to mention it? 'I hope I'm not in your way,' she said, putting down her glass.

'Not at all. I'm delighted you're here. I have to admit I spent the weekend alternately worrying about my grandmother and worrying about my briefcase – *and* yours, of course. I kept leaving her room in the hospital to go and phone this Anne-Marie. My grandfather must have thought I had St Vitus's Dance! Are you hungry, by the way? I don't know about you, but it seems an age since I've eaten.'

'Well, I wouldn't say no to a biscuit.'

He laughed. 'I'm not sure I've got any. But there is some Christmas cake. That's Grandmama again. She always makes a separate one, just for me. Do pour yourself more brandy. I won't be long.'

The last thing she needed was more brandy to fuddle her brain. While he was gone she took out the manuscript (which fortunately wasn't even creased) and assessed its length: she would have to skim-read in order to finish it and still allow time to write the report. She began reading there and then – every minute counted.

'It's not exactly a feast,' James said apologetically as he came back with a tray. 'I'm afraid the cupboard's rather bare.' He passed her a plate, exquisitely painted with blue peacocks. The small round cake, with only a tiny wedge missing, didn't have the usual Father Christmas standing on the top but a slender silver angel, complete with halo and harp. The words 'Peace on Earth' were iced around its feet, with heavenly rays streaming from the letters.

'It's beautiful,' she said, feeling a twinge of envy. One of her grandmothers had died twenty years ago, and the other kept her distance and certainly wouldn't be bothered icing fancy cakes.

He lifted the angel off the cake and held it out to show her. 'This chap's incredibly old. Grandma found him in a little Viennese antique shop – or "it", I should say, since angels have no gender.'

In fact, the figure looked distinctly female, with long blond ringlets and flowing lacy gown – a stark contrast to James himself. He had pushed his sleeves up, exposing sinewy arms, stippled with dark hairs. Gender was somehow on her mind.

James attacked the cake with a knife, which failed to pierce the icing. 'Oh dear, it's solid as a rock! Tell you what, we'll forget the icing and just eat the cake. That looks fairly OK.'

'Mm, delicious,' she said, biting into the densely fruited slice he gave her. Surreptitiously she watched him eat, again noticing contradictions: he took small fastidious bites yet swallowed with a sort of greedy pleasure. And, despite the taut lines of his face, his mouth had a sensual quality, seeming almost to caress the cake.

'Yes, it is good, isn't it?' he said. 'And extremely alcoholic!' He scooped up a stray raisin, glistening black, like his eyes. 'I've unearthed a couple of pears as well, and – what are these things called? I can never remember.'

'Lychees,' she said, wondering if they too dated from Christmas. Their nubbly brown jackets did look very shrivelled.

He began peeling a pear, revealing a plump cream curve of flesh beneath the pock-marked skin. Her eyes kept straying back to him as he deftly removed the peel in a single coiling ribbon. Juice was dribbling down his hands, although he didn't seem to notice; his full attention focused on the knife. He cut the pear into four, then leaned forward to slip the pieces on to her plate.

His closeness was disconcerting; the jeans tight across his thighs. Was she *mad*? In the middle of a crisis she was letting herself be distracted by a man. Yet she desired him – it was a fact. It was also crazy. Totally crazy. She'd only just met him. She knew nothing about him. She already had a boyfriend. As for James, he probably had scores of women. The strain of the weekend had clearly robbed her of her senses.

Again she watched as he peeled one of the lychees, breaking fragments of the brittle shell from the moist, translucent flesh. Then he passed the naked fruit to her on another of the peacock plates. In her mouth the texture felt almost obscene – solid yet silky wet. She realized to her consternation that her cheeks were scarlet and she was burning hot all over. The brandy must have gone to her head.

Slowly she sucked the stone clean. All this was far too intimate. Why had he peeled the fruit for her? It was what you did for a lover or a child, and she was neither. Right now her sole concern ought to be Christine's manuscript, not adolescent fantasies. Time was ticking on.

Suddenly the phone rang. James got up to answer it, his first non-committal 'hello' changing to a warmer tone. 'Hold on,' he said, then turned to her. 'Excuse me – I'll take this in the other room.'

The room seemed empty when he'd gone. Furious at her stupidity she got out the book once more, but not a word of it sank in as she sat speculating about James's mystery caller. Was that why he'd been racing home: his girlfriend had arranged to phone?

Angry with him now as well, she banged the plate down on the tray. She must set off home this instant, even if it meant walking. She had only a few hours to produce what might be the most important piece of work of her career.

Abruptly, she jumped to her feet as he returned. 'I'm sorry,' she said, 'I really must go. I have to write a report on this manuscript by eight o'clock tomorrow morning and I haven't even read it yet.'

'Let me try the cab firm again. As a matter of fact I have some work to do myself.'

His reply was calm and civil, unlike her own flustered outburst. None the less, she felt hurt by the prompt dismissal. There was no interest from *his* side – that was plain enough. She was so confused, she couldn't decide whether she wanted the cab to whisk her away immediately or whether she was hoping for a longer delay. She must be out of her mind. Her job was on the line, yet she was jeopardizing everything for the sake of a stranger she would never see again.

He replaced the receiver with a frown. 'They're going to be another fifteen minutes, minimum. But look, you're welcome to work here. I'll clear the desk and you can make a start. In fact if you don't think it rude I'll do the same. I have a meeting to prepare for in the morning.'

'Well, you have the desk then. I only have to jot down a few notes, so I'm fine where I am.' Hardly fine. How on earth would she concentrate with him so close?

'Do you need a pen or paper?'

'No, I've got it all in here, thanks.'

'Coffee? Tea?'

'No, nothing. Really.' Was he simply being polite, or did his words imply that they might be working together for longer than fifteen minutes? If only . . .

Of course the wretched taxi was sure to arrive just as they had settled down . . . But she *must* stop thinking about James and get back to Luis, the hero of the book. It struck her that in certain ways the two were alike: both dark, intense, seductive men, although not conventionally good-looking.

Pencil poised, she turned back to the beginning. If she started at page one again, she might find it easier to concentrate. Amazingly, it worked, and she was soon thoroughly absorbed, almost forgetting that she was reading as a critic and not simply for enjoyment. Glancing up briefly, she saw that James was equally engrossed. Indeed the house was conducive to work, being blissfully peaceful compared with the Clapham flat – no noisy traffic or shuddering trains, no intrusive stereo pounding from downstairs; only the faint drone of the fan heater and an occasional rustle of paper. James neither spoke nor fidgeted – the perfect workmate whose depth of concentration seemed to inspire her own. She read swiftly on, not pausing until the end of Chapter 3, the point where Caterina falls in love with Luis. Reading it on Friday, she had found it improbably quick; now, though, she was less sure. You *could* be smitten within a few minutes – it happened even in the classics. And love at first sight needn't be a cliché. If two people were thrown together by unusual circumstances and then kept together by a twist of the plot – well, anything might happen.

4

The managing director of Shaw Hilliard raised a hand for silence. The talk and laughter subsided as he stepped forward, flanked by Christine and a couple of other senior staff. 'Ladies and gentlemen, I'm delighted to welcome Francesca de Romero, who's come all the way from São Paulo to be with us this evening.'

Alison craned her neck to get a view of the author, who wore a skin-tight scarlet dress with a feather boa tossed across one shoulder. Her dark hair was coiled on top of her head and studded with silk flowers. Such glamour and confidence were intimidating in a twenty-year-old.

'As you know,' the MD continued, 'Shaw Hilliard won this auction against formidable competition. It seems that every publisher in town was fighting tooth and nail to get their hands on the novel.'

Alison shivered involuntarily at the memory: Christine ashen-faced and chain-smoking as the bids rose – and rose – to astronomical sums. Gradually the others dropped out, and in the end it was a battle to the death between Shaw Hilliard and a huge international conglomerate.

'Our success was not just a triumph but a privilege. Everyone in house, myself included, is tremendously enthusiastic about this novel's merits. It's a terrific read and also has great literary potential. We see an exciting future for its author.' He smiled at Francesca, motioning her forward. 'Ladies and gentlemen, will you please raise your glasses and drink a toast to . . .' he paused for effect, 'Francesca de Romero.'

'Francesca de Romero,' Alison murmured, adding *sotto voce*, 'My author, *my* book.' She took a sip of champagne, swirling it in her mouth. She loved that sensation of tiny pinprick bubbles exploding on her tongue. Her whole body was effervescent – a magnum of Dom Perignon. The heady atmosphere had affected her. Indeed just being in the board-room and meeting the top brass made her feel she had arrived, at last.

On the wood-panelled wall hung a portrait of the original Mr Hilliard: Tobias Joseph Leopold, a Victorian grandee, whose mutton-chop whiskers and exuberant grey beard provided ample compensation for his bald pate. A bowl of hothouse flowers had been placed beneath his por-trait, although whether in tribute to him or to Francesca, Alison wasn't sure. She gazed at the flamboyant display – speckly lilies with long pow-dery yellow tongues, and some luscious purple orchids. The noise level was rising again as people resumed their drinking and chatting. She hovered near a group of marketing people, still feeling rather over-awed, then suddenly spotted Christine coming purposefully towards her with Francesca de Romero in tow. She took another gulp of champagne, for courage.

'Francesca, may I introduce my assistant editor, Alison Ward?' Christine spoke in a gushing, almost obsequious tone Alison rarely heard her use. 'Alison will be working on your novel with me.'

'Hi! Great to meet you, Alison.' The dark eyes gazed into hers – James's eyes, lustrous-black. Francesca could almost be James's sister: tall, slender, spirited and with some elusive quality which marked her as special.

'Alison wrote the initial report on your book,' Christine continued in the same unfamiliar purr. 'And she had nothing but praise for it.'

Not quite true, thought Alison – there had been a few adverse comments. Christine had judged the report thorough and well-balanced: high acclaim indeed. Although James was the one who deserved it. After she had left his flat, his charisma had stayed with her, all the way to Clapham and right on through the night; the words pouring out effortlessly as she worked on her report. And the feeling of exultation had persisted the next morning, despite the fact that she hadn't slept a wink.

'Yes, the novel enthralled me,' she confided to Francesca, now that Christine had been cornered by the sales director and was safely out of earshot. 'Your characters are so alive. I couldn't get them out of my mind, long after I'd finished the book. And the way you describe their love is incredibly moving. That sense of their being driven by some force outside themselves. You feel if they resist they could sacrifice everything.'

Francesca nodded eagerly. 'And even if they don't resist they may still lose everything. But it doesn't matter. It's worth it. They'll go to any lengths.'

'Absolutely. Love makes you a different person. Your standards change. You become determined, reckless. You feel you could commit murder to get the man you want.'

Francesca laughed. 'I can see you speak from experience! Did you know that the ancient Greeks believed falling in love was inspired by the gods? Because of the wild irrational feelings that take you over and make you almost crazy.'

So the gods were to blame, Alison thought wryly, for that state of triumphant madness which had seized her eighteen days ago and refused to go away. She was desperate to see James again. Countless times she had picked up the phone and dialled his number, only to put it down before he answered. If he wanted to see *her*, he'd get in touch himself. But then the craziness would sweep over her with even greater force, and she would find herself writing passionate letters to him in her head. And the unsettling thing was that, always before, she had distrusted such extremes of feeling, preferring to be in control. Wild infatuations were all very well in books or films but too painful in reality.

A heavily built man with a drinker's ruddy complexion suddenly materialized and slid his bulk between her and Francesca. 'Oh, I say,' he joked, '"Lady in Red" times two!'

'Yes,' said Francesca, 'isn't it a coincidence? Alison and I have chosen exactly the same colour.'

Alison glanced down at the scarlet dress she had bought specially for tonight. It was more slinky and seductive than the normal style of thing she wore – James's influence again.

Having paid a glut of compliments to Francesca, the man turned his attention to her. 'I don't think we've met. I'm Martin Wallace.'

The name rang a bell – the new head of marketing – which meant she was willing to ignore his oily manner. 'And I'm Alison Ward,' she smiled. 'Christine's new assistant editor.' It gave her a thrill each time she said it. Events had certainly moved fast these past two weeks. She even had a proper office now – well, sharing with another girl but infinitely better than the cubby-hole.

More people started flocking round Francesca: the publicity director, someone from the rights department, the senior sales manager and another couple of editors. A fortnight ago Alison would have stepped aside, intimidated, but now she stood her ground. She had as much right to be here as anyone else. Indeed more. Without her report, Christine would never have bid, and Francesca would be celebrating at some rival publishing house.

'What are your plans for the book, Ruth?' she asked the publicity director, gratified by her own assurance. Up till now, Ruth – like Christine – had been a formidable character, to be approached (if at all) with deference.

'Oh, we'll give her the full works – features in the women's pages, profiles in the glossies and the Sunday supplements. Any chat shows we can get. And a launch party, of course. And maybe –'

'Alison!' Francesca butted in. 'I'm in London for a fortnight. Perhaps we could meet for lunch? I'd love to have a longer talk.'

'Yes, that would be great.' She hoped Christine hadn't heard – she might regard it as trespassing. Not that Christine and Francesca had much in common. She couldn't imagine them having deep discussions about the madness of love, for example.

Out of the corner of her eye she could see the photographer taking shots of them all. Normally photographers embarrassed her, but tonight was different. She felt confident, exotic, even on a par with Francesca, and James was the reason, once again. If she could have bid for *him* in an auction the sky would have been the limit, and somehow his worth had rubbed off on her.

Two hours later, she floated down the stairs and out of the building into the refreshing evening air. She walked on past the tube, too elated to return tamely to a claustrophobic flat. Besides, Jim had said he'd ring at nine to see if she was back, and she had no desire to speak to him. Their relationship was precarious at the moment. Jim (and indeed all other men she'd known prior to James) seemed immature and pedestrian. Maybe Francesca was right about a godlike force controlling things – that points failure at Waterloo, for instance, which had thrown her and James together. He had been on his way to Kingston Hospital to visit his grandmother, and if there hadn't been a hold-up he would have gone by train, not tube.

She stopped in her tracks, struck by an idea. She could ring and ask how his grandmother was – a perfectly natural inquiry. Of course he might just say, 'She's fine' and 'Thanks for asking' and then ring off, and she would be back to square one with even less excuse to phone again. If only she had accepted the loan of that sweater, then she would have had to return it. Perhaps she could call *without* an excuse; pretend she just happened to be passing. Except acting on blind impulse was unwise, to say the least, and it would only reinforce Linda's opinion that she was in the grip of a dangerous obsession.

'Anyway, what about poor Jim?' Linda had persisted, voicing her own unspoken guilt. Yes, poor doggedly faithful Jim. She loathed the thought of hurting him, yet her longing for James seemed to override all scruples.

'You don't understand,' she had told Linda. 'I've been waiting my whole life to meet a man like James.'

'But you don't *know* what he's like, Al. You were only with him for an hour.'

Ironically, she could sympathize with Linda's point of view. This sudden passion for a virtual stranger did seem irrational, excessive and little short of a teenage crush. Yet in truth she had never felt more adult. Love, in teenage terms, was often a matter of boasting and giggles, whereas for her it had assumed an almost frightening intensity. Her hour with James seemed more exhilarating than Christine winning the auction; more important than her own promotion.

She had reached Covent Garden Piazza, where the sky had room to spread itself. A tiny sliver of raw moon was etched against its dark expanse, looking far too young and frail to be out alone amidst such vastness.

'Mind where you're going!' A passer-by bumped into her.

'Sorry,' she said peaceably. Nothing could annoy her tonight. James's energy invigorated her – and London. The piazza was pulsing with life: waiters bustling to and fro in crowded cafés, music pounding from pubs, gold necklaces of light flickering and twinkling along the roof of the old market building.

She stopped to look in a bookshop window. Francesca de Romero's novel would be displayed there in November, perhaps the centrepiece. And *she* would have played a part in getting it into print. She and Francesca might even be friends by then – anything was possible the way she felt just now.

One book in the window caught her eye: *Who Dares Wins*, a thriller about the SAS. She hadn't dared a thing with James. It was all unfulfilled speculations, unposted letters, aborted phone-calls, even attempts at poetry, clumsy and unfinished. She turned on her heel and walked briskly along Garrick Street in the direction of the tube. Forget phoning, forget letters. Who dares wins. She was going to see him – this minute.

The lights were on downstairs, for once, at number seventeen; a soft amber glow shining through the curtains in the front. The Walwyns, she presumed. James had told her that they were friends of his parents who spent much of their time in the country and had become increasingly nervous about leaving the London house unoccupied. After a couple of recent break-ins they had decided to let the top floor. James seemed the ideal tenant and it had suited him to move – his previous flat was miles from a tube and noisy. The first time she had come here he was still in the process of moving in, but things had obviously progressed. There was now a second bell, marked 'J. Egerton, Top Flat'. Strange how much courage she needed to ring. Each time she was about to, something stayed her hand. Suppose he were downstairs with the Walwyns having an after-dinner drink? Or, worse, upstairs with some female in bed. That phone-call he'd had while she was there: it was bound to have been a woman – midnight calls implied intimacy. He might even be expecting her now and would be disappointed – angry – to find an uninvited guest on the doorstep.

She turned away. Linda was right: she was behaving out of character, worryingly so. As a rule she wouldn't dream of lurking like this outside someone's house, making an utter fool of herself. She had her pride, after all.

And yet this *wasn't* 'as a rule'. What she felt for James took no account of rules. She had to see him, if only to cure the obsession. It was more than likely she had exaggerated his attractions in her mind, and in reality he would shrink to normal size. There was no need to stay – she would just say her piece and leave.

Tentatively she pressed the bell. The sound of footsteps pounding downstairs rekindled her misgivings. Should she turn and run?

The door opened. She was face to face with a different man – tall, lean, intense, but older and more businesslike, in a dark suit and crisp white shirt. She gazed at him, unspeaking. He looked elegant, distinguished and even more desirable, although he did seem slightly puzzled. Perhaps he didn't recognize her in her make-up and best clothes.

'It . . . it's Alison,' she said.

'Oh, *Alison*. Of course. Do come in.'

'Well, I can't stop . . . I was just passing . . .' The words came out in jerky gasps and were clichés anyway. She cleared her throat, began again. 'I, er, wondered if you'd found a . . . a notebook. It was in my briefcase – I mean, Anne-Marie's briefcase. You know, the one you picked up on the tube. It's not valuable or anything, but she's making rather a fuss about it.'

'Oh Lord!' He sounded genuinely concerned, which made the lie seem all the worse. She hated lying, having been forced to do it so often in her childhood to cover up for her father.

He ushered her inside. 'You know, I don't recall seeing a notebook. And I did check the briefcase thoroughly.'

'It's only very small. Perhaps you missed it, or . . .'

'Well, I *was* a bit het up that weekend, so I suppose I could have done. And there's just a chance it might be at the hospital. I certainly had the briefcase there and I did take some things out.' His frown of dismay increased her guilt. 'I could have sworn I put everything back, but . . . I'd better ring the hospital. Do come up and I'll get on to them right away.'

'Thanks.' She followed him into the hall.

'Mind you, it's a while ago now,' James observed as he led the way upstairs. 'I only hope they've still got it.'

'I'm sorry, I should have come before. But what with Easter and everything . . .' She had spent Easter with her parents, but although she was physically in Leicestershire her mind remained with James, conjecturing where he might be and, more importantly, with whom. 'How's your grandmother, by the way?' she asked, remembering her original plan.

'Oh, loads better, thank you. In fact, I was with them on Easter Sunday, and she was well enough to go out to lunch.'

'That must be a relief.' A relief for Alison, too. She wanted everything in his life to be serene. Far from curing her obsession, just seeing him again had brought all the violent feelings surging back. Whatever Linda might say, this was different. Special. Real.

When he opened the door to his flat, she saw more furniture had been installed: an antique bureau in the corner and a mahogany table with four chairs. On her previous visit the place had offered no clue about his lifestyle: no photographs or trinkets and an almost empty bookcase. Now, though, there were scores of books, neatly arranged by size, and also a couple of framed photos on the mantlepiece. Yet the overall impression was still one of restraint. Everything was tidy, everything well bred – a contrast to Hunston where she had been cooped up for four days with her parents' constant bickering and the accumulated clutter of twenty years.

'Let me take your coat.'

As she slipped it off her shoulders, the scarlet dress was revealed – again she was introducing a note of strident colour into the sobriety of his flat. Yet she wanted him to admire the dress, even to cast a surreptitious glance at her cleavage, as Martin Wallace had done. Instead he was draping her coat carefully over a chair.

'Do sit down. Can I get you something? Tea? Coffee? A glass of wine?'

She hesitated. She had drunk enough alcohol already. It would be appalling to become loud or giggly and ruin this one chance to make her mark. 'I'd love a coffee, if it's no trouble.'

'Of course not. I'll put it on and it can be perking while I phone the hospital.'

The instant he left the room she jumped up to look at the photos. Only one concerned her: a dark-haired girl about his age, with attractive features and a sensitive face. Was this the girlfriend she'd imagined? It could even be his ex-wife. Except he'd hardly keep an ex-wife's photo on the mantlepiece. Maybe she was his fiancée, the entrancing, brilliant woman he adored.

By the time he came back she was sitting on the sofa again, unsuccessfully trying to conceal the expanse of stockinged leg on show. Did she look cheap in his eyes? The woman in the photo would have worn a more subtle dress – a designer creation, most likely. And she would probably have a Sloaney voice and be knowledgeable enough about modern art to make perceptive comments on his paintings.

'Now then, the hospital . . . I know I've got the number somewhere.'

She watched him flick through his Filofax. His fingers were almost effeminate: long and slim and tapering. Yet everything else about him was resolutely male – heavy brows, dark-shadowed chin, lean, athletic build. The suit showed off his figure to perfection and the white shirt made his hair seem blacker still.

'Got it!' he said, moving to the phone. 'But first you'd better give me a few more details about this notebook.'

'It's, er, blue. Spiral-bound. Quite small.' The duplicity was hateful. All she wanted to say was: 'Forget the stupid notebook. Sit down here and talk. Tell me all about yourself.'

He dialled the number and, after a few seconds, mouthed 'Answerphone' and raised his eyes to heaven. Answering-machines seemed to play a major role in their relationship.

It took some time to establish that no notebook had been found. He was transferred from one department to another, remaining calm and courteous throughout. She admired the way he treated everyone – operators, strangers – with such good-humoured patience. Next he phoned his grandparents to ask if they had seen the notebook. She sensed the depth of affection in his voice – a bantering tone almost, more suited to a lover – and felt absurdly jealous.

'No luck there either, I'm afraid. I really am sorry. If it doesn't turn up, will you be in trouble?'

'Er, no.' How could she tell him that Anne-Marie didn't even work at Shaw Hilliard any more? She had walked out after a blazing row with Christine about the Glyn Griffiths fiasco. In fact, that was why *she* had been promoted. Christine had decided after top-level consultations that it would be easier and less expensive to give her Anne-Marie's job than to have to advertise for someone from outside.

'What happened about that manuscript?' James asked, as if reading her mind. 'Did you manage to finish your report?'

'Yes. And we won the auction. It went for three hundred thousand pounds.'

'I say, congratulations! You must be awfully pleased.'

'Yes, I am,' she smiled, thinking how different his reaction was from her mother's cry of outrage: 'It's absolutely wicked! How could any book be worth so much? Madge next door is living on a pittance. She can hardly afford to feed her cat.' Her mother (who never opened a book from one year to another) would gladly see the British Library close down if it would keep Madge next door in Kit-e-Kat. She noticed James's books all looked rather scholarly; some were even leather-bound.

'And that's just the start,' she told him. 'Now they're busy negotiating the international rights. The sale to the States alone could well fetch a million dollars. And there's lots of interest from the film world.'

'It *does* sound exciting.'

'Oh, it is. We've just been celebrating actually. I'm on my way back from the party.' Finsbury was hardly on the way back from Covent Garden. She only hoped he wouldn't ask where the party had been held.

Fortunately he remembered the coffee and disappeared into the kitchen.

While he was gone she had another quick look round. On the mantlepiece she found a postcard from someone called Jeremy – no rival there, thank God – and a rather grand wedding invitation: Rear Admiral and Mrs Edward Fraser-Moore requested the pleasure of his company at the marriage of their daughter Rosamund . . . She fingered the embossed black script. The wedding was on Saturday week at a church called St Etheldreda's, Ely Place, and the reception was in the Painted Hall at the Royal Naval College, Greenwich. Glumly she stood the card on the mantlepiece again. No way was she in *that* league.

James served the coffee in delicate porcelain cups, with a matching milk jug and sugar bowl. In the Clapham flat, milk stayed in its bottle, sugar in its packet and coffee was Tesco's instant. Jim didn't even know how to *make* coffee. He could just about manage to put a teaspoon of powder in a mug, but when it came to percolators . . .

No, that was unkind and unworthy. She had been happy enough with Jim – in fact, pleased to have a steady, serious boyfriend after a succession of rather tenuous relationships at college. Yet her adolescent fantasies had invariably featured a dark, intense, cultured man who whisked her off to Tibet or Istanbul, prised the world open for her and presented her with the pearl. Jim was sandy-haired and freckly and with him she'd not been further afield than Hunston (to visit her parents) and Newbury (to visit his).

'So what happens now with the book?' James asked, as he passed her milk and sugar. 'Is it your responsibility to see it into print?'

She was tempted to say yes. Instead she answered honestly that, in spite of her promotion, she still worked for Christine in a fairly lowly position with no authors of her own as yet. 'But I will be reading manuscripts,' she added. Which was quite enough about *her*.

However, questioned about his own work his response was jocular: 'You know what they say about accountants – as boring as they come! Your job sounds much more interesting.'

Next she inquired about his family, hoping that might shed some light on his age. He was older than her, certainly, but how much?

'I have three sisters – two older, one younger.'

'And brothers?'

'No. I was the only boy.'

'Were you spoiled when you were little, then?'

He laughed. 'I expect so. How about you? Do you come from a big family?'

'No, I'm an only child.' She regretted her solitary childhood. Brothers and sisters would have taken the onus off her. Instead, she had been the sole focus of her parents' hopes and ambitions and appealed to by each as an ally in their frequent rows. But she had no wish to go into that. Meeting James had changed her, fired her with a desire to transform herself from scratch. She might not be in his league at present, but anything was possible if you worked at it with enough commitment. The heroine of Francesca's novel had battled against overwhelming odds to win the man she loved, and she would do the same. One thing she was determined on: before the evening was out she and James must have arranged to meet again.

5

Alison emerged from the tube and consulted her A–Z. Ely Place looked tiny on the map, an unobtrusive cul-de-sac off Charterhouse Street. It was only ten minutes' walk away, which in normal circumstances would have meant a pleasant stroll in the early morning sunshine, but she was too agitated to take much in until she reached her destination. Away from the fret of traffic and the blare of unsightly hoardings, Ely Place had an air of cloistered elegance, with its quaint, old-fashioned lamp-posts, and well-coiffed bay trees standing guard outside graciously proportioned houses. However, there was no sign of a church, although the invitation had definitely said St Etheldreda's, Ely Place.

She walked on a little further past imposing façades with porticoed front doors flanked by black and gold railings, and suddenly saw a huge traceried Gothic window, all but trapped, it appeared, between the adjacent buildings. This was it, the church – but what an extraordinary position. She had expected a frontage, open space of some kind. Even City churches had at least a strip of grass, if not a proper graveyard, but St

Etheldreda's seemed overpowered by the structures rudely elbowing it on each side. It gave the impression of being a foundling, abandoned far from its natural habitat, and certainly didn't look grand enough to house a society wedding.

She was miles too early, of course (having lain awake all last night in a mixture of fear and anticipation), and there was nobody around yet – no priest or vicar, no guests in wedding finery. She might as well kill time in a café and return at a more suitable hour.

She wandered back along Holborn, then down Leather Lane, looking for somewhere open on a Saturday. The only place she could find was a rough workmen's caff and, as she entered, several heads turned. Her outfit – a smart black skirt and velvet top – made her conspicuous amidst the donkey jackets and jeans. She sat at a plastic-topped table and ordered a coffee. Most people were alone, like her, perhaps spinning out their eggs and bacon because they had nowhere else to go. The smell of frying churned her stomach – or was it nerves at the thought of seeing James again? He had affected her like a drug, one with dangerous side-effects. And the enormity of what she was doing added to her apprehension. Her experience of fashionable weddings was nil. In fact, she had only been to two weddings in her life, and both were in registry offices.

She made the coffee last as long possible, trying to avoid the eyes of the other customers and the attentions of the waitress, who kept clumping over to see if she wanted anything else. The man at the next table reminded her of her father – not just the way he smoked with such single-minded devotion, using his greasy plate as an ashtray, but his solid build, jowly face and thatch of salt-and-pepper hair. She felt an unexpected homesickness as she suddenly remembered her first bleak day at grammar school, when she had wanted to cling on to him and never let him go. That scholarship (a source of self-satisfaction for her parents) had in fact cut her off from her friends in the village and left her with the feeling that she didn't quite belong, either at home or at school. Gradually, inexorably, she had grown away from her parents, as her interests changed and broadened. Poetry, her father stated, was a total waste of time; philosophy worse still: 'What on earth's the point of *that*, pray? It won't get you a decent job.' Now she felt caught between two worlds. James had read Classics at Cambridge.

'Hm, a good catch, then,' Linda had said drily. 'No wonder you're smitten.'

She was secretly hurt, if not insulted, at Linda's implication of social climbing. James meant far more than that – he was everything she respected in a man: caring and family-minded and well-mannered and sincere but also dynamic and exciting. Admittedly she didn't know much about him, apart from Cambridge and accountancy and a close circle of relatives, but she was certain at an instinctive level that this was the man she was destined to love.

She had been thinking night and day about love, aware that prior to James it was a word she had largely distrusted – her father had used it too often to disguise selfishness or lust. Whatever else, it had been blunted through overuse, yet the concept itself was . . .

'Can I get you some toast? Or a refill?' The waitress's tone was brusque.

Evidently she had spun out one small coffee long enough. She left some money on the table and picked her way back along the lane, side-stepping dustbin bags, broken crates and hazardous gaps in the pavement. The buildings were old and dingy, many covered in graffiti – a marked contrast to the tasteful privilege of Ely Place.

She stopped outside its gated entrance, surprised at the strength of the sun veneering the grey City idling in weekend sloth. Perfect weather for a wedding – bright and crisp, with a confident blue sky.

At the church there were now more signs of life: a few sleek limousines parked opposite and a group of ushers waiting just outside. She froze – she hadn't reckoned on ushers. But one of them was approaching, immaculate in morning suit and white carnation.

'Hello,' he said, 'you're nice and early.'

She murmured a greeting, hoping her clothes didn't smell of bacon fat.

'Bride or groom?' he asked.

'Er, groom.'

'Fine. Do you know the church?'

'No, I don't.'

'Well, you go in by the side door here and follow the cloister until you come to the church door proper at the end. Sit on the right, anywhere you like except the front three rows. There'll be plenty of choice,' he smiled. 'You're practically the first.'

As she had intended. Yet it was madness to sit alone in the church, exposed to public scrutiny. She hadn't expected a set-up like this, with nowhere to hide, no escape route. Too late to change her mind, though – the usher was gesturing with his top hat towards a small side door. Walking through, she found herself in a stone-flagged passage leading to a short flight of steep stone steps. The church door was at the top and to the right, set beneath a Gothic arch which, although impressive, again looked oddly cramped, as if this beleaguered church had no room to breathe or spread itself. Opposite the door was a small winding staircase marked 'Private', screened by a stone wall. At that moment, she heard muffled voices from the far end of the passage. The priest? Or some official who might ask her awkward questions? Without stopping to think, she darted behind the stone wall and crouched out of sight halfway up the stairs.

Regaining her breath, she noticed a trail of dust on her skirt and brushed it off impatiently. This cloak-and-dagger stuff was quite absurd. Yet she had to admit the hiding-place was ideal, concealing her completely while affording a perfect view of the church door just below. There was no need for her to enter the church at all. She would simply stay here and watch for James's arrival.

As the voices grew louder she straightened up a little and peered over the top of the wall. A couple were approaching, walking up the flight of stone steps – he in a dress uniform, she in an exotic feathered hat, and with a white corsage pinned to her dress. As they turned to enter the church Alison was so close to them from her vantage-point above that she could see the age spots on the man's bald head and the woman's pearl-drop earrings. Behind them came a family: parents shepherding four little girls. The children were dressed alike in velvet-collared coats, white socks and black patent shoes – a veritable fashion parade in miniature. Reaching the top of the steps, one of the girls glanced up at the wall, as if conscious of an unseen watcher. Alison shrank back. Perhaps she wasn't as safe as she thought. She had no idea where the staircase led. Someone might appear at any minute, coming from a belfry or a gallery . . .

But now there was more noise from the passageway. Warily she looked out and saw a large contingent of men in morning suits, all well under thirty. Friends of the groom perhaps. James was not among them, nor in the group which followed – a motley crew of young and old, talking animatedly. Soon guests were arriving thick and fast and, as the flight of stone steps created a bottleneck, she imagined the passage must be fairly congested by now. She wondered how such numbers would fit into the church, although she hadn't actually seen inside it. She needed her full attention to scan all comers, otherwise she might miss James. The wedding was due to start in ten minutes, and still he wasn't here. Perhaps he wasn't coming after all and this whole risky endeavour had been a waste of time. Indeed, as the minutes ticked on, she regretted her folly more and more. In the early hours of this morning her plan had seemed perfectly reasonable. She had never intended to reveal herself, just to turn up early and wait a short distance from the church, to see whether he was on his own or with a woman. If the latter, she would leave the field to her rival and graciously withdraw. Well, maybe not graciously but at least she would have the tact to stop pursuing him. She disapproved of pushy women who inflicted themselves on men who weren't remotely interested. Yet James *had* seemed interested that evening in his flat. In fact, he had inspired her to flights of eloquence, laughing at her jokes, asking more about her job and certainly in no hurry to get rid of her. When she left, long after midnight, she was positive he would phone the following day.

Nine days had passed. No phone-call.

Hearing the tap-tap of a stick, she looked cautiously over the wall again. The crowd was now reduced to a few stragglers – one of them an elderly lady trying to climb the first of the steps. She wore an old-fashioned Persian lamb coat and matching hat. All at once a much younger man materialized at her side and took her arm: a tall, slim, dark-haired man. *James!* And his grandmother. Alison scarcely dared believe her eyes as the pair negotiated the next few steps. But then, sick with disappointment, she realized that it wasn't James after all. Like a traveller in a desert starving after nine days without food, she had conjured up a mirage. Yet she knew she was overreacting, ludicrously so. Even if he turned up on his own it wouldn't prove a thing. He might still have a girlfriend who hadn't been invited or simply couldn't come. In any case, she could hardly jump out and accost him.

She sat crouched on the staircase, appalled at her behaviour. What in God's name was she *doing* here, gatecrashing somebody's wedding? If James should spot her he would be furious, disgusted. She must go back to Clapham – back to reality – before she lost all self-respect. She was already in danger of losing her friends. Linda was sick of hearing James's name, and Jim was increasingly suspicious, even if he was too decent to ask questions.

Suddenly the organ, which had been rumbling quietly in the background, struck up the opening chords of the wedding march. She scrambled to her feet, determined to leave before the wedding began. Impossible: her way was barred by the bridal party processing steadily towards her.

She couldn't help but stare. So this was Rosamund – perhaps a friend of James's, even a relative. They might have played together as children or gone to the same school. Or maybe her father, the Rear Admiral, was a friend of James's parents. He looked impressive, certainly: a well-built man in full naval regalia and sporting a row of medals. And the bride could have stepped straight out of the pages of the *Tatler*, in her Edwardian-style dress with its high neck and full flounced sleeves. The sweeping train was carried by a posse of bridesmaids, mostly under-fives, in dark green velvet gowns with circlets of flowers on their heads. As the procession turned to enter the church Alison felt even more ashamed at spying on them at such close quarters. She could actually smell the bride's perfume and could almost have reached down and touched the silk rosebuds wreathed in her dark hair.

Once the last pair of bridesmaids had vanished inside the church, leaving the coast clear, she dashed down the staircase, intent on escape, then down the flight of stone steps. But halfway along the passage something made her stop and, marvelling at her audacity, she walked back to the open door of the church and slipped inside.

The sight that greeted her took her breath away. The interior of the church was magical: a treasure house, a masterpiece. She was astounded at its size, its simple splendour, its blaze of coloured glass – a secret gem hidden in an unprepossessing carapace.

The sun, streaming through the great east window, cast patches of hazy blue and red on the ancient pale stone walls. The glass itself glowed like precious jewels, and all along the window-sills candles were alight, interspersed with posies of spring flowers. An unseen choir was singing – their voices swooped and soared, pursuing each other in glorious counterpoint. Although the words were unintelligible she recognized the drama in them, the majesty, intensity. Such was the mood of joy and triumph, her worries seemed to fall away as thundering organ and jubilant choir uplifted her to a place that knew no fear.

She crept in a little further and stood unnoticed in the back pew, as near to the aisle as possible, so she could see what was happening at the other end of the church. There appeared to be one main priest, an imposing, white-haired figure wearing sumptuous vestments encrusted with gold embroidery. Behind him came a group of men and boys, in full-length purple robes with short white gowns on top and bronze medals round their necks. Some were carrying silver candlesticks, one a silver crucifix, one an open book. Moving with stately grace they positioned themselves to the right of the altar, while the priest stood facing the bride and groom.

'Welcome, my dear friends,' he said, addressing the congregation. 'Welcome to St Etheldreda's, which has stood on this hallowed site for seven hundred years. Perhaps some of you are unaware that this is the oldest Catholic church in London. And we're in a church today because marriage is a sacrament. Don't imagine,' he continued in his deeply resonant voice, 'that you're only here as passive spectators. You play an essential role in the ceremony. We need you to bear witness as Rosamund and Mark promise to love and serve each other throughout their life and to be faithful to each other unto death.'

Rather different from the reality, Alison reflected. Most of her friends' parents were divorced, including Jim's and Linda's, and her own parents only stayed together because her father despised lawyers almost more than priests.

'Rosamund and Mark have chosen to have their Nuptial Mass in Latin, the ancient language which befits this ancient church. So please be seated for the singing of the *Kyrie* and *Gloria* . . .'

In a dream, she sat down. Conscience dictated she should leave, but the lure of the music proved too strong. Being in church was a new experience for her, and only now did she realize what a deprivation that had been. She had always longed for tradition, for something to sweep her beyond the drably mundane – and here it was in all its glory. To think that some fortunate people enjoyed this sort of ceremonial as a regular part of their lives. Perhaps James was a Catholic and this was his church. It wasn't far from his flat.

Good heavens, James! She had actually forgotten him. And for all she knew, he might be here, only feet away. She began checking every head in every pew – an exacting task, to say the least – but eventually satisfied herself that he wasn't in the congregation. Which was something of a relief. If he were indeed sitting here she would have to leave at once, and she couldn't bear to miss this exquisite music. She had no idea what it was, but there was such tremendous spirit in it – a full-frontal attack on one's ears and mind and heart. Certain phrases seemed to be repeated, tossed back and forth between the voices like children playing ball, then, after a crescendo with the choir imploring *en masse*, came a sudden dramatic silence, as if the whole church were holding its breath.

She shivered with pleasure, astonished that so many people, children included, could maintain such a reverent hush. Then a solo soprano pierced the silence with an impassioned cry, and immediately other voices joined in, weaving and entwining, while the organ boomed a majestic accompaniment. This is how heaven must be, she thought – this ecstatic, powerful sound, this sense of being transported to another world. Shafts of sunlight filtered through the windows and mingled with the incense to create a hazy film which heightened the feeling of unreality. And the colours in the magnificent east window exploded into even richer life: claret red, kingfisher blue, electric green, magenta. She feasted her eyes on the glass. In the centre, a troop of angels clustered around a seated Christ. Their golden wings seemed aflame, blazing with the splendour of the music. The rest of the window thronged with scenes and people – regal figures holding staves or scrolls and, above them, abstract shapes like Catherine wheels spinning in shell-bursts of colour.

She gazed up at the soaring stone arches framing every window; the crumbling stone itself, so venerably old; the striking life-sized statues standing in niches round the church walls, who appeared to be real historical characters wearing hats and ruffs. The nearest, just above and to her left, was, she fancied, eyeing her sternly, as if aware that she was here without an invitation. She looked the other way. She couldn't leave at this point – the singing had just reached a climax with a final peal from the organ, and a young man in a brocade waistcoat got up from the front pew and went to stand at a lectern in front of the altar. It would be rude to creep out when he was obviously about to speak.

'The first reading is from the Song of Songs,' he announced, and after a moment's pause, began. '"Hold me close to thy heart, close as a locket or a bracelet fits. Not death itself is so strong as love, not the grave itself cruel as love unrequited. The torch that lights it is a blaze of fire."'

She was entranced by the poetic words, which perfectly expressed her own private sentiments. Her thoughts returned to James as she imagined herself a locket round his neck, a bracelet on his wrist. The images became more erotic: the two of them braceleted together, naked and entwined.

Guiltily she scrambled to her feet. Everyone else was standing while she lay heart to heart with James. She had missed part of the service; the priest's words a backdrop for her fantasy. And now the marriage proper was about to begin. The tall white-haired priest was standing in front of the bridal couple, and the best man had stepped forward with the ring.

'Mark' – the priest's voice echoed through the church – 'Wilt thou take Rosamund here present to thy lawful wife, according to the rites of our holy Mother the Church?'

Alison hung on every word. How much more inspiring this was than the brief rubric of the registry office, with its added indignity of a queue system – one bride hustled off the scene only seconds before the next arrived. Here, as the vows were recited, the pace was measured, the language solemn.

'The ring,' explained the priest, 'is a symbol of fidelity, which binds husband and wife together. And it shares the symbolism of the circle as completeness and fulfilment – another important attribute of marriage.'

Alison glanced at the ring she was wearing: pretty in its way, but devoid of such sacred meaning it remained a mere piece of jewellery.

'With this ring,' said Mark, turning to his bride, 'I thee wed. This gold and silver I thee give. With my body I thee worship . . .'

Struck by the beauty of the words once more, she repeated them in her head, although it was *James* who was speaking in his soft, distinguished voice, vowing to worship her with his body. But just at that moment a little boy in the pew in front turned round and fixed her with a hostile stare. She shifted uneasily. She had no right to be here. The priest was about to give his address – an address intended for the bride and groom and their families and friends, not for an intruder. She dragged herself up from the pew and was on the point of tiptoeing out when the priest's voice seemed to summon her back.

'Love' – the word rang out like a clarion call – 'is the most important thing in life. More important than money, status or career. None of that is permanent and none of us is essential in our profession. Only love is permanent. Only in love will we find true and lasting fulfilment. Love is at the heart of human life.'

She stood transfixed. This was the truth; the one great truth people chose to forget. Linda would dismiss it as a cliché, and her parents too would scoff, but she had an uncanny premonition that the priest's words were directed at her particularly. Intruder though she was, she knew now she had to stay for the rest of the service; gather up this wealth of joy and colour and store it away for the future. She would need courage and perseverance to fight for that ideal, against Linda's so-called common sense and the easy cynicism of the world.

'Rosamund and Mark,' the priest concluded. 'You no longer have problems in your life – you have only challenges. With your love to sustain you – and God to sustain your love – you cannot but succeed.' He laid his hands briefly on their heads, then returned to the altar and began chanting aloud in Latin.

She watched the ritual unfold, listening to the mysterious words, strange yet sublime. The men in purple robes glided to and fro, bowing solemnly to each other as they played their well-rehearsed part in the service. Even the young boys were remarkably dignified – one refilling the incense, another handing the priest a gold vessel. (What a contrast to the foul-mouthed kids who terrorized the street in Clapham.)

There was a sudden stirring fanfare from the organ, and the choir erupted in a tumult of sound which ran like an electric charge through her body and her mind. This music was like *love*, she thought: the same drama, passion, clamour; the same surges of sheer joy interspersed with yearning tenderness. Most of her life had been spent in a grey, uncertain world like a photographic negative, but now she was being 'developed' into brilliant singing colour – the colour of the music, the brilliance of the glass. She might not understand the words or the meaning of the ritual, but one thing she knew beyond all doubt: she would be married in this church – with this priest, this choir, this music – and remain faithful to her marriage vows till death.

6

The photographer appeared to be having trouble fitting the battalion of relatives into the rather truncated space outside the church. And the bridesmaids were becoming restive, dashing about and trying to escape. Alison stood watching from the other side of Ely Place, where she had concealed herself between two cars. She had planned to leave as soon as the service was over, but somehow it was impossible. The beauty of the service had left her on a high, and she couldn't just return to an ordinary Saturday at the flat. Besides, this was James's world and many of the people milling about in the close might well be his friends.

'Ah, Father!' The photographer seemed relieved as the priest appeared from the side door. 'If you'd like to slip in there beside the bride – that's it. Now, keep still everybody. And could you manage another smile?'

Alison gazed at the priest, who was still wearing his elaborate vestments – a work of art in themselves; the heavy, ivory-coloured damask embroidered with Easter lilies and an embossed gold chalice resplendent in the centre. The registrar at her schoolfriend's wedding had worn a shiny blue suit, and they had taken the photos in the car park against a concrete wall.

'Excuse me, young lady . . .'

Alison felt a hand on her shoulder. A daunting-looking woman in an ostrich-feather hat had come up right behind her. The blood rushed to her cheeks. Was she about to be ejected?

'Are you Janet McGrath, my dear?'

'Er, no, I'm not.'

'Oh, do forgive me. I thought as you were on your own . . . Apparently she's come all the way from Scotland and doesn't know a soul here, except Rosamund, of course. I was told to keep a look-out for her, but so far I've drawn a blank.'

As the woman turned to walk away, Alison suddenly blurted out, 'Actually, I'm looking for someone, too. James Egerton. Is he here, do you know?'

'Who, my dear?'

'James Egerton.' She swallowed, appalled at her temerity. 'My . . . flat-mate is an old friend of his from Cambridge. She wanted me to give him a message.'

'No, I can't say I've heard the name. Hold on, I'll ask my friend. Muriel,' she called to another portly female in a swathe of yellow chiffon, 'd'you know a James Egerton?'

Muriel shook her head. 'Sorry, it doesn't ring a bell. Try Claire. She's bound to know.'

'Good idea. Claire!' The woman's voice rang out imperiously. 'We're looking for a Mr James Egerton. You haven't seen him, have you?'

By now Alison regretted having asked. Her tentative whisper was being bellowed to all and sundry, and she had been flushed out of her hiding place and exposed to general view.

'No. Never heard of him.'

'James Egerton?' said a male voice. 'He's a friend of Suzanne's. They were at Emmanuel together.'

'Suzanne?' Alison turned eagerly to the young man who had spoken. 'Is she here, by any chance?'

'Yes. We came together, although I'm not sure where she's got to.' He looked up and down the crowded close, where clusters of guests stood chatting and laughing, enjoying the spring sunshine. Some of the outfits, Alison reckoned, must have cost more than she earned in a month. This chap, however, looked, frankly, a bit of a mess – his hair untidy, his tie askew.

'Seen Suzanne?' he asked an older man, another of the naval contingent in uniform and medals.

'Yes, I was talking to her a minute ago. She said she was going to get something from her car.'

Alison felt more and more self-conscious at being the centre of attention. At this rate, it was only a matter of time before she was rumbled.

'Well, her car's parked just a little further down.' The young man turned to her with a smile. 'I'll introduce you. I'm Douglas, by the way.'

'And I'm . . . Alison.' She was aware that her palm was damp as she shook his hand.

'Nice to meet you, Alison. Were you at school with Rosamund as well? I've already met at least three old St Margaret's girls.'

Fortunately at that moment he spotted Suzanne, who was leaning against a steel-blue Volvo, surreptitiously smoking. 'You haven't seen this, OK?' she said, cupping a guilty hand around the cigarette. 'I'm meant to have given up. But, good grief, that service was so long I was absolutely gasping.'

Douglas laughed. 'She's always giving up smoking, you know,' he confided to Alison. 'It's become almost a hobby for her. Never mind, we've all got to die of something. Suzanne, this is Alison. She's a friend of Rosamund's.'

Alison glanced furtively over her shoulder, thankful that Rosamund was still busy posing for the photographer. It was madness taking risks like this. Suppose someone asked her about the Fraser-Moores. She would have to resort to fabrication again.

Suzanne smiled a greeting. 'Cigarette?' she offered.

'No thanks. I don't smoke.'

'That's what everybody says these days. We smokers are an endangered species!'

'Oh, all my friends smoke,' Alison said quickly. Anything to find favour with Suzanne. 'And my father's a sixty-a-day man.'

'Mine too,' said Suzanne. 'And he has no intention of dying before his hundredth birthday.'

'Which reminds me,' said Douglas. 'I'm meant to be looking after Mrs Phelps. She's ninety-seven, would you believe! I'll leave you two together.'

'How long have you known Rosamund?' Suzanne asked when Douglas had gone.

'Oh, I, er, met her quite recently.'

'I have to say I was surprised she had a Nuptial Mass. I mean, she's been living with Mark for years. It seems a tad hypocritical, don't you think?'

Alison nodded uneasily.

'Especially a *Latin* Mass. Personally, I find that rather pretentious in this day and age. But let's be charitable and put it down to her father's influence. And since he's paying for the whole shindig, I guess he's entitled to his little whims. All the same,' she shrugged, 'I wish he hadn't inflicted it on us. If I have to go to Mass – which admittedly is a rare event these days – I prefer it short and sharp.'

'Me too.' Alison was on dangerous ground. It would probably be safer to jump right in and ask about James. Every other subject was a minefield. She cleared her throat nervously. 'Douglas tells me you're a friend of James Egerton.'

'Why, yes, I am. Do you know him?'

'Yes. No. I mean . . . it's my . . . flatmate. She lost touch with him after Cambridge and she wanted . . . wondered . . .'

'Was she at Emmanuel? In that case, I might have known her. What's her name?'

'Er, Francesca.' (Last week, the real Francesca had met her for lunch before flying back to Brazil.) 'Francesca . . . Lloyd.'

Suzanne frowned, as if trying to recall the name. 'What was she reading?'

'English.'

'Oh, I see. James and I did classics, and us lot did rather tend to stick together.' She shaded her eyes against the sun. 'Rosamund's so lucky with the weather. If this had been last weekend, we'd have all been in winter woollies.'

'I think Francesca's hoping to see him again.' Alison refused to be sidetracked by the weather. 'In fact,' she forced a laugh, 'I suspect she's still a little bit in love with him.'

'Aren't we all?' Suzanne laughed too. 'God, I nearly died when he went off to be a priest. What a waste!'

Alison stared in disbelief. 'A . . . a priest?'

'Yes. Didn't Francesca tell you? Straight after finals he went back to his old school to join the monks. We weren't really that surprised, to be honest. He was a bit like a monk even at Cambridge. I mean, in the vacs, when normal people pop off to Greece or Tuscany, James would go to Lourdes and trundle sick kids around in wheelchairs, bless him. Mind you, he did have lots of girlfriends. Women seemed to swarm around him. A friend of mine at Emmanuel was badly smitten, I can tell you, but she didn't stand a chance. It was no sex before marriage, and marriage only to a good Catholic girl. Poor Philippa hadn't even been baptized. Her parents were rampant atheists.'

Alison struggled for words. 'Is he . . . still a priest?' How could that be possible when he *said* he was an accountant – and dressed in ordinary clothes and lived in an ordinary flat? Although didn't priests wear mufti these days? And perhaps he was involved in some sort of financial work for the church . . .

'Pierre!' Suzanne stubbed out her cigarette and rushed over to greet an angular man in a black shirt and white three-piece suit. 'How wonderful to see you. I'd no idea you were coming.'

'I only made it by the skin of my teeth! The journey was a nightmare.' He kissed her on both cheeks and gave a formal bow to Alison.

'Alison, this is my friend Pierre. He owns a restaurant in Paris. How's it going, *mon ange*? When we last met you were having trouble with the decorators.'

'Oh, that's all sorted out. I'm having trouble with the chef now!'

Alison waited in tense silence while Suzanne and Pierre discussed the problems of finding reliable staff.

'Alison, I'm sorry to be so rude,' Suzanne said, at last. 'Pierre and I haven't seen each other for . . . how long is it, *chéri?*'

'Eighteen months?'

'More. I remember now, it was Annette's twenty-first. You know, that ghastly do in Antibes when they hired a yacht and half of us were seasick.'

Alison glanced over her shoulder again. The photographer must have finished, since the regimented group was breaking up and the chauffeur of the wedding car (a vintage Rolls-Royce the colour of Jersey cream) was standing to attention, awaiting the bride and groom. They would all be leaving for the reception – the Painted Hall at the Royal Naval College. Impossible to gatecrash that. Yet she just had to find out about James. If he *were* a priest it changed everything; put him completely out of her reach.

'Ah, we seem to be on the way at last,' Suzanne said eagerly, observing the general movement towards the cars. 'I'll give you a lift, Pierre. And how about you, Alison? Have you any transport?'

'Er, no.'

'Well do come with us. There's plenty of room.'

'Thank you, but I . . . I can't come to the reception. I've got to . . . see my mother. She's not well.' Lies and more lies. She was horrified at how glibly they came out. Yet in the pursuit of James they seemed justified. *Anything* seemed justified. Desperately she turned to Suzanne. 'Could I ask you one last question about James?'

'James?'

'James Egerton.'

'Oh, *him*. I'm sorry, I'd forgotten your poor flatmate. Actually, he should be here. He told me he was coming.'

'He's not ill, is he?' Gruesome images flashed across her mind – heart attacks, car accidents.

'Not that I've heard.' Suzanne's mind was elsewhere. She was rummaging in her handbag, presumably looking for car keys.

Alison felt uncomfortable pestering Suzanne, but if she didn't get some answers, she would never sleep tonight, let alone concentrate on work. 'Is he still a priest? You didn't say.'

'Heavens, no! It didn't work out. He left about five years ago and decided to go into accountancy, of all things.' Now she had found her keys Suzanne seemed more communicative again. 'Sounds fearfully boring, doesn't it? I mean, he was absolutely brilliant at Cambridge. He got a double first and wrote plays and poetry and stuff. Personally, I blame the monks. I'm sure they broke his spirit.'

'Francesca's dying to know if he's . . . married or engaged or . . .?' Alison just had to get the question in. Pierre was already walking round to the passenger side and any minute her sole source of information would be gone.

'No.' Suzanne shook her head. 'He never seems to meet the right woman. He *was* involved with someone a few months ago. But same old story. She wouldn't convert to Catholicism. Besides which I don't think she was all that keen on marrying a man who's still a virgin at the age of thirty-two.'

'*What?*' Pierre's head bobbed up from the other side of the car. 'You're joking, of course?'

'No. Cross my heart! He must be the only Catholic left who actually believes every word our dear Pope says.'

'I assumed virgins were extinct.' Pierre shuddered delicately. 'Especially the male of the species. Certainly they are in France.'

'Yes, in England too, apart from poor old James. *Saint* James, I should say. Actually I think it's rather sweet that he's celibate. If you ask me, he's in love with God.' Suzanne unlocked the car. 'Come on, Pierre. I don't want to be late. It's a long enough trek to Greenwich as it is. *Au revoir*, Alison. Maybe see you around.'

'Mm. Yes . . . goodbye.' Dumbly she watched them drive away. James – an ex-priest, a celibate in love with God. She didn't stand a chance. Like Philippa she had never been baptized.

'Excuse me, can I offer you a lift?' An elderly man in a morning suit smiled at her as he unlocked his silver Jaguar.

Politely she declined. She must leave at once before he – or anyone else – could ask more awkward questions. She hurried out of Ely Place and crossed the road against the lights, causing several cars to hoot impatiently. Her mind was in such turmoil she hardly knew what she was doing. Did she really want a man who sounded so peculiar – a virgin of thirty-two, for heaven's sake? Perhaps there was something wrong with him. It might not be religious scruples at all, but an abnormally low sex-drive. Or he might be gay and denying it.

None the less, he was brilliant. Suzanne had said so categorically, and she didn't seem the type to give unwarranted praise. And compassionate. How many people would spend their vacations wheeling sick children around Lourdes? And what was wrong with strict principles? If someone was a Catholic, better they took it seriously than flouted the rules. And he was popular – that was obvious.

But what would he see in *her*? The agnostic daughter of parents who dismissed all religion as claptrap. The only good work she had ever done was visiting old people as part of a school project. And as for her degree, she had scraped a second from a middle-brow, middle-of-the-road Midlands university (as the *Sunday Times* had once described Leicester). Despite Linda's insinuations, it wasn't a matter of bettering herself. All her life she had felt an indefinable longing. Sometimes, as a child, she would sit alone in the field beyond the house and wish she were a star or a cloud – not only to escape her parents' quarrelling but because stars were brighter and clouds were higher than grubby little girls. And today she had found what she was seeking: in St Etheldreda's Church, with its music and its poetry, its view of another dimension beyond mere clay and clod. And James was part of it.

She looked up at the sky, now a brilliant blue, more like August than mid-April. In her head she could hear the choir again, their exquisite voices soaring over London, transforming it into a colony of heaven. She was seized with a wild happiness. Whatever the problems ahead and whatever the gulf between them – even wider than before – James was free. She had no rival. Except God.

7

Alison pushed aside the curtain and looked out at the sky. The day seemed suspended between night and morning; a few stars still doggedly shining, yet the first pink flush of dawn already lightening the murky blue. The lamp-posts cast their own harsh light on cars, pavement, fences, interspersed with swathes of darkness. The houses opposite had black and blinded windows; the whole street quiet, deserted. Only the sparrows were astir; cocksure and almost truculent as they twittered in the eaves. She was as wide awake as they were and twice as energetic. Only the thought of Linda's Sunday morning lie-in stopped her from hurtling down the stairs and running all the way to the common and back.

She remained at the window watching the almost imperceptible change in the blue from indigo to navy, and a few more tentative pink brush-strokes feathering the clouds. How slow the process was. If *she* were the dawn, she would break instantly, dramatically, in a dazzling sunburst of light. Unfortunately she had work to do. She pulled a sweater over her nightdress, picked up the manuscript from the dressing-table and climbed back into bed with it to keep warm. She had already read a hundred pages and could finish it in a couple of hours before Linda opened her eyes. It was a rather pedestrian story of two elderly sisters in York and, so far, she was inclined to reject it. Such power to make or break an author sometimes made her feel uneasy, although on the whole she was thrilled at how well the job was going. Even Christine seemed to have mellowed, and Francesca de Romero had kept in touch from Brazil. There had been a long letter just two days ago.

She began reading again, aware of the light nudging through the skimpy curtains, slowly increasing in intensity until the sun was streaming into the room. She ploughed on to the end, making notes from time to time, pleasantly surprised by the ingenious dénouement. Perhaps it wasn't so bad after all. She would have a rethink over a cup of tea before writing her report. She crept into the kitchen – more a cupboard really, where only one person could stand and work in comfort. The hob was not a pleasant sight. Whatever Linda had cooked last night (scrambled eggs, chicken soup?) had overflowed the saucepan and left a hardened yellowy crust. She attacked it with a scouring pad and then decided she might as well clean the whole oven. If only the flat had the elegance of James's place. Yet a few simple changes would improve it no end – fresh paint on the walls, new curtains perhaps, even some decent furniture from one of the second-hand shops down the road.

She rummaged under the sink for the oven-cleaner. Instead she found jars of mouldering shoe cream, ancient tins of paint with rusted-on lids, a headless doll and a pair of mud-caked trainers. Ignoring the kettle panting to a boil, she turfed out the useless items, tidied the remainder, then proceeded to do likewise with all the drawers and cupboards. It was hard work but worth the effort. If James should ever come here she wanted the place to look cared for. Next she scrubbed the worktops, washed the floor and cleaned the tiny window. She was about to start on the oven when Linda appeared at the door, bleary-eyed.

'What the fuck's going on?'

'I'm spring-cleaning.'

'At this ungodly hour? You woke me up.'

'I'm sorry. I did try to be quiet. D'you want a cup of tea?'

'OK,' said Linda grudgingly, 'but I'm going back to bed. Can you bring it in?'

''Course. Toast as well?'

'Not in the middle of the night, thanks.'

'Don't be daft – look at that sun! Let's go out and enjoy it later on. How about a trip to Kew?'

'We're going to the launderette, remember?'

'That won't take all day.'

'*And* Sainsbury's.'

'Oh, Linda, don't be such a grouch.'

'Well, I'm knackered. So would *you* be, after only three hours' sleep.'

Not true. Nothing could dampen her spirits now she knew that James was free – well, free in a sense. She switched on the news, which was full of dismal reports from the Gulf, and chronicles of redundancies at home. Given such gloom, it seemed callous to feel elated, so she retuned to Capital. They were playing 'River Deep, Mountain High' and she stood motionless to listen. Since meeting James the words of love songs, which used to pass her by, had acquired new force and meaning.

The song ended, although its exuberant mood remained with her. Ignoring the disc-jockey's babble she continued to hum the tune while she made the tea, seeing James in her mind, hearing the timbre of his voice.

Once the tea had brewed she poured two cups and took them into Linda's room, picking her way between the usual piles of unread newspapers and drifts of discarded clothes. Linda had never been noted for her tidiness but she had other, more important qualities. Who else would have listened so patiently to her endless ramblings on the subject of James?

'Stay a minute,' Linda said. 'There's something I have to tell you. Jim rang late last night after you'd gone to bed. I think he was checking up on you. He sounded pretty desperate.'

'Oh no!' Jim was spending the weekend in Newbury with his parents, much to her relief. 'I hope you told him I was in bed. Alone.'

''Course. I'd have said that anyway. On the other hand, you can't blame him for worrying.'

'But what am I meant to *do*?' It was extraordinary how her view of Jim had changed. He had always been a good-humoured, easy-going type, ready with a joke, but now all that seemed rather shallow. He had no burning ideals, no desire to give up time to help the sick, nor did he write poetry and plays. But then neither did *she*, for God's sake. She was being horribly unfair. And also boring Linda to tears with her continual talk of James – he might almost be a third person in the flat. Yet an awareness of her faults helped not a jot.

Linda took a sip of tea and leaned back against the pillows. 'Al, don't take this the wrong way, but I feel I ought to warn you.'

'What about?'

'James, of course. Look, think about it. Any bloke of thirty-two who's never had his end away is seriously bad news.'

'You didn't say that last night.'

'How could I? You were deaf to reason, floating around all starry-eyed. Although *why* I can't imagine. He sounds a complete arsehole.'

'You're just prejudiced. You haven't even met him.'

'I wouldn't want to, thanks. He must be hopelessly insecure if he has to have his girlfriends toe the party line. Religious maniacs – who needs them? And Catholics are the worst. They're anti everything – abortion, contraception, divorce, pleasure, sex . . .'

'It's not like that now. Things are changing.'

'Well, up to a point, I suppose. Remember that weird girl at college, Stephanie? *She* was a Catholic and by the end of the first term she'd slept with practically every bloke on the campus, tutors included. And she was on the pill. But that shows how fanatical James must be, if he insists on doing everything by the book.'

'He's got principles, that's all.'

Linda waited for a train to finish rattling past. 'Hitler had principles,' she said witheringly.

'Don't be ridiculous! James is a thoroughly good man. He used to take sick children to Lourdes.'

'That's not exactly a recommendation. The place is about as holy as Disneyland. And a total con. I mean, all those poor deluded wretches hoping for miracles. If God's so fucking good, why does he make them ill in the first place? D'you know, if he *did* exist I think I'd probably sue him.'

'You're just as biased as James, in your way.'

'Look, Al, it's *you* I care about. I couldn't bear to see you landed with umpteen children and throwing away your life on a bloke who's a closet gay.'

'He'd hardly father umpteen children if he's gay.'

They both laughed, and the tension was broken. They sat drinking their tea – companionably Alison thought, until Linda put her cup down and returned to the attack.

'This stuff about him being a priest. It sounds a bit creepy to me. I mean, why did he leave? Did you bother to ask?'

'Suzanne said it didn't work out.'

'I bet it didn't! He probably got the push for interfering with little boys.'

'Don't be so vile.'

'Listen,' Linda persisted. 'It's not just sex. He's bound to be into abstinence in general – no booze, no –'

'That's not true,' Alison retorted. 'When I went to his flat the first thing he did was offer me a brandy.' Yet she remembered the bare cupboard, the uneaten Christmas cake. She had to admit he was extremely thin. And had he actually *drunk* his brandy?

'You only want him because he's unavailable. It's a classic situation. If he was showering you with chocolates and flowers and phoning every minute you'd soon be fed up to the back teeth.'

Give me the chance, Alison thought. Forget phoning every minute – one call would be enough.

'*I* know what.' Linda giggled suddenly. 'Why don't you seduce him? Pop the virgin's cherry. Then you can find out what he's like in bed before you burn your boats.'

'Oh, Linda, I *couldn't*. He'd never let himself be tempted. That's why I admire him.'

Linda yawned hugely. 'I give up,' she said. 'You've got the whole thing out of proportion. It's like talking to a brick wall.'

Alison recalled a pet phrase of her mother's: 'all things in moderation'. Tepid applause instead of a standing ovation; a dry biscuit rather than a seven-course meal awash in cream and brandy; a penny-whistle in place of a grand orchestra. Real love *was* excessive, by its very nature. If you felt moderately about someone (as she did – or had done – about Jim) you could leave them or lose them without suffering despair, whereas the thought of never seeing James again made her physically ill. Sometimes her longing for him was so acute she felt in need of a crash helmet to protect her from its impact. But how could Linda understand? She discarded men like beach shoes – fun for a season, then of no more use. 'I'll leave you to catch up on your sleep,' she said, making for the door.

'Some chance, if you're planning a blitzkrieg on the flat.'

'It's OK, keep your hair on. I've got a report to write first. And I won't make a sound, I promise.'

'Thanks. Wake me at eleven, will you, and we'll go to the launderette.'

'I can hardly wait!'

'It's brute necessity, I'm afraid. I've run out of clean knickers.'

And you've also run out of patience, Alison didn't say, vowing not to mention James again – all day.

'Ready?' Linda called.

'Hold on, I'm just stripping the bed.'

'Al, you did your sheets last week. Can't they wait till next Sunday?'

'No.' She could hardly admit to Linda that she wanted to wash Jim off the sheets. It seemed wrong to be still sleeping with him when her heart and mind were riveted on James. In fact the only way to endure it was to imagine he *was* James. She would shut her eyes and change his voice and body, invent a whole new repertoire – slower, more erotic . . . In her fantasies James was highly sensual, but Linda's words had aggravated the niggling doubts first planted by Suzanne. Suppose he *were* gay, or prudish and abstemious? And yes, why had he left the priesthood? And he did seem overly tied up with his family. On her second visit he had talked at greater length about his parents and grandparents and had barely mentioned friends of his own age. But why fret about such things when she didn't stand a chance in any case? Quite apart from the religious aspect, she had slept with three men – hardly excessive compared with her contemporaries – but to James it would seem promiscuous.

'Buck up!' said Linda, barging into her room. 'If we don't get a move on all the machines will be taken.'

'You're a fine one to talk, sleeping till eleven. I don't know how you do it with those trains.'

'Oh, I'm used to the trains. I probably couldn't sleep without them now. It's you spring-cleaning that gets me. What on earth came over you?'

Alison ignored the question and set off downstairs, sprinting ahead with the heavy laundry bag.

'Wait!' said Linda, emerging into the sunshine and undoing the jacket she'd just put on. 'I don't need this. It's really warm.'

'I told you, Linda, we should be in the country.'

'That reminds me – you know the couple who lived opposite? Well, they've moved again, to Ross-on-Wye this time. And Karen says . . .'

Alison wasn't listening. As they crossed the road into Ivor Street, she spotted a sign saying 'Catholic Church'. Strange she hadn't noticed it before. James would be at Mass this morning, maybe with his family. She could have gone herself, to see what it was like. There must be dozens of Catholic churches in London, although probably none in St Etheldreda's class. She gave a surreptitious glance at her watch. Ten to twelve. Not as late as she'd thought. 'Er, Linda?' she said.

'What?'

'I know I'm being a pain, but could you bear to do the wash on your own? I'll do it next week, I promise.'

'Why? What's up?'

'There's just something I have to do.'

Linda stopped in her tracks. 'It's that bloody James again. Come on, Al, admit it.'

'No, honestly, it's not.'

'What is it then? You can't just skive off and not tell me where you're going.'

'I'll tell you when I get back. Meet you at Sainsbury's at half past one, OK?' Before Linda could object she dashed across the street and started running towards the tube.

She arrived out of breath in Ely Place, only slowing down as she walked along the stone-flagged passage and up the flight of steps. Too late. The church was empty, save for a middle-aged man kneeling near the back. The Mass must have ended recently, though – a smell of incense lingered in the air, tickling her nostrils, spicy and insistent.

She ventured a little further in this time and sat level with the man on the other side of the aisle. Without a congregation the church looked still more beautiful. It was easier to see its structure, its simple satisfying shape, and to admire the ancient wooden roof soaring high above. As she gazed at the stained glass she suddenly felt ravenous. She had been up for hours and eaten nothing. The clear bright colours reminded her of fruit drops, and she could almost feel the yellow fizzing on her tongue like sherbet lemons; the green as tart as fresh limes.

The man appeared to be praying; eyes closed, head bowed, lips moving silently. She watched him, fascinated. She was a virgin when it came to prayer. Was that how James would pray, with such intense concentration? Did he ever come here? Or did he attend a church closer to his flat?

She started at the sound of footsteps, almost imagining that he'd come in. She turned to see the priest, the one who had conducted yesterday's wedding. He was now wearing a plain black suit but looked every bit as distinguished as in his vestments.

'I've come to turn the lights off. I hope I'm not disturbing you.' Even addressing only the two of them his voice had resonance.

The man got up from his knees. 'No, Father. I'm just leaving.'

'So am I,' she mumbled quickly, following them out to the passage. The man hurried off immediately, leaving her and the priest alone. Any minute he too would be gone, to his lunch or home or whatever. She hesitated, caught his eye. His kindly glance seemed to be inviting her to speak. 'Er, Father' – the word sounded strange and even traitorous on her lips – 'I . . . I want to become a Catholic.'

8

'Look, this probably sounds awfully ignorant, but what exactly *is* the soul? I've never been quite sure.'

Father Gregory leaned back in his chair. His face was in shadow, but his silver hair was highlighted by the lamp. 'That's a very good point, Alison – not ignorant in the least. The soul is the spiritual principle in man, the part of greatest value. And, you know, it's not a genetic thing, inherited from your parents, like the colour of your hair or your eyes. It's created directly by God.'

'I see.' She wasn't sure she did; none the less she liked the thought of possessing something independent of her parents; something they could neither spoil nor take away.

'And the soul,' the priest declared, 'is immortal, and will be reunited with your body at the final Resurrection. It ties up with what we were discussing last time – the fact that God made you in His own likeness and designed you for everlasting happiness.'

She nodded. Previously such ideas had seemed preposterous; no more than wishful thinking. But her view of things was changing, and changing quite dramatically. She was no longer a nonentity, shambling towards extinction, but someone with an immortal soul, created to be with God for all eternity. Her life had gained a sense of purpose, new structure and security. And she was now answerable to Another, which transformed everything she did.

'Being made in God's image isn't a matter of anatomy, of course. We resemble Him in our will and in our ability to love.'

Yes, she thought, love *is* divine. Supreme. Sublime. Beyond explanation.

'Do you remember what I told you, Alison? That if you believe, you become God's daughter.'

How could she forget? The phrase was so enthralling. A new, all-powerful Father who knew her through and through and actually loved her enough to die for her. Indeed, she had two new fathers. Father Gregory himself was exactly the sort of parent she would have wished for in her teens, when her own father's sordid entanglements (and the consequent lies and quarrels) had been the cause of so much pain.

There was a familiar scratching at the door, and she and the priest exchanged a smile.

'That'll be Percy, right on cue! He always seems to know when you're here.' The priest got up to let him in. Percy, an elderly blue Persian cat, had already established himself as an integral part of her instruction – a heavy purring presence on her lap, more concerned, it had to be said, with the warmth of her body than with any intangible soul.

'Are you sure he's not a nuisance?'

'No, I like him being here.' The whole ambience was special: the ancient room with its quaintly sloping floor and marble fireplace; the prints and portraits crowding the ochre walls, including one of Father Gregory himself – a huge gilt-framed study in oils. The table they were sitting at had once belonged to Sir Edward Elgar, but instead of being treated as a museum piece it was simply part of the furniture.

'Father,' she said, returning to the matter in hand, 'I still don't find it easy to pray. I suspect I'm going about it all wrong.'

'You're too hard on yourself, my dear. I'm sure you're doing extremely well. Just set aside some time each day, as I suggested. But, you know, you can also pray anywhere and everywhere – walking down the street, making a cup of coffee, doing the washing-up. Just dedicating those simple actions to God turns them into prayer.'

'OK,' she said uncertainly. He didn't seem to understand the sheer embarrassment of praying. As soon as she began she would hear her father's voice taunting in her head. 'My parents don't know I'm taking instruction,' she suddenly blurted out. 'I haven't dared tell them yet.'

'Now you mustn't worry on that score. I'm sure they love you and want only your happiness.'

Dubiously she looked at Percy, curled up on her lap. Her parents had refused to let her have a cat when she was little. Or a pair of roller skates. And later, her happiness seemed to count for less than their convenience. Her father had even interfered in her choice of university. She had been offered a place at Bristol, but he'd insisted Leicester would be better: she could save money by living at home. It was perfectly obvious he just wanted someone to be there with her mother when he was away on his 'business trips'.

'Besides, you're an adult and this is your free choice.'

Was one ever free, she wondered – free from the fear of criticism, or of causing more unhappiness? How could she have decamped to Bristol, leaving her mother on her own to fall apart? Yet she had missed so much at college by not living in: communal suppers, bedtime chats, the important networking and bonding rituals she had always envied Linda. She had led two separate lives, shedding her college persona every evening and reinhabiting it next day; never quite knowing who she was.

Father Gregory was surveying her intently. 'Alison, if you think there might be a problem, would you like me to get in touch with them and try to explain things from your point of view?'

'Oh, no,' she said hastily. She had no wish to embroil this mild-mannered priest in her parents' prejudice. She was determined to keep him to herself, as part of her private London life. Indeed it made her feel valued that he should lavish so much time and trouble on her. Apparently in many churches you were taught as part of a formal group and according to a set rite; not granted these intimate tête-à-têtes. It was as if Father Gregory was her personal tutor coaching her through a second degree, not at uninspiring Leicester but in the setting of an exquisite Gothic church. Her head was bursting with new words and concepts – the Trinity, Atonement, transubstantiation, the communion of saints. Best of all, she was drawing closer to James, in learning to understand his outlook and beliefs. The irony was, he didn't even know. She hadn't seen him since the night of Francesca's party, five weeks ago exactly, and her one overriding concern in life was how to re-establish contact with him.

'There's plenty of time for your parents to come round.' Father Gregory glanced at his diary, lying open on the table next to the New Testament and the new catechism. 'We're talking about having your reception in mid-November, aren't we, and that gives us a good six months.'

Six months and she would be received into the Church. The prospect seemed suddenly frightening. Becoming a Catholic was almost like assuming a different nationality. Indeed, it was even possible to take a new name, as part of the baptismal rite. The idea both intrigued and appalled her. Wouldn't it mean losing one's identity? Not that she was particularly fond of the name Alison – her parents' grudging compromise when she was already two weeks old. Up till then her mother wanted Deborah, while her father fought for Julie ('fought' being the operative word). But at least a change of name was optional, unlike those doctrines and dogmas she was compelled to believe, and the Creed she would have to recite in public before she was baptized. She hadn't yet confided to Father Gregory that she had nagging doubts about some of them. The Ascension, for example, sounded downright bizarre.

'And talking of your reception,' the priest continued, breaking into her thoughts, 'I don't know if I've mentioned this already, but you're going to need a sponsor.'

'No, you haven't mentioned it, Father.'

'Well, the sponsor plays an important part in the ceremony, as your witness and support. And of course in your case they'd also be acting as a godparent, since you haven't been baptized. As well as being there at the reception they can help you during the process of instruction – if they have the time, that is. They can pray with you and for you, accompany you to Mass and so on. Do you know any practising Catholics?'

Her rhythmic stroking of Percy's fur stopped abruptly. She gripped the arm of her chair.

'You mustn't be afraid to ask. To be a sponsor is a great privilege and any good Catholic would regard it as such.'

She stared at him, unspeaking. He was offering the solution to her problem.

'If you like, I can easily find you someone from the parish. In fact there's a very nice young woman called Agnes. I know you'd get on well.'

'Does it have to be a woman?'

'Oh, no. Anyone you choose, so long as they've been confirmed and are committed to their faith.'

'Well, I do know a man . . . He's very devout.'

'And does he live reasonably near here?'

'Oh, yes. And he works quite near as well.' She was so keyed up she hardly heard what Father Gregory was saying. How could James refuse if it was a matter of her immortal soul? *And* a privilege. They would pray together, sit side by side at Mass. She could even dash round to his flat as soon as this session was over and ask him there and then. No – that would put him on the spot. Better to write him a letter, apologize for troubling him but explain that he was the only Catholic she knew.

'Well, perhaps you'd contact your friend, and let me know what he says.'

'Yes, of course.'

'And now, let's return to the soul . . .'

His words were wasted on her since she could think of nothing but James. All at once Percy gave an indignant mew and sprang off her lap. She realized that she'd been clutching the poor creature too tightly in an attempt to conceal her emotions from Father Gregory. It was a relief when the priest stood up, indicating that the session was over.

'See you next week,' he smiled, opening the door for her. 'And don't worry about anything meanwhile. You're making very satisfactory progress. Oh, and by the way, if you still find praying difficult, why not simply sit in the church and soak up the atmosphere? You could do that after each of our sessions, if only for a few minutes.'

Following his advice, she went straight down to the church. She was beginning to feel at home there, now she attended the lunchtime Mass several times a week. It provided an oasis of serenity and she could be back at work within the hour. She had even made friends with some of the regular Mass-goers, which gave her a sense of belonging. For the first time in her life she was part of a group with shared ideals.

Tonight the church was empty and she walked right up to the front. When she had the place to herself she liked to pretend it was her own private chapel, with Father Gregory constantly on call to comfort or advise. Even without him she never felt alone. All the thousands who had worshipped here through seven centuries were still present in a way. She was proud to be one of their number and to be enlisting in a faith which some had valued enough to die for. The life-size statues surrounding her were, she'd discovered, martyrs. She knew something of their history now and could put a name to each. Her favourites weren't the priests and friars (heroic though they might be), but the ordinary people – a seamstress and a boatman, hanged on Tyburn Tree. All *she* had to contend with was her parents' irritation, not the gallows or the stake.

The stained-glass windows, too, were full of history and drama. And although in this artificial light the glass looked almost black, with only hints and gleams of colour, she was now familiar enough with it to clothe the blurred shapes in their dramatic daytime radiance: angels clustered round Christ the King. Angels had a strict hierarchy, Father Gregory said: nine different ranks, all depicted in this window, along with St Etheldreda.

And Etheldreda herself was no longer just an unknown figure with a mouthful of a name – and a rather comical name at that. In her day, apparently, she had been as famous as Mother Teresa and had worked scores of miracles, including raising people from the dead. (In which case it shouldn't tax her powers unduly to exert influence on James.)

Alison knelt in front of her statue, which stood on a plinth to the right of the altar. 'St Etheldreda . . .' she murmured, casting a furtive glance over her shoulder. Thank heavens Linda couldn't see her – *she* would think it ludicrous addressing a hunk of plaster; even more so as it represented the patron saint of chastity. St Etheldreda had somehow kept her virginity intact through two marriages and finally escaped her second husband's advances by becoming a nun.

'What a load of cobblers,' she could almost hear Linda saying. 'I expect the woman was frigid, and just wanted an excuse to kick her old man out of bed.'

Linda was so dismissive. 'Bollocks!' was her reaction to the story of the saint's body being discovered incorrupt five hundred years after her death. And as for the relic preserved here in the church: 'There's no *proof* it's her hand, for fuck's sake. It could just as well be a few old bones from the butcher.'

Perhaps it would be wiser not to discuss religion with Linda. It only aggravated the doubts she was trying to suppress. If all the great Doctors of the Church (and James himself with his double first) could accept Catholic doctrine, then why couldn't she? And if praying to a statue did seem peculiar, it was only because she was new to it. All new pursuits felt strange at the beginning, even walking, as a toddler, or starting one's first job.

'St Etheldreda,' Alison continued, determined to drown Linda's voice, 'if you could use your powers on James . . .' Again she broke off. Wasn't it childish and manipulative to make these sorts of bargains? True prayer, she had learned, meant praising God, not demanding favours. Yet if St Etheldreda could somehow intervene on her behalf, in return she would stop sleeping with Jim *and* come off the pill.

Neither would be easy. Jim was still anxiously clinging, and she had been taking the pill for years. Father Gregory's instruction hadn't touched on sex so far, but doubtless he'd get round to it. And she would certainly feel less awkward if she could tell him truthfully that she was no longer in a relationship.

'Help me,' she implored, aware how distressing it would be trying to explain the situation to Jim, for whom sex meant everything.

The statue's eyes seemed to look beyond her, unseeing, almost hostile. Perhaps it was insensitive mentioning sex at all to a saint who had gone to such lengths to avoid it.

She got up from her knees, fighting an awful temptation to laugh. Linda accused her of having lost her sense of humour and, yes, she had been rather preoccupied of late, but giggling in church was hardly a solution – she'd better leave before she disgraced herself. She couldn't concentrate in any case. She was starving hungry and had come straight from the office without time for so much as a coffee. St Etheldreda was reputed to have eaten only one small meal a day, but self-denial on that scale probably needed years of training. In fact, far from praying, she began to imagine sizzling steaks, pizzas oozing melted cheese, sausages and chips . . .

She walked back down the aisle, turning as she reached the door to make one last desperate plea. 'St Etheldreda, I beg you, persuade James to be my sponsor and I'll follow your example and live on bread and water for a week.'

9

'So what made you decide to take instruction?' James asked, taking a sip of his drink.

Alison studied the pattern on her side-plate to avoid his dark, distracting eyes. When Father Gregory had put the same question, the answer had been simple: her first experience of St Etheldreda's had shown clearly that something was lacking in her life. But, face to face with James, her spontaneous reaction was: It's *your* religion, so it must be right.

'I suppose I realized my life was empty and . . .' No, that made her seem shallow, unworthy of his time.

James put his glass down, still looking at her intently. 'You see, I remember you telling me you'd never been to church.'

Had she said that? How stupid. No wonder he hadn't phoned.

'It was my parents, really,' she explained, instantly regretting her words. She was an adult now, so why bring her parents into it? 'I mean, religion never struck me as particularly important.' Another crass remark, to someone who valued religion above all else.

James sat silent, unsmiling. He had probably already realized how superficial she was and decided not to be her sponsor. She noticed he had barely touched his drink. Perhaps he *was* ascetic and judgemental, as Linda kept saying. His iron-grey suit gave him an air of severity, reinforced by his haircut – shorter than ever, as if he was determined it shouldn't straggle out of control.

Nervously she started again. 'There . . . there seemed so many other things to worry about – you know, finding a job and a place to live.' She was making a total hash of this, and she hadn't said anything remotely intelligent. Playing for time, she leaned down in the pretence of looking in her bag and somehow managed to knock over her drink. Horrified, she watched the stain creep across the starched white tablecloth. '*Oh, no!* I'm terribly sorry.'

'Don't worry.' James was all concern, using his napkin to mop up the mess and assuring her it didn't matter. Two waiters swiftly appeared and began whisking away cutlery and glasses to replace the tablecloth.

Alison felt mortified, and to make matters worse the people at the next table were observing the scene with interest. 'I'm sorry,' she murmured again. James must think her a clumsy oaf and was probably wishing he had never come. He was obviously snowed under with work: he had asked if she minded eating as late as nine o'clock, and even then he had come straight from the office. *She* had arrived ridiculously early and had to kill time wandering around in the rain.

'Shit,' she muttered, under her breath, glancing down in dismay. 'I've spilt some on my dress as well.' It served her right for wasting so much money on another unsuitable outfit. He was dressed for a business meeting, she for partying.

'Will it stain, do you think?' James seemed genuinely worried. 'Perhaps you ought to go to the Ladies and try to get it off.'

'No, honestly. It's fine.' She'd spent enough time there already, redoing her face and hair after the ravages of the rain. 'It's just that I feel an awful mess and –'

'Alison, you look stunning.'

She stared at him incredulously. Was she hearing right? Yet now that she dared to hold his gaze she realized his expression wasn't stern, as she'd imagined, but admiring and even affectionate. Such was her relief, it was all she could do not to leap up and shout, 'Say it again. Again!'

'Let me get you another drink.'

'No, really, James, I'll wait till you've finished yours.'

'That won't take long,' he smiled, picking up his glass.

Hardly an ascetic's remark, she thought happily, watching as he drained it.

'Two more of these,' he told the waiter, then turned back to her. 'You can't imagine how glad I was to get away from the office. It's been a pretty frightful day.'

'Mine too,' she said, not revealing that he was the cause of it. From the moment she'd got up (after practically no sleep) she'd been as nervous as a prisoner awaiting sentence; unable to think of anything except her nine o'clock appointment in the dock.

'Oh dear. Was one of your authors throwing a tantrum?'

'No, nothing like that. Just – you know – stressful.'

He nodded. 'I do know. I had a obnoxious client to deal with. He's hell bent on suing the Inland Revenue and expects *me* to provide the evidence. But I shan't let him spoil the evening.' Laughing, he picked up the menu. 'Shall we order, Alison? Have you decided what you'd like? The sole *parmigiana* sounds good. Or the fillet steak with brandy.'

Two of the most expensive items, she noted guiltily. She had only intended meeting him for a coffee or a drink, but he said he owed her dinner in return for bringing back his briefcase. 'I think I'll have pasta,' she said. 'The spaghetti with clams.'

Halfway through the second drink she began to relax and notice her surroundings, which up till now had been little more than a blur. On the wall opposite was a painted window looking on to a painted sea – the Mediterranean, presumably, since the restaurant was called Bella Sicilia. The water was a deep turquoise blue and the horizon seemed to extend for ever, lost in shimmering haze.

'Tell me more about your work, Alison. What happened with that book by Francesca de Romero?'

She was surprised and flattered that he should remember the name after all these weeks. 'Oh, it's gone into production now. It'll be published in November.' The same month as her reception into the Church, although that was something she dared not mention again for fear of seeming to pressurize him.

'And are you still working for the dreaded Christine?'

So he remembered Christine too. *And* her reputation. 'Yes. She's mellowed a bit, thank goodness! I'm getting out of the office more these days – meeting authors, lunching with literary agents . . .' It sounded rather grander than the reality. The only author she had met so far was an elderly no-hoper foisted on her when Christine had an unexpected visit from Shaw Hilliard's latest wunderkind.

'You know, I've always wanted to write. Although I suppose everybody says that, don't they?'

She laughed. 'Too right! But luckily most of them never actually get round to it. We're swamped with manuscripts as it is.' She recalled Suzanne saying that James had written poetry at Cambridge. If only she could ask to see his work, it would give them another excuse to meet.

'And how are you getting on with Father Gregory?'

'Er, fine,' she said, somewhat fazed by the change of subject. 'I do find some things difficult, but he says it's normal to have doubts.'

'Oh, he's right. I've never known anyone who didn't – if they're honest, anyway. I've had a struggle at times, especially when I was younger. Although I was told in no uncertain terms that doubts were sinful and had to be suppressed.'

'But isn't that rather a cop-out?'

'Yes, I suppose it is. On the other hand, engaging with the doubts head-on isn't much help either.' The waiter brought him a clean napkin, which he shook out and spread on his lap. 'Over the years I've come to see the limitations of reason. Logical analysis can only go so far. There's another level of truth, which is more intuitive – allied with things like music and art.'

'Yes, that I can accept – I think! What throws me is the problem of evil. Oh, I know the pat answer is that it's a result of man's free will. But what about that cyclone in Bangladesh? It's killed two hundred thousand people so far.' The gruesome television images flashed into her mind: rubble-strewn streets, stunned and weeping women. 'How can a God who's all-powerful and all-good allow such a thing to happen?'

'There is no answer, Alison, to suffering on that scale. People have been trying to come up with one since time immemorial, and I know I burned a lot of midnight oil in the same vain exercise. The only solution, as I see it now, is to counter evil by a contrary force.'

'How do you mean?'

'By love,' he said simply. 'A word that's rather demeaned these days, alas. When you think about the concept of loving our neighbour as ourself it's absolutely mind-blowing. It could transform the world overnight – no more war or poverty or inhumanity. Oh, I know that sounds impossibly naïve, but if we all started in a small way . . .'

Naïvety was *her* failing – according to Linda. But perhaps it wasn't a failing after all. 'I suppose that ties in with the idea of souls. The way they give people greater value. I really like the thought of everyone being sort of . . . precious, however poor or wretched they are. Father Gregory was telling me about a shelter for the homeless, near St Etheldreda's. It's run by the Franciscans, and he says they treat each person who turns up there as if he were Christ himself. No matter how dirty or drunk they might be, they're all cherished and shown respect.' She paused for breath. Was she talking too much now, having been too constrained at first? No, James seemed interested, his eyes on hers, his hands cupped around his glass. 'And d'you know, the idea of the soul has even changed the way I read. If characters in novels have souls, their lives gain a new dimension. And they're less expendable. I've noticed it with Catholic writers like Graham Greene and Evelyn Waugh.'

'And it's true of Dostoevsky, of course. In *Crime and Punishment* he gives an apparent criminal a truly noble soul . . .' James broke off as a waiter arrived with the starters.

Dostoevsky was forgotten while she watched him eat an artichoke – his slender fingers plucking off each leaf and dipping it in the sauce before transferring it to his mouth. Each action was performed with that combination of delicacy and enthusiasm she remembered from the evening in his flat.

'And going back to the subject of doubts, Dostoevsky was plagued by them. But he talked about "the furnace of doubt" as actually leading to religious faith.'

She nodded. They were so close she could see his long black lashes and the shadow on his chin. Her eye followed another artichoke leaf as it

85

touched his lips, disappeared into his mouth. Would he ever kiss her?

'You see, without a God, man's nothing more than an evolutionary accident, a combination of genes. But given the religious view of life, people can transcend their genes and be heroic, even holy.' He wiped his fingers neatly on the napkin, then smoothed it on his lap again. 'In fact Father Gregory's what I'd call a holy man. And one of the finest priests around. Somehow he manages to steer a middle course between the two extremes – the dyed-in-the-wool reactionaries who still can't accept Mass in the vernacular, and the lunatic fringe who don't even believe in God.'

'I find him rather strict,' she said, trying to keep her mind on the absent Father Gregory rather than the all too physically present James. 'He's always tremendously kind, but he does seem to emphasize the rules.'

'Oh, but he must, don't you see? That's one of the strengths of Catholicism – it doesn't alter its stand simply because something's inconvenient or difficult. Don't get me wrong, Alison. I'm certainly not a conservative, with either a big C or a small, but I've come to the conclusion that a reactionary Church can sometimes be an advantage. Otherwise the essential doctrines get watered down, and while you're bending over backwards trying to please everyone you lose the concept of absolute truth.'

A concept which disturbed her. Absolutes of any kind seemed dictatorial and could provide a justification for intolerance. Yet she was about to join an absolutist Church. Clearly she needed more instruction – and further contact with James. A dream she'd had last night came suddenly to mind. James was beating her with a golden whip – a strangely gentle beating, as if it was a sort of initiation, performed in the most loving fashion. On waking she'd felt disconcerted: ashamed and aroused at once.

'I'm not saying for a minute that there haven't been scandals and corruption. And evil Popes, of course. But the Church has survived, despite all those abuses. In fact it's the only institution, political or otherwise, that's lasted two thousand years. And it's kept alive a vision – something beyond brute force or mere materialism. Ah,' he said, 'here's the wine.'

Once the waiter had gone she took a cautious sip of Frascati. She hadn't really drunk a great deal, but already she was finding it hard to concentrate on matters of religion. She gazed at the painted sea, imagining herself and James in Sicily, lying thigh to thigh on a secluded beach . . .

'And think of the art it's inspired – all those wonderful cathedrals and the centuries of church music. And paintings, sculpture, altarpieces . . .'

She was relieved to see the main course arrive. Although the starters had been large she still felt ravenous. The hunger was for *him* – a desire to strip him leaf by leaf until she reached his soft, unguarded heart.

His manners were impeccable. He anticipated her every need; refilling her water glass, offering bread, butter, salt and pepper, salad dressing. (Jim would have tucked into his own food straight away.) And he was so courteous with the waiters – precious souls, evidently, not mere serving staff.

'How's the spaghetti?' he asked.

'Delicious. Lots of clams.'

'Believe it or not, I once tried making clam chowder. It was rather a disaster, though!'

'Oh, do you like to cook?'

'Well, I'd hardly call it cooking. But when I left Ampleforth . . .' He broke off suddenly and put his knife and fork down. 'Alison, I probably didn't tell you that I spent some time in a monastery, training to be a monk, and later a priest.'

'Oh, really?' Her surprise was not entirely feigned. She had assumed he would never mention it.

'The life was fairly strict, but we were spoiled as regards food. Meals appeared magically on the table, just as they did at school and university. It was only when I returned to secular life I realized it was high time I learned to fend for myself.'

'Why *did* you leave?' She half dreaded the answer.

He sat in silence, looking down at the table.

'I'm sorry,' she said hastily. 'Perhaps I shouldn't have asked.'

'No, it's quite all right. It's just difficult to explain. And anyway I wouldn't want to bore you.'

No risk of that, she thought.

'You see, it was a question of . . . celibacy, and that whole debate is such a thorny issue at the moment. I do firmly believe in celibacy for priests, but I've been attacked before now for saying so.'

She gave a nervous laugh. 'Well, *I* shan't attack you. I don't know enough about it.'

'It's a wonderful ideal, Alison, and one I sincerely aspired to. But after a year as a novice and three more years studying philosophy and theology I felt less and less sure that I'd actually have the strength. One of the duties of priests is conducting marriage services and I knew I . . . I'd feel a certain envy for the couple. And when I was doing baptisms I might even be resentful because I couldn't have children of my own.'

Her food lay untouched as she let his words sink in. He actually wanted marriage and a family. She could have hugged him for sheer joy. Instead she said quietly, 'So you never became a priest?'

'No. I left before my final vows.'

'But weren't you devastated? I mean, after all that training – just having to walk away?'

'Oh, it wasn't like that. I got so much out of it. The sense of belonging, for a start. The Benedictine Order is another institution that's survived for hundreds of years. And it's probably not an overstatement to say it helped keep Western civilization alive and kicking! I still feel part of that, especially when I go back to see the monks, which I do from time to time. In fact I regard Ampleforth almost as a second home. I was at school there first, you see. And so were my father and grandfather. You could say it's in the family.'

Her mind buzzed with speculations, less about his family or Ampleforth (which she'd never actually heard of) than about his chastity. If he had found it a struggle in a monastery, wouldn't it be nigh impossible in the world? Perhaps Suzanne had been mistaken. In any case, who could say for certain whether a man was a virgin or not? At least the subject was more broachable now that he'd brought it up himself, and without embarrassment. 'James, talking of, er, celibacy, there's something I want to ask you.'

'Yes?'

James was the perfect listener, giving her his undivided attention, yet that only made it harder to steer the conversation to his sex-life. She took an indirect route. 'Father Gregory's been explaining the Church's position on things like sex and birth control, but as far as I can gather most Catholics follow their conscience these days, rather than the rules, and – you know – sleep around and . . .' It had all come out in a garbled rush, and she was actually blushing, for heaven's sake.

'Yes, many do,' he said calmly, 'but by no means all. And it's not just a question of rules. I personally believe that sex should be restricted to marriage, but I see it as an ideal, something that makes for a better society. It isn't easy – Lord, no! I find it a constant battle, but worth the effort. Lots of my friends have affairs and I wouldn't dream of condemning them, although it doesn't seem to make them any happier. I think the Church is actually rather wise in latching on to our deep psychological need for security and trust.'

Her mother had never had either, she reflected. If religion protected women by sanctifying marriage, perhaps chastity was not such a bad idea. And the fact that it was a struggle for him showed there was nothing wrong with his sex-drive.

'I mean, compared with the years of training for the priesthood, it seems incongruous that people can get married without any preparation whatsoever. After all, marriage involves a partner and children. It affects the whole next generation. But forgive me, your food's getting cold and I'm rattling on like the Father James I never was!'

She was glad he could laugh at himself. He wasn't strait-laced, as Linda thought. On the contrary, far from being a constraint, his religion seemed a genuine source of joy – shining in his voice when he spoke of it (unlike the religious cranks she had learned to avoid at university, who tended to be dreary in the extreme). And his view on affairs did have a certain validity. A hectic sex-life was assumed these days to be normal, healthy and good fun, yet it hadn't made her father very happy. Or Linda, for that matter. In fact just last week when Father Gregory's instruction had touched on sex – describing it as a sacred act between two committed, devoted people – she realized how far her own experiences fell short of that ideal. Imagine having sex with someone who regarded it as sacred; someone you could trust a hundred per cent!

She twirled more spaghetti on to her fork. The sauce was rich and creamy, in contrast to the crisp light wine. As she ate and drank she suddenly recalled her vow to St Etheldreda – bread and water for a week if he agreed to be her sponsor. They had skated round the topic, discussing religion only in general terms. And judging by what she'd said so far she would hardly seem a worthy candidate for admission to his Church. 'James,' she said tentatively, 'I wondered if you'd thought any more about – you know – being my sponsor?'

'But of *course* I will, Alison. I thought that was understood. It would be a tremendous honour.'

She sat looking at the painted sea, the Mediterranean sun blazing triumphantly down, making everything sparkle. The horizon of her life stretched alluringly ahead, unclouded now that James was part of it. She imagined them away together – not difficult in this setting. The dark-haired waiters jabbering in Italian provided authentic local colour as she walked hand in hand with James through the streets of Agrigento. The scene changed to their *pensione*: James slipping the dress off her shoulders, kissing her bare back . . .

'I envy you, in a sense, you know. You'll receive three sacraments on one day. And being an adult it'll have greater meaning for you.'

She hoped he wouldn't notice how hot and restless she was. Paradoxically, his allusion to a 'constant battle' had been more of a turn-on than an actual physical touch. In her mind she could see him with an erection. Did he ignore it, she wondered, or rush off and take a cold shower? It seemed such an awful waste.

'It's probably heretical to say this, but I think the importance of the sacraments is rather lost on children. I remember when I made my First Communion all I could think of was the humiliation of having to wear a frilly white shirt my grandmother had bought for the occasion.'

She laughed, picturing her own reception – his hand on her shoulder as they stood side by side in front of the altar, almost like bride and groom. 'I must admit I found the whole concept of a sacrament somewhat baffling at first. It was a bit like the Cheshire cat, if you'll forgive the analogy. Just as I thought I'd understood what Father Gregory meant, it would disappear again.'

Now it was James's turn to laugh. 'It may help if you think of the ordinary things we need for day-to-day survival – bread, wine, water, light – as being given a sort of spiritual charge and taking on new meaning.'

She warmed to the idea. The Church had an ingenious knack of bringing the supernatural within reach. And James too seemed more in reach. The two of them were drawing closer, discussing subjects which expanded her horizons (although most of her friends, Linda in particular, would probably dismiss them as either boring or irrelevant).

She refused dessert and coffee, just sipped her water and nibbled her bread, giving silent thanks to St Etheldreda.

'Are you sure you won't have anything else? How about a brandy?'

'No, honestly, I couldn't.' He had eaten his sole *parmigiana* with relish, she noted. No punishment of the flesh in that regard, at least.

'Well, if you don't mind,' he said, glancing at his watch, 'I'll get off fairly shortly. It's my sister's birthday tomorrow and I'm spending the weekend with them in Guildford. She's having a big shindig in the evening. It's partly for her and partly for my other sister, Nicola, who's going to Argentina next week to teach at a school in the middle of nowhere.'

'That sounds adventurous!'

'Well, it's certainly a change from Reigate Junior.'

'So she lives in Surrey too?'

'Yes. All my family seem to have landed up there. Which makes it handy for family gatherings.'

'It sounds as if you have them often.'

'Oh, absolutely. Any excuse for a party.'

Rather different from her own family: small, scattered and mutually suspicious. If only she could accompany him to Guildford and meet his relatives. She couldn't bear the thought that the evening was about to end, especially as she might not see him again till November. Father Gregory had said that people receiving private instruction didn't really need their sponsors until the reception. A sponsor *could* play a more active role, but it was purely optional.

James was now getting out his credit card and handing it to the waiter. Don't go, she pleaded silently.

He rose to his feet. 'You didn't have a coat, did you?'

She shook her head, feeling like a child going back to school after the most idyllic Christmas holiday. Perhaps she should take the initiative and invite him to supper at the flat one evening. But the place was so unprepossessing, and anyway she would have to bribe Linda to go out.

He steered her to the door amidst a chorus of 'Arrivederci' from the waiters. 'Arrivederci,' she echoed, although addressing it to him.

Outside the night was dark and blustery, unseasonably cold for May.

'Can I walk you to the tube?'

'Thanks. And thank you again for dinner. It was a really marvellous evening.'

'My pleasure,' he said formally. Already he seemed to be receding; his face lost in shadow, his voice inaudible in the traffic.

If only the tube were miles away . . . But they were there in a couple of minutes.

'Goodbye, then, Alison.'

'Goodbye.'

'Oh, by the way, next weekend I'm in London, for a change. If you're free on the Sunday I wondered if you'd like to go to Mass at St Etheldreda's? The eleven o'clock is always a sung Mass in Latin, and as it's Trinity Sunday it should be rather special. They're doing the *Missa Solemnis* – lots of pomp and splendour!'

'Yes, I'd love that, James.' How could her voice sound so calm when inside she was singing with all the jubilation of a dozen massed choirs?

'And we could have lunch afterwards, if you can spare the time, that is.'

Spare the time! Was he *mad*?

'It might be easier if you came round to my flat first. Then we can walk to St Etheldreda's together. I know it's a bit of a trek, but it's pleasant at weekends when there's not much traffic about – especially if the sun shines.'

Of course the sun would shine. It would never rain again, not for years and years. The Meteorological Office would be astounded; holiday-makers would exult; farmers and gardeners complain. Only *she* would know that James could affect the weather, affect the stars, the tides.

'Well, what d'you think?'

'Mm. Yes. Lovely. Thank you.' The trite monosyllables were all he heard. But beyond them she was pouring out a paean of praise to St Etheldreda – her own private miracle-worker.

Bread and water tomorrow, she promised her, as she floated down the steps to the tube.

10

'Fancy a coffee? I'm knackered.'

Alison hesitated. They'd been shopping all day. Well, *Linda* had – spending money she couldn't afford on skirts, tops, jackets, shoes. It was high time they went home. There was some urgent editing to do, and anyway she wanted to get ready for tomorrow.

'Al, are you listening? I said do you want a coffee?'

'Mm, all right.' Better a coffee than another row.

'You *do* sound keen,' Linda said sarcastically.

'Sorry. There's a café upstairs, isn't there? I'll treat you to scones and cream.'

The café was crowded with Saturday shoppers and seemed almost noisier than Oxford Street three floors below. Throaty sputterings from the espresso machine rose above the Muzak and general buzz of conversation. Only one table was free, next to a mother and her brood of children, the youngest of whom was banging the tray of its high-chair and screaming for attention. Linda raised her eyes to heaven as she stacked the clutch of carrier -bags in the corner.

Comfort shopping, Alison thought, pulling up her chair. Linda was manless at present and worried about her job after a recent spate of sackings. Whenever she felt insecure her shopaholic tendencies would surface with a vengeance.

'You're very quiet,' Alison remarked.

'I'm thinking.'

'What about?'

'Well, James, if you really want to know. Listen, Al, this isn't easy . . .' She frowned into her cup. 'To put it bluntly, I didn't like him.'

Alison stared at her in horror. 'But you said you *did* last night.'

'Only because you were so desperate for me to approve. I didn't dare say anything else.'

'So you lied to me?'

With intense concentration Linda spooned the froth off her cappuccino. 'Al, you don't realize how difficult it is for me to tell you what I think. Every time you've mentioned James this morning – which must be hundreds, actually – I've tried to be honest. But if I utter the slightest breath of criticism you're immediately up in arms. On the other hand, if I *don't* say something I'm scared you'll make a terrible mistake.'

'OK.' Alison faced her across the table. 'What's wrong with him? Let's hear it.'

'He's too serious. Sanctimonious.'

'That really is unfair. We all had a laugh and a joke –'

'*We* laughed – you and me. He didn't. I watched him.'

'Well, he was probably shy. And no wonder. You were so provocative, winding him up like that.'

'If a bloke can't take a bit of fun.'

'It wasn't fun. It was deliberately unkind. Besides, I don't see how you can judge him when he was only there about half an hour.'

'Yes, I noticed he couldn't wait to leave. The first time he's ever been to the flat and he's off before he's finished his drink.'

'He had an appointment, Linda. You can hardly blame him for that. Punctuality's a virtue, you know. For normal people, anyway.'

'Oh, I'm sure he's full of virtues – to the point of priggishness. But priggishness I can take, just about. What I didn't like was his sinister side.'

'Sinister? What on earth are you talking about?'

'It's hard to explain. But all that politeness and formality is sort of . . . creepy and unreal. I'm sure it's just a front. You said you don't really know him. Well, I suspect he won't *let* you know him, because he doesn't want you to see what's underneath.'

'Linda, you're off your head.'

'And you're completely biased.'

'Well, we'll have to agree to differ then.'

'Al, just allow yourself to face the possibility, if only for a second, that he might not be the paragon you think.'

Alison banged her cup on its saucer. 'I don't want to discuss it.'

Linda looked hurt and sat staring into space.

The silence grew uncomfortable. Nowadays there seemed to be more and more things they couldn't discuss. Alison watched two women at an adjoining table, chattering and joking. She and Linda had been like that – before James. Her life was rigorously divided into before James and after. He had caused a seismic shift.

'I suppose it's Mass again tomorrow, is it?' Linda said at last.

'Yes.'

'With James?'

'Yes.'

'Sunday used to be *our* day, Al. Now it's bloody God's.'

'I'm sorry, Linda, honestly.' She *was* sorry. Linda's latest man had turned out to be married with three kids. It was possible she was jealous; maligning James only because he was single and available.

'I just hate to see you being brainwashed by this Father whatever his name is.'

'Gregory.'

'Yes. If you ask me, you're in love with him almost as much as James. Isn't it rather adolescent having a crush on a priest?'

Alison ignored this last remark. 'It's not brainwashing,' she said. Linda lacked an understanding of religion, rather as some people lacked a musical ear. Certain subjects were off-limits for her – bread and wine turning into God, for instance. *She* found it quite astonishing, and charged with the mystery and magic she had sought since childhood (although as far as she could gather most Catholics took it for granted).

'Well, you're always spouting secondhand opinions these days.'

'They're not secondhand. They're *my* opinions.' Certainly James had influenced her. But that was only natural when he knew so much more about the Church. He had also helped allay her doubts, principally through his honest admission that some things you had to take on trust.

'Al, I've known you nearly six years now and you never believed any of this stuff before.'

'OK, I've changed my mind. There's no law against that, is there?'

'It's more than changing your mind. You've become a different person. I hardly recognize you. Take sex, for example.'

'All right, take sex. It's a good example. I *do* see it differently, but mainly because of Dad. If he'd had something to believe in, it might have stopped him screwing around. Don't worry – I won't bore you with it all again. It's just that I keep remembering little things. Like the times he used to pick me up from school with one of his fancy women in tow. He'd make me promise not to breathe a word to Mum, but then *she'd* ask if I'd seen him out with anyone. It was an awful position to be in. I was forever having to lie to stop them rowing.' She stirred her coffee vigorously, although she couldn't remember whether she had sugared it or not. 'Thinking about it now, I realize it even affected the way I chose my boyfriends. I'd only go out with safe, boring ones, so they wouldn't be like Dad. Yet underneath I was dying for somebody passionate and romantic.' Until she met James she had assumed that certain qualities were mutually exclusive. If a man was faithful and dependable he couldn't be charismatic.

Linda hacked her scone in half. 'Why are you doing it again, then?'

'Doing what again?'

'Well, you can't get more safe and boring than James.'

Alison gave an exasperated sigh. 'You just said he was sinister. You can't have it both ways.'

'OK, perhaps I'm wrong. I might be jumping to conclusions after one short meeting. Why don't you ask him to pick you up tomorrow and come and have breakfast first? I'll make a supreme effort and sacrifice my Sunday lie-in, in the interests of getting to know your paragon of virtue.'

'No, Linda. It . . . it won't work.'

'Why not?'

'Because Clapham's miles from St Etheldreda's, and anyway . . .' Distractedly, she spooned more sugar into her coffee. The truth was she couldn't face another session like last night's. All three of them had been on edge and had somehow displayed their worst side – even James. He *had* left rather abruptly, but that wasn't surprising after Linda's vituperative comments on religion and sex. 'Linda, please, let's not keep arguing. I know you're upset about Neil. And you've every right to be. He's treated you like shit.'

Linda shrugged. 'Don't they all?'

'No. That's just it – they *don't* all. James wouldn't, for a start. He's different, though. He's never slept with anyone. But it takes guts to admit that, especially for a bloke. You'd think he'd be terrified of people taking the mick. Most men would, I bet. They'd lie through their teeth about how great they are in bed. I have to say I admire him, if only for his courage.'

'The bloody man's obviously a saint – chaste, unselfish, virtuous, good-looking. And now courageous with it.'

'Do you think he *is* good-looking, Linda?'

'Not bad. At least he's tall.'

'What d'you mean, "at least"?'

'Well, personally, I'm not struck on lean, cadaverous types.'

'Look who's talking!'

'I'm slim. He's skin and bone.'

'He's *not*. You're just determined to find fault.'

'OK, he's got nice eyes, I'll grant you that.'

'I can't believe it! Something positive at last.'

'Nice eyes won't get you far, though.' Linda turned her attention to her plate, prising open the tiny plastic pots of jam and cream. 'But what does my opinion matter? I might as well shut up.'

'Yes, perhaps you'd better. Because I'm going to marry him.'

Linda stared, the scone suspended halfway to her mouth. 'He's *asked* you?'

'Not yet. I've got to become a Catholic first.'

'And then he'll ask you?'

Alison nodded, amazed at her own certainty. Yet the new confidence sprang directly from the new beliefs.

'You're out of your mind. Seriously, Al, I'm worried about you. This is like some sort of sickness – except you're too blind to see it.'

'No, I'm perfectly sane. James is the man I want to spend my life with. He may not feel the same about me, but if there's anything I can do to change that I'll do it.'

'Including becoming a Muslim, I suppose.'

Alison grinned. 'Not quite.' What Linda failed to grasp was that when you were in love there was an overriding need to see the world through the beloved's eyes; to share his creed, his convictions.

'And what if he turns out to be useless in bed? Catholics don't believe in divorce, remember. You'll be stuck with him for ever.'

'He won't be useless.'

'How d'you know? He hasn't even kissed you yet. That's a bit odd as well, isn't it?'

She shook her head. It was part of James's courtesy and consideration. He would never pounce. Or presume. And when he did kiss her (any day now, she was sure) it would surpass all the kisses in films and books which had so thrilled her in her teens. She was acutely aware of his sexuality – not repressed, not odd, just waiting in reserve. It was hard to explain, especially to someone as sceptical as Linda, but the way he spoke, moved, ate, even prayed, all suggested a depth of passion in him. And she could see it in his eyes: a blazing intensity, ready to ignite.

Linda gave a sudden laugh. 'What is it they say about chastity? – that it's the most unnatural of all sexual perversions.'

Alison refused to be drawn and sat sipping her coffee in silence.

'All right, Al, let's be serious. Say he *is* a fantastic lay, what about contraception? They don't hold with that either, you know.'

Again Alison said nothing. The Church's hard line on birth control did strike her as irrational, even primitive. James was too caring and unselfish to saddle her with hordes of kids. None the less . . .

'Imagine being stuck at home all day, ankle-deep in nappies.' Linda eyed the baby in the high-chair, still banging with its spoon – a podgy red-faced creature with little in the way of hair. 'You can wave goodbye to your career, for a start.'

She wished Linda wouldn't rub it in. Her ambition was to become a senior editor, commissioning books of her own. Yet James had waited all these years for marriage and a family. Would it be fair on him to delay it even further? And she so longed to have his children – dark, talented, enchanting children – more souls for God, as Father Gregory put it. She found the concept awe-inspiring: that an ordinary mortal like her could actually play a part in God's work of creation. But again, most Catholics seemed to accept it with maddening nonchalance.

'I suppose you could always go back on the pill, secretly, of course. Then all you have to do is rush off to confession each week. Hey, have you heard the one about the woman who goes to confession and says, "Bless me, Father, for I have sinned – a pound of carrots, two tins of beans . . . Oh heavens, Father, I've left my sins at Tesco's!"'

Alison laughed, relieved to hear Linda sounding more like her old self. 'Have you any other shopping to do?'

'Just some tights. Why, d'you want to go home?'

'I ought to really. I've got a couple of manuscripts to read.'

'Soft touch *you* are, mate. You should charge overtime.'

'It's part of the job. I'm used to it.'

Linda scraped the last of the cream from its pot and spread it on her remaining piece of scone. 'Just let me finish this. It's too good to waste. By the way,' she said, between bites, 'you haven't mentioned Jim all afternoon. How's he getting on with this Carole woman?'

'Haven't a clue.'

'You *mind*, Alison, don't you?'

'No.' She pushed away her own scone. She shouldn't lie – not now. According to Father Gregory even white lies eroded trust. 'Well, yes, I do a bit.'

'Come off it! You gave him the push. You can't expect him to live like a nun just because *you* choose to.'

Justified or not, she did feel a sense of betrayal. It was the first serious relationship she'd had (although, with the advent of James, 'serious' had assumed a different meaning). And since hearing about Carole – a secretary and blonde – she had suffered guilt, resentment and sadness in succession. It was as if Jim had only valued her for sex and now that he'd found a substitute she had become defunct, extinct. 'Look, I . . . I'd rather not talk about it.'

'You keep saying that. What *can* we talk about?'

What indeed, Alison wondered, when every subject seemed to lead back to James.

Linda wiped her mouth with a paper napkin, leaving an imprint of red lipstick. 'I've got a horrible feeling, Al, you're going to live to regret Jim. You were so well suited, I thought. Whereas you and James have almost nothing in common. He's ten years older, for one thing, and –'

'Nine,' she corrected – another white lie. James would be thirty-three next week.

'And public school and Cambridge . . .'

'That's not exactly a criminal offence.'

'Oh, come on, Al, you know what I mean. Marriage works better if both partners are from roughly the same background.'

'I don't see why.' True, she and Jim had jogged along companionably enough. She might even have moved in with him long term if she hadn't been lightning-struck by the real thing. Thousands of people must settle for someone not quite right and perhaps never be aware of what they had missed. Scrunching up her napkin, she tossed it on the table. 'Jim's a good, solid, decent sort – I'm not denying that. But it's like comparing . . .' She broke off, searching for a simile. All the ones she could think of – a pocket-torch contrasted with the sun; a molehill with Mount Olympus – would have Linda hooting in derision.

'At least Jim's independent and stands on his own feet. James sounds an utter wimp, from what you've said – always running home to Mummy. Or wanting Granny to kiss him better.'

Without a word Alison snatched up half the carrier-bags and stalked out of the café.

Linda ran to catch her up. 'Alison, I refuse to let James destroy our friendship.'

'Well, don't keep slagging him off then.'

Linda linked arms with her in a gesture of conciliation, and they strolled on through the dress department until Linda jerked to a stop in front of a mirror. 'God, what a fright!' she exclaimed, making a rude face at herself.

'Don't be silly. You look fine. That new haircut suits you.'

'Mm. I'm not sure about the fringe.'

They stood side by side surveying themselves: Linda tall, fair and slender, with delicate skin and striking slate-blue eyes; Alison shorter and dark-eyed, and more rounded where Linda was angular. Never would she have described herself as beautiful, but, now that James had said it not once but twice, she was almost inclined to believe him. Last week he'd even told her she had the most gorgeous hair he'd ever seen.

'Come on,' Linda muttered. 'Or we'll crack the bloody mirror!'

As they continued through Bridalwear in search of the escalator Linda clutched at Alison's arm. 'Please tell me you're not getting married! You don't want to end up looking like *that*, do you?' She was gazing aghast at a mannequin swathed in yards and yards of tulle.

'The bridesmaid's worse,' laughed Alison, pointing to a child-size model in salmon-coloured flounces.

'You know, you always swore you wouldn't even contemplate marriage until you were twenty-eight at least.' Linda's voice now had a resentful edge. 'Remember that time at college when Claire talked about settling down, you said the very words made you cringe.'

Alison did remember. But there hadn't been a James at college. 'Well,

I've changed my mind,' she said quietly. 'I want to be married in St Etheldreda's exactly this time next year.'

'You may want it, chum, but it's not going to happen. James has agreed to be your sponsor, not your husband. Hey, wait!' She hurried after Alison, who was making for the escalator. 'I'm prepared to bet you, actually. Fifty quid – no, five hundred. It's so unlikely I can afford to be rash.'

'OK,' Alison turned to face her. 'You're on. I'm afraid you're going to lose, though. So keep the beginning of June free. I'll let you off the pink frills, but you've got to be the bridesmaid.'

II

11

'And now you may kiss the bride.'

James bent his head towards Alison's upturned face. She felt a little shy of kissing him in front of Father Gregory and the whole hushed congregation. But once he held her close they were alone in their own private space, bounded by his arms. The kiss was restrained yet promised more – more tonight, and always. Despite the stone-cool breath of the old church walls she could feel the heat of his body through the formal morning suit. He was imprisoned in a starched white shirt, tight waistcoat, heavy frock-coat – whereas her arms and neck were bare; her naked skin caressed by snowy silk. His chin grazed against her face. However closely he shaved, defiant stubble would spring back within hours. The defiance seemed to spice the kiss, already tangy with incense and the fondant sweetness of freesias. His waistcoat buttons were pressing into her breasts, a strange and secret arousal. Tonight he would be bone of her bones and flesh of her flesh. His first time – and in a sense hers, too: the first time it would be sacred.

Reluctantly she pulled away. Father Gregory was waiting to exchange the sign of peace with them. 'Peace be with you,' he murmured, shaking James's hand and kissing her with the warmth of a true father. Then the younger priest assisting him gave her a chaste kiss on the cheek and the elder shook her hand. She couldn't quite get used to the fact that James had priests in the family, and no ordinary priests either. His Uncle John – *Monsignor* John – was a member of the Roman Curia and a leading light in the Sacred Congregation for the Doctrine of the Faith, while his cousin Adrian, a Jesuit, combined a Cambridge lectureship in theology with frequent religious broadcasts on radio and television.

'Kiss *me*!' demanded Charlotte, the smallest of the bridesmaids, stepping on Alison's train in her excitement.

Alison complied, kissing the trio of James's young nieces and lastly the chief bridesmaid, Linda – yes, in pink.

'Well, that's it, kiddo,' Linda hissed in her ear. 'No going back now!'

'No,' she mouthed, 'never.'

Then her husband of ten minutes led her from the sanctuary to the front pews where their families were sitting, only a few feet away. She was compelled by her elaborate dress to hold herself erect and move in slow and stately fashion; the train swish-swishing behind her. Her head felt strangely heavy with her hair swept up in coils and secured by half a hundred pins, and on top of that a flower-wreath and long veil. It was as if her new identity as Mrs Egerton would not admit of waist-length hair loose and unadorned. Nor, indeed, of any dress save the most expensive in the shop – a present from her father and therefore doubly precious. He had raided his pension fund to pay for it so that no one should say she was unworthy of the Egertons.

She paused at the altar-rails and looked down the length of the church, almost surprised at the number of guests. Every pew was crammed, and some people were even standing at the back. An hour ago, processing up the aisle on her father's arm, she hadn't dared glance right or left but fixed her eye on James, a reassuring beacon at the altar. And now they were man and wife! She shivered with excitement, glad of the anchor of his arm to stop her floating away on a tide of dizzy joy. The church had caught her mood and seemed to throb with light and colour; candles flickering on the window-sills, spears of sunlight sizzling through the glass. The figures in the windows – angels, martyrs, saints – had sprung to three-dimensional life and were rejoicing with the guests. Indeed she imagined the whole heavenly host joining in with the choir – *her* choir today – singing in her honour.

'*Dona nobis pacem,*' the luscious voices entreated, as members of the congregation exchanged the sign of peace, turning to their neighbours to shake hands or embrace. The required greeting 'Peace be with you' would hardly be apt for her parents – peace had featured seldom in their lives. Her mother had been ill again and her blue dress hung in folds on her scraggy figure. The over-ambitious hat dwarfed her small, pale face and was a shade too dark for the suit. Alison hugged her fiercely. 'I love you, Mum,' she whispered. James's love for *her* was tinder, igniting other, barely smouldering loves into full flame.

Even her father was smiling; his hostility to priests and papists overcome by triumph at his daughter's match. 'She's marrying class,' he'd been boasting to half of Leicestershire. But now, stepping forward to kiss her, he seemed overawed by her finery and handled her like glass. 'I'm so proud of you,' he said, his voice low and almost deferential.

She gave his hand a squeeze, moved by this unaccustomed praise. He had aged, she noticed sadly: his hair greying at the temples, and his morning suit (borrowed from a friend) straining across the beginnings of a paunch.

James led her across the aisle to *his* parents in the opposite pew: Anthony tall and distinguished; Evelyn exuding confidence in her oyster-coloured two-piece and flawlessly matching hat. Alison found her intimidating and always felt a little awkward about her own modest social background. Yet her in-laws seemed delighted that James had found a suitable bride at last – suitable meaning Catholic and devout.

The rest of his family remained a blur of smiling faces. There wasn't time to greet them all, as the priests were waiting to give Communion. She and James returned to the sanctuary and knelt in front of the altar, in the very spot where she had made her First Communion in November. Then, as now, there was a sense of being special – special even to God, the focus of attention. And on both occasions the sun had shone. Even an icy winter's day had managed to produce a clear blue sky to mark her new life through the Church – new life through James, as she saw it. He had stood at her side for the ceremony and, together, they had gone up to the altar to sign her Declaration of Faith. That same evening he'd proposed. Now 17 November was a double anniversary.

'The body of Christ,' Father Gregory intoned, placing the Host in her hand.

'Thanks be to God.' Her response had never been more heartfelt. Thank you, Lord, she repeated silently, for the gift of James. Her soulmate, literally.

Next Monsignor John offered her the chalice – an eighteenth-century golden cup engraved with trailing vines. She took a sip of wine, trying to formulate a prayer worthy of the astounding fact that she was drinking Christ's blood. But, like the skittish young bridesmaids fidgeting behind her, she was too excited to pray.

She stole a glance at James, who had just received the bread and wine and was kneeling with his eyes closed, still and undistracted. Such devotion to his God induced a stab of jealousy, but suddenly the choir burst forth, singing her favourite hymn.

> *'Lord, let sweet converse bind*
> *Lover unto lover . . .'*

She touched the gold ring on her finger. She was bound to him already, as he to her. At that moment he opened his eyes and clasped her hand in his. She returned the secret pressure of his fingers. Still hours to go before they were alone and she would have his devotion to herself . . .

The organ thundered fortissimo into the final verse of the hymn.

> *'Grant us love's eternal three –*
> *Friendship, rapture, constancy . . .'*

Friendship, rapture, constancy. What more could she ask of marriage?

III

12

'I'm sorry, Mrs Egerton, we appear to have come to the end of the road –
at least as far as drug treatment's concerned.'

Alison fixed her eyes on Mr Prescott's hands linked together on the
desk – plump, pink hands with stubby fingers. The end of the road
sounded so bleak, so final.

'I do realize how disappointing it must be after all this time.'

He was clearly trying to sympathize, but his tone had no real warmth.
And the words were too trite for her shattered hopes, and the months
and months of soul-destroying side-effects.

'As I told you at the outset, it was rather a shot in the dark.'

Again the clichés grated. A shot in the dark suggested something brief
and impulsive, not three wasted years. She shivered, although the room
was pleasantly warm: well proportioned, with a high ceiling and fine fur-
nishings. And Mr Prescott, too, was suavely elegant, with discreet gold
cufflinks showing on crisp white cuffs. He probably had several children
himself and a wife who produced them effortlessly without recourse to
drugs or tests. She knew nothing of his private life, whereas he knew *her*
more intimately than James did: her anatomy, her hormonal state, the
intricacies of her menstrual cycle. His fleshy hands had trespassed inside
her body, exploring her womb and ovaries and fallopian tubes, probing
with brutish instruments. However wretched or even assaulted she might
feel, she had become a willing victim, undergoing every procedure he
suggested.

'Isn't there any other drug I could try?'

'No, I'm afraid there's a limit to what we can use and how long we can
use it.'

'Well, any other tests, then?'

He shook his head. 'You've had every possible investigation. And, as
you know, everything seems to be working as it should. That's partly the
trouble. It's often harder to treat a patient if we can't find anything
specifically wrong.'

She met his eyes, looked away. She almost wished she *did* have
blocked tubes, or something relatively straightforward that could be corrected by a simple operation.

'No, the next step is IVF, but I know that poses problems for you.'

'Not for me,' she said bitterly. 'For the Pope.'

He gave an embarrassed laugh. 'Yes, technically the Church does disapprove of it, but' – he paused and adjusted his tie – 'strictly off the record, Mrs Egerton, I have quite a few Catholic patients who are so desperate to conceive they turn a blind eye to that.' He uncapped his pen and scribbled something on the notes. 'Surely even the Pope couldn't object if the intention is to create new life?'

He could and he does, she thought. And so did their parish priest – another ultra-conservative. Father Peter's response to her plea for guidance had been to quote some pompous papal encyclical (already ten years out of date, she'd discovered later). What made it all the more galling was that, as far as she could gather, many Catholics didn't even know it *was* banned – or perhaps didn't want to know.

'Of course the success rate of IVF is still comparatively low and I ought to warn you it *is* expensive. But it would certainly improve your chances.'

She nodded, well aware of the statistics.

'And short of that, I'm afraid there's nothing more I can suggest.'

'All right, I'll discuss it with my husband.' She wouldn't, though. James had suffered enough already. If only he could have been here and not stuck with a client who had flown from New York for the day. He had been wonderfully supportive through all the proddings and pokings. Each time her period came, flushing out yet another month's hopes, he would hold her close and be wise enough to say nothing. There *were* no words of comfort, and other people's attempts were often maddening if not patronizing: Give it time. Don't think about it. Relax and it'll happen.

Mr Prescott looked up from his notes. 'Even without IVF you mustn't lose hope, my dear. Let's see – you're thirty, aren't you? Many patients don't start tests until well into their thirties. And it's quite common these days for women to give birth in their forties. So,' he smiled, 'you've got years ahead of you.'

Yes, she thought, years of tense and timetabled sex; years of frantically counting days and dates, only to be frustrated; years of envying every pregnant woman, every mother pushing a pram. And with each month that passed, her chances would diminish. By thirty-five a woman was only half as fertile as at twenty-one. And by forty there was a one-in-three chance of infertility. Besides, James would be too old to start a family at fifty-odd.

'Well, Mrs Egerton' – the brisk tone indicated her time was up – 'I suggest you speak to your husband again about the possibility of IVF. And then, if you'd like to come back and see me together, just give my secretary a ring.'

'Thank you.' She forced a smile. It was hardly *his* fault they'd got nowhere.

He ushered her out of his office, where his secretary took over and accompanied her downstairs and right to the front door – all part of the service. However depressing the outcome, she was extremely lucky to be going private. The first two years' tests and treatment had been on the National Health, where the waiting-room *was* for waiting (standing room only, sometimes) – anything up to a couple of hours. In fact on the NHS waiting was an art form: waiting for the initial appointment, waiting for the results of tests, waiting to get treatment, waiting to see if it worked. Chequebook medicine dissolved queues as if by magic: appointments on demand, test results within days and a tasteful waiting-room where you barely had time to get settled on the sofa with the latest issue of *Vogue* before you were summoned to your consultation.

Outside it was cold and blustery. The wind whipped her hair against her face as she stood dithering on the pavement. There was no point returning to an empty house, especially as James would be out till late. She could call in at Shaw Hilliard – although eleven o'clock in the morning was hardly the ideal time for social chit-chat in a busy publisher's. Anyway it was always rather awkward having to admit she wasn't pregnant yet, when that was the reason she'd given up the job. It had been a difficult decision and one she'd only taken because her GP had suggested, almost as a last resort, that a less stressful way of life might improve her chances of conception. Even at the time she knew it was clutching at straws, yet, as James himself had pointed out, her work *had* become very pressured (and part-time not allowed), so reluctantly she had handed in her notice. Now she regretted it bitterly, having fallen between two stools and ended up as neither editor nor mother.

She walked slowly along Harley Street, still unsure where to go. All her London friends worked, and her neighbours in Surrey who *were* at home would be busy with their children. She couldn't cope with children. Not just now. There was always Oxford Street and the shops, which would kill an hour or two, but the Christmas decorations were up and she wasn't in the mood for Christmas: another child, another birth.

She waited at the traffic lights, watching the stream of cars. It was such a faceless area – no character or colour – just strangers hurrying past and the impatient hooting traffic.

A taxi was cruising towards the lights, and on impulse she flagged it down. 'Conyers Road,' she told the driver, feeling a sudden desire to see the old flat. They had been so happy there, never doubting they would have children; indeed, trying to stave them off for the first year or so. How ironic it seemed now – all that calculating and temperature-taking to work out the safe period. No other Catholics she knew would dream of subjecting themselves to such a palaver, but tended to dismiss the Church's official line as unrealistic and out of date, and use contraception like everybody else. Although in fact she hadn't really minded being the odd one out. If anything it had brought her and James closer. And sex was more exciting for being restricted. Even on the 'forbidden' days there was a tantalizing pleasure in going so far and no further, and James had developed the technique to an art.

'What number, lady?'

'Seventeen. It's a bit further, on the right.'

Once the cab had driven off she stood looking up at the house. She missed it terribly. True, the flat had been rather cramped for two, but they were both at work all day, and anyway she associated it with that idyllic time when her body had been her own – and James's – not demonstration fodder in a hospital. Often she would race home from the office, as if weeks had passed since they'd last met, instead of one brief day. She would run upstairs to find him. Was he in? Yes! They'd hug, they'd kiss, they'd delay their meal for hours, making up for James's years of chastity. And weekends were even better. They would stay in bed till lunchtime and, finally venturing out of doors, would walk with arms entwined and haunches touching, as if their bodies still craved contact with each other, even in public, in the street.

Perhaps she hadn't conceived because she already had too much – not just James's love but friends, health, money – and the added blessing of children risked making her complacent. Or it could simply be God's will, as James's grandmother claimed.

God's will was dreadfully hard.

She noticed several changes in the house: different coloured paint, new curtains at the windows and a rash of entry bells by the front door. The Walwyns had moved, too, and the property was now split into flats. Yet she still felt a sense of ownership – and pride. Their first home as man and wife was honoured, in her mind at least, by a commemorative blue plaque.

It was too cold to stand around, so she walked on along the familiar streets, past the Village Buttery, the delicatessen and the old-fashioned bakery where she and James bought gingerbread men. Once he had remarked that you couldn't buy gingerbread *women*, and she had made him some the following weekend; voluptuous creatures with glacé-cherry nipples and vermicelli pubic hair – as dark and thick as her own. He had licked it off, then bitten into their gingery breasts . . .

The gingerbread men were still on sale in the window. She was tempted to buy him a couple, but didn't dare go into the shops for fear of joky questions about gooseberry bushes and the patter of tiny feet. People were so tactless.

From Amwell Street she turned into River Street, named for the City's first water supply, established here by Thomas Myddelton, a seventeenth-century goldsmith. James owned an old engraving of the waterworks which showed gushing springs, green fields, and sheep and cows grazing on the bank of a reservoir. The cows had calves, the sheep had lambs, the grass was long and lush. Compared with such fecundity her own barrenness seemed all the more pronounced. Of course, no one used the word barren these days, but the dictionary definition was hideously apt: 'sterile, incapable of bearing fruit; unprofitable; without result'.

She strolled on into Myddelton Square, where she and James used to sit in the summer, soaking up the sun – the only garden they had. Today it looked cold and bare, the wind stripping the leaves from the trees and whirling them about in a storm of withered brown. The flowerbeds had an air of neglect. Convolvulus choked the rose bushes and nothing was in bloom save a single shrivelled chrysanthemum. She skirted a dead bird on the path, recalling the Gospel verse about God taking note of every sparrow that fell – hard to believe in her present desolate state. If God was so compassionate, why couldn't He avert floods, famines, earthquakes, war and, yes, childlessness?

She found her and James's favourite bench already occupied. A large, shapeless woman was slumped there, wearing an old army greatcoat and trainers with no laces. Alison smiled as she sat down, but the woman seemed lost in her own world, mumbling to herself and rummaging in a plastic bag held protectively on her lap. Another outcast from life, Alison reflected wryly, with neither job nor children, whiling away the days on a damp bench spattered with bird-droppings. They sat stiffly, side by side; the wind a third, unwelcome presence, intent on pestering them. It blew leaves in flurries over her shoes; tugged at her hair with the same relentlessness as the questions nagging at her mind. Should she accept God's will with good grace? Adopt a child? Return to work and forget about babies? Defy the Church and embark on IVF?

It struck her as absurd that a celibate, unmarried Pope could lay down the law on such matters. How could he comprehend the all-consuming desire for a child, the way it took over your life, removed the pleasure from lovemaking, drove you to despair? She kicked at a stone, watching it ricochet over the path as she thought of the papal encyclical – its constipated language, its irrational distinctions between artificial and so-called natural. Conception, it insisted, must take place via the sexual act and not in a laboratory. IVF it condemned as a commercial transaction, degrading both to child and parents. Yet the women she'd met at the clinic regarded their *in vitro* babies as the most precious things in the world, not as the 'artefacts' or 'objects' described in the encyclical. And if *she* had been permitted the procedure, she too might be a mother by now, not a barren, sterile, unproductive . . .

'No!' It was a shout.

Alison jumped, although the woman was evidently not addressing her but some invisible opponent. None the less, the interruption served to rouse her from self-pity – and from distorting the statistics. IVF wasn't a panacea. One patient she'd met had practically bankrupted herself and ruined her health by seven successive attempts – all failures. James had already spent a fortune on infertility treatments without a word of complaint. In retrospect, it seemed a shocking waste – not only of money, of life. She felt she had left her youth behind in Conyers Road and was now menopausal at the age of thirty; the hot flushes, headaches and thinning hair all a direct result of the drugs. Did she really want to soldier on any longer, being pumped full of hormones and spending half her time in hospital? Besides, asking James to ignore the papal ruling would cause him an unbearable conflict of loyalties, and she loved him too much for that. Even the fact that he was so different from the majority of Catholics was part of his attraction. He refused to compromise on what he believed was right just because it might suit him personally.

She closed her eyes and tried to pray, as *he* would – pray for strength, acceptance. Instead of criticizing the Pope she should give thanks for her happy marriage and for a husband with high ideals who was also exceptionally faithful and caring. Many men lost patience with the whole frustrating rigmarole, and some were so oppressed by the sense of failure they actually walked out on their wives.

'Lord, help me,' she murmured, 'to accept Your will, as James does.'

She should be grateful to the Church as well, which provided her with purpose in life and value in her own right, regardless of whether she had a child or a job. She was important to God, and that counted for a lot.

'Thy will be done,' she whispered, over and over, until she could say it with conviction, more or less.

She stole another look at the woman beside her, who was still railing against an unseen persecutor. Her hands were swollen with chilblains, her greasy hair unkempt, and she was probably homeless and alone in the world. Spurred by a pang of conscience, Alison took a ten-pound note from her purse and pushed it into her hand, then got up and quickly walked away, embarrassed to be playing Lady Bountiful. But her own life was a bed of roses in comparison – a healthy bank balance, a big house in Surrey and James's supportive family close by. In fact there was nothing to stop her calling on Helen right now. She couldn't put it off for ever. Matthew was already two weeks old, and so far only James had seen him. She must steel herself to go, and on the way to Waterloo she'd buy something special for the baby. And afterwards, when she got back home, she would chuck out all the temperature charts, the pill bottles and syringes, the ovulation predictor kits and books on infertility, and she would start again: turn envy into love and concentrate on being a devoted aunt to her six nieces and new nephew.

'More cheese? Or fruit? Or there's yogurt in the fridge.'

'No, nothing more, thanks, Helen.'

'Coffee?'

'Mm. Lovely. I'll make it.'

'No, you stay put. You look tired.'

'Tired doing nothing,' Alison smiled. 'You've been waiting on me hand and foot. Thanks for a marvellous lunch.'

'It was only pot luck.'

But offered with real love, she thought. Helen was like James in many ways, not only in their looks – dark colouring and tall, lean build – but in their kindness and sensitivity: Matthew had been whisked upstairs the minute she arrived. Yet there was no escaping the baby paraphernalia: cot-sheets drying on the airer, Moses basket in the corner, nappy-pail, toy rabbit – things *she* would never need.

Helen saw her glance at Fiona's drawing of 'Mummy' pinned up on the cupboard door. 'Let's take our coffee in the other room,' she suggested.

But the sitting-room was no better: full of photos of the children – Helen's four and Pauline's three – at various stages of development. Alison's eyes kept returning to the twins, prancing in their ballet gear or solemn in school blazers. To give birth to twins seemed both miraculous and unfair.

'How's James?' asked Helen, when they were settled on the sofa.

'Busy!'

'But are things OK?'

'Oh, yes. Although I do feel guilty all the time. You know – not producing. He wants a child so badly, Helen. Some men aren't that bothered. Obviously they're upset on their wife's behalf, but that's as far as it goes. With James it's absolutely central. He's always longed to be a father. But of course, you know that as well as I do.'

'He's certainly a fantastic uncle. My lot all adore him.'

'That's it, you see. I feel I'm letting him down.'

'No more than him letting *you* down. I mean, it's no one's fault, is it, if there's nothing wrong with either of you?'

'Yes, but it's shaken his confidence badly. And I can't bear him to blame himself.'

Helen squeezed her hand. 'It's just as hard for you, my love. We must simply go on praying – that's the most important thing. I've started another novena for you, and Philip offers up his Friday Mass each week.'

'Thank you,' she said, gratified by such concern. The whole of James's family were praying for them, and Cecilia had even gone on pilgrimage to Lourdes. She was famous for her pilgrimages and, according to family lore, had been the force behind several near-miracles. Indeed, when James himself was born, dangerously premature, Cecilia's prayers had saved him – and his mother.

'And honestly, Alison, he's so much happier these days, in spite of everything you've gone through. Before he met you there was something missing in his life.'

'He seemed perfectly content to me.'

'He was content, that's true. But now he's . . . he's . . . fulfilled, I suppose the word is. You're so good for him, in –' There was a sudden wail from upstairs. 'Oh dear, I knew it couldn't last. I'd better go and feed him before he screams the place down. You stay here and have your coffee in peace.'

Alison obeyed. She *was* tired. The years of dashed hopes had come to a head today, leaving her almost shell-shocked. She sat back against the sofa cushions, making a conscious effort to relax. She liked this room – its warm colours and modern paintings and its view of the back garden with the majestic cedar tree. And it was always remarkably tidy, considering the onslaught it must get from sticky hands and muddy shoes, but that was the Egertons – they all had elegant, uncluttered homes. She remembered her apprehension on first taking James to Hunston, about the shambles of her parents' house and, worse, the fear they might erupt into a quarrel. Somehow, though, he had brought out the best in them. They had behaved almost like a normal happy couple and even managed to avoid the vexed question of religion. (Presumably Catholicism was acceptable if it improved a daughter's prospects.) And she was profoundly grateful that they seemed to accept her childlessness with so little disappointment, even if her father's way of expressing it was hardly the soul of tact: 'You've married well. What more do you want? Children can wreck marriages.'

Her eyes strayed to the grand piano, where most of the photos were clustered, including one of the new baby. Matthew was a 'mistake', conceived when Helen was forty. Such mistakes seemed even more miraculous than twins. Not only that – Helen had gone on working until she was thirty-one, managing to have a career *and* a family.

She got up and went to the window. More evidence of children: the garden swing, the sandpit. Yet it was shameful to be jealous when Helen was so caring – more a sister than a sister-in-law. James's family had accepted her wholeheartedly, when they might have been rather dubious about the daughter of a sales rep marrying the son of a QC. And she was touched that they were all praying for her to conceive. Indeed the fervour of their prayers contrasted with her own lacklustre efforts. She must work harder at her faith; pray with more sense of hope; become more involved in parish work. After all, James did the church accounts and chaired the parish council, on top of a full-time job. They were desperate for help in the crèche. She would volunteer tomorrow. It was no good avoiding babies for the rest of her life just because she couldn't have one herself.

She ran upstairs and tapped at the nursery door. No time like the present.

'Come in,' Helen called. 'I'm just feeding him.'

She slipped into the room, trying not to look at Helen's bared breast. *She* would never have that experience – a child suckling from her, bonded as closely as two people could be.

'May I hold him?' she asked, when Helen had finished feeding.

Helen looked at her anxiously. 'Are you sure you – ?'

'Yes!' Her own vehemence surprised her. But this was James's favourite sister's baby, mistake or no.

Helen put him into her arms and she sat tense with fear, fear of her own feelings and of his vulnerability. He seemed so tiny lying there, half asleep yet nuzzling instinctively for her breast. Tears slid down her face.

'Oh, Alison, don't upset yourself. Here, let me take him.'

She shook her head. He smelt warm and milky; his eyes were tight shut, his fingers curled. Tentatively she stroked his fuzz of jet black hair. This could be her and James's child – dark, trusting, special.

'Don't cry,' said Helen gently. 'Let's go down and put him in his pram. I have to fetch the girls from school any minute. Or would you rather stay here?'

'No, I . . . I'm all right now.' She carried him downstairs and laid him in his pram. 'I'm sorry,' she said, wiping her eyes. 'I don't know what came over me.'

Helen gave her a hug. 'Don't worry. I understand, especially today of all days when you've just seen Mr Prescott. Look, I hate to rush you, darling, but it's already five past three. Are you sure you want to come, though? You could stay here and put your feet up for a while.'

'No, I'd like to push the pram.' Now that she had finally met her nephew she was keen to get to know him and for him to get to know her.

'Have you thought any more about adoption?' Helen asked, as they took the short cut through the recreation ground.

'Yes, but we've decided against it for the moment. Apparently it can be just as stressful as trying to have your own. We've heard these awful stories – you know, waiting around for years and being inspected by all and sundry, only to be turned down in the end.'

'But wouldn't you and James be in a better position than most? You both have so much to give.'

'It isn't just the waiting, Helen. Even if we were approved there's very little chance of a baby – only an older child, who's likely to have a lot of problems. It's not their fault, poor things. They've been moved from pillar to post, or stuck in dreadful children's homes for years and often been sexually abused as well.' She manoeuvred the pram with care round a deep rut in the path. 'I know we ought to offer one a home, but I'm not sure I'd be able to cope – particularly if they were handicapped or seriously disturbed. No, I think what I'll do is go back to work and forget about babies for a while. If I can *get* a job, that is.'

'Wouldn't Shaw Hilliard take you back?'

'I doubt it. The new MD's been laying people off in droves.'

'Well, don't start job-hunting straight away. You need time to get all those drugs out of your system. Can't you and James wangle a holiday?'

'Not at the moment. He's up to his eyes.'

'Go on your own then. To a health farm or something.'

'No fear! I'd be bored stiff. I need to keep busy too. In fact I've just had a thought – why don't you come to *us* this Christmas and let me do the cooking for a change?'

Helen laughed. 'It sounds like heaven! But all the tribe are coming to me.'

'No, I meant all of them – the whole family.'

'But we're talking about twenty-odd people. Remember Mummy always brings Gordon from the church, and sometimes a couple of others.'

'That's OK.'

'Gordon's ninety-six, you realize, and pretty gaga.'

'Don't worry. At least he'll keep my mind off babies!'

'But, Alison, there'll be seven children, including three under-fives.'

She looked down at Matthew sleeping in his pram. What better way to be a proper aunt? She could buy an enormous Christmas tree and hang it with toys for the children; make Christmas puddings with real silver charms inside, and a cake with an angel on top. She knew James would love the idea, and he deserved a decent Christmas. He had put up with her weeping, irritable self all the time she'd been on the drugs, but once off them she would soon get back to normal. Christmas *wasn't* a barren time – she must rejoice in it like everyone else.

They were now in sight of the school, and children were streaming out of the gates to their waiting mothers. Fiona was one of the first, followed closely by the twins. All three ignored Helen and rushed up to their Auntie Alison with cries of delight.

'Have you brought us sweets?'

'Can we play the tree game?'

'Are you staying for tea? Oh, *please*! And will you put us to bed?'

She kissed them in turn and handed out the chocolate bears she'd bought, which produced still more excitement. She was lucky to have Helen's children to love. *And* Pauline's. Aunts could be special too – almost as special as mothers.

13

'A child is born for us, a son is . . .'

The rest of the antiphon was drowned by Cecilia's coughing. Alison smiled at her sympathetically, but the older woman's eyes were on the altar. As hers should be.

'Let us call to mind our sins,' said Father Peter, who was visibly perspiring in the overheated church.

Alison's mind was a long way from her sins. She was concerned about the turkey. Should she have basted it again before they left?

'I confess to Almighty God . . .'

She joined in halfheartedly. Why couldn't *God* be sorry for a change, especially today? She had woken in the early hours, bubbling with excitement at the thought of her wonderful Christmas present for James: the news that she was pregnant. After six glorious weeks she was sure. Didn't people say that when you gave up hope it happened? Then she saw the bloodstains on the sheet. She could have crawled into a hole and wept.

Numbly she gazed at the plastic poinsettias and the lurid banners proclaiming 'Peace on Earth'. Peace was not in evidence. The church was full of noisy children, and the baby in the pew in front kept up a constant wail, to the obvious consternation of its mother. Mothers and babies were the theme of the day – indeed *virgin* mothers and babies. Was it a sin to resent the Mother of God for producing a child without even having sex, let alone fertility treatment?

The first and second readings, she realized, had completely passed her by, and as for the Gospel all she heard was the word 'son'. Her own son would have been born in August. This last week he'd become almost a physical presence, as she imagined him growing cell by cell. Deliberately, she hadn't told James – hard though it had been – wanting to save the good tidings for Christmas Day and to be absolutely certain before she raised his hopes. Her period had been late before, in the summer, and after rejoicing prematurely for a whole ecstatic week James's disappointment had seemed almost worse than hers.

She leaned back against the pew, still only half aware of what was happening in the Mass, simply standing up or sitting down when the others stood or sat. Cecilia was coughing again, trying to muffle the noise in her handkerchief. Many of the congregation seemed to have bad colds, and various splutterings and sneezings punctuated Father Peter's sermon. He had none of Father Gregory's natural eloquence, just as this red-brick church lacked the beauty of St Etheldreda's. Every Christmas since their marriage she and James had attended Midnight Mass there, turning up early to be sure of getting a seat. Some people came from miles away, just to hear the choir. Here there was no choir, only the amateurish warblings of a tone-deaf congregation.

What a rotten snob she was! Religion wasn't a matter of stirring music or fine architecture. God was still God, red brick or no. Yet today she was angry with Him. She had worked so hard in the crèche, pouring out her love on other people's offspring as she gradually dared to believe in the reality of her own child. But those spots of blood this morning had shattered everything. It seemed more like an abortion – brutish, murderous.

All of a sudden her stomach rumbled – loud enough for the whole church to hear. Francis noticed her embarrassment and squeezed her hand affectionately. It was a bonus to have acquired a grandfather by marriage – both of hers had died before she was born. And secretly she preferred him to Cecilia, who was rather overbearing and formidably devout.

The congregation rose to their feet for the Creed. How dreary they all looked, she thought, in their macs and shapeless anoraks. The weather had kept up a steady drizzle since dawn, as if it begrudged the joy of Christmas.

'We believe in one holy catholic and apostolic church . . .'

Her voice was all but inaudible beside James's confident tone. Spiritually she had always felt inferior to him and sometimes wondered if he was disappointed that she had failed to develop a more mature and positive faith.

When it came to the 'Our Father' she was reluctant to join in at all. Fathers were a let-down – the loving Father God who continued to deny her a child; Father Peter who drank too much and viewed any new idea with deep suspicion; Father Martin O'Connor, splashed all over the papers this week for serial child abuse.

'Lord, forgive me,' she murmured, appalled at such thoughts when they were nearly at the Consecration, the most sacred part of the Mass. If

Cecilia could have seen into her mind she would have disowned her on the spot. She made a brief act of contrition before going up to Communion, hoping God would understand her misery today. Apart from period pains she had a bad headache and sore throat and suspected she was going down with flu.

James was already standing beside Father Peter, holding a ciborium. He had recently become a Eucharistic minister, much to Cecilia's delight. The prospect of receiving Holy Communion from the hand of her own grandson was one of the reasons she and Francis had decided to stay overnight, rather than attend their own church in Esher.

'The body of Christ,' James said, placing a Host on his grandmother's tongue. (Cecilia had never accepted Communion in the hand, regarding it as disrespectful.)

'Amen,' she responded, bowing her head in devotion to God – and James.

'The body of Christ,' he repeated to his wife.

No! she suddenly wanted to shout, it *isn't* the body of Christ. It's just a mouthful of wheat and air. The blasphemy was so shocking she forgot to say Amen. James gave her an anxious glance, but she quickly turned away and took Cecilia's arm again, to help her back to the pew. She knelt beside her, head bowed, eyes closed but, far from praying, her mind was in turmoil. Her entire faith appeared to have collapsed. Loving fathers, miracles, resurrections, virgin births, all had lost their meaning.

She'd had doubts for months but suppressed them. Only now had she come face to face with the terrifying fact that she no longer believed a word of it. Yet how could she admit her loss of faith? James (and Father Peter) would refuse to accept it as such, seeing it instead as a short-term spiritual crisis to be overcome by determined, ceaseless prayer. In her present state prayer seemed a waste of time, if not a mockery – an outrageous point of view for someone whose life was so embedded in the Church. Most of their friends were Catholics, and more and more of their leisure time was spent on church activities. She could do without the friends – some of them were frankly rather dull – but no way could she do without James. He was her rock and anchor, her closest friend, her soul-mate. Soul-mate! What an irony when even souls had a religious connotation. A huge gulf had opened up between them.

Although dimly conscious of the noises in the church – the shuffling feet of communicants returning from the altar, the babble of bored children – she had lost all track of time as she wrestled with her dilemma. 'Lord, help my unbelief,' she prayed, knowing no one was listening. No one was *there* to listen.

In a daze she stood for the final hymn: 'Once in Royal David's City'. She mouthed the words, but no sound would come. Mother. Baby. Lord of All . . . Francis's and Cecilia's voices rose, spirited if frail.

> *'Christian children all must be*
> *Mild, obedient, good as He . . .'*

Why should she be good? She was sick of obeying the Church; following papal encyclicals to the letter while most Catholics ignored them; a thirty-year-old Christian child saying 'Yes, Father, no, Father, three bags full, Father.'

Francis was looking at her curiously, and she realized that her fists were clenched. What in heaven's name was wrong with her? Was she cracking up?

I *do* believe, she told herself, I *will* believe. The alternative was grim – it meant either becoming an outcast or living a lie the rest of her life.

'May Almighty God bless you,' Father Peter intoned, 'the Father, the Son and the Holy Spirit.'

Mechanically she crossed herself, although what use was a blessing if there was no one with the power to bless?

'The Mass is ended.' Father Peter raised his voice to be heard above the footsteps of those already making for the door. 'Go in peace to love and serve the Lord.'

Impossible, she thought.

Francis clapped his hands for silence, although no one took much notice. The children were fighting over their Christmas presents, the adults deep in conversation, oblivious of the call for quiet. Evelyn came to her father's rescue – as headmistress of a large girls' school she was used to commanding attention.

Sidestepping the toys on the carpet, Francis took up a position in the centre of the room. With his clipped voice and white moustache he had the manner of an elderly colonel addressing the troops. 'I'd like to propose a toast to our charming hostess,' he said. 'I know for a fact she's been working since the crack of dawn today to prepare our Christmas lunch. *And* most of last week. So let's all raise our glasses and drink to Alison. God bless her!'

'Thank you,' Alison smiled. 'It's really nice to have you here . . .' Somehow she must carry on as planned. Thankfully everything was under control – potatoes crisp, turkey nicely browned, Christmas puddings simmering, wine chilling in the fridge. She had sought to model herself on the well-organized Egertons, and in that respect (if no other) they could be proud of her today. Yet as she stared at the sea of faces she felt a surge of panic, realizing the full horror of her situation. Every single person here was enmeshed in the faith. Anthony, like his son, was a Eucharistic minister, Francis a Knight of St Columba, Evelyn in charge of nine hundred Catholic girls. Sylvia ran a prayer group, Graham was a fund-raiser for a local Catholic charity, and even the now doddery Gordon had once been the church organist. And the children were no less committed: the twins were altar girls, Amy was about to make her First Communion, Rebecca had played the part of Mary in the school nativity play, and Matthew had recently been baptized. And Cecilia, the matriarch, most pious of them all, would rather her granddaughter-in-law dropped dead than renounced the precious gift of faith – a gift the Egertons had kept alight for centuries. One ancestor had been martyred for his beliefs; another had founded a religious order. How could she stand against all that?

'I'm hungry,' Rebecca complained, chewing the end of her ponytail. 'When's lunch?'

'Now!' said Alison. 'You children have been very patient. And if you'd like to go and wash your hands . . .' She turned to James. 'Darling, would you be an angel and get everybody seated while I dish up?'

Helen, Pauline and Evelyn came out to help. The kitchen was stiflingly hot and her head burned and throbbed as if she were running a temperature. She would never manage to eat, but if she could just survive the meal . . .

'Right, that's the lot.' She sprinkled toasted almonds on the sprouts and handed the dish to Pauline. 'Do go and sit down. I'll be with you in a tick.'

She escaped into the garden, taking some scraps for the birds as a pretext, glad of the slap of cold air against her face. Her dwindling faith seemed to have left her short of oxygen and feverish with guilt. The sky was swollen with rain-clouds, their oppressive greyness belying this morning's Mass with its many references to light. And the garden lay waterlogged and bleak. A large family house and garden had seemed the obvious choice when James was transferred from the City and made a tax partner at the firm's East Surrey branch – an ideal time, they had felt, to try for a baby. Four years on, they were still rattling around on their own here.

She tossed the scraps on to the lawn and almost at once a flock of gulls descended in a flurry of white wings and raucous cries. They swooped and fluttered around her, jostling each other and squabbling over the food. Gulls were rare in the garden, except for the odd one or two, but now it resembled a beach invaded by a mob. She, as gracious hostess, couldn't express her feelings, but the frantic birds were doing it for her.

She felt a touch on her shoulder and turned to see it was James. She clung to him, aware of his concern. How could she hide anything from him when he was so attuned to her moods? It had been hard enough to disguise her elation about the assumed pregnancy, but deceiving him long term was quite another matter and utterly abhorrent. He had never lied to her and she knew he never would. He treated her with the utmost respect, as someone created by God and therefore to be cherished. But that was the trouble. If she cut herself off from God, would James still love her? Was it even fair to expect him to?

'Darling, are you all right?'

She hugged him tighter, and suddenly noticed a grey hair – his first – glinting against the black. He'd been having a really stressful time at work, and one of his oldest friends had died of cancer less than a fortnight ago. She couldn't burden him with *more* problems. Sometimes love was more important than truth, and he it was who had taught her what love meant. In fact she was beginning to wonder if she had ever believed in anything but all-loving James himself.

She watched the gulls wheel out of sight, their powerful wing-beats drumming in her head. If only she could go with them; vanish across the sea, a mindless creature who had never heard of God. Or love.

'We'd better go back in, darling. They're all waiting to start lunch and I didn't know where you were.'

She hesitated. Before the ordeal of lunch there would be grace: the whole tribe sitting with bowed heads while Francis asked God to bless their food, bless them – and, most likely, *her* in particular.

'You do seem awfully hot. I'm worried about you, my love.'

'I'm . . . fine.'

'Honestly?'

'Honestly.' She kissed him – a passionate, almost desperate kiss. This was only the first of the lies.

14

Hearing the rattle of the letter-box, Alison ran into the hall. Most of the letters were for James, but there were three for her, including the all-important one franked Macmillan. She kissed the envelope for luck before tearing it open.

'Dear Ms Egerton, Thank you for attending the interview last week for the post of commissioning editor. We regret . . .'

She let it fall on the table. Each rejection lowered her self-esteem another notch. There weren't that many openings just now in publishing, and being away for six months hadn't helped.

She scanned the second letter – a reminder of the Third World Trade and Craft Fair she had promised to help organize. If Macmillan didn't want her St Anselm's certainly did. Apart from doing three days a week in the crèche, she was working as a fund-raiser for Project Peru and had also agreed in a weak moment to help Father Peter set up a new database. Frankly it annoyed her, the way he regarded women as an inferior species yet relied on them to do his donkey work. And not just women, either. If James were paid for all the time he put in on the parish council (*and* the church accounts) he would have amassed a small fortune by now.

The third letter, airmail with a row of gaudy stamps, was from

Francesca de Romero. Working on Francesca's novels at Shaw Hilliard, she had taken a proprietorial pride in her success, but now an insidious touch of envy had crept into the equation. Francesca had everything going for her – fame, wealth, a second, glamorous husband and, last September, the ultimate achievement: a baby. Her own letters must seem dreary in comparison, especially this past year. Still, envy or no, she couldn't help smiling at Francesca's hilarious description of Zach in his high-chair, his face, hands and even hair liberally smeared with carrot purée.

The clock in the hall chimed the quarter. Another hour before she was due at the presbytery. She left the letter on the table with the rest. Its half-dozen pages, mostly detailing Zach's achievements, had made her feel inadequate, coming on top of publishers' rejections. She decided to use the time to put in some piano practice as an antidote to joblessness and babies. The piano lessons (an inspired Christmas present from James) were proving an absorbing challenge, and even the daily scales hadn't yet become a chore. She just wished the piano wasn't in James's study, which was uncomfortably full of God: theological books on the shelves, photos of Ampleforth . . .

She wandered in and stood at the window, watching the fast-falling snow. Its swirling energy put her own idleness to shame. Winter seemed to have lasted for an age, although in fact she dreaded the spring this year. Lent and Easter meant so much to James, but Redemption and Resurrection were now only words for her.

Sitting at the piano, she studiously avoided the photograph of James as a monk, formidable in his long black hooded robe. Ironic really – an ex-monk married to an atheist. Perhaps she had inherited her parents' irreligious genes; their aggressive ones as well. Sometimes she found herself actually longing for a row, a real cathartic screaming match. But James would never row, let alone scream. She ought to be grateful for his love. She *was* grateful. All the same . . .

She ran through a few scales, envying him his natural talent. Last night he'd been playing Brahms and the music was still open on the piano: a piece marked *ma non troppo*. Apparently Brahms used that marking so frequently some critics had called him unadventurous and afraid of emotional extremes. Yet wasn't *James* a bit like that, she thought disloyally? Or at least had become so recently. Their marriage was almost stultifyingly perfect; their life becalmed in dull commuter-land, surrounded by church worthies.

She ran her hand along the keys. Worthy, hell! Hypocrites, a lot of them; supposedly intelligent but not daring to examine their faith in case it fell apart. Half the women in the parish were taking the pill for 'health' reasons and simply ignored Father Peter's blathering about the evils of contraception. And they turned a blind eye when their teenage children sneaked off to find another priest with more liberal views on sex. And all the seething conflict was suppressed beneath a façade of unity. Although who was she to condemn them? – the arch-hypocrite, bowing and scraping to a Church she no longer believed in.

She crashed a chord on the piano. The only way to escape was to find a proper job and, if publishing had nothing to offer except further blows to her confidence, perhaps secretarial work would be a safer bet. There were plenty of agencies around – she could even try one now, before Father Peter lumbered her with helping on the church-cleaning rota or the First Communion programme. As she was leafing through the Yellow Pages the phone rang.

'Linda!' she exclaimed. 'How lovely to hear from you.'

'Well, I got fed up waiting to hear from *you*. Didn't you get my Christmas card?'

'Mm, yes.' With so much else on her mind, she had genuinely forgotten about Linda being back in London.

'So how's things? It's ages since you've written. Any news on the sprog front?'

'No. 'Fraid not. In fact I'm looking for a job. Congratulations on yours, by the way.'

'Thanks. I have to say it's great to be back in civilization. Walsall was unspeakable.'

'I'm sorry. I said I'd come and see you, didn't I?' She hadn't even got as far as looking up the train times. The trouble was, their lives had diverged by more than just geography.

'Forget Walsall. It was a disaster. Let's get together in London – soon. What're you doing tonight?'

'Nothing much.'

'Good. One of the girls I work with is thirty today, so we're going to the Bar Latino in Soho – us and a few others. Why don't you come too?'

'Won't I be in the way?'

''Course not. They're a smashing crowd. You'll like them. And anyway you and I can meet first. Come to the office around seven and we'll go and have a pizza.'

She hesitated, not wanting to rouse Linda's scorn by mentioning James or his dinner. 'I'm not sure how I'll get there. I mean, the snow may –'

'Snow? What snow? The sun's shining here.'

'You're kidding!'

'No, honestly. Would I lie to you? There's even a blue sky.'

Blue sky seemed a promising omen, although she was still worried about the trains. 'What about getting back? I presume it'll be fairly late.'

'Simple. Stay the night. I'm dying to show you the flat. In fact stay the whole weekend. And on Sunday we'll go to my new health club and lie around in the jacuzzi all day.'

It was tempting, certainly, a weekend of indulgence. Just to avoid Sunday Mass would be pleasure enough. Every time she went to Communion she felt horrendous guilt. And a lazy weekend was a rarity. Even on Saturdays they had started getting up for early Mass.

'OK, I'd love to come. What do I wear?'

'Anything you like. It's pretty casual. But dress up if you want. Have you anything vaguely Spanish?'

Only a mantilla, she thought, brought back by Cecilia from a pilgrimage to Santiago de Compostela, for her to wear at Mass. (Cecilia belonged to that generation which considered it shocking for women to enter a church bareheaded.)

'OK, see you later, Al. We're on the second floor. You'll see the sign – Midas Marketing.'

Alison rang off, smiling foolishly. She *would* dress up. She might even brave the snow and go out and buy a new dress, something frivolous. Their social life just now was anything but frivolous; bogged down in Justice and Peace meetings, humdrum parish suppers and the odd charity concert or barn dance to raise funds for the church. She still missed Conyers Road – the scores of bohemian pubs near by, ethnic restaurants of every description and the arty Islington crowd. After moving they had kept up with their London friends and with the latest plays and films. Only in the last two years had James become so pressured he had neither time nor energy to flog up to town after work. But *she* was bursting with energy. Linda's phone-call had dispelled her former lethargy. Enough of *ma non troppo*; tonight would be *molto vivace*.

Her breasts were clamped to Mario's chest. The top four buttons of his shirt were undone, revealing a tangle of dark hair. He was short and rather tubby, but those were minor defects compared with his superlative skill as a dancer. He steered her round the tiny dance floor in a near fault-less tango, although she had never done the tango in her life. It could have been mayhem in such a crowded space, but Mario wove an expert path between the other couples, and somehow she was able to follow all his movements and even avoid treading on his feet. In lieu of conver-sation (neither spoke the other's language) he flashed her ardent smiles. Words weren't necessary. The music was enough – an irresistibly sensual rhythm with abrupt and thrilling pauses.

After performing an elaborate twirl he eased her gently backwards until she was almost lying horizontal. Supporting her with the flat of his hand against her spine, he rocked to and fro, gazing deep into her eyes. Amazingly she felt no hint of embarrassment in such an extravagant pos-ition. With Mario as her partner she had acquired something of his skill and grace. He had complete mastery over her body, combining passion with precision as he manoeuvred it this way and that. One minute he twirled her away from him, spinning her under his arm; the next he pulled her close again and danced cheek to cheek, executing tiny fiddly steps which by some miraculous instinct she managed to do too.

He used his legs to guide her as well as his arms – his powerful thighs pressing into hers. She had never danced so intimately with anyone. Their two bodies were fused groin to groin and she had the strange sen-sation that his blood was flowing through her veins, his heart beating for them both. His strong hand was gripping hers, bare skin against bare skin; his thick hair brushing her face as he drew her towards him in yet another dramatic pause. Their sweat was mingling, their breath was mingling – even their smells: her scent, his pungent hair oil and cumin-flavoured smiles. And all the while the music urged them on; wild, tempestuous music dispelling the dark and cold of London. She felt that any moment they might burst out of this crowded basement and tango right across the South – Spain, Mexico, Brazil. She could already sense the warm night air on her skin, smell the bougainvillaea, see the stars emblazoning the southern sky. Easy to imagine she was there, with so many dark-haired, dark-eyed people whirling round her, and snatches of their languages, mysteriously foreign. She too felt foreign tonight, an exotic señorita, light-hearted, fancy free. Who cared about God – or babies? All that mattered was the music, its seductive glide suddenly changing to a stomping, strutting anger. Anger was dangerous and forbidden but a wonderful release. She was dancing her defiance – against the Church and Father Peter and useless Mr Prescott. Mario had saved her, reminded her she was still a woman, as glamorous, as fêted, as Francesca de Romero.

The tune ended with a passionate fanfare. He spun her into a pirouette and, with a gallant bow, escorted her from the dance floor to a shadowy corner away from the crush. There he broke into a torrent of words, not one of which she understood.

She smiled and shook her head, but suddenly he lunged forward and kissed her on the mouth. His leech-like tongue attached itself to hers, and she realized with horror that far from finding it repugnant she was beginning to respond. His very insistence excited her; the urgent feel of his erection thrusting against her flimsy dress; his reckless indifference to the fact they were in a public place. She half expected him to tear off his clothes and pull her down on top of him.

He shoved his hand up her skirt and only when his fingers fumbled at her pants did she pull away, appalled. What the hell was she doing? James would never forgive her.

Mario gave a cry of protest and grabbed at her again. She practically had to fight him off, straightening her dress as she fled back to the bar.

Linda had evidently been watching and gave a rueful smile. 'Al, I warned you this was a pick-up joint. We thought we'd lost you with *that* one!'

'He . . . he was such a good dancer,' she said lamely, and everybody laughed.

'Let me get you another drink.' Bruce, flamboyantly gay, had already established a rapport with the winsome, fresh-faced barman. 'I reckon you need it, my sweet.'

'Well, I'm not sure if . . .' The tequilas must be lethal. After only one she had allowed a total stranger to maul her. Still, the others were knocking it back – especially Jane, the birthday girl – and she didn't want to seem a spoilsport in comparison. Anyway she'd had enough of boring Perrier during her time on the fertility drugs. As far as she could gather, none of Linda's crowd had children – nor wanted them. In their circle, life was for enjoyment. And all around them people were laughing, flirting, drinking, which made her realize how long it was since *she* had felt as happy as that.

'You like dance?'

A natty little fellow in tight white jeans and cowboy boots had materialized in front of her.

'Not just now, thanks.'

'God, it's like bees round a honeypot,' Linda remarked. 'Some people have all the luck.'

'I'd dance with you, Linda,' Bruce said, returning from the bar with the drinks, 'but I'm afraid I have two left feet. Besides, Stephen would be jealous, wouldn't you, my treasure?' Stephen, his partner, was a rather lugubrious-looking man with sad-spaniel eyes and a droopy moustache.

'Al, I don't believe it!' Linda nudged her in the ribs. 'Here comes another one. It's that dress, you know. It's barely decent.'

Alison tugged at her silver mini-skirt. She actually rather liked it, especially the little pelmet frill which flared out when she danced. 'I'm sorry,' she said to the Che Guevara type who had squeezed his way to their table. 'I'm just recovering my breath.' It gave her a buzz to have men flocking round (even if she turned them down). The years of infertility had destroyed her confidence, made her feel a failure and a freak.

'I wish I'd had time to dress up.' Michelle glanced disparagingly at her creased grey office skirt. 'I didn't leave work till half past eight .'

'Good grief! On a Friday?' Linda took a swig of her margarita. 'We wouldn't stand for that, would we, Stephen?'

'Certainly not. In fact I've decided work doesn't agree with me. I intend to pack it in when I'm thirty.'

'Oh yes? And what are you going to live on, pray?'

'Bruce, of course!'

The two men slipped their arms round each other. Alison recalled Linda's recent remark about all the men in London being married, gay or impossible. The men in Walsall she hadn't mentioned yet. They'd had less than half an hour on their own – the trains *had* been delayed and several cancelled altogether.

Someone else now breezed up – a blue-eyed, fair-haired man, wearing a white blouson thing above black hipster trousers.

Linda gave him a hug. 'Great! You made it.'

'Yeah, I've just finished, thank Christ. I did the early shift, so I should have been here hours ago.'

'Come and sit down. This is Craig, everyone. He works behind the bar at Bacchus when he's not slaving away at his masterpiece. Craig, you must meet Alison. She's in publishing.'

'*Was*,' Alison corrected.

'Well, you're going back soon, aren't you?'

'If anyone will have me – yes.'

'I'll have you,' chorused Bruce and Stephen, who were now drinking from the same glass with two straws.

She grinned at them as she made room for Craig. 'What sort of thing do you write?' she asked him.

'Well, it's my first attempt, to be honest – a travel book, but sort of fictionalized, and –'

'Don't be so bloody modest,' Linda interrupted. 'He's been all over the world. And got into stuff like sweat lodges and voodoo.'

'And lived to tell the tale,' said Bruce, eyeing him speculatively. With his pale skin and floppy hair Craig did look slightly girlish.

'It was a close shave at times,' Craig admitted with a grin. 'I was nearly murdered by a drunken Mongolian herdsman.'

'My dear, Herne Hill just can't compare.' Bruce fished the lemon slice out of his glass and ate it, rind and all. 'The only danger there is crossing the road against the lights.'

Alison laughed. 'I once edited a novel set in Herne Hill.'

'There can't have been much plot then. It's the doziest place in London.'

'What about Muswell Hill?' said Stephen.

'That's not dozy, angel. That's dead.'

Alison's attention was caught by a handsome Afro-Caribbean man swaggering towards the dance floor in a wide-brimmed black hat and dark glasses. White Englishmen like Craig tended to look anaemic against such competition. Another interesting type was standing opposite, his swarthy, gypsyish face crowned startlingly by a cascade of bleached-blond hair. His body was swaying to the music, and she too found her feet were tapping and her fingers drumming on the table. The beat was so compelling it seemed to demand a physical response. Although she couldn't understand the lyrics, the husky, yearning voices could only be singing of love, and became practically orgasmic as they throbbed towards a climax with wild shouts of '*Olé!*'

The swarthy character was leering at her openly, his gaze lingering on her breasts. Although embarrassed by his scrutiny she also felt elated that she could still actually turn heads. It was probably the boots as much as the dress – thigh-high suede she had found half-price in a sale this afternoon and bought for the sheer hell of it.

'Oh, listen!' Craig exclaimed, stubbing out his cigarette. 'It's a salsa. I've just got to have a bash. I've been taking lessons these last few weeks. My girlfriend talked me into it.'

So he wasn't gay, she thought. Still, not her type – too wishy-washy. 'Alison, do you salsa?' He was already on his feet.

She shook her head. 'I'd love to, but I wouldn't know where to begin.'

'Go on! Try,' said Linda. 'You looked incredible doing that tango. A few sequins and you could be on *Come Dancing*'.

'OK,' she laughed. 'Why not?'

Linda also jumped up. 'Come on, Jane, I've had enough of sitting here like a lemon. Let's dance.'

Bruce rolled his eyes in mock horror. 'Oo-er! I didn't know you were *that* way inclined. Fancy you never letting on, ducky.'

Linda gave him a friendly punch, then led Jane into the mass of dancers, even denser than before. Several obvious experts were performing with enviable panache, hampered by the stumbling amateurs. Jane and Linda made a pretence of joining in, until suddenly an oily little man stepped forward, seized Jane by the hand and swept her away into the crowd.

'Never mind, Linda.' Craig linked his arm through hers. 'Join *us*.'

Professional it wasn't. The salsa was fast and required perfect co-ordination, whereas she and Linda kept bumping into each other. Craig, however, was more proficient and even managed some fancy footwork.

'Wow! Snake-hips,' Linda panted. 'You're putting us to shame.'

Alison tried to copy him, flinging herself into the spirit of the thing. There was a marvellous sense of freedom in submitting to the rhythm, feeling it pulsate to her very core. She had been imprisoned so long in her head, worrying about infertility and loss of faith, but now her physical self had taken over and she was just rippling body and flashing feet.

'I've had enough of this lark,' Linda wailed, pulling Craig to a halt. 'I need a drink.' She staggered from the dance floor, followed by the other two. They had to push their way through the throng of onlookers now standing seven deep.

'Shall we go on somewhere less frenetic?' Linda suggested. 'How about Cheers in Covent Garden? You can hear yourself speak there and it's open until three.'

'Yeah, I know it,' Craig said. 'They do good food as well.'

'Is that OK with you, Al?' Linda asked.

'Yes, fine,' she said, delighted at the thought of staying out till three, with no worries about getting up for Mass. Their Surrey village would be dead to the world by now, whereas she had achieved a miraculous Resurrection.

15

'So what happened to Roy?' Alison asked, adjusting her towel as she lay back on the recliner.

'God, don't mention him!'

'But I thought you said –'

'He was just about OK before he took up golf. That ruined everything. He'd spend hours watching videos about the correct grip and the right position and what-have-you. But when it came to positions in bed he didn't have a clue. Believe me, Al, golf's a sex substitute. Roy even had this club called Golden Ram Tour Grind!'

Alison laughed and took a sip of tropical fruit juice, in keeping with their surroundings: exotic plants, pink parasols and a mural of a sun-kissed beach complete with palm trees and macaws. Snug in Linda's luxurious health club it was hard to credit that the temperature outside was only a scant degree above freezing.

'One night I blew my top. He was glued to the box the whole evening, watching the Ryder Cup. And suddenly he lets out this blood-curdling shriek and leaps ten foot in the air. And all because some creep got a hole in one. He never used to say a *word* in bed – he just pumped away in grim silence. Yet all that fucking passion for a golf ball.'

Alison's laugh was more restrained this time. Linda's swearing, which she'd barely noticed in the old days, was beginning to grate on her nerves. The Egertons' influence, no doubt. Cecilia would be horrified by Linda – not just her language but the affairs and the abortions. And she would have no compunction in damning Bruce and Stephen as perverts. ('Gay' for Cecilia still meant merry.)

'I can't get away from sportsmen, Al. If it's not golf it's fucking rugby.'

'You need an intellectual type.'

'No thanks. I've had one of those. He was writing this thing on Princess Di – royal, romantic, beautiful and dead before the wrinkles set in. I didn't stand a chance.'

Linda did look older, Alison realized with a pang. Strange that only a couple of years should make a difference, but then Linda was probably thinking the same about her. After all, thirty was a watershed and apparently in biological terms you had passed your prime at twenty.

'Anyway, how about you and James?' Linda asked. 'You've hardly mentioned him.'

No, she thought. Deliberately. It would be embarrassing to admit she'd lost her faith when Linda had warned her from the start that she was converting for all the wrong reasons. Besides, it seemed disloyal to tell her friend but not her husband. 'We're . . . fine.'

'And what are you going to do about the job? I mean, if nothing else comes up?'

'God knows. That's the most depressing part. It might help if I'd had more experience.'

'Well, say you have. Everyone lies on their CV.'

'They'd only check. And I'm telling enough lies as it is.'

'How do you mean?'

She hesitated. Even if Linda said 'I told you so' it would be a relief to confide in someone at last. Keeping silent so long had proved a terrible strain. 'Well, promise not to breathe a word.'

'Promise. But I can guess what you're going to say – you're having an affair.'

'I am *not!*' she retorted. 'I wouldn't dream of it.'

Linda looked almost disappointed. 'What, then?'

'Oh, never mind.'

'Don't be silly. I want to know.'

'It's nothing.'

'Why bring it up then?'

'Look, I'm sorry. You . . . you won't understand.'

'That's nice, I must say. I've told *you* enough.'

True, Alison thought – even the grisly details of two abortions, extremely painful to listen to, given her own circumstances. Still, Linda meant well. They had always shared their traumas. She took a long, slow draught of fruit juice, debating whether to speak or not. The abrupt gurgling noise of the straw in the bottom of the empty glass seemed to trigger a decision, and suddenly she began pouring out the story.

She felt better at once, just getting it off her chest. And Linda did seem sympathetic.

'Shit! What a mess. No wonder you're in a state.'

'And the awful thing is, I can't see any end to it. I mean, do I carry on pretending to James until one of us drops dead?'

'No, that's crazy. You'll have to tell him. Surely he'll understand?'

'That's just it – I don't know if he will. Religion's such an in-built thing with him he'll be devastated. And his family will go ballistic. They'll want me to talk to a priest – Father Gregory, most likely. But I know already that won't work. Most priests take the line that doubts are normal and you simply have to ignore them and carry on regardless. But if you applied that to something evil, like, say, Hitler and the Nazis, it could be extremely dangerous.'

'Come off it, Al. That's going a bit far.'

'It's the same principle, though. If you can't examine a subject impar-

140

tially you're lying to yourself. Which is just as bad as lying to everyone else.' She lowered her voice as a young man sauntered past, eyeing Linda's bikini with interest. They had tried to find a secluded spot away from the jacuzzi and the swimming pool, but waiters were plying back and forth with trays of drinks, and people were stopping to admire the statue of a naked nymph flaunting beside the fishpond. An odd setting for a discussion on religion.

'Look,' said Linda, once the man was out of earshot, 'does it matter what James's family think? You're not married to *them*, are you?'

Yes, in a way I am, she thought. Having no siblings of her own, she had become the little sister; part of a loving, stable clan that accepted her and cherished her. But the position could easily change. They must already be disappointed by her failure to conceive and, although they never made the slightest allusion to what she saw as her undistinguished background, they would be far less sympathetic if they knew she'd renounced her faith. 'I'm actually very fond of them and –'

'But, if the relationship means anything, surely they won't drop you just because your thinking's moved on a bit?'

'They won't see it like that. For them the Church is divinely inspired.'

'Bollocks! How about all these scandals – priests abusing little boys and running off with parishioners' wives? Which incidentally is the Pope's fault in the first place, for insisting that a priest can only be a person with a phallus – on condition he doesn't use it! You can hardly blame them if they're so frustrated they go off the rails.'

Alison managed a weak smile. 'They say it's not the players that count, it's the play. They're convinced that theirs is the one true Church – you know, founded on a rock and all that stuff. And scandals only make them more determined to *keep* it rock-solid. They're forever worrying about the thin end of the wedge – watering things down till there's nothing of any substance left. If you believe in Truth with a capital T, there can't be any compromise.'

'Yeah, and you end up burning heretics.'

Alison nodded. Even pious Cecilia wouldn't go quite as far as condemning her to the stake, but she would certainly be shocked to the core. And Francis scarcely less so. He had told her once that when he was young he would no more have dreamed of marrying a non-Catholic than marrying a divorcee. Even converts he probably considered dubious, and converts who reneged would be quite beyond the pale. 'It's difficult for you to imagine how extreme they are, Linda, especially compared with most Catholics. Take the people I know in our church – they're all fairly easy-going and turn a deaf ear to a lot of what the Pope says. And the majority of priests are careful not to be too dogmatic, otherwise people would leave in droves. They tend to say follow your conscience, which really means do what you like but keep quiet about it. Just my luck,' she grimaced, 'that Father Peter should be one of the old school, and James's family, too – well, not so much his sisters, but his parents and grandparents definitely. They're like some kind of Catholic fundamentalists, living a life of total obedience and always putting duty before rights. A lot of the things you take for granted, like sex outside marriage or abortion or divorce, are anathema to them.'

'Well, if you ask me, it's high time they dragged themselves into the twentieth century.'

'Yes, but what other people regard as progress they oppose on principle. Cecilia even objects to the word "partner", except in the strict business sense. She said if I ever see it on a form I must cross it out and put "husband" or "wife" instead, to show I believe in the sanctity of marriage.'

Linda shuddered. 'Weird. I just couldn't live with a man like that.'

'Oh, James isn't like that. He's a different generation and much less narrow anyway. He's religious in the best sense – charitable and decent and . . .'

Linda didn't seem convinced. The trouble with virtue was that it invariably sounded dull. James *lived* his faith, and that wasn't dull but challenging and rare. He treated everyone he met with profound respect and courtesy, be it a window-cleaner, a traffic warden or the old biddies at St Anselm's. She found that genuinely moving, but Linda shrugged it off as affectation. Admittedly she sometimes felt annoyed with him herself (his very goodness, measured against her own deceit, could be a source of irritation), but if Linda said a word against him she would instantly spring to his defence.

'Well, if he's so damned decent, Al, it beats me why you can't just tell him the truth.'

'Because . . .' Alison cast around for words. 'It . . . it would change our whole relationship, all the little details of our life. For instance, James and I pray together every night and morning. At present I'm just kneeling there going through the motions and feeling an utter hypocrite, but it's still part of our routine, something we've always done, and I know he values it.'

Linda stared at her aghast. 'For fuck's sake, Al! You mean to say you and James actually kneel down by your bed each night and say your prayers, like Christopher Robin?'

Alison flushed. Thank heavens she had never revealed that James even prayed as a prelude to sex. Father Gregory had suggested that since lovemaking was a gift from God it would be a fitting gesture to ask His blessing on it. At the time it had seemed erotic, almost part of the foreplay. Now she resented God as a threesome in the marriage. 'Prayer's important to him, Linda. Which isn't surprising, given his background. He wouldn't be here at all if it wasn't for prayer. When he was born, the obstetrician gave him up for dead, but Cecilia overturned the laws of nature – so the family claim.' Alison used her straw to hook the slice of lemon from her glass. 'Francis says she can even control the weather. If she prays for sun, God makes sure it shines.'

'Well, He rather slipped up today, then.'

'Oh, she'll only do it for some vital event.'

'Like the church fête, I suppose,' Linda said with heavy sarcasm. 'But tell me, if her prayers are so amazing why aren't you pregnant by now? She must have droned her way through several million rosaries on your behalf.'

Alison bit into the lemon slice, wincing at its tartness. 'You know,' she said reflectively, 'it's probably just as well we can't have children. I'd have to bring them up Catholic, which means Catholic schools, indoctrination . . . Nicola's girls are taught about God as a *fact*, like DNA or the First World War or something.'

'Look, what you need at the moment, Al, is not a kid but a complete change of scene. This religious thing is getting out of all proportion.'

'It'll be better when I get a job.'

'Well, don't settle for typing letters all day. Stick out for what you want. Anyway I reckon having an affair's a bloody good idea. Christ! After what you've been through, you deserve a bit of fun.'

'Oh, I *couldn't*, Linda. I love James. That's the trouble. If he didn't mean so much to me, I wouldn't be in this state. He's absolutely central to my life. I'd never cheat on him. Ever. Besides . . .' She broke off as a little girl came up to inspect the fish: exquisite creatures with rainbow-coloured bodies and transparent trailing fins, gliding to and fro among the water-lily leaves. Just watching them was therapeutic; their slow and languorous movement gradually helping her unwind. It was a waste of the day to sit agonizing over God when she could be relaxing in the pool.

'Let's change the subject, OK? You've been great, Linda, honestly, but I want to make the most of this place. It's a treat for me to have a Sunday off. Normally I'd be cooking lunch for the in-laws.'

'That reminds me – we haven't had *our* lunch. What d'you fancy? There's the Four Seasons Restaurant, very posh with flunkeys, or the poolside caff where they let you wear bikinis.'

'Oh, the caff, please. But can we have a swim first?'

''Course. They keep the pool at ninety-two degrees. It's like having a warm bath.'

'Fantastic! It seems incredible to be sitting here in swimsuits when there's sleet and snow outside.' 'Outside' had disappeared – the noise and fumes and traffic and bitter January weather all strictly barred from this Caribbean-on-Thames.

'Hey, I've just thought,' said Linda, 'if the trains are still haywire, maybe you won't be able to get back. So you can stay with me for *weeks* and we'll go out every night and live it up.'

Alison laughed. It was a tempting prospect – to escape from Surrey and mix with normal, cheerful people who weren't the slightest bit concerned by the issues that worried *her*: bishops burning condoms in AIDS-ridden Third World countries; theologians excommunicated for not toeing the Catholic line; a God of Love who evaded blame for Dunblane and Lockerbie by holding man's free will responsible. She jumped up from the recliner. 'Race you to the pool!'

She arrived there just a fraction before Linda and dived straight in. It was a wonderful sensation – the warm, caressing water sweeping anxiety away. She stayed down till the last possible moment and surfaced as a different, carefree person, like everybody else: couples playing ball, children splashing and laughing, lovers kissing in huddles.

She turned on her back and floated lazily. She was no longer even bothered about missing Mass this morning or drinking too much last night. Seeing Linda was a tonic. Not only was she a generous friend (paying for everything today and refusing to take a penny), she had her priorities right: life was for living.

16

'Bless me, Father, for I have sinned.'

He *wasn't* a father and she *hadn't* sinned. None the less, she went grimly on. It had been a tremendous struggle to come here, so she had to see it through. 'Father, I've been having doubts. Doubts about – well, everything.'

'We all have doubts, my dear.' He sounded kind and unperturbed, although his voice was rather croaky. 'But God loves us even through our doubts.'

'I . . . I don't *believe* in God.'

'You may feel you don't, but religion isn't about feeling, it's about commitment and perseverance. Doubts are often God's way of testing our faith.' Suddenly he sneezed, an explosive noise that made her jump. 'Oh, I do beg your pardon. I'm afraid I have a cold. Now, as I was saying, doubts are normal. Even St Thérèse of Lisieux doubted God's existence. But it didn't stop her praying. You need to say "Jesus, I trust in you" and repeat it over and over.'

Brainwashing, she thought.

'Are you managing to pray?'

'No, Father.'

'Well, you know, you can't treat God as a sort of lucky charm and just take Him out when you need Him. If you're sick, you go to a doctor and you follow doctor's orders, even if you don't like the medicine. Jesus is the great healer . . .'

I'm *not* sick, she wanted to shout. And I've followed doctors' orders for five useless, wasted years.

'Perhaps you're making too much of the doubts. As Cardinal Newman said, "Ten thousand difficulties don't make one doubt." If you think of them as difficulties I'm sure you'll find them easier to overcome.'

Maybe. But only at the cost of distorting her own reality. It was like her parents again. They too had refused to acknowledge her feelings or allow her to work out truth for herself. What *they* thought became the canon, whether about politics, art, life or the superiority of all things British – beer, bread, climate, sport. Yet at least now she could discount their views, whereas she couldn't discount James's. She loved him. Passionately. Which made an enormous difference. This confession itself was an act of love – James would want her to go.

'Father, I haven't told my husband about these doubts – difficulties. Yet I hate deceiving him. Should I tell him, do you think?'

'Do you and your husband have a good relationship?'

'Yes,' she said vehemently. There were no doubts on that score. She might resent his eternal busyness and his saintly self-control (when *she* was close to screaming in frustration from the strain of bottling things up), but he was still her rock, her anchor.

'And you truly love each other?'

'Yes.'

'Well, there you are, you see. That shows you're much closer to God than you imagine. Wherever love is, God is present.'

Why, she wondered, couldn't love exist as a purely human value? Yet James's love for her was so much part of his love for God that she couldn't divorce herself from God without losing him in the process. A terrible dilemma: she either sacrificed her integrity or sacrificed her marriage. Yet, ironically, the ideal of Christian marriage was to allow each partner to become their true self; neither dominating the other. How could James not dominate when he had the full force of scripture, revelation and canon law on his side? In the Church's eyes she was merely in error.

'On balance, I'd say it's best to tell your husband. Share your worries with him. And ask him to pray for you.'

James would take the praying as a serious responsibility. He might even try to go to Mass in his lunch-hour every day, when he simply couldn't spare the time. He was under more and more pressure at work. Was it fair to burden him further?

The priest was blowing his nose. All she could see of him was a shadowy profile and the gleam of a bald head. There they were, two strangers whose paths might never cross again, yet she was expected to entrust him with the most intimate details of her life. Still, better a stranger than Father Gregory, who would have been dreadfully disappointed in her after all the time he had lavished on her instruction. And Father Peter was out of the question. She had made a point of driving miles to a church where she wasn't known as a stalwart of the parish. And now she was here she ought to be making more effort, putting the questions James would want her to ask. 'Should I continue going to Communion, Father? It feels rather hypocritical.'

'As I said, try to ignore your feelings. God might seem distant, yet in fact He's very close to you. Allow Him into your life and this period will pass. You need the spiritual food of the Eucharist to build up your spiritual health, so, yes, do continue to go.'

He appeared incapable of understanding that concepts like the Eucharist meant nothing to her any more – nothing to most people, come to that. She glanced up at the Crucifix hanging just above her: a naked criminal on a gibbet, Linda had once said. She shivered. The dim, confining space was becoming claustrophobic, and she was conscious of the people waiting outside. She was holding them up. Worse, what if they could hear what she was saying? Confessional boxes never seemed private enough, and this one had neither door nor curtain.

The priest began coughing – a dry, ticklish sort of cough. He apologized, cleared his throat. 'I think we need to talk this over in more detail. My name's Father Luke and you can contact me at any time. If you'd like to come to my house we can have a little chat.'

God forbid! Father Luke was kind, but simple – simplistic. They could have 'little chats' *ad infinitum* and still be speaking different languages. 'You mean you can't give me absolution now?'

'It depends if you want it, my dear.'

For James's sake she did want it, yet if there *were* no God, what power had Father Luke to absolve anyone from anything? Divested of the status of God's representative on earth, he was just an old man with a bunged-up nose. 'Well, it's difficult to want it, Father, if I feel –'

'Feelings again,' he tutted. '*I* believe in absolution, and I also believe that the more you take advantage of the sacraments the stronger your own faith will become. The Church withholds absolution only if someone refuses to change. Are you at least *open* to a change of heart?'

'Yes, Father.' His insistence was grinding her down. It would be the same at home, notwithstanding the fact that James was probably vastly more intelligent than this priest. Whatever the Church might claim to the contrary, intelligence and faith belonged to separate spheres.

'Good. Now is there anything else you need to confess?'

Anger, she thought, with *you*, for assuring me that God is close and loving when He's distant and non-existent. And for dismissing my doubts as unreal. Yes, and scores of other sins – cynicism, resentment, missing Sunday Mass, envy of women with jobs, envy of women with babies. Just this morning her period had started – as always a source of mingled grief and bitterness. Although officially they had given up trying to conceive, her mind was constantly on her cycle. James too would be upset. Since the débâcle at Christmas he had made her promise to tell him if she was even a day or two late, saying he'd rather have his hopes dashed than not share things with her. Yet there was so much they couldn't share now.

'I've been telling lies,' she said wearily, realizing she hadn't answered the priest.

'Lies entangle us still more. We must always seek to live in the truth. As it says in St John's Gospel, "The truth will set us free."'

Whose truth, though? Theologians'? Scientists'? Philosophers'? Could any of them come close? Maybe human beings had to settle for just fragments of relative truths.

To her horror she felt her nose beginning to run, and she had forgotten to bring a handkerchief. Surreptitiously she wiped it with her hand, feeling like a grubby child. She could hardly have caught the priest's cold in the space of a few minutes. Perhaps it was an involuntary show of sympathy for a frail old man cooped up on Saturday morning in this draughty mausoleum of a church, charged with the saving of souls. Most people would be in the rival cathedrals of St Sainsbury and St Tesco; warm, bright shrines to the God of consumerism.

'Now, for your penance I'd like you to say three Our Fathers. And ask God the Father to send the Holy Spirit into your heart.'

Churchmen had poured out reams of words on the Holy Spirit, and when Father Gregory had first explained the mystery of the Trinity she'd been fascinated, not – as now – sceptical and impatient. How could she have changed so much? Once, confession too had seemed awesome – one's sins forgiven, however grave; guilt erased; the slate wiped clean. Yet today she felt more guilty than ever for receiving another sacrament in a state of secret rebellion.

'I absolve you from your sins in the name of the Father and of the Son and . . .'

She emerged blinking into the light of the church and went to kneel at the back. There were only two people waiting for confession, both elderly, both women. These days even good Catholics rarely went to confession. James, of course, was untypical: he went once a month. But since she was here for his sake, there was no point in asking advice if she didn't intend to follow it. This evening she would tell him everything, before she lost her nerve. Admittedly it wasn't the ideal time – he'd be tired after the conference – but there *was* no ideal time.

Dutifully she recited the three Our Fathers, although the words seemed to stick in her throat: Father again. Sins again. Thy will be done.

It was a relief to leave the church and drive back home, despite the heavy rain which threw up clouds of spray and reduced visibility to two semicircles of windscreen.

At the local newsagent's she stopped to pick up the *Bookseller* she'd ordered. Following Linda's advice she was sticking out for a job in publishing, and preferably at the same level as when she'd left. It had taken her long enough to get there, so why chuck it all away?

As soon as she got in she scanned the recruitment pages. Only one commissioning editor's post was advertised, and that was in Bristol; otherwise just a couple for editorial assistants (glorified secretaries) and for a desk editor in a small academic publisher's which required a knowledge of physics. Well, there was always Monday's *Media Guardian*, and meanwhile she'd ring Joanna to see if there was anything going at HarperCollins. It was often worth trying the grapevine first.

'Sure. I'll ask around,' Joanna promised. 'How would maternity cover suit you? That occasionally crops up, if you don't mind a short-term contract.'

'I'd consider it, certainly.' It would tide her over for several months, even if she was back to square one when the contract expired. Also there might be a chance of freelancing, although that meant being stuck at home, and it was the companionship she craved as much as the work.

She drifted into the study and sat down at the piano. She had neglected it of late, perhaps a subconscious reaction against the Egertons, for whom musical expertise was a *sine qua non* of any civilized person. But today she didn't feel civilized – nor did she want to be.

After a few minutes' discordant banging she gave up, finding it hard to concentrate on that or anything. On impulse she rang Linda. A man's voice answered, and when Linda eventually came to the phone she sounded out of breath.

'I'm sorry, am I interrupting something?'

'No, it's OK. Just a sec.' Linda broke off to talk to someone else and Alison heard noises in the background: laughter, music, a babble of competing voices.

'What's going on? An orgy?'

Linda giggled. 'Not quite. I've got a few friends round. We're going out for lunch in a while. Why not come too? Bring James if you like. It's ages since I've seen him.'

'He's not here. He's tied up all day, speaking at a conference on taxation.'

'Well, whatever turns him on . . . Still, at least it means *you're* free. I'll expect you in an hour or so.'

'No, wait . . .' She had planned to cook a special dinner for James, to soften the blow. And there was Cecilia's curtain material to pick up and drop round to her. 'I don't think I can. I've got loads of boring chores to do.'

'They'll keep! Shut up, Craig, I can't hear. OK, I'll tell her. Listen, Al – Craig says he's almost finished this book he's writing and he wants to know, does he need an agent or should he send it straight to a publisher?'

'Well, an agent would certainly help. But the problem is . . .'

'Look, why don't you come over, and you can talk to him yourself. He's desperate for advice.'

'Frankly, Linda, he doesn't stand much chance of getting an agent *or* a publisher. Not in the present climate.'

'That's a bit of a bummer. Can't you say something positive?'

'I'm just being realistic, to save him wasting his time. There's a glut of travel books at the moment, so unless his is really outstanding . . .'

'It may be. He's included lots of stuff about Mongolia –'

'Mongolia's been done to death. First there was that TV series and then a –'

'But Craig's approach is different. He set out to see if someone from the West could live like a primitive herdsman. And he's taken some fantastic photos.'

'Photos don't sound very primitive to me. I can't imagine Mongolian herdsmen wandering around festooned with cameras, like a bunch of Japanese tourists.'

'What's bugging you today, Al? You're not usually like this.'

'I know. I'm sorry. Things are rather . . . difficult.'

'Why? What's up?'

'I've decided to tell James,' she blurted out, 'about not believing. Tonight. When he comes in. I've got to get it over with.'

'Oh God! Suppose he goes berserk?'

'Honestly, Linda, you're the one who told me he wouldn't.'

'Did I? Well, that settles it – you *must* come over. We need to psych you up, give you a stiff drink or three. Don't worry, you'll be back in plenty of time. We'll have a quick lunch, then send you on your way ready to do battle with the Pope himself.'

It sounded most unlikely, yet preferable to spending the day alone, worrying about James's reaction. Cecilia's curtains could wait. 'All right,' she said. 'I'll come, but don't expect me to be good company.'

'Excuse the mess.' Craig pushed open the front gate, which was hanging on one hinge. In the patch of garden, among copious weeds, were several bulging dustbin bags and an abandoned supermarket trolley. 'If I'd known you were coming I'd have tidied up.' He ran down the steps to the basement and unlocked a battered door.

'Like hell you would,' said Linda. 'Your place is always a tip.'

'I need a wife.'

'We *all* need wives.' Linda picked her way through the cluttered bedsit and cleared a space on the sofa, the garishly patterned cover of which couldn't disguise the bumps and dips. 'Here, Al, sit down.'

'Thanks.' She lowered herself gingerly, in case of broken springs.

'I'll make coffee if you like, Craig,' Linda offered, 'while you show Alison your *magnum opus*.'

'God, don't call it that. You'll make me nervous.'

'And so you should be. Alison's a top-notch editor, used to dealing with the likes of Martin Amis.'

'Hardly,' Alison said. 'I'm beginning to think I'd be lucky to get a job editing the phone book.'

'Don't be silly. You've only been trying a couple of months.' Linda located the kettle, hidden behind a pile of magazines. 'Coffee, Al? Craig, where's the milk?'

'Sorry, there isn't any.'

'It'll have to be black then. What about sugar?'

Craig produced the crumpled remains of a packet.

'Thanks. Now scat. Alison's in a rush.'

Involuntarily Alison glanced at her watch. Lunch had taken longer than intended, although it *had* been fun – so much so she'd actually forgotten the evening's ordeal. None the less, she must leave soon and start preparing the expiatory dinner for James.

Craig lit a cigarette, tossing the match on the floor. 'Let me just sort the pages out. They seem to have got into a muddle.'

It didn't sound too promising and, if the manuscript was as messy as the room, most publishers would reject it out of hand. Craig's bed was unmade and, in the absence of shelves or wardrobes, more black dustbin bags stood haphazardly about, overflowing with books and clothes. It seemed odd that he chose to live in student squalor when he must be in his mid-twenties. There was a pervasive smell of stale smoke and unwashed clothes. Maybe the window didn't open. It was barred, like a prison, and looked out on to the street, where people's top halves occasionally bobbed past, while their legs remained invisible behind a low brick wall.

Craig was still shuffling pages, apparently reluctant to hand them over. 'You may think it's a load of crap. I've never written anything before, you see.'

His nervousness was catching. If it *was* bad, she'd have to break it to him, which might well cause offence. She knew from experience how touchy aspiring authors were. Many people thought they could write, then produced some pathetic effort which had no earthly chance of selling.

'Coffee up.' Linda passed her a mug with a pair of protuberant pink breasts on one side. 'You two'll have to share a spoon. I can't find any others. And get a move on, Craig. We said half an hour, not all night.'

'Coming.' He thrust a stack of now well-ordered pages into Alison's hands.

She leafed through them in surprise. They were impeccably neat; the paper an expensive vellum and his printer obviously state of the art. He had lavished all his devotion on the manuscript while neglecting himself and his surroundings. His jeans were torn, his long fair hair untidy.

He flicked a worm of ash into his palm. 'While you're having a quick read-through I'll see if I can dig the photos out. A mate of mine was looking at them last night and I'm not sure where they've got to.'

She nodded, already engrossed in the writing. Craig's prose style was extraordinary: edgy and electrifying. The book started in full flood with the protagonist rising at dawn to take part in a shamanistic rite with a Mongolian medicine man, then moved on to breakfast in the gher: hard salty curds washed down with mares' milk vodka.

Suggestions and improvements were already flooding into her mind. After her years at Shaw Hilliard she couldn't read so much as the back of a cereal packet without a metaphorical blue pencil at the ready. Craig's book cried out for editing. It was far better than she'd dared hope, but it needed discipline. The sentences tumbled pell-mell over each other and some passages were indigestibly complex.

She suddenly realized he was watching her, the photographs forgotten, an anxious expression on his face.

'Well,' he said, 'what d'you think?'

She had learned long ago not to over-praise a book before reading it right through. However, she smiled at him encouragingly. 'There's some good stuff here.'

'You mean there might be a chance of getting it published?'

There was such longing in his voice she was loath to disappoint him. Yet it was crazy to raise an author's hopes before even the sniff of a contract was in the offing. 'I honestly can't say until I've finished it.'

'Couldn't you stay and read a bit more? Oh, *please*.'

She consulted her watch again. If she cut corners on James's dinner she could spare another half-hour. After all, a three-course lunch was provided at the conference. And it did feel good to be needed. There was a sense of exhilaration – even power – in reading an interesting manuscript, finding ways to improve it and influence its final shape. For the past six months she had been deprived of all that. 'Linda, would you mind? Or are you bored just sitting around?'

'No. Go ahead. I'll read too. Craig, chuck me that *Time Out*, will you? I'll have a flick through the Lonely Hearts. Who knows, I may find that Sagittarian yacht-owning whisky-distiller I've been searching for all my life.'

Alison grinned and turned to Craig, who had eventually tracked down the photographs and was sitting on the floor sorting them into piles. 'Would it be OK if I made a few notes on the pages – ideas, suggestions?'

'Please do. I desperately need some input. At times I felt completely at sea, not knowing if I was doing it right.'

'Can I borrow a pencil? I find it best to jot down first impressions straight away. It's a funny thing, but on the second reading one's reaction is never the same.'

Chapter 2 changed abruptly in style. If Craig started getting too experimental, it might alienate a mainstream publisher. However, the content was absorbing: the protagonist's attempt to shed his First World values and possessions (camera and tape recorder excepted) and live a Third World existence. She began scribbling in the margins, just odd words so as not to interrupt the narrative flow. She could elaborate on them later – the important thing was to get the general gist.

It was very much a young man's book – intense, showy and opinionated, but those were assets. There was nothing worse than passionless prose. Indeed she was so caught up in Craig's exuberant word-painting – transported from London SE11 to the awesome expanse of the steppe, stretching thousands of miles, lonely, parched and treeless – that she was startled when he spoke.

'Perhaps you ought to see the photos. They'd make it much more vivid.'

She laughed. 'It's vivid enough already. Heavens! Is that the time? I'm sorry, Craig, but I really must leave.'

He was hovering at her side, dropping ash on the sofa. 'Oh, do just read to Chapter 10. That was a hell of a challenge. You see, I –'

'Craig, give us a break!' Linda flung down the *Time Out*. 'Alison came for a nice relaxing lunch, not to flog her arse off for you and your bloody book.'

'It's OK,' she assured him. 'I'm enjoying it. In fact I'll take the manuscript home with me if you like and work on it next week.'

'God, that would be fantastic.'

'I hope you can pay her bill,' Linda put in tartly.

He looked aghast. 'Oh, I hadn't realized . . .'

'Don't be silly. Just buy me a drink. I've actually been considering freelance work, and this'll be good practice.' (And far more satisfying than Father Peter's projects.) 'I'll give you a ring when I've finished and maybe we can arrange to meet.'

'I can't believe my luck!' He tore the flap off his empty cigarette packet and scribbled down his phone number. 'I'm on the late shift next week, so I'll be around till about five in the afternoon.'

'Fine. And now I've got to dash.'

'I'll walk you to the tube,' said Linda. 'It's stopped raining, thank God.'

Once Craig had closed the front door, Linda gave her an appraising look. 'You seem better – more relaxed.'

'I am.' One of the advantages of editing was the total concentration it required. Personal problems simply faded into the background.

'You sure you'll be OK this evening? We haven't had much chance to talk it over.'

'Don't worry. I've got things more in proportion now. You were right – it did me good to get out.'

'I'm always right,' Linda said smugly. 'Just follow Auntie Linda's advice and everything'll be OK. And listen, Al, if James gets bolshie tonight just give me a bell and I'll come straight round and sort him out.'

17

'I'm sorry, Craig, this chapter really doesn't work. I told you last time, you can't keep changing perspectives. It's muddling for the reader.'

'*I* like it.' There was an edge of defiance in his voice.

'What's the point asking me to help if you don't take a blind bit of notice?'

'I rewrote all that first section, didn't I? And anyway . . .' His words were drowned by another burst of drilling from outside. 'Bloody hell!' He strode to the window and looked out. 'Not again! I thought they'd finished. Why the fuck do they have to dig the road up when we're trying to work? Let's have a cup of coffee and hope they piss off soon.'

'Good idea.' A hot drink would ease her throat. She had caught the priest's cold, which had lingered for a fortnight and left her with an irritable cough. She unwrapped a cough sweet, the only sustenance she was likely to get. They had finished the biscuits earlier on – a grand total of three dampish custard creams.

She got up to stretch her legs, wincing at the noise from the street. The whole bedsit seemed to shudder with the pounding of the drill. Through the window-bars she could see the torsoes of the workmen, clad in orange safety jerkins – great hulking chaps with sinewy hands and bull-necks. Craig was a stripling in comparison. His shrunken sweatshirt only served to emphasize his narrow shoulders, and left a gap above the top of his jeans, revealing bare and bony ribs. Still, whatever his sartorial failings he had at least tidied the room. There was even a new poster covering the damp stain on the wall: a photo of a pear, with 'APPLE' printed underneath.

He handed her a mug of coffee. 'Look, don't think I'm ungrateful. I'm a bit on edge, that's all.'

'So I realize.' Both of them were on edge. As well as feeling hungry and off-colour she was increasingly worn down by the strain of lying to James. And this morning's unpleasant scene in the crèche had been just about the last straw. It was hard enough looking after other people's children, without having to restrain a hysterical mother from laying into her two-year-old.

Craig was leafing gloomily through the pages of his manuscript.

'There seems to be so much wrong with this sodding book I'm beginning to lose heart.'

'Well, don't. It's good. It needs some work, but that's normal. Even experienced writers often revise through umpteen drafts.'

'I haven't got time for that.'

'You'll have to make time, Craig – if you're serious, that is.' Like him she had to shout above the uproar from the street. The screeching of the drill was rising in pitch until the noise became an assault. Then it stopped abruptly, only to begin again a few seconds later with another nerve-jangling barrage. It might be better to cut their losses and arrange a session for next week – the last one, she hoped secretly. She had enough on her plate at the moment, with Cecilia so unwell.

Craig sat close to her on the sofa and spoke loudly into her ear. 'You don't think I'm wasting my time, do you?'

She shook her head impatiently. They'd had the same conversation last Tuesday. She longed to get back to working with proper professional authors who didn't regard revision as an insult. If only next week's interview at Heinemann would lead to a definite offer. Each rejection sapped her confidence, made her more dispirited.

Another ear-splitting salvo exploded through the room. She drained her coffee and stood up. 'Craig, this is ridiculous. We can't hear ourselves speak. Let's call it quits and meet some other time.'

'When? I'm on the early shift next week and *you* can't do the evenings.'

'Oh, I'm sure I can manage one. I'll have a word with James. Give me a ring, OK? Now where's my briefcase?'

'Here.' Before she could move, he darted forward to pick it up, and held it behind his back. 'Come and get it,' he taunted.

'Don't be stupid, Craig.' She tried to wrest it from him, but he dropped it to the floor and nudged it out of reach with his foot. Then without warning he pulled her towards him and jammed his mouth against hers. The kiss was so violent that she felt a sort of roar reverberating through her mouth, echoed by the noise of the machines outside. He seemed to be consuming her whole body, swallowing her right down inside him. His breath tasted of nicotine and coffee – harsh tastes like the harsh kiss. She struggled with him wildly, hitting out at random. But he grabbed her wrists and held them. 'Steady on, woman. It was only a kiss, for God's sake.'

'I don't want a kiss. Let me go.' How dare he call her woman! Viciously she kicked his shins, but he didn't loosen his grip. So much anger was welling up inside her she was like a loaded gun about to discharge.

With a sudden sharp movement she freed herself, then tried to fend him off with feet and fists. He was much stronger than he looked, his arms as hard as steel as they fought. But she stood her ground and parried blow for blow, troubled by the growing realization that this violence wasn't altogether unwelcome. It had triggered a release in her, put an end to her recent passivity. She almost *needed* the sheer physical aggression. Craig had galvanized some unknown, unused part of her, unleashing a passion close to rage and turning her into the belligerent child she had never been allowed to be. There was an added tension in the sound of their laboured breathing; hers swift and snatched, his slower and more rasping. Despite the racket outside, it seemed to be the only noise in the room; increasing in intensity like an expression of her defiance. She smelt a whiff of acrid sweat. His? Or hers perhaps. She was no longer a demure and well-behaved woman but an uncontrollable animal.

Suddenly he pushed her down on the sofa, as if signalling an unspoken truce, and they lay still but wary, recovering their breath. He knelt above her, deliberately holding her gaze, unblinking, insolent. His long floppy hair dangled over her face. She tugged a strand of it: soft, blond, boyish hair, joltingly different from James's short dark crop. Only now had he become flesh and blood; not just Linda's friend, a barman and potential author, but disturbingly real – and male. It was as if she were seeing him for the very first time, and seeing him in close-up: the golden gleam of stubble on his chin, the Adam's apple pulsing in his throat, the surprising darkness of his lashes, fringing baby-blue eyes. All at once, she laughed. Craig, the macho baby.

'What's so funny?

'Everything.'

'OK, how's this for a bit of a giggle?' He pulled her sweater up and dragged it over her head. Enraged, she tried to stop him, but he pinioned her arms, then slipped his hands beneath her back and scrabbled to unfasten her bra. She realized to her horror that she was responding to his groping, urgent touch. Instinctively she covered her chest with her hands, yet that other secret part of her *wanted* to be naked. Unrestricted. Exposed. He prised her hands away and started kissing her breasts – hurting again, working his mouth fiercely from one nipple to the other. She accepted the pain willingly, as a distraction from the chaos in her mind, and, hardly aware what she was doing, thrust herself against him.

'Let's fuck.' He was already yanking down his jeans.

The crude word jarred. Yet she found herself staring at his penis in disgusted fascination. It was standing out red, swollen and imperious, in such contrast to his pale and slender body that it seemed to have an existence all its own. And not just an existence – an iron determination. She and Craig were powerless to oppose it.

He wrenched her skirt down, and her tights and pants came with it. He tossed them aside and pulled her to her feet, steering her towards the bureau. With one hand he forced a drawer open and reached for something inside. When he turned to face her again, his penis was armoured in black rubber. It was so long since she had seen a condom she shrank back involuntarily. The very blackness of it was menacing. But he seized her by the shoulder and jerked her round the other way, and as he propelled her back towards the sofa she could feel the rubber penis hard against her buttocks. She fell to her knees, her face pressed into the musty cushions, her hair trapped beneath his hands. He tried to ram in from behind, probing clumsily at first and forcing her to open her legs. She heard herself cry out in rage as he began drilling her and drilling her. She was furious, furious – with him and everyone; sick of all the lies and the rejections, the piddling daily round of duty and pretence. This was her revenge; this brutish, frenzied fucking. *Fucking*, yes, she liked the word. It made her a different person – feckless, irresponsible, someone who didn't give a damn about God or jobs or babies.

'Be quiet, woman!' Craig panted, scratching his nails down her back. 'You'll deafen the whole road.'

'I *shan't* be quiet!' she yelled.

After the weeks of enforced silence and deception she had to let everything out. The workmen, too, were shouting; their uncouth voices hammering out a rhythm above the bombardment from the street. They seemed to have materialized inside the room; their rough mouths on her nipples, their calloused hands clutching at her back. She tried to throw them off, jack-knifing her body, but suddenly there was a cry from Craig and a long, slow, juddering spasm.

The drill outside throbbed and bludgeoned on. She lay motionless, his damp body sprawled over hers. It was difficult to breathe. Her nose was blocked, her mouth dry and bruised. She gave a painful cough.

Then, all at once, the drilling stopped. Silence poured into the room – an intrusion, an affront – becoming gradually so taut she flinched at the tiny creak of the sofa springs as Craig shifted his weight.

She closed her eyes, not daring to look at his nakedness or face the enormity of what had happened. It *couldn't* have happened. She and James were devoted to each other. Faithful. Happily married. She must have been possessed by some terrible evil to betray him so unspeakably. Yet nothing could ever undo it. Her vile and reckless behaviour this one brief afternoon would remain an indelible stain on their marriage.

Tears streamed down her face. Tears of shame and self-disgust.

'Dear God,' she mouthed, 'forgive me.'

Then she remembered with a crushing desolation that there *was* no God.

No forgiveness.

18

'Are you sure there's nothing I can do, Cecilia? Shopping? Hoovering?'

'No, my dear. The shopping you did on Wednesday should keep us going for a month! You sit still – you look tired. You've been wonderful these last two weeks. Francis and I really do appreciate it.'

Wonderful. If only they knew . . .

'And I think I'm on the mend at last, thank the good Lord. My chest feels much less tight.'

'Well, don't get up too soon. You know what the doctor said. When's he coming next?'

'Monday.'

The day of her interview at Heinemann. Not that she'd given it any thought. She had other things on her mind – like yesterday. Just being with Cecilia made her even more ashamed. On top of the bedside cabinet with the medicines and Lucozade lay Cecilia's rosary and missal. Indeed Cecilia regarded illness as a chance for extra prayer. And she received Communion daily in this room. Alison studiously avoided looking at the 'altar': a small table covered with a white lace cloth, on which stood two white candles in ornate silver candlesticks. The very thought of Communion brought her out in a cold sweat. How could she go this Sunday – or ever again?

'Pass me my bedjacket, would you, my dear? It's getting a little chilly.'

'Yes, of course. Would you like the fire on?'

'No, I prefer the room fairly cool.'

Alison helped her on with the bedjacket, noticing how parchment-pale Cecilia's cheeks were. The iron-grey hair was scraped back in its habitual chignon; the nightdress pristine white. Even ill in bed Cecilia liked to observe the proprieties. And as with physical, so with mental. However frail she might be, she would never waver in her mission to defend the family faith. Alison knew that, so long as she had breath, every grandchild and great-grandchild would be taught by strict example to uphold their religious heritage.

'And perhaps you could tidy up the bed a bit. You know I like things straight.'

She did indeed. Cecilia's house was impeccable and the bed already perfectly tidy. Still, she smoothed the quilt to show willing and picked one tiny errant feather off the pillow. Her grandparents-in-law had slept together in this double bed for nearly sixty-six years, utterly faithful to each other. For them adultery was a mortal sin, a grave offence against God.

There was a sound of footsteps on the landing and Francis called, 'Alison, be a pet and open the door.'

He was carrying a tray of tea and toast, laid out Cecilia-style with the best bone china and an embroidered linen tray-cloth.

'I thought you might be peckish,' he said, smiling at her fondly as he put the tray on the dressing table. 'And I'm sure *you* need a drink, sweetheart.' He plumped up Cecilia's pillows and handed her a cup of tea.

Sweetheart. James called her that, often. How could she have betrayed such a loving, blameless man? There was no excuse. None. She wasn't starved of sex – far from it. She didn't even fancy Craig. It had been like a sort of rape, except that no way was she a hapless victim . . .

'There's Cecilia's home-made raspberry jam, if you'd like it on your toast.' Francis passed her the dish and the toast, but she had lost her appetite. Last night when James was worried about her eating almost nothing, she'd had to pretend she was suffering from an upset stomach.

'Tell me more about this job you're hoping to get.' Francis always took an interest in what she did.

'Well, it's not ideal. I'd be earning less than I was at Shaw Hilliard, and I wouldn't be commissioning books, but on the other hand . . .' How would she face Craig again? And what if he bragged about the incident? Somehow it might get back to James. She had lain awake all night in utter dread.

'What time's your interview?'

'Eleven thirty.'

'We'll be thinking of you,' Cecilia said. 'And I'll say a special prayer to St John the Apostle. He's the patron saint of publishers.'

'Oh, really? I didn't know there was one.'

'Yes, one of the saints I most admire. Our Lady was very fortunate in having him to care for her after Our Lord had . . . gone.'

Alison nodded politely. Cecilia, too, had John the Apostle to care for her – indeed the whole battalion of saints. Cecilia was never alone. Her guardian angel hovered permanently at her side, and God Himself was within whispering distance. *She* had no such comfort, but felt a terrifying isolation, cut off from James, from everyone. She didn't dare confide even in Linda, who would never understand the depth of her shame.

'And I'll pray to St Cecilia, of course.'

They all glanced up involuntarily at the reproduction over the bed – Raphael's depiction of Cecilia's name-saint. Like St Etheldreda, she had vowed her chastity to God and thus refused to consummate her marriage, and she was eventually martyred by a pagan Roman emperor. Alison would have found it extremely disconcerting to have a virgin martyr watching the goings-on in the marriage bed, but Francis and Cecilia had no such reservations. (There was even a crucifix in the kitchen, where her own parents had a cartoon calendar.) She and James

162

had seen the original Raphael in Bologna soon after their wedding – the first of many such trips. He had expanded her horizons, sharing his favourite artists with her, making up for her years of cultural famine. And she had repaid him by letting a virtual stranger shag her like an animal on heat.

'You'll never believe this, Alison . . .' Cecilia anchored a slipping hair-pin – they too were kept under rigid control, 'but I read a piece in the paper claiming St Cecilia didn't *exist*! She's just a legend, they said. But of course it was written by one of those atheists. I think it's quite disgraceful the way they cast aspersions on God's saints. First St George was –'

The doorbell interrupted her.

'Ah, that'll be Father Michael,' said Francis. 'I'll go and let him in.'

Alison froze. Another priest . . .

'Put the cups back on the tray, dear,' Cecilia instructed. 'He's come to give me Holy Communion and we don't want the place looking a mess.'

Alison did as she was told, although not in a million years would Cecilia's room look a mess. 'I thought your priest was Father John?'

'Yes, he is. Father Michael's the new curate. I haven't met him yet, but Francis went to Mass this morning and had a word with him afterwards. Apparently he's just taken over the Communion round. I have to say I *was* expecting him earlier, but no doubt he's very busy.'

'Well . . . I'll be going then.' If she could just get downstairs before the priest came up . . .

'No, do stay, my dear. I'm sure he'd like to meet you. And could you light the candles, please? There's a match on the table there.'

Alison lit them with shaking hands. 'Actually, I . . . have to go to Sains-bury's. I've just remembered, we've run out of –'

Too late. A large, untidy man, roughly her own age, strode into the room with Francis in his wake. Apart from a clerical collar, just visible at his neck, he looked nothing like a priest. He was encased in a black leather motorcycle jacket, heavy trousers and boots, and a gleaming red crash-helmet was tucked under one arm. But what struck her most was his hair – long and rather greasy and tied back in a ponytail. She noticed Cecilia gazing at it in horror, obviously alarmed at this irruption into her orderly room.

'Hi!' He put his crash-helmet on the floor and unzipped the jacket with a rasping noise to reveal a garish purple jersey. Then he breezed up to the bed and shook Cecilia's hand. 'I'm Mike Greville.'

It was some moments before she recovered her composure. 'How do you do, Father Michael,' she said, with a perceptible chill in her voice. Cecilia was unfailingly polite, to priests above all, but apart from her shock at his appearance she expected to be addressed by name. 'Thank you for coming, Father,' she continued. 'To tell the truth, I'd almost given you up.' She turned to smile at Alison, her tone softening. 'This is Alison, my grandson's wife. She became a Catholic five years ago. It was a very beautiful service, wasn't it, my dear?'

'Er, yes, Cecilia.'

'Nice to meet you.' The priest grasped her hand firmly – too firmly. No wonder Cecilia had winced. He was like a bear let loose in a dainty dolls' house. He took out of his pocket what looked like a large gold watch-case but which opened to reveal a Host. He laid it on the white-clothed table and bowed in front of it. 'Alison, would you like to receive Communion as well?'

'Yes. No . . .' She was floundering. 'I mean, you . . . you've only brought one Host.'

'No problem. I can break it in two.'

'But what about Francis?'

'He received Communion this morning,' Cecilia informed her. 'And anyway it's the presence of Christ that matters, not the size of the Host.'

'Yes, of . . . course.'

'Righty-ho. Let's get going, shall we?'

She had no knowledge of the protocol for Communion at home. Cecilia's hands were joined and her head bowed reverently, and Francis was kneeling by the bed. Best to copy them. But as she knelt and joined her hands she was instantly reminded of last night. Then, too, she had been on her knees . . .

Father Michael heaved off his leather jacket and put it with the helmet in an untidy heap on the floor. From another pocket he produced a long white stole which he looped around his neck. It looked most incongruous against the baggy jersey but, unabashed, he began the rite in his loud estuary English voice. 'The peace of the Lord be with you always.'

'And also with you,' Francis and Cecilia replied in unison.

Alison mumbled something inaudible. No chance of peace. Not now.

Father Michael smiled at her encouragingly. 'That greeting is a reminder of Christ's presence. He's actually with us in this room. Remember His promise that where two or three are gathered in His name, He too will be there.'

She tensed, picturing Christ beside her in person, His all-seeing eye outraged at the obscene images in her head.

'My brother and sisters,' the priest continued, 'to prepare ourselves for this celebration, let us call to mind our sins.'

Alison tried to fight off more unnerving visions of Craig: the black-rubber penis rearing up, the shock of pubic hair . . .

She heard Francis and Cecilia joining in the 'I confess', but when she followed suit her voice was no more than a croak. Never had words seemed so apt: 'I have sinned, through my own fault, in my thoughts and in my words, in what I have done, and what I have failed to do . . .' In the background Craig was shouting, 'Let's fuck!', his final juddering gasp somehow entangled with the words of absolution.

'May almighty God have mercy on us, forgive us our sins and . . .'

If only it could be that gloriously simple – adultery wiped out at a stroke.

'And now a reading from the holy Gospel according to John. Alison, perhaps *you'd* like to read it for us?' He passed her the small booklet and indicated the passage.

Nodding dumbly, she stammered the first line. 'J . . . Jesus says, "Anyone who does eat my Flesh and drink my Blood . . ."' For the other three the Host *was* Christ, literally and physically – a full-grown man encapsulated in a wafer of bread. How could she ever have believed something so preposterous? How could they?

Somehow she stumbled to the end of the reading and returned the booklet to the priest. But there was still the Our Father to come; the confident voices of the other three drowning her faint whisper.

Then Father Michael took the Host from its gold case and held it up in front of them. 'This is the Lamb of God . . .'

'Lord, I am not worthy to receive you,' Cecilia responded, 'but only say the word and I shall be healed.'

Alison stayed silent. A mere word could never heal the sin she had committed. She recalled her honeymoon. On that first night, James – like Craig – had come abruptly, within minutes. But there the similarities ended. True to the vows of the marriage service, he had worshipped her body, approaching it with tenderness and awe – an extraordinary combination of the sacred and the sensual. And she had been the first for him. Neither his body nor his mind bore the traces of another woman. Craig had a girlfriend, whom she had also betrayed.

Father Michael broke the Host into two and distributed half each to the women. Alison all but choked on her piece, despite its tiny size. It wasn't Christ in her mouth but Craig – Craig blocking her throat, Craig shoving his imperious body right down into her belly. Her cheeks were flaming. How could they not notice? But the priest continued praying, unperturbed, and was soon intoning the final blessing.

'Thanks be to God,' said Francis. After a reverent interval of silence, he rose from his knees and thanked the priest as well. 'Can I get you a cup of tea, Father, or do you have to rush off?'

'No, I've finished my Communion round. I purposely left you till last so I could stay and have a chat. Father John's told me so much about you.'

'Let *me* make the tea,' Alison offered quickly.

Francis touched her arm affectionately. 'No, you stay put, my dear, and talk to Father Michael. I won't be long.'

'Do call me Mike. Everybody does.'

'I'm sorry, Father Michael, I can't abide abbreviations.' Cecilia gave a delicate shudder. 'My husband has always been Francis and my elder son Anthony. I should never have permitted Tony. And as for *Al*' – her voice rose in horror – 'an abomination.'

'So, *Alison*,' said the priest, 'tell me about yourself.'

'Well, I . . . work in publishing – used to, anyway. And we live in Elmleigh, near Reigate. And, er . . .'

Cecilia came to the rescue. 'They moved to Surrey five years ago, when James was made a partner in his accountancy firm. That's my grandson there.' She pointed proudly to a photograph on the dressing-table which showed a much younger James. He looked so eager, so trusting, Alison couldn't bear to meet his eyes.

'He's very precious to me,' Cecilia continued. 'In fact, I call him my miracle baby. When he was born, you see, neither he nor his mother were expected to live.'

Alison let the familiar story wash over her. Cecilia had looked after James for the whole of his first year, while his mother remained seriously ill, and throughout his childhood she had played a major part in his upbringing, especially his spiritual development. She regarded him almost as her own child, whom God had been gracious enough to save, using her as the instrument.

Could it have been a miracle, she wondered? There had been reports in the news which showed prayer could be effective, even with cancer patients, although no one seemed to know why. Whatever – James had been saved. And it was actually something of a miracle that he had married her at all. He deserved the most special of wives, not an atheist, a slut. She suddenly imagined Cecilia watching as she wrenched off her clothes and grappled with Craig on the sofa. She must never, ever, see him again. She didn't need a priest or a God to make a firm purpose of amendment. From this day on she would be faithful to James, until death.

19

'Watch out!' said Craig. 'You'll squash the grapes.' He picked up the large cluster from where it had rolled beneath her thigh and, dangling it above his face, sucked each grape into his mouth in quick succession.

'Don't you dare spit out the pips this time. They prickle.'

'Look who's talking!' He crunched them noisily. 'God knows what I'm lying on . . .' He groped into the bed and held up a piece of cheese rind. 'Did we finish the cheese, by the way?'

'*You* did. I never had a single bite.' His greed maddened her, his way of grabbing everything he wanted – her included. 'Surely you're not still hungry?'

'Famished.' He suddenly clamped his mouth to hers. She could taste grapes, red wine, pungent Gorgonzola. His mouth was always so fierce. He had to overmaster her. And she derived a perverse and painful pleasure from fighting back, slamming hard against him. He reached for a condom – a green one. They had been through every colour in the pack.

'Look,' he said. 'A Martian. Your little green man.'

'Not so little.' Deftly she helped roll it on.

'Flattery will get you everywhere. OK, green for go!' He shoved in, covering her mouth with his hand. Muzzling her was part of the procedure. She bit his palm, thrust her pelvis against his, appalled, as always, at how much anger was mixed with the excitement – anger with him for making her want to do it; worse, making her enjoy it. Anger with the Church for locking her in a religious prison and throwing away the key. Anger with James for being so damned *good*.

'You're fantastic, woman,' he panted, his head thrown back, his face contorted. 'My cock's so deep inside you it's splitting you in half.'

She should be shocked by his crude commentaries. She *was* shocked, yet at the same time goaded on. Sex with Craig wasn't a solemn sacrament; it was a free-for-all, a sport. 'Split me in half, then!' she shouted through the gag of his hand, shutting her eyes to relish the sensations: his cock ramming up inside her, his mouth hungry on her breasts. 'Yes!' she gasped. 'Now. Christ! *Yes*.'

It was the first time she had come before him. Only moments before, though. His body jerked and shuddered, then he pulled out abruptly and removed the condom. She had come to like the condoms – different colours, different flavours and textures. And it was an incredible relief to forget the whole business of conception. Sex couldn't be a failure if you weren't trying for a baby. Another sin, in Cecilia's eyes. To hell with Cecilia.

He lay back beside her, his hair flopping in his eyes.

'Still hungry?' she taunted, reaching out for the last cluster of grapes. Plucking one off she held it against his lips. He swallowed, grazing her finger with his teeth. Dangerous. Delicious. She fed him another, wondering what he'd feel if he knew how deeply she resented him. Resented and desired him. Everything in opposites: disgust and elation; bravado and despair.

'You're a brilliant fuck,' he said, chewing.

'I bet you say that to them all.'

'What do you mean, all?'

'Well, your girlfriend.'

'That's over.'

'Really?' She levered herself up on one elbow and gave him a searching look, trying to gauge whether he was telling the truth. 'Why?'

'I prefer you.'

Being preferred to a nineteen-year-old was extremely flattering when you were thirty. Except she didn't feel thirty with Craig. He made her younger, turned her from a respectable married woman into a randy adolescent. Sometimes they played crazy games or wrestled naked on the floor. At home she felt old and stale; here she was new-hatched.

He pulled her down on top of him. 'I know – let's pretend we've just met. You come into the bar and I serve you with a drink and say, "I fancy you, babe. Get your knickers off."'

She giggled. 'We can't, Craig. I'll be late.'

'Go on. Just one kiss. I take you out the back and you find you can't resist and –'

'I *can* resist. I must.'

'And then, guess what happens? Th-i-s.'

'Stop it, Craig. I've got to go.'

'Spoilsport! You're always rushing away.'

She took his hand and kissed that instead, smooching her mouth across his knuckles. The skin was smooth, and tasted warm and salty. He had tiny golden hairs on the backs of his fingers, even on his thumbs. She licked them like a cat, continued licking sensuously along the inside of his wrist.

'I thought you said you had to go,' he murmured.

She pushed him off and jumped to her feet. What in God's name was she *doing*? Blatantly arousing him (and herself) when part of her could happily have murdered him. Her conflicting emotions went far beyond resentment and desire – it was more like brute fury ranged against drooling lust.

Shakily she walked over to the window. Rain was pattering on the glass but she hadn't noticed it till now. In Craig's cramped divan there wasn't room for weather. The light was beginning to fade. It must be getting on for four – time to return to reality.

Or was *this* reality: a crumpled bed littered with grape pips and flakes of bread? At least he'd thought to buy some food today, even if he'd devoured the lion's share. He was learning. And she was learning – vile truths about herself.

She retrieved her clothes from the floor. Her blouse was inside out, her skirt entangled with his jeans. It was the same every time – she couldn't wait to fling her things off and become that other person: tempestuously out of control. Control was James's province.

She went along to the bathroom, gasping at the shock of cold water as she dabbed between her legs with an anonymous red flannel. (Craig shared the bathroom with five others in the house.) The only towel was stained with paint, so she didn't dry herself, although she did rinse her burning mouth. No one had ever kissed her like Craig – kisses that hurt, that stayed on her mouth all night, overlaid with James's more tender kisses. No, she mustn't think of James. If she didn't keep the two men strictly separate she would go mad with guilt and confusion.

She was already mad, in the grip of a monstrous aberration. She had become a divided personality; at home devout and dutiful and here the shameless slut. Each time she vowed to stop, the headstrong part of her would somehow succeed in taking over; the part she hadn't known was there. It was terrifying, gross.

She buttoned her blouse, fastened her skirt: conventional clothes that seemed to belong to someone else – the pious little soul who assisted Father Peter, the steadfast wife to James.

Shivering, she returned to the other room, where Craig was sprawled on the sofa gnawing the last knob of bread. 'Do you mind if I don't walk you to the tube?' he said. 'I'm bushed.'

'Yeah, I do mind. Get dressed, you lazy sod!' She'd even begun to copy his speech. James had set her high standards; Craig was dragging her down.

'It's you who's shagged me out.' He pulled on his jeans and sweater and shook his hair back into place. Craig could do some things more quickly than any man she knew. She watched him lace his battered trainers – a world away from James's smart black leather shoes. Yet, strangely, she found the trainers erotic: their faint but gamey smell; the outline of his long naked toes imprinted in each one. Craig rarely bothered with socks, and sometimes left off his underpants – as now. That was another secret turn-on: his casual, brazen maleness; denim yanked up over a sticky, unwashed cock.

'OK, ready,' he said. 'When'll I see you again?'

'I'll phone.'

'And you'll read that last bit I rewrote?'

'Don't I always?'

'Yeah. Thanks.' He hugged her briefly. 'The book's getting better, isn't it?'

'Much.' His recent acquiescence had surprised her – almost every suggestion accepted without argument. It was as if, having mastered her in bed, he had no need to fight about the book. And it *was* better, infinitely. That, at least, gave her guilt-free pleasure. In her relationship with James he was the teacher, she the pupil, but with Craig the roles were reversed. He deferred to her as his editor. She hadn't got the job at Heinemann – Craig was now her job.

The train to Reigate was overheated and stuffy. The faceless commuters opposite were entrenched behind their early evening papers. She had bought a *Standard* herself, but reading was impossible. The journey home was always the worst part: the shame, the fear of being found out, the renewed and near-desperate determination never to see Craig again. It was almost as difficult to believe in free will as in the Virgin Birth. This last fortnight she had never felt less free. In spite of the mounting guilt and wretchedness she seemed compelled to steal back to his bed. Sometimes she suspected it was another way of punishing herself. If she weighed the shame and guilt against the crudely reckless pleasure, she knew which way the scales would tip.

At Clapham Junction a woman with a baby got into the carriage. Alison took in every detail: the baby's fuzz of hair, its solemn long-lashed eyes, the pudgy hands, plump cheeks. Childlessness was still so hard to bear. She continued to work in the crèche, devoting herself to other people's children, almost as an atonement. Sin and penance; sin and penance. Even the sin was a sort of penance – the sordid bedsit, the brutish rutting – but perhaps better that than love and romance, which would have been a still greater betrayal.

The train rattled on its way, seeming to gather speed with every station it passed. If only it would shoot past Reigate without stopping and take her to the end of the line. What she dreaded most was James's kiss of welcome when he walked into the house. She felt all the more despicable because he knew where she had been. He trusted her implicitly, indeed often praised her kindness in helping a tiro author with his book. She wouldn't admit it to a soul, but such unquestioning trust annoyed her. It was part of that goodness she had once so much admired. She still admired it. Only the other, devious part of her longed for him to understand that some people were *bad* – depraved, deceitful, beyond forgiveness.

As soon as she got home she ran a scalding bath, washed her hair, cleaned her teeth, changed every stitch of clothing. Then she set about making dinner. Cooking, too, was an atonement. Since she'd met Craig, James had enjoyed more elaborate meals than at any time in their marriage.

'Mm, that smells good,' he said, sniffing the air, after giving her the customary kiss. 'How was your day?'

'Fine. We had two new arrivals in the crèche this morning: Silas and Seymour. I ask you! – imagine saddling babies with names like that.'

James didn't laugh – he was busy pouring drinks. 'And how's Craig's book progressing?'

She swallowed. 'Quite . . . well. How was *your* day?'

'Frustrating. Elaine's causing a few headaches, as always. On top of everything else she's just discovered that the firm's been underpaying its VAT.'

'What, deliberately?'

'Good heavens, no! In error. But it's still an awful embarrassment.'

She tried to provide a sympathetic ear – the least she could do – although neither VAT nor Elaine were exactly her favourite subjects. The wretched woman (apparently head-hunted from Customs and Excise and made a junior partner) had initiated extra partner meetings, mostly in the evenings, which meant James's days were longer still.

'And guess who has to pay the balance?'

'Not you, surely? That can't be fair.'

'Well, all the partners, between us. Anyway, enough of Elaine. All I can say is thank the Lord it's Friday. Although I'm afraid I have to see a client tomorrow.'

'What, again?'

'I'm sorry,' he said, following her into the kitchen. 'I know I've been neglecting you. But look – next weekend, why don't we go away somewhere? How do you fancy a trip to Paris?'

'There's no need, honestly.'

'But I'd like to take you somewhere. Things have been so hectic recently we've hardly seen each other. And it would do you good to have a change of scene. We can go somewhere more exotic if you want. Istanbul? St Petersburg? You choose.'

'St Petersburg's a bit far for the weekend!'

'Well, how about finding a nice hotel and doing nothing for a couple of days? You do seem awfully tired, darling.' He eased the spatula from her hand and turned her round to face him. 'I'm worried about you actually. You're not your usual self.'

What *was* her usual self, though? The self he'd married? Or had that too been a fake? As he held her close she was tempted in a split second of madness to give him a blow-by-blow account of her afternoon with Craig. The moment passed. She hadn't even told him yet about her problems with the faith. She had lost her nerve at the last minute, and now there was so much to confess – lies piled on lies.

'Where's it to be then?' James topped up his whisky. He was drinking more these days, apparently concerned about *her* as well as work. Could he be suspicious? That first evening she'd come home with scratch marks on her back. Although she'd taken the utmost care to conceal them, her very furtiveness might have put him on his guard.

He was still waiting for her to answer. 'I . . . I'll think about it, OK?' she said, busying herself with the knives and forks. Wherever they chose to go he would try to make it perfect – cherish her, pamper her, turn it into a honeymoon. She didn't deserve that, didn't even want it. The sex would be too loving, and there would be the usual hopeless hope for a baby. The longer she went without conceiving, the more she resented even trying. It was irrational and unfair, but she couldn't help herself.

'We did say we'd go back to Venice. I know it's cold in February, but the advantage is that it won't be packed with tourists.'

'It might be flooded, though.' She realized with another stab of guilt that if Craig had suggested a weekend away – in Venice, Blackpool, Timbuktu – she would have accepted with alacrity. No Sunday Mass, no night and morning prayers, no love and tenderness; above all, no deceit.

'Damn!' said James. 'There's the phone. It'll probably be Bill Fraser about the arrangements for tomorrow. I'll take it in the study.'

While he was gone she stood at the kitchen window, gazing out unseeingly. Did there have to be so much deceit? Why couldn't she *tell* him about her loss of faith, not in the convoluted words she had rehearsed so many times but just as a simple fact? She owed him that, at least.

As soon as she heard him put the phone down she went along to the study. 'Darling,' she said, 'there's something I need to –'

'Not now,' he snapped.

Stung by this brusqueness – unheard of for James – she retreated to the door. He looked preoccupied and tense, sitting at his desk, scribbling a note on the pad. 'Did you sort it out with Bill?' she asked when he glanced up.

'Who?'

'Bill Fraser.'

'No. It . . . it wasn't him.'

She waited, but he volunteered no more information. Had it been bad news? Certainly, his mood had changed. And she noticed with surprise that his shoes were dull and scuffed, when as a rule he polished them meticulously. It was only a tiny detail, yet so out of character she went cold with fear. She could see Craig's trainers again, lying on the carpet where he'd kicked them off in his haste; their insistent tongues protruding from hungry, gaping mouths. James *must* have guessed. Why else should he be so tetchy? Perhaps the offer of a weekend abroad was an excuse to confront her on neutral ground, away from distractions like the phone.

She trailed back to the kitchen, somehow managing to burn herself as she dished up the vegetables. The pain barely registered – there was too much on her mind.

'James?' she called nervously. 'Supper's ready when you are.'

He failed to come – that, too, was unlike him. But if he was wrestling with mistrust and jealousy . . .

She called again, almost wishing she could forget supper and sneak out of the house. Just facing him across the table and making normal conversation seemed an impossible ordeal. However, when he appeared he was smiling, as if nothing untoward had happened, although the smile, like hers, could be false.

'What are we having?'

'Garlic mushrooms to start, then sole *Véronique*.'

'Is that the one with grapes?'

She nodded.

'Great! My favourite.'

Yes, she thought, the one thing – the only thing – James and Craig had in common was a passion for grapes.

20

'No, it's not a Gainsborough – just in his style. Charming, though, isn't it?'

She nodded. Almost too charming. A large, aristocratic family, arrayed in their Sunday best, posed beneath a noble oak; an Arcadian landscape undulating into the distance. A couple of pampered spaniels frolicked at their feet, and one of the small daughters, dressed in frills and flounces, cradled a pet rabbit on her lap. 'All that's missing is the cat!'

James laughed. 'They're called conversation pieces, these eighteenth-century groups. I suppose they worked out cheaper than lots of individual portraits.'

'This bunch don't look exactly strapped for cash.'

'Oh, no. The whole idea was to display their wealth. See the house in the background? It's almost as big as this one. Actually I think we've seen everything now, but I'd just like to pop back to the library and have another look at that ceiling. Do you mind?'

'Of course not.' She had made the weekend James's treat, which was why they were in Oxfordshire (rather than Paris or Venice) looking round Sir William Barnaby's mansion. Barney, an acquaintance of the Egertons', had died last year, leaving his house to the nation. James had long wanted to see the art collection, so she had suggested it herself – a small sacrifice, considering.

She was glad to leave the painting, which reminded her of the Egertons – a distinguished family in elegant surroundings, every blade of grass in place, every oak leaf manicured. Yet their serenity masked a steely control imposed on every member. She was the weed in the flowerbed, the unpruned tree – the wayward element threatening their ordered system.

James took her arm as they strolled back to the library. Having all this time alone with him only made her more uneasy: she had to be constantly on guard against incriminating herself. She feigned an interest in the magnificent library ceiling where naked gods lolled on a painted sky, but naked bodies reminded her of Craig. It was madness to have spent so long with him yesterday.

'They say Barney owned fifty thousand books. I can well believe it, can't you?'

She glanced at the crowded shelves: books on science, religion, philosophy, full of 'facts' and theories. Full of lies. Wherever she turned these days she seemed to be faced with more and more untruths – politicians' evasions, advertisers' hype, statistics massaged, models airbrushed, even medical researchers paid to produce the right results – all reflecting her own lies. She was deceiving Craig as well as James. He thought she was unhappily married, practically on the brink of divorce. But then he was deceiving *her*: Linda had seen him with a new girlfriend just a couple of days back, the pair of them kissing quite openly. For all she knew, he might have several women on the go. The very notion provoked a surge of jealousy. Ridiculous, irrational. Craig meant nothing to her. And yet . . .

'You look as if you're wilting, darling. How about a cup of tea?'

'Mm, that would be nice.' It was as if she were with a stranger, making formal conversation. Except *she* was the stranger. James was still the man she had married, cultured and considerate. Although in fact he did seem noticeably tense. Even touring the house, he had wandered somewhat distractedly from one room to the next, rather than studying each exhibit with his usual focused attention. And at breakfast he'd spent for ever deciding what to have, then changed his mind when they brought it. She had feared at first he must have discovered something about Craig, but that was hardly likely when he was treating her so lovingly. It was more probable he'd guessed she was having problems with her faith. Any normal Catholic wife would have told her husband right away, but the longer

176

one put off such a thing the more of a hurdle it became. She dreaded the repercussions, especially as James was bound to insist that she saw a priest. How could she talk honestly to a priest without Craig coming into it?

They walked across the courtyard to the teashop. The first daffodils were in bloom, planted in rustic tubs, and the waxen petals of a showy pink magnolia made a burst of colour against the wall. The weather was capricious, veering from flurries of rain to flashes of shy sun. Marrying James had meant an adjustment to the calendar – March was no longer spring but Lent. James was presumably doing his customary Lenten penances, although this was the first year he hadn't suggested a joint endeavour. Another indication, perhaps, that he knew about her godless state of mind. Which made it all the more pointless to conceal it. She could always refuse to see a priest; tell James she needed time to work things out on her own.

'You sit down. I'll get the tea.'

He returned with a tray and a single piece of cake. 'Your favourite,' he smiled. 'Chocolate fudge.'

'Thank you,' she said politely. She couldn't eat – she was trying to summon the courage to speak. At least it would be one deception resolved.

The silence seemed to build and build, despite the rattle of cups behind the counter and the chatter of people at other tables. There was art even here, mostly modern works. A grotesquely distorted portrait hung opposite. She felt it must be *her*: a single eye, instead of two, jaw pulled out of shape, mouth gaping in a scream as she contemplated the weekend ahead – tonight's long, leisurely dinner, followed by long, leisurely sex.

'Alison . . .' James leaned across and took her hand. 'What's wrong?'

This was her chance. She opened her mouth, but the words refused to come. It was too dangerous: suppose she let slip something about Craig? After all, the two were interlinked. If she hadn't lost her faith she would never have embarked on an affair. 'Nothing's wrong,' she said defensively. 'Why should it be?'

'Look, we haven't talked for ages. It's my fault – I accept that. I've let work get on top of me. But I realize things aren't good for you at the moment and I, well, wondered if . . .'

Someone in the teashop laughed. Unnerving sound.

'. . . if we ought to consider adoption again.'

'Adoption?'

'Yes. I know we decided against it, temporarily at least. But since you've stopped the fertility drugs you seem to have lost heart. I do understand. It must be awfully hard for you, seeing all the nieces and nephews and looking after Matthew.'

'No, I enjoy it.'

'But if we put our names down for adoption and pulled as many strings as possible, who knows, we might be lucky. It would be so marvellous to have a child of our own.'

'We might *not* be lucky, though, and frankly I couldn't cope with any more rejections.'

'Aren't you being rather negative?' There was a hint of irritation in his voice. 'Those people we met at the Johnsons' were offered a child in the end.'

'Yes, a child. Not a baby.'

'Actually there *are* babies available. I heard only the other day that –'

'James,' she cut in, 'have you forgotten what the social worker said – that the chance of getting a baby is less than one in a hundred?'

'Well, surely any chance is better than none. Besides, I thought we'd agreed that we wouldn't rule out an older child altogether.'

'We didn't agree anything.'

Although he refrained from contradicting her, he frowned impatiently. 'I still can't see why the age of the child should matter quite so much.'

'It doesn't. It's just that . . .' She stabbed the cake with her fork. He could hardly be expected to understand that she couldn't consider a child of *any* age until she was rid of Craig. If she and James applied formally to adopt, a full-scale investigation would begin: interviews, home visits, checks with the police. She felt quite enough of a criminal as it was, without all those pryings and probings.

She glanced anxiously at James. It wasn't like him to be edgy, and he had never called her negative before. Did he really not suspect?

'We could just put out some feelers – maybe join one of those support groups for prospective adopters. It wouldn't commit us to anything and at least we'd get more idea of –'

'James, I feel I need a longer rest from even thinking about babies.'

'But you *are* thinking about them, aren't you?'

She was thinking about Craig. She broke off a piece of the cake and crumbled it to nothing. 'If I could only get back to work I'd have less time to think.'

'By the way, what happened about that job in Watford? You didn't tell me.'

'Well, I only decided yesterday. It really isn't practicable. Watford's too far *and* a horrendous journey. I wouldn't be home till eight or nine at night.'

'I could help, though – do more about the house, cook supper, if you like.'

She squeezed his hand. 'You're an angel.' What an irony that the sole job for which she'd been shortlisted was in the Religious Books Division of a large general publisher. They wanted a committed Christian, not surprisingly. Despite that proviso – and the distance – it was tempting. The salary and prospects were good, and she could probably bluff her way at work just as convincingly as at home. (She was beginning to realize how many so-called Christians stifled their doubts rather than confronted them. A friend in the parish had admitted recently that she clung to a childlike belief in a kindly Father-God, just to avoid the chaos of a meaningless world.) However, integrity had triumphed and she'd made up her mind to phone first thing Monday morning and turn down the second interview. Integrity? It was a nerve even to think in such terms.

James picked up her empty sugar packet and put it on the tray, tidy as always. 'Don't you like the cake?'

'Yes. It's . . . lovely.' In fact it made her stomach heave: the dark moist pores oozing chocolate grease; the sludge of icing glistening queasily on top. She forced a mouthful down, somehow managing to drop her fork in the process.

James retrieved it from the floor. 'Could you be so kind as to bring another?' he asked a girl who was passing with a tray of dirty cups.

'You can get one yourself. It's self-service.'

'There's no need to be rude,' James said testily.

'Look, it doesn't matter,' Alison muttered.

'It *does* matter. I won't have people treating me like that.'

179

The words set up threatening echoes. It was *her* he was addressing, not the waitress – he must know she was deceiving him and this was a veiled warning. The girl herself merely gave him a withering look.

'Let's go, James,' Alison whispered.

His own voice seemed unnaturally loud. 'I don't see why we should be driven out for requesting a clean fork.'

'It's not that. I . . . need the loo.'

He pushed his chair back and stalked towards the door. She followed in alarm. James was never temperamental. Maybe she had upset him even more by refusing to consider adoption.

She disappeared into the ladies', almost glad to get away from his unaccustomed anger. It was extremely disconcerting not to know what he was thinking, when previously they had always been in tune. He might be just worried about work, of course. Safer to believe that than face the grim alternatives.

She stood rinsing her hands at the basin, mesmerized by the running tap. Somehow she must salvage the weekend, avoid a confrontation.

When she emerged, James was nowhere to be seen. He's *gone*, she thought. He does know. He's taken his revenge and left.

She walked to the end of the path, panicking as she pictured life without him: forlorn and one-dimensional. How would she endure it? Don't be stupid, she told herself. He wouldn't go, not like that, in any case: simply vanish without a word. Whatever else, he was rational and responsible – at least he had been for the last six years.

She scanned the gardens to right and left: no sign of him there either, so she hurried back to the café. Turning the corner she suddenly spotted him standing beside an empty bench, apparently staring into nothing. She felt relief and yet dismay. Why wasn't he looking for *her*? Or had he forgotten she existed? Nervously she went over and touched him on the shoulder. 'James, are you OK?'

He jumped. 'Yes. Fine.'

'I . . . wondered if you'd like to see that film. The one you said had such good reviews.'

'Oh, *Zero Day*, you mean.'

'Yes.'

'But it's on in Oxford. That's twenty miles.'

'No problem. We've plenty of time.'

'All right then. If you want.'

'But do *you* want, James?'

'I don't mind.'

Strange he should show no enthusiasm when it was a director he particularly admired.

'It'll be like the old days,' she said with a determined smile. 'Weekends away, films in the afternoon . . .'

No, nothing like the old days.

James unfolded his damask napkin with a flourish. 'Look at the size of these things – they're nearly as big as tablecloths.'

'Mm. It's all frightfully plush, isn't it? Did you notice the waiter's white gloves? I thought they'd gone out with horse-drawn carriages!'

They had decided to have dinner in their room. It would be romantic, as James put it. He seemed his normal self again, thank God. The film had certainly helped. Although the story was sad, it had forged a bond between them, and for a precious two hours they had shared the same intense emotions, laughing and crying in exactly the same places. Perhaps she had imagined his suspicions; read too much into an uncharacteristic contretemps with a waitress.

She lifted the silver cover off the dish. 'Oh, James – *lobster*! And look at that gorgeous chocolatey pudding.' He had chosen the dinner: all her favourite things. Surely he wouldn't spoil her like this if he thought she was having an affair. There was even a bottle of Bollinger, despite the fact it was Lent. He hadn't mentioned religion once, not even where they'd go to Mass in the morning. Which might imply that he knew about her doubts (if nothing else). Maybe he felt compassion for her predicament and was trying to make it easier for her to confide in him without fear of recrimination. But that wouldn't explain his earlier ill humour and, anyway, she had no wish to get involved in a deep spiritual discussion – not now. It was hard enough ousting Craig from the room when everything seemed to serve as a reminder. The sumptuous food, for instance, was a farcical contrast to the bits and pieces he'd produced last night – leftovers, no doubt, from some other woman's meal. And the velvet drapes and thick-pile carpet were a world away from his shabby bedsit. She was sitting facing the enormous bed (twice the size of his divan) – a constant baleful presence. The past couple of weeks she had managed to avoid sex with James, pleading stomach cramps or headaches, but tonight there was no escape. This dinner was part of the slow erotic build-up she had so loved on honeymoon: the privacy, the champagne, the warm, inviting room, the delicious decadence of eating in their dressing-gowns.

She cast around for a subject that would be both safe and unerotic. 'Tell me about Elaine,' she said, finally plumping for VAT as an ideal turn-off. 'Is the situation still as bad?'

For some reason he looked startled. 'What situation?'

'Well, I thought you said you were both working on the same client whose books were in a terrible mess.'

'Oh, I see. Yes.' He wiped his mouth with the napkin, although he hadn't touched his food. 'She's found a lot of anomalies in the VAT returns and seems to hold me responsible, although I've told her umpteen times I didn't deal with the VAT side.' Now he was twisting the napkin between his fingers, pulling it this way and that. 'And her being hand in glove with Lionel doesn't help. He's the one who hired her from Customs and Excise, so naturally he's inclined to back her. They seem to think fourteen-hour days are standard practice.'

'Hasn't she any sort of home life? Is she married, or . . .?'

Again that look of apprehension.

'I . . . I'm not sure. Although I suspect she misses the Civil Service. It's not so well paid, of course, and hedged about with rules and regulations, but there's much more structure and security and more sense of camaraderie than in a small accountancy firm.' At last he put his napkin back on his lap, smoothing out the creases. 'I feel sorry for her in a way. She's rather a fish out of water at Garrard Ross.'

Alison helped herself to salad, then passed the dish to James. Trust him to feel sorry for the very person at the root of all his problems.

'Anyway, enough of Elaine,' he said, taking half a tomato and a solitary lettuce leaf. 'You've been wonderfully patient, darling.'

'Well, it isn't your fault, is it?' His long hours had been useful sometimes – last night, for example. Yet she did resent his busyness – his work for the church as well as for Garrard Ross. Might her fling with Craig be some kind of retaliation? How unfair though and how cruel. She owed this lifestyle to James: four-star hotels, exotic dinners . . . And it was his service to others which had attracted her in the first place. He hadn't changed in that respect.

She prised the flesh out of a lobster claw with the fiddly silver pick and swallowed a few morsels. James, too, she noticed, had barely eaten anything. Both of them were dissembling; both pretending nothing was wrong. She longed to be back in the comforting darkness of the cinema, where there was no need for conversation and where traumas happened only to celluloid characters and could be righted by a simple twist of the plot.

James was pouring the champagne. 'To our second honeymoon,' he said, touching his glass to hers.

Was he being sarcastic? He looked sincere enough, although *she* felt close to tears, recalling their first honeymoon. Things had been so different then. Now an invisible steel wall seemed to rear between them, cutting off all communication.

She took a sip from her glass, feeling the tiny frantic bubbles tingle against her lips. Expensive champagne it might be, yet to her it was as flat and insipid as tap-water.

James drew her towards him and kissed her. His mouth tasted joltingly clean; no trace of the rich dinner; no nicotine or garlic breath, like Craig. Craig was still here between them in the bed, making James seem strange: too tall, too dark, too gentle in his lovemaking. Yet how could a man she had known a mere six weeks displace a husband of six years? And what if James could smell Craig on her body, or even Craig's other women – their sweat, their juices, fused with hers? She pulled away.

'Darling, what *is* it? What's wrong?'

Wordlessly she shook her head. Making love was meant to be the closest you could get to another person, yet Craig scarcely knew her, nor she him. Perhaps the ultimate degree of intimacy wasn't sex at all but absolute trust – the capacity to confide one's deepest secrets. In which case she was no longer intimate with anyone. Even Linda believed that she and Craig were simply working on the manuscript together.

'Whatever it is, I'll try to understand.'

183

Yes, he would – she knew that. But understanding had its limits. Knowledge of a wife's affair could destroy a man. And a marriage. She shivered.

'You're cold. Snuggle up and I'll keep you warm.' He put his arms around her and she lay rigid, as if trapped. In the silence she was aware of the faintest noises: a vibration from the radiator, muffled footsteps passing the door. And almost imperceptible sounds from his body as he held her close: his rhythmic heartbeat, whispered breathing. One flesh, the marriage service ordained, yet she had never felt more distant from him. It was Craig's noises she could hear: the vulgar, swearing build-up as he came, followed by the triumphant cry.

'*Alison* . . .'

She jumped. James's tone was bitter. Could he read her mind?

'Look, we can't go on like this.' The bitterness subsided into despair.

'Like . . . what?'

'Well, you've been so . . . so odd these last few weeks. I can't get near you – in bed, or any other way. I mean, yesterday morning, when I tried to kiss you, you said you had a migraine and –'

'I did. I felt lousy. It lasted all day.'

'So why did you go out and stay out till nearly midnight?'

Because Craig had a day off, she didn't say. 'It cleared up. Unexpectedly. And then Linda rang – I told you – and asked me to . . .' The lies were pathetic – she wasn't even convincing herself. Feeling horribly exposed, she turned on him instead, spitefully putting him in the wrong. 'Anyway, *you*'re the one that's odd, not me. I've never known you like this before – carping and suspicious and accusing me of things. You can't blame me for going out when you're always late home from the office. Even this weekend you've been bad-tempered. Snapping at that poor girl in the café and mooning around the gardens in a sulk. Why bother to come away if you're too busy to enjoy it?'

She turned to face the wall, her back a hostile barrier. Her malicious words hung in the air, poisoning the room. James, too, turned over: they were now lying back to back. The very unnaturalness of the position seemed ominous. Everything might break apart. Yet she couldn't bring herself to make amends – she was too demoralized, too fraught. All the tensions of the day had come to a head: outwardly a pleasant day – good

184

food and time to themselves – but at its core rotten, like a rosy apple seething with maggots.

She heard him sit up; waited grimly for his angry response.

'Alison, I'm *sorry*. You're right. I have been selfish. And unreasonable today. Forgive me.'

She swallowed. Selfish? Earning the money to keep her while she stole off to Kennington. Unreasonable? Compared with her he was the very soul of reason and good judgement. She should be begging forgiveness from him, not the other way round. There was such compunction in his voice she could hardly bear to listen.

'Just . . . just give me a moment,' she stammered. 'I need a glass of water.' She slipped into the bathroom, trembling from the sense that she had only narrowly averted a disaster. The more she thought about the risks she had taken, the more aghast she was: coming home so late last night; refusing to let James touch her. Whatever his problems – at work or with Elaine – he had made it clear he loved her. The weekend itself was proof of his devotion. Craig was merely using her for his own self-serving ends – using her body and her help on the book. Craig made love with his cock; James with his mind and soul and body, his tenderness and concern. Three weeks ago, she had vowed never to see Craig again. A vow broken the very next day.

She stared at her naked body, a blurred reflection in the black marble walls. She was no better than her father, who picked quarrels to divert attention from his affairs. As a result, her parents lived in a state of continual bickering and mistrust.

She turned away from her shadow-self, suddenly knowing what she must do. She would go for that second interview in Watford and take the job if they offered it. The long day and the long journey would actually be a bonus, leaving no time or energy for Craig. And by working at her faith – literally, editing religious books – that faith might even return. If not, well, safety *was* more precious than integrity – at least where James was concerned.

She walked back into the bedroom and lay beside her husband, holding him so tightly their flesh and bones and boundaries seemed to dissolve into each other. That was how it must be.

'I'm sorry, too,' she told him. 'I'm the one who's been selfish.' And far worse than you, she added silently, kissing her fingers and laying the kiss against his lips. Then, with tantalizing flicks of her tongue she traced an inch-by-inch pathway along his neck and throat, across his chest and slowly, slowly down. 'I love you, James,' she murmured. 'More than anything on earth.'

Even truth, she didn't add.

21

'Hello, I'm Mrs Egerton.' She hoped she sounded confident. 'I'm here to see Amanda Clark.'

'Would you take a seat, please. I'll let her know you've arrived.'

Alison perched on the edge of the black leatherette sofa. The reception area was elegant but furnished rather sombrely; the book jackets in the display-stands providing the only splash of colour. She leafed through a copy of *Publishing News*, trying to take her mind off the current family crises: Cecilia rushed to hospital suffering from pneumonia, Amy with her leg in plaster. James had urged her to be positive and trust that she would get the job. She was even wearing his watch, for luck – bought just before his own successful interview at Garrard Ross. She took a deep breath and imagined herself arriving here each morning, working with interesting authors, commissioning worthwhile books. Home life was pretty grim of late and a job – any job – would mean an escape from tedious parish work, from Father Peter, still floundering in the mysteries of his computer, and above all from Craig, furious at being rejected. Even James was increasingly tense – in fact downright irritable at times. Of course, he was worried about Cecilia and the ongoing war of nerves with Elaine, but she suspected there was more to it than that. He was sleeping badly and . . .

'Mrs Egerton? They're ready for you now.'

Quickly she stood up, recognizing the lanky, red-haired girl as Amanda Clark's assistant.

'It's in Mr Vaughan's office this time,' the girl explained, as they took the lift to the top floor.

Alison swallowed. Edward Vaughan was managing director of the Religious Books Division and, according to the grapevine, exacting and cantankerous. She was ushered into an imposing room with floor-to-ceiling bookshelves and a selection of plants which looked as if they'd come from Kew Gardens' Tropical House. Amanda Clark was sitting at a large mahogany table, between two middle-aged men. Alison was introduced. The stout, balding one was Mr Vaughan; the other, slimmer and dark-eyed, was the publishing director, Paul Chalfont. She was motioned to a chair across the table from them, where she felt like a prisoner facing a firing squad.

After a few brief pleasantries Mr Vaughan began the interrogation, frequently interrupting before she could do justice to herself.

'So, Mrs Egerton, what makes you think you can contribute to the success of this division?'

'Your experience appears to be solely in fiction. Do you *know* the religious market? The sort of books that sell?'

'And what would you consider the most important criteria for . . .?'

She had done her homework and managed to give authoritative replies – when he let her have the chance. Mostly he cut in before she could finish, or changed the subject disconcertingly. Perhaps he was assessing how she reacted under pressure, so she made a conscious effort to keep calm. Then the publishing director took over – a less irascible type altogether, although his first question rather threw her. Was she familiar with the religious press: the *Church Times*, for instance, or *Christianity* and *Renewal*?

The last two she had never heard of, but she elaborated on the several Catholic papers she did know and regularly read.

'Quite honestly, we'd prefer an Anglican,' Mr Chalfont said. 'Amanda's Catholic, too, you see, so it's a matter of balance in the editorial team.'

'And we are a little worried about the fact that you live in Reigate,' Amanda smiled sympathetically. 'Our last editor often had trouble getting here on time, especially when the train strikes were on. And she only lived in Ealing.'

Alison explained the new and quicker route she'd found, but already she was beginning to lose heart. Why had they bothered to call her for a second interview if they foresaw so many problems?

'And I understand,' said Mr Vaughan, fixing her with an unsettling gaze, 'that you took six months off to try to start a family.'

'Well, yes, but . . .' How stupid to have *told* Amanda that! She had only done so to justify the gap in her CV. And in any case she had stressed her intention to devote herself to her career now that pregnancy was no longer an option.

Undeterred, Mr Vaughan went on. 'I know these days it's not considered politically correct to bring the matter up, but, to put it bluntly, Mrs Egerton, if we were to offer you the job how could we be sure you wouldn't be leaving us before the year is out?'

She bristled, trying to think of a suitably terse rejoinder without actually being rude. He deserved a put-down for asking sexist questions.

Fortunately Amanda came to the rescue and steered them to safer ground. Even so, she could feel her heart pounding, and it took great willpower not to fluster.

'Right, we'll be in touch, Mrs Egerton.' The managing director stood up, indicating that the ordeal was at an end. Her job prospects, too, by the look of it. The first interview with Amanda had been friendly and low-key and left her feeling hopeful. Now she doubted whether they would ever meet again. It was Amanda, pleasant as always, who saw her out to reception and thanked her profusely for coming.

'Thank *you*.' She forced a farewell smile, her face as stiff as a mask. Today's experience had been gruelling, yet interviews were a necessary evil unless she settled for being a home-body, dutiful and dull.

In the foyer she lingered by the books – books she would never be involved in now as begetter and midwife. Or was that being defeatist? After all, Mr Vaughan would grill every candidate in the same belligerent fashion, so she might still be in with a chance. As James had said, be positive and . . .

'Alison!'

She started. She didn't know anyone here. Turning, she caught her breath. Surely it couldn't be . . . He had put on weight and looked tired and drawn. And yet the sandy hair was as thick as ever, and there was that familiar little dimple on his chin. 'Jim!' she exclaimed. 'What are *you* doing here?'

'I was about to ask you the same thing.'

'I'm trying to get a job. I've just had an interview.'

'Good God! Perhaps we'll be working together then – I'm production manager in the Trade Division. I started in July.'

'Congratulations. I'd no idea you . . .' The words petered out. Why should she know anything about him? They had lost touch years ago. He had never forgiven her for leaving him for James.

There was a brief embarrassed silence before Jim found his voice again. 'This calls for a drink. You're not rushing off, are you?'

'Well, I . . .'

'Come on, just a quick one. It's such a coincidence. I mean, why a job in this neck of the woods?'

She smiled. 'Desperation.'

'Which department?'

'Religious Books,' she said, a shade defensively.

'Just up your street.'

She didn't contradict him. In fact she hardly knew what to say. They had parted on the worst of terms.

'There's a wine bar round the corner.' Jim was buttoning his coat. It had a button missing, she noticed.

As he held the door for her she gave him a quick glance. His healthy glow had gone, and he looked pale beneath the freckles, and older than his years. Perhaps promotion was proving a strain. On the other hand, it was only just after five and he was obviously on his way home. James never got away before seven at the earliest. She remembered with a shiver that the last time Jim had mentioned James it was to express the wish that he rot in hell.

'No, I *haven't* told James. I daren't, Jim.'

'He must have guessed, though, surely?'

'Well, yes, I'm terrified he has. But he's so on edge, it makes it very difficult to bring the subject up.'

'You told *me* OK.'

'You're different.' She avoided his eyes. It was disloyal to carp about James, but after a couple of glasses of wine she had suddenly found herself blurting out her problems with Catholicism. Jim had been surprisingly sympathetic, given his sceptical attitude to religion: having managed without it all his life he couldn't understand why other people should make such a song and dance about it.

'You see, James isn't like most Catholics,' she explained, 'who tend to go to Mass only when it suits them, and cherry-pick the bits of the faith they like and disregard the rest. Mind you, I shouldn't complain. It was James's high ideals that attracted me in the first place.'

'You're telling me,' Jim said feelingly. 'I tried to warn you, but –'

'I don't regret it, Jim,' she said, wondering, traitorously, if she did.

'So why is he in such a tizz? What's the matter with the bloke?'

'I wish I knew. It can't just be pressure of work – he's used to that by now. But he's sort of . . . distracted all the time and doesn't hear what I say. It's weird, because he used to be such a good listener. But' – she poked at an olive with her cocktail-stick – 'I don't want to bore you with all this.'

'Don't be silly. I'm interested – just sorry you're not happier.' He gave a rueful laugh. 'I thought you'd be on cloud nine, with your wealthy, brilliant husband.'

'He's still brilliant,' she said quickly. 'And we *are* happy. It's just that sometimes the whole religious thing gets on top of me. I mean, my little niece broke her leg last week, and the main concern the family seem to have is whether she'll miss her First Communion. They regard it as the most important day of her life. I ask you! How can something you do at the age of seven be more important than your wedding day, or the day you give birth to a child, or . . .? I'm sorry,' she said, 'I must get off my hobby horse. How old are *your* children?'

'Gareth's five, Hugh's nearly three and Robin's eighteen months.'

'All boys?'

'Yes.' Tactfully he spared her further details. He had learned earlier about her infertility and shown great understanding.

In fact only now did she realize that she had talked more or less non-stop about herself. Ashamed, she asked about his career.

'I left Hodder three years ago and went to Random House, but it didn't work out too well. Actually, I'm still matey with a guy there. I could give him a bell, if you like, and see if there's anything going on the editorial side.'

'Thanks, Jim. I'd appreciate it.'

'But, as I said, don't give up hope of *this* job.'

'What, Religious Books without a religion? Bit ironic, don't you think?'

'They won't have to know, though, will they? Given your talent for pretence.'

'Thanks a bunch! I'm sure I won't get it anyway. Everything's against me – my experience, the journey . . . Where do you live, by the way?'

'About two miles up the road.'

'You moved to *Watford*?'

'You needn't sound so horrified. We don't wear skins and woad, you know!'

She laughed. 'It's just that I remember how you loved living in London.'

'Yeah, but Watford's cheaper, and I've got an ex-wife with expensive tastes to support, not to mention the three boys.'

'Oh, Jim, I'm sorry. You didn't say you were divorced.'

He shrugged. 'It's not something I'm particularly proud of.'

'But surely you can talk to me about it. I've told *you* enough.'

'No, let's get off the subject before I have us both in tears!'

'Oh, Jim . . . Is it that bad?'

He waved away her sympathy and helped himself to a handful of nuts. He hadn't changed, she noted wryly. James would have offered the dish to her first.

'How's Linda?' he asked, munching. 'Are you still in touch?'

'Yes. And things are going fine. She's landed a great job – *and* a new bloke, Derek. So she's been rather out of circulation.'

'Did she ever get married?'

'Are you kidding? You know Linda's views on marriage.'

'What about this Derek? Do they live together?'

'Oh, no. She only met him a fortnight ago. Mind you, she's completely obsessed. Whenever I phone, it's Derek this and Derek that.' It was true she was missing Linda and their usual heart-to-hearts, but Jim made a welcome substitute. Certainly she felt more relaxed than at home. Just to stop lying was a relief. Not that she could tell Jim about Craig, even though his vindictiveness was causing her such pain. His bruised ego, both as lover and as author, had made him . . .

'Hey, d'you remember Fritzie?' Jim said with a laugh. 'I wonder what happened to her.'

191

'God knows.' She felt a sudden pang for the old days, when there was nothing more to worry about than which film to see or party to go to. Fritzie had been an inveterate party-giver. 'Another drink?' she suggested. 'I'll get these.'

'No, I'd better not. Carole's always nagging me about drinking too much.'

'Carole?'

'My ex-wife.'

'Yes, of course.' She had a vague recollection of a slender, hard-eyed woman she'd met only once – and disliked.

'D'you know, she even told Gareth I wasn't safe to drive him, can you believe! She's always sticking the knife in or trying to turn the kids against me.'

'Oh, Jim, I am sorry. That sounds appalling.'

'God, Alison, you don't know the half of it. Actually, I'd like to ask your advice on something. Why don't we go and have a bite to eat? I know it's early, but I didn't have time for lunch.'

She hesitated. It would be unkind to refuse, especially as she had encouraged him to confide in her. 'Well, I mustn't be too long. And I'd better give James a ring.'

She just caught him at the office. She had forgotten he was leaving early to visit Cecilia in hospital. 'But what about *your* dinner, darling?' she asked.

'Don't worry, I'll get something in the hospital canteen. And when you get back you can tell me all about the interview. Love you, darling.'

'Love you,' she said mechanically. As she put the phone down, it struck her that if she'd married Jim she might have three children by now. Would she be happier? Would *he*?

She followed him out of the wine bar. Traitorous thoughts again. James was blameless in all this. She had brought the whole thing on herself. And no way did she regret marrying him. As the vows said, for better, for worse.

'But why did you marry her if you didn't love her?'

Jim broke his roll in half, scattering crumbs on the cloth. 'Do you really want to know?'

'Of course.' She put down her knife and fork. She wasn't hungry anyway – not at half past six. The restaurant was practically empty and they had picked a secluded table at the back.

'Because I married on the rebound. Damned obvious, isn't it? It was *you* I loved, Alison. I was so shattered when you chucked me, I grabbed the first woman who showed interest.'

'But, Jim, I . . . I thought –'

'You *didn't* think. You didn't even care. No one existed for you but James. And now look – we're both unhappy.'

'But, Jim, I'm not unhappy.'

'Oh, no? You've spent the last hour telling me how shitty things are at home.'

'It's not James, though, it's –'

'Of course it's James. You said you're scared of him, and – '

'Not of him. Don't be stupid. Our marriage is very good.'

'Like hell it is. You can't tell him anything, you hate his family –'

'I don't hate them. Far from it. I –'

'Alison, for God's sake. You're contradicting every single thing you've said.'

'Well, OK, there are a few problems. But only minor ones.'

'Minor? No job, no faith, no children?'

Put like that, it did sound hopeless. She let out a sudden cry – of grief, frustration, anger – startled by her own lack of inhibition. Both waitresses had turned to stare.

'Alison, I'm sorry. It wasn't fair to snap at you.' Jim leaned across the table and took her hands in his. 'I'm sorry,' he repeated. 'I . . . I'm a bit cut up myself, to tell the truth. It's Gareth's birthday today and that bitch won't let me see him.'

She squeezed his hand, not trusting herself to speak. The restaurant was in a basement (an unwelcome reminder of Craig's bedsit), with mirrored walls and fake candle-lamps. Her myriad reflections showed all the different people she'd become: the smiling, dutiful Catholic to Cecilia, the traitorous slut to Craig, the unhappy wife to Jim . . .

Jim was gazing into her eyes. 'And it was such a shock seeing you, after all this time. I thought I was *over* you, for Christ's sake.'

Tears slid down her face. A new source of guilt, to add to all the rest –

driving Jim into a loveless marriage, cutting him off from his sons. Once, he had been the office clown, the eternal optimist. Now he looked almost haggard.

Tenderly he lifted a strand of hair that had fallen over her eyes and stroked it back into place. 'I feel terrible upsetting you like this. I didn't mean to, honestly. I love you, Alison.'

'Please don't say that.'

'It's true. And if there's any chance of our getting back together . . .'

'Jim, you have to understand – I'd never leave James. Ever. He's the most important thing in my life.'

'So why the hell are you crying?'

She stared at herself in the mirror. Her face seemed to blur like that shadow-self she had left behind in Oxfordshire. How *could* she leave it behind? The damage was done.

'Alison, what's wrong?'

Last weekend, James had asked her the same. And, as then, she dared not answer. It was the most dreadful strain keeping Craig a secret – from Jim, from James, from Linda. The situation was almost worse now that she had given him up. It had been hard enough to make the break, without his histrionics. She'd had a week of anxious days and sleepless nights; even wondering at times if she might tip over the edge.

The evenings in the hospital didn't help. She sat there like a plaster saint, mouthing words of comfort to Cecilia, playing the virtuous wife to James, while Craig's vile, abusive phone-calls replayed in her head . . .

'Alison, you've got to tell me what's wrong.'

'It's Craig!' she shouted suddenly, alarming herself as much as Jim. It was as if a dam had burst by the very utterance of her lover's name, sweeping away a tide of debris.

'Who's Craig?'

'Oh, Jim, I haven't dared breathe a word to anyone, but I . . . I've been having an affair. With a man I don't even like.'

'Bloody hell!' Jim put his head in his hands.

'And when I said I couldn't see him any more, he went berserk and –'

'Look, I don't want to hear this. Can't you understand? I've told you, I *love* you. Doesn't that mean anything?'

'Yes, of course it does. I'm sorry. But I . . . I'm not free to –'

'You were free enough to screw this bastard Craig.'

'I wasn't. I mean, I shouldn't. I can't tell you how guilty I feel.' Guilty on all counts. She had upset Jim now as well as James. And Craig. Blighted everything she touched. And even if she tried to make amends it was likely to misfire. Any overture to Jim would give him false encouragement, and the same applied to Craig if she offered more help on the book. Yet the greater her loyalty to James, the greater the rancour of the other two.

Jim flung his napkin on the table and rose abruptly to his feet. 'Let's go.'

'Go? Go where?'

'Anywhere. So long as it's less public. We can't talk here.' He snapped his fingers for the waitress and pushed a couple of £20 notes into her hand. Without waiting for change, he steered Alison upstairs, moving with the urgency of a man escaping a fire.

Outside it was dark and wet, and they stood huddled in the rain. Finally he broke the silence. 'We'll go to my place,' he said.

'No, Jim, we can't. It . . . it wouldn't be wise. And anyway I ought to get back.'

'I thought James wasn't coming home till late.'

'Not that late. Before me, anyway. The journey takes an age.'

'I'll drive you.'

'No, honestly. Reigate's an awful long way. And it'd be even longer by car.'

'Well, I'll take you to the station then.'

'Thanks, but there's no need. It's only round the corner.'

'No, I don't mean Watford, I mean Victoria.'

'But that's miles!'

He shrugged. 'I'm sure I can forgo *Frasier* for once.'

She managed a weak smile. 'I'm sorry,' she said with genuine remorse. 'For everything.'

'Don't be. It was fantastic seeing you. You look so beautiful. Your hair . . .' He ran his hand slowly down the length of it. 'I'm glad you never cut it. It's amazing.'

'Jim, please – no compliments. And no touching. We can't go back to how it was.' She stepped away from him and set off purposefully, fighting the exhaustion that had settled on her recently like a heavy, stifling shroud. However late she got in, she must make it up to James: listen to him, cosset him. She was still committed to the new regime she had decided on in Oxfordshire: she was bound to him and him alone.

In seconds Jim was beside her again. 'Look, I'm not pretending we can simply pick up where we left off, but what I *do* feel –'

'Jim,' she said frantically, 'if you love me, then let me go straight home. *Please.*'

He let out a great sigh, tilting his head back and exposing his face to the rain. Then he shook his wet hair, shook his whole body, as if trying to rid himself of a relentless stinging insect. 'OK,' he said. 'I . . . I promise to keep my distance, if you say that's what you want. Fuck it, though' – his voice rose in frustration – 'why does your smart-arse of a husband always have to win?'

Ignoring this outburst, she touched his arm in gratitude.

Instantly, he softened, taking her hand in his. 'Oh, Alison, if only . . .'

She prised the hand away. 'Look, we'd better hurry. I mustn't miss the train.'

'And neither must you break your neck. I'll drive you to Victoria, as I said. No – I insist.' With evident, almost heart-wrenching effort he assumed a joky tone. 'Don't worry, I'll be on my best behaviour: the perfect chauffeur – eyes on the road at all times and not a word unless I'm spoken to.'

She opened her eyes to blackness, aware only of pain – a metal hammer pounding through her skull. A relentless, raging thirst. Her tongue felt thick and furred, and her body ached, yet seemed not to be her body but out of her control. She sat up gingerly, holding her throbbing head. Was *she* moving, or was it the room swaying? She groped for the bedside lamp. It wasn't there. Instead her hand encountered skin, warm skin – an arm, by the feel of it. Blind in the darkness, she traced the arm to a shoulder and slowly down to a chest. 'James?' she whispered.

Silence.

Desperate for a pee, she blundered to the door and somehow found her way to the bathroom, staring in confusion at the unfamiliar walls.

And when she washed her hands the soap smelt wrong and the towels were yellow, not blue. She wrapped herself in the largest and ventured out again, finding another unknown room. Yet her clothes were there, in a jumble on the floor. And someone else's clothes – white shirt, grey jacket and trousers. She sank on to the sofa, catching the eye of one of the boys in the photo. Jim's sons. Their names came to her instantly: Gareth, Hugh and Robin. Strange she should remember them when all the rest was hazy. But she had wept over the photo. And so had Jim. It was Gareth's birthday and the expensive present he'd bought him lay on the sideboard, still wrapped in Mickey Mouse paper.

Next to it stood two coffee mugs, two glasses and an empty brandy bottle. The haze began to clear. Yes, they had come here for a coffee – Jim wanted to sober up before he drove her back. Just half an hour, he'd said. There wasn't a clock in the room, but she knew she'd seen a watch – on the floor, beside the clothes. Two watches, in fact. She stooped and peered at them. They were men's watches, almost identical, with Roman numerals and metal straps. Half past two, they said.

Half past *two*? It couldn't be. They had only stopped for a quick coffee. She was going to catch the 9.01 from Victoria.

She picked up both the watches. One must be James's. He had lent it to her for luck. But which?

She stumbled back to the bedroom. A muffled voice said, 'Darling, are you there?'

Only James called her darling. She gripped the watches more tightly. For luck.

The bedside lamp snapped on and a shaft of light fell across the bed. She gazed in shock at the freckled chest, the sandy pubic hair, the penis curled limp between his legs.

It was all coming back now, but distorted as in a dream – the dim light in the sitting-room and the gentle patter of rain against the window; the hot, sweet coffee slipping down her throat. And then the brandy – liquid velvet – and the soft, hypnotic music and the silky feel of his shirt against her face. He had held her close and stroked her hair. Nothing wrong in that. He was just consoling her; consoling himself

197

because he couldn't see Gareth on his birthday.

'Darling, do come back to bed.' The voice was slurred, and she saw the hand fumble for the light switch. In an instant she would be swallowed up in darkness again, blanked out.

She let both watches fall. It would be terrible to muddle them. 'James,' she sobbed, 'I . . . I've lost your watch.'

Lost everything.

IV

22

'This weather's unbelievable!' Francesca peeled off her jersey, exposing her arms to the sun. 'Last time I was here in the spring it snowed for a solid week. I'm not likely to forget. All the planes were grounded and I got stuck in Edinburgh.'

Alison sugared her coffee and stirred it vigorously. 'It must seem odd, staying in one place for a change.'

'Odd but preferable,' Francesca laughed. 'Those author tours are a terrible strain. And lonely. Oh, I know we have our entourage, but when it comes to the crunch it's just the poor beleaguered writer facing the audience or the television cameras.'

'Don't you miss the pizzazz, though?'

'Not really. In fact, looking back, there's a certain irony to it all. My books brought me everything I wanted – money, fame, you name it. And because of that I met Stefan. Yet our marriage was so awful, I felt it was the price I had to pay for success – fate stepping in and taking me down a peg. My first marriage was bad enough, but Stefan . . .' She rolled her eyes. 'Let's not talk about it. I don't want to spoil the afternoon. I'm so glad you persuaded me to come here, rather than meet in London. Your house is really lovely.'

'Yes, we like it.'

'And thanks again for the lunch.'

'It was only very simple.' Alison was aware how stiff she sounded, but she wasn't finding it easy to relax. Francesca had been her usual friendly self and, although their meetings over the years, as editor and author, had been too sporadic to allow a deeper relationship, it was *she* who was at fault today, imprisoned in her private hell of guilt. Even at lunch she hadn't dared have any wine in case it loosened her tongue. Not that sticking to water was any deprivation – she never wanted to touch alcohol again.

Francesca stretched luxuriously in her deck-chair. 'How's James?' she asked. 'You've hardly mentioned him.'

'Oh, haven't I?' She feigned surprise. She had no wish to talk about James, who was still strangely tense and distracted. 'His grandmother's been very ill, so he's rather down at the moment. He spends most evenings at the hospital.'

'Oh, I *am* sorry. It sounds as if they're very close.'

'Mm. They are.' Unhealthily so, she thought. If only she had some idea of what was wrong with him. Could he be ill himself? One evening last week she had somehow found the courage to start telling him about her doubts, but he'd been so distant and withdrawn she'd given up after a couple of fumbling sentences. In any case her loss of faith now seemed almost trivial when weighed against her other offences.

'And have you managed to find a job yet?'

'Well, actually, I was offered one last week.'

'That's good news! When do you start?'

'I don't. I turned it down. It's in Watford, you see, and it's really too far to travel.' The distance was immaterial compared with the problem of Jim working there. She nudged the conversation back to Francesca. 'Have you got another book on the go?'

'I'm afraid not – however remiss that may sound to an editor! You see, since I had Zach I've realized that writing was a sort of . . . substitute. I just can't tell you, Alison, what an extraordinary experience childbirth is. It's so *intense*, you're completely taken over, submerged in the sensations. Everything else disappears – thoughts, worries, even other people. It's just you and the pain on your own. And the pain *is* atrocious, no doubt about it, but then suddenly it's gone and you feel the most indescribable joy.' Francesca hugged herself at the memory. 'It put things into perspective, made my writing seem – well, immature. I'd been pontificating about love in my books, but I didn't know what real love was until I held Zach in my arms. I was absolutely besotted with him, Alison. Words I'd normally be wary of using, like miracle and rapture, began to take on meaning. I must admit I do feel guilty letting Shaw Hilliard down after all they've done for me, but . . .'

'I shouldn't worry. You've made them enough money, for heaven's sake.' This rapturous talk of babies made her want to switch off. Besides, she was pretty sure Francesca would return to writing once the idyll of motherhood paled.

'Alison!' Gail's head appeared over the hedge. 'Oh, I'm sorry. I didn't realize you had visitors. I was going to ask if you'd seen Sammy's shuttlecock? He thinks it's in your garden – down the far end, he says.'

'I'll go and have a look. No, of course it's no bother.'

She found it by the garden swing – bought, along with the Wendy house, for the use of visiting nieces and nephews. In fact their garden was better equipped than Gail's, who had a brood of four. Practically everyone in the road had children. And took them for granted, of course.

'Thanks, Alison. I'll tell Sammy to be more careful in future. Marvellous weather, isn't it?'

'Mm. Lovely.' No doubt Gail regarded her as a normal, decent woman, a good neighbour and regular church-goer; she would be utterly disgusted if she could have seen her lying sozzled in Jim's bed – and then with Craig again only two days later. She was disgusted herself. Admittedly, she had never intended for a single moment to go to bed with Jim and, as for Craig, she had submitted out of fear. None the less, she seemed trapped in a vicious downward spiral and was appalled at the depths to which she had sunk.

She returned listlessly to the patio, resuming the role of friend and hostess – a veil of respectability masking the foulness inside. 'More coffee?'

'No, I'm fine.' Francesca handed her a small leather-bound album. 'Look, I forgot to show you these. Isn't he gorgeous?'

Alison gazed from the baby in the photographs to his mother in the chair. Yes, both were beautiful: black hair, dark lustrous eyes. Francesca had changed little in the seven years they had known each other. If anything, she looked younger today and uncharacteristically casual in T-shirt and blue jeans.

'That's another irony. My marriage went wrong almost from day one, yet without Stefan I wouldn't have Zach. He's even like his father in some ways – the best ways, I hasten to add.'

'Weren't you tempted to bring him with you?'

'Yes, I did consider it, especially as none of my English relatives have had a chance to see him yet. But I thought two long flights in the space of a week wouldn't be a good idea. And anyway a funeral's hardly the right time, with the family so distraught. I'm sure babies can pick up vibes, you know, even when they're tiny.'

'Were you OK, Francesca? She was your favourite aunt, wasn't she?'

'Well, I did cry buckets, but she was ninety, after all, and crippled with arthritis, so it was a happy release, I suppose. And I'm very glad I made the trip. At first I was tempted just to send flowers and leave it at that. Talking of flowers, you must have enough here for a dozen funerals! I wish *I* had all this space.'

'It's really too big for just two of us.'

There was a moment's awkward silence. Tactfully Francesca put the photograph album back into her bag. 'Do you do the gardening yourself, or have someone in to help?'

'No. James and I do it between us.' Or used to. James had lost interest of late. Normally, his passion for neatness and order would have him enthusiastically sweeping fallen leaves, dead-heading daffodils and pruning the shrubs along the drive. Now he left it all to her. She didn't mind the work – it was the change in him that hurt.

'Alison, I seem to remember, last time we met you were thinking about adoption. What happened? You never said.'

'We didn't actually apply, in the end.'

'Oh, I see. Why not?'

'It's such a long-winded procedure. And terribly intrusive. You have to be vetted by a social worker, and they scrutinize every little detail – right down to questions on your sex-life and how your parents treated *you*.'

'Yes, but you can understand their point. People have to be so careful nowadays, with all this stuff about child abuse.'

'Mm, I grant you that. But it makes it really depressing if you're rejected in the long run. You see, when the social worker's finished her report – which can take ages in itself – it goes to an adoption panel, who have the final say. They're frightfully strict and can still turn you down, in spite of a pretty favourable report. And there's no right of appeal. That's it – end of story.'

'Surely it's better to try, though?'

Alison plucked the flower-head from a geranium and pulled off the petals, one by one. 'It's . . . not a good time at the moment.' The last few weeks were ample proof that she had no right even to consider adoption. The disturbed children who were likely to be offered needed a stable, responsible mother, not a drunken slut opening her legs for all and sundry. She should never have gone to Jim's place. And even with Craig, there was no excuse. She could have brazened it out instead of yielding to the threat of blackmail.

She jumped up from the garden seat. 'How about a walk? The country's very pretty round here, and we ought to make the most of the weather.'

'Yes, good idea. I'm still a bit jet-lagged, and they say exercise does help.'

Alison put the cups on a tray and took them into the house. 'I'll just lock up, OK?'

'Right,' she said, re-emerging, 'which do you prefer – fields, woods or a stroll round the village?'

'Oh, woods, I think. Nice and cool.'

They cut through the back garden and followed the overgrown path. Most of the trees were still bare, but the hawthorns in the hedgerow were beginning to crinkle into fierce-green leaf, and dandelions made vulgar yellow splodges in the grass. Alison bent to pick one. A dribble of milky juice oozed from its stem on to her hand. She dropped it instantly. Everything conspired to bring back memories of Jim – or Craig. A tree had fallen and been caught by the branches of its neighbour, one cradled in the other's arms. And the sticky buds on a horse chestnut seemed to swell and glisten as she passed. Another tree was being strangled by a growth of ivy, clinging to it, clutching it, winding its relentless tendrils round every twig and branch.

'You're very quiet,' Francesca remarked.

'Sorry. I was just . . . enjoying the scenery.'

'Yes, lovely, isn't it? I'll think of this tomorrow when I'm cooped up on the plane.'

'Still, you must be looking forward to seeing Zach again.'

'You bet! The only thing I don't miss is the dirty nappies.'

Alison skirted a muddy puddle on the path. 'That's funny, I've just remembered a dream I had last night. It went completely out of my head until you mentioned nappies. I found a baby and –'

'*Found* one?'

'Yes, just lying by the roadside. Forget fertility treatment, adoption panels and all that sort of palaver. He was in this hamper thing and I simply picked him up and took him home, and from then on he was mine. And the weird thing was, he never dirtied his nappies. Stupid, wasn't it?'

'Not at all. Dreams can be very significant.' Francesca stopped and looked her intently. 'I think perhaps it's telling you that babies don't have to be associated with "shit" – you know, difficulties, doctors, all that palaver, as you say – and maybe you could get one through adoption more easily than you think.'

'Quite honestly, Francesca, I'd rather not try.'

'Isn't that a bit defeatist?'

She didn't answer. James had said much the same and probably thought her heartless too. There were thousands of children waiting for homes – older children, abandoned children, desperate for a 'forever family'. She'd been moved to tears by their pictures in the adoption magazines: the determined smiles that couldn't disguise the hurt in their eyes. Yet what use were tears if she didn't help? And now it was too late. Any adoption agency, knowing what she'd done, would reject her out of hand.

'There must be some solution,' Francesca persisted. 'Have you and James considered a child from overseas – a little Brazilian orphan, for example?'

'Well, yes, we did look into it, but overseas adoption is even more of an ordeal. Apparently you can spend a fortune on lawyers, battling through mountains of red tape, and still not get a child. In any case . . .' She turned away, avoiding Francesca's eye. 'I . . . don't think I'm cut out to be a mother.'

'Rubbish! Look how you mothered my books – the love and care you lavished on them.'

She gave a hollow laugh. 'Books are different.'

'Yes, but you have all the right qualities for bringing up a child – patience, intelligence, sensitivity . . .'

'Francesca, you're embarrassing me!'

'Well, it's true. Besides, you can't know until you *are* a mother. I wasn't all that keen myself until I had Zach. But he changed everything. Maybe your dream is a good omen. Funnily enough, I dreamed I was pregnant just ten days after I conceived. My period wasn't late and I had no symptoms whatsoever, but I just felt . . . well – different. It's hard to explain, but I *knew*, deep down inside, as if my body was telling me, as well as the dream. I do believe women have these very strong gut instincts, only we're so blinded by modern technology we tend to ignore them. If only we were more confident we'd tune in to that inner self and be aware of things on a totally different level.'

Alison stood stock-still. The world itself seemed to have juddered to a halt. She stared in shock at a clump of cow parsley in the shelter of the hedge. The tiny hairs on its stems were magnified into monstrous bristles; its delicate leaves giant palms; nature itself reflecting the enormity of Francesca's words, their electrifying truth. There *was* a level at which you knew things. Instinctively, unerringly. But you were blinded not only by technology but by sheer unadulterated terror. She closed her eyes against the sun. Blackness, brilliance, both at once.

'Alison, are you all right?'

She nodded. Francesca's voice seemed to come from far away.

'Well, let's walk on. It's such a beautiful day, I'm really enjoying it.'

A beautiful day? Alison opened her eyes, flinching at the glare. The sky was laser-blue; the sharp greens pierced and stung. She laid her hand on her stomach. Flat. Slim. Not an ounce of spare flesh. She had lost weight recently. Lost her appetite.

'Alison, what's wrong?' Francesca was looking at her strangely. 'Aren't you feeling well?'

'No. I mean, yes. I . . . I think we'd better turn back.'

'But why? We've only been out a few minutes.'

'It just that I . . . I promised to pick up a prescription for James. From the chemist. He's been sleeping badly and . . .' The words were jumbled, unconvincing.

Francesca glanced at her watch. 'But it's only ten past four. You've plenty of time.'

'They might close early. I'd hate James to think I forgot. I'm sorry to cut things short, Francesca, but I really would prefer to get back straight away.'

'OK.'

She deserved the terse reply. She was being rude and selfish. Upsetting people, as usual, even a guest. She forced a smile, although her face felt taut: a mask. 'I'm sorry,' she repeated. 'Are you sure you don't mind?'

Francesca shook her head. 'Don't worry. It'll actually suit me to get off a bit earlier, then I can make a start on my packing. You'd never believe the amount of stuff I brought for five days! Of course, half of it I haven't worn. Hey, Alison, slow down! You'll break your neck.'

She waited impatiently for Francesca to catch up, chafing at every moment lost. She *had* to get to the chemist's in time, but it wasn't simply that.

Her life had changed, for ever.

23

'You see, I did this pregnancy test – the sort you buy at the chemist's – and it came out . . . positive. I still can't quite believe it. I know they're meant to be accurate, but I wondered if it might be a false positive.'

Mr Prescott leaned back in his chair. 'That's most unlikely, Mrs Egerton, if you followed the instructions correctly.'

'Oh yes, I was scrupulously careful. But somehow I have doubts about the result. You see, I was sure I was pregnant last December and that was a false alarm – my period was late. But they've been regular since then. I did the test two days before my next one was due. Was that too early, d'you think?'

He shook his head. 'Doing the test too early might give you a false negative. But you say yours was positive. Still, if you're concerned, my dear, why don't we do another test, here and now, to put your mind at rest. Sister!'

A stout, cheerful-looking woman appeared from the adjoining treatment room, her tight navy uniform emphasizing her ship's prow of a bosom. 'Yes, Mr Prescott?'

'Could you arrange for Mrs Egerton to give us a specimen?'

'Yes, of course.' She ushered Alison along the passage, chatting brightly about the weather. For Alison, there *was* no weather, no outside world at all. Everything had contracted to her womb. Was an egg cell implanted there, which was growing and dividing? Three days ago she had been absolutely certain, influenced by Francesca's talk of gut instincts. But now she was less sure. Gut instincts could be misleading, as she knew from past experience. In December, she had all but ordered the pram, before being brought down to earth with a bang. Perhaps she was deluding herself once more, letting her imagination run wild.

'Mind you, they say it's going to rain at the weekend.'

'Oh, really?'

'Well, I suppose we have to expect April showers at this time of year.'

'Yes. I suppose so.' Her legs seemed made of Plasticine and it was all she could do to keep up with the nurse, let alone discuss the weekend forecast. As she locked the toilet door she found herself praying to the God she no longer believed in. 'Let it be all right.' A pointless prayer anyway: whatever the result it couldn't be all right.

After handing over the sample she was left sitting on her own while Mr Prescott and the nurse went into the treatment room. Their muffled voices reached her through the partition – there was even a chuckle from the nurse. How could anyone be so insensitive as to laugh at a time like this? She counted the seconds in her head in a vain attempt to keep calm. The test took only a minute so she should know the verdict at once. Yet after counting thousands of seconds here she was, still waiting.

She examined the carpet instead, every tiny detail: the way the blue shaded into purple, the pattern of interlocking curves. Perhaps she *had* done the first test wrong, being in such a state, or simply misread it. As she had misread the 'signs' from her body. She had no actual symptoms – swollen breasts, nausea – but had let herself be swayed by irrational hunches. Yet if her period should start tomorrow she'd be devastated and would actively mourn the child that never was. She remembered meeting an IVF patient who'd told her that she'd consciously tried to foster a bond with the embryos from the very moment they were implanted. For the next two weeks she had talked to her babies and played them soothing music; she had even given them names. Then her period came and the poor woman felt literally bereaved. Alison could sympathize wholeheartedly.

She consulted her watch. Almost eight minutes had passed. What was going on? Was something wrong with the test? Maybe she'd caught some infection. She knew Craig had other women, and so might Jim now that he was divorced. How would she keep it from James, she thought with mounting alarm – keep *everything* from James?

And then, at last, Mr Prescott reappeared, a broad smile on his face. 'I'm delighted to confirm, Mrs Egerton, that you are definitely pregnant. Congratulations! It's wonderful news, isn't it?'

She sat in stunned silence. Wonderful. Appalling. And still totally incredible. She couldn't take it in. This must be happening to someone else or happening in a dream. Yet Mr Prescott looked real enough – square shoulders, stocky build – even if everything in her head seemed out of focus.

He was looking at her quizzically. 'You seem a little concerned, my dear. Is anything wrong? If you're worried about the pregnancy I can put your mind at rest. It should be completely trouble-free. You're young and healthy, and we found no problems when we did the investigations.'

Completely trouble-free . . . He didn't know the half of it.

'But while you're here I'd like to examine you – take your blood pressure and so on. Where do you want to have the baby, by the way? At the East Surrey?'

She stared at him in consternation. He was already arranging the confinement when she was less than two weeks pregnant. 'Er, yes,' she stammered.

'Fine. I'll write to your GP and let him know.'

No, don't, she pleaded silently. Why was he rushing everything? Her GP was James's too. She needed much more time to decide what to say, what to do.

Mr Prescott scribbled something on her notes and looked up, frowning slightly. 'You are happy about the news, I take it, Mrs Egerton?'

She gripped the arm of the chair, seized by a ridiculous urge to race out into the street and announce at the top of her voice, 'I'm pregnant, I'm pregnant, I'm really, really pregnant!' A miracle had happened in her life and the problems had simply faded into oblivion.

'Mrs Egerton . . .?'

'Oh, *yes*,' she said, 'I'm so happy I could fly!'

'Alison, you've got to get rid of it.'

'Are you crazy? I want this baby more than anything I've wanted in my life.'

'But if you think it might be Jim's . . .' Linda was fiddling with a dish of paper-clips, spilling half of them on the desk. 'Look, abortion's a piece of cake these days. I should know.'

'Linda, I'm sorry but I don't believe in abortion. That's one of the few things I agree with the Church about. Anyway, how could I even consider it after trying all this time?'

'But what if James finds out? He'd never forgive you.'

She pushed her cup away. Linda had made her a coffee, but even the smell of it turned her stomach. 'I know. I can't think about anything else.'

'Mind you, knowing Jim, he's not likely to rat on you. I'm sure you could get away with it.'

She shifted uneasily in her chair. 'It's . . . not just Jim I'm worried about.'

'What d'you mean?'

'Oh, Linda . . .' She put her head in her hands; her voice a muffled wail. 'I don't know what to *do*.'

Linda came to sit beside her. 'What is it? What's the matter?'

'It's no good, I can't tell you.'

'For Christ's sake, Al! You ring me in a total panic and drag me out of a meeting and now you say you can't tell me.'

There was a sudden shrill from the phone. Linda snatched it up. 'No, Valerie, I can't take calls at the moment. Tell people I'm busy until, say, twelve fifteen.' She replaced the receiver and turned to Alison. 'OK, we've got half an hour.'

'Look, it doesn't matter. I shouldn't have bothered you when you're up to your eyes.'

'Al, if I haven't got time for my oldest friend . . .' Linda gave her a comforting pat on the shoulder. 'I'm sorry if I sounded sharp. It's nothing to do with you – just a bit of hassle with a bloke here. I can see you're in a shit-awful state, and I want to help, believe me. But I can't unless you open up.'

Alison sat twisting her watch round and round on her wrist.

'Come on, what is it?'

'You won't be shocked?'

'Am I ever?'

'This time you may be. I . . . I've . . .' She took a deep breath and made herself go on. 'I've been having an affair with Craig.'

'*Craig?*'

'Well, not an affair exactly. The sex sort of . . . happened while we were working on the book. We got a bit carried away. And then it became a regular thing.'

211

Linda was staring at her in amazement. 'I'm not shocked, Al, I'm gob-smacked. Why on earth didn't you tell me before?'

'I suppose I felt ashamed. I mean, he's *your* friend and younger than me and –'

'So what? I wasn't exactly lusting after him. And actually I wouldn't have –'

'Let me finish, Linda. This is difficult enough. What I'm trying to say is that . . . that he always used a condom. Except once – when neither of us thought we'd . . . You see, by then I'd told him it had to stop. But he went berserk. I don't think it was *me* he cared about so much as his precious book.'

She went over to the window and stood staring blindly out. It was easier to talk without Linda's eyes on her face. 'Anyway, he wanted to see me one last time, to discuss publishers and things, and when I said no he . . . he threatened to tell James. He was probably bluffing, but I didn't dare take the risk. In fact, I was so terrified I *did* agree to meet him. But not at his place. That would be asking for trouble. I picked him up at the bar after he'd finished work, and we were supposed to be going for a drink, but . . .' She shivered, clutched the window-frame. She could feel the dank chill of the cellar again; smell the acrid smell of the beer. The place was like a prison; the oppressively low ceiling crisscrossed with danger-ous-looking wires; the flagstones scarred and pitted. Craig had tricked her into going down there, asking if she'd give him a hand taking some bottles upstairs. The steps were steep and narrow, and when the door slammed behind them she heard him turn the key. He stood facing her between two rows of huge steel barrels, each with a thin plastic tube feed-ing the beer up to the bar above. They were like the transparent tubing hospitals used for blood transfusions and drip-feeds. She felt faint at the sight of the brownish-coloured liquid, imagining it pumping into her – a transfusion not of blood but fear.

He gripped her arm, his fingers digging into her flesh. 'Get this straight, Alison. I won't stand for this sort of shit. You can't just pick people up and dump them again when it suits you.' The harsh whirr of the cooling fan added menace to his voice. 'And why does your husband mean so fucking much all of a sudden, when you said your marriage was practically over?'

212

'I didn't say that.' Her arms were covered with goose-pimples. She was standing directly in front of the fan and couldn't stop shivering.

'On the verge of divorce, you told me.'

'Craig that's not true. I never mentioned divorce.'

'You implied it. You've been stringing me along the whole fucking time, haven't you? Pretending you liked my book and saying what great things you could do for it. And then – bingo! – the novelty wears off and you can't be bothered any more. How am I supposed to feel, for Christ's sake?' He gave a bitter laugh. 'Maybe I should meet this famous husband of yours. I'll *need* an accountant if the book takes off.'

'Craig, don't be stupid.'

'Oh, stupid now, am I? I don't think James would think so. I'm sure we'd get on well. After all, we do have *you* in common. What a gas, talking to a bloke about his wife, comparing notes . . .'

Fear prickled down her spine. She was in his power, in every sense. This cellar was his realm, and even if she shouted for help nobody would hear. In any case he'd probably told the other staff to keep out of the way. 'Look, Craig . . .' Her voice was all but lost beneath the grumble of the fan. It seemed to mock her feeble protests; take Craig's side against her. 'I . . . will help with the book.'

'Oh, big deal! She'll help me. Aren't I the lucky guy? Do I go down on my knees and kiss her feet?'

'Craig, *please*, can't we behave like adults?'

'Yeah. Good idea. I'd like that.' He yanked her towards him, pressing his groin into hers.

She tried to knee him off, appalled that a vicious quarrel could arouse him.

'Aha – playing hard to get, are we? I quite enjoy that little game. As a matter of fact I've always fancied a quick fuck down here. Great atmosphere, don't you think?' He pushed her roughly on to a pile of dirty sacking.

'Craig . . .' Her voice was shrill with fear as she struggled to escape his grip. 'I've told you, it's over.'

'Oh, come on, sweetie, just one last time.'

She was astonished at the sudden change in tone – softer, almost affectionate. He even ran a gentle finger round the outline of her lips.

213

'Tell you what,' he whispered, 'how about a compromise. You guarantee to get me a publisher, and I won't say anything to James.'

'I can't guarantee it, Craig. No one can.'

'You can try. You must have loads of friends in the business.'

'OK. I'll try.'

'Promise?'

'Mm.'

'Let's seal it with a kiss.'

'*No*, Craig. I'll do my best to help you with the book, but that's as far as it goes.'

Before she knew what was happening she was face down on the sacking and his hand was groping up her skirt, feeling for the waistband of her tights. She tried to fight him off, remembering all the other times. Just part of the game, she had thought. But today it wasn't a game. If she resisted she would get hurt – and not just physically. Better an ordeal of five minutes than a husband lost for ever.

She closed her eyes and the thrumming of the fan swelled into a roar. The stale smell of beer seemed to have permeated her clothes and hair – she could even taste it in her mouth. She lay motionless, her legs cold, exposed, the hessian rough against her cheek. It took less than five minutes and didn't hurt particularly. She was lucky in a sense. He could have murdered her.

'Alison, my God! He could have . . . *murdered* you.'

'Yes.'

'I just don't know what to say. It makes me feel sick to my stomach. And Craig of all people . . . I didn't think he'd hurt a fly. You could take him to court, you realize, make him pay, the bastard!'

'Are you mad, Linda? I don't want anyone to know.'

'But you can't let him get away with it.'

'I've no alternative. He could be the . . . the father of my baby.'

'Oh, no!' Linda shook her head in disgust. 'In that case, you *must* get rid of it. You can't take the risk. Just think, every time you look at the kid it'll remind you of – '

'Linda,' she cut in, 'I'm going to have this child, whatever. I've made up my mind.'

'But suppose Craig threatens you again?'

'I don't think he will. Believe it or not, we parted on quite reasonable terms.'

'You're joking!'

'No, honestly. I said if I was going to succeed in getting him a publisher, it was essential for us to be seen as two professionals – author and editor, or author and agent, whatever he likes to call it – and not as romantically involved in any way. Otherwise people would think I was pushing the book for that reason, rather than on its merits. It seemed to convince him, thank heavens.'

'How can you be sure? He sounds positively psychotic to me.'

'Not so much psychotic as obsessed with his book. What you have to understand, Linda, is that for him it's much more than just a book – it's a passport to fame and fortune. He has visions of a Porsche in the drive and Hollywood producers flocking round his door.'

'Surely he can't be that naïve? I thought most writers starved in garrets.'

Alison managed a weak smile. 'Not quite. There are exceptions. Take this builder chap who's been in the news. He's – '

'What builder chap?'

'You know, the guy from Sunderland who made a million on his first novel.'

'Never heard of him.'

'Oh, come on, Linda, you must have. He was splashed all over the papers. Anyway, it's given Craig the completely false impression that unknown authors earn six-figure advances as a matter of course. He's in this dead-end job at the moment and he thinks I'm the one who can get him out of it. So when I said I wouldn't help him any more he accused me of being a callous bitch and depriving him of a future.'

Linda bent a paper-clip out of shape and jabbed it against her palm. 'I can understand him having ambition and wanting to make pots of money, however remote his chances, but what I don't get is why you let him screw you.'

Alison flushed, and avoided giving a direct answer. 'I've come to the conclusion that it was a male power thing. I was in control, you see – the editor, giving him advice. At the beginning that was fine. But he gradually came to resent it. So he used sex to make us equal again, and then he could accept the situation.'

'Yeah, you were definitely a cut above his usual kind of girlfriends. He tends to go out with airheads, so you must have seemed a bit daunting.'

'Hardly. Craig's not easily daunted. But he did once say he liked the fact that I was older than him. And married. And had a proper career. He said it boosted his ego. I can't think why, but – '

'I can! His last girlfriend worked in Boots and looked about thirteen. He'd have seen you as a good catch. So it would come as a nasty shock when you dumped him.'

'Well, I tried not to hurt his pride by – '

'Al, it still beats me why you got involved in the first place. What was in it for you? I mean, if you didn't even fancy him, why the hell did you do it?'

'I don't know,' she snapped, discomfited by Linda's questions, which echoed what she had repeatedly asked herself. It would be glib to say she was miserable and angry – so were many people, and for more compelling reasons. Maybe it was a sort of self-inflicted punishment. Or a way of getting at James because secretly she blamed him for their childlessness. Or a way of getting at God. But there were other, less negative motives. 'This'll probably sound weird, Linda, but what I liked about Craig was that he let me be myself. I didn't have to pretend, not even when we were having sex.'

'But surely you don't pretend with James, do you?'

'No, but . . .' She frowned. 'It's hard to explain. You see, making love with James always has to be so *good* – each of us concerned about the other's pleasure and trying to make it perfect every time.'

'Christ, Al, most women would give their eye teeth for that!'

'Yes, I know it sounds terribly ungrateful, but it can sometimes be a strain. And anyway there's this wild, rebellious bit of me which doesn't *want* to be good – or unselfish or considerate or even halfway decent. Craig encouraged that. Shit, *he* was selfish enough! He did exactly what he wanted and to hell with whether I'd come or not. But I did come, Linda, because I found it . . . well – exciting. I think I actually liked him being violent. Oh, I don't mean in the cellar – that was vile. But at his bedsit.' She stared down at her hands, ashamed of such an admission. 'And the most ironic thing of all is that sex with Craig wasn't connected with babies – or so I thought. With James I can never forget what time of the month it is. When you've spent years and years studying every detail

216

of your cycle, knowing exactly when you ovulate, you can't switch off and pretend it doesn't matter. It's constantly there, in the back of your mind, turning sex into a sort of . . . test. You're always thinking: maybe this time . . . But with Craig I could forget all that.'

She sank down on the window-seat, exhausted suddenly after living on her nerves all day. Faint sounds filtered through from the adjoining offices: voices raised in argument, a continually ringing phone. Outside, a florist's van was unloading gladioli, a reminder of the stiff-necked bouquet she had taken to Cecilia in hospital. 'Linda, you've no idea,' she said vehemently, 'how sick and tired I am of going through the motions of being a good Catholic. It makes me feel an utter fraud. That was another thing about Craig. He couldn't care less about religion. In fact he wouldn't have given a toss if I did something quite outrageous like screwing the Pope or dancing naked on the altar of Westminster fucking Cathedral. Excuse my language but, well – that's the point. It's all the bloody *rules* . . . Everything's set in stone – what you're allowed to say, or do, or even think. And James's family have their own battery of rules, on top of the Church's. No swearing, needless to say. And being charitable and community-minded and volunteering for things you loathe. And the priest is always right, even if he's practically brain-dead . . .'

'Al, I've never *heard* you like this.'

'I know. I'm sorry. I'd better push off. I didn't mean to stay this long. I'm probably boring you to death.'

'Don't be silly. Look, it's nearly half past twelve. Let's both get out of here. I'll take an early lunch. Where d'you fancy – a wine bar?'

'You choose. I don't think I could eat anything. And I suppose I shouldn't drink now I'm pregnant.'

'God, what a bore! *I* shan't ever have kids.'

Alison laughed. 'Drink's the least of my problems.'

'We could go to the park, if you like. I'll buy a Coke and a sandwich and we can sit on a bench and enjoy London's lovely fumes.'

'OK.'

Linda picked up her jacket. 'I'll just tell Valerie I'm off. Are you all right?' she asked. 'You look completely bushed.'

Alison smiled wanly. 'I've hardly slept a wink the last few nights. As they say – no peace for the wicked.'

'Don't worry, Al – we'll sort it out. I'll help all I can. When's the baby due, by the way?'

'December.' She stopped dead in her tracks, only now taking in the full impact of the test result. 'Linda, do you realize, I'll have a baby by Christmas!'

She watched the pigeons scavenging round their feet, pecking at Linda's discarded sandwich crusts. 'Let's talk about *you*, for a change. How are things with Derek?'

'Fantastic. I just hope it lasts. You know, the other night I was working it out and the longest relationship I've ever had was fourteen months. So by those standards you've done damned well with James.'

'Don't! I can't bear to think about leaving him.'

'Leaving him? Why should you? Just pass the baby off as his. You wouldn't be the only one. Didn't you see that thing on TV about the incredibly high number of babies born to married couples that aren't fathered by the husband? And no one's any the wiser.'

'But it seems such an awful deceit.'

Linda ignored her interruption. 'And they said it was much the same with animals. Field-mice, squirrels, rabbits, you name it – they're all bonking away like fury. *And* birds.'

'I thought birds were supposed to mate for life.'

'Yeah, that was the general idea. But it's wrong, apparently. They sleep around just the same as we do. Take sparrows.' She had noticed one fighting for its share of bread amidst the flurry of pigeons. 'They can have several mates on the go at once, so it's anybody's guess which male fertilizes the eggs.'

'I'm not a sparrow,' Alison retorted, 'and I do happen to have ideals, Linda, even if I haven't lived up to them. And anyway I *love* James, which makes an enormous difference.'

'Are you sure you love him, though? I mean, you've just been saying how dreadful all the rules are and what a sham your life is because you don't believe in the God crap any longer.'

'Maybe. But that's the point. If I didn't love him it wouldn't be so bad. I could just shrug it off and go my own way without feeling such a traitor. And I do desperately want him as the baby's father. He'll be a marvellous father, I know. I've always wanted his children.' She pressed her hand into the rough, ridged surface of the bench. 'But if it *isn't* his . . .'

'Who's to know?'

'*I* will. And I don't think I could live with myself. It's bad enough faking the religious thing, but . . .' She had snagged her hand on a splinter of wood and tiny beads of blood were oozing through the skin. 'It's *my* fault, Linda. No one else's. I really don't deserve James. In fact I'm beginning to think that the only decent way out is to tell him the truth, then go and set up on my own with the baby.'

'That's plain daft!' Linda crumpled up her sandwich wrapper and threw it into the bin. 'You'll destroy him. And his bloody family. And you'll land up in some seedy bedsit without a penny to your name.'

'Perhaps that's a kind of justice, though. After all, I brought it on myself.'

'Forget yourself. Think of the kid. He needs security. You know how I feel about my Dad doing a bunk before I was out of nappies. It affected the whole family, me especially. I'm sure that's why I can't make it with men – I don't trust the buggers. Why inflict that on your own child? Whatever *you* might have done, he's innocent. There's not just one simple morality, you know.'

Alison glanced at the people strolling along the path – a young couple hand in hand enjoying the April sunshine; a man with a pair of poodles in fussy tartan coats. It was a perfect day to be out – the trees budding into leaf, the sky a tranquil blue. Yet it felt like darkest winter in her head. 'If I stay with James my whole life will be a lie. I'll have to have the baby baptized and bring it up a Catholic.'

'For Christ's sake, Al, the most important thing is making sure the poor kid has a father. And two pennies to rub together. If *my* father hadn't pissed off, we wouldn't have been on the breadline for the next fifteen years.'

Alison sat in silence. She had always understood Linda's deep psychological need for a highly-paid job, to save her from financial dependence on a man. But what right had *she* to continue living off James? 'It still seems so wrong to deceive him.'

'Come off it, Al, we all tell lies. It's part of being human. And sometimes it's a darn sight kinder than the truth. Why upset everyone else just because you're on some self-punishment kick? You won't be allowed a divorce, which means James'll be stuck on his own for the rest of his life, lonely and depressed. And if the baby *is* his, he'll be deprived of his own child.'

'And if it isn't?'

Linda sighed in exasperation. 'Listen, you were planning to adopt once, weren't you? So James was willing to love a child who wasn't his.'

'That's a different thing entirely. There's no deceit involved.'

'OK, what about AID? You told me you'd have had that if you could. Well, isn't what you've done a sort of AID, with Craig or Jim as the donor?'

'The Church won't allow AID, though.'

'Shit, we're back to the bloody Church! Which is constantly changing its mind. I know that from a guy in our accounts department. *He's* Catholic, but he's divorced, and he remarried a few months ago in church. He had to shop around until eventually he found a priest who'd do the wedding. And he was telling me the other day that the liberal faction are just waiting for this Pope to die, so he can be replaced by a more progressive one. Well, that could happen any time, and then AID might be permitted. In which case James would agree to you finding a donor, wouldn't he?'

'Well, yes, I suppose he would. He said he'd do anything to have a child.'

'There you are then. Let's face it, more and more babies are going to be born in future to people who aren't their biological parents – sperm donation, egg donation, surrogate mothers, all that sort of thing. And sooner or later the Church is bound to adapt. Anyway what really matters is that the parents want the child and love it. Which James *will*.'

Linda was right, Alison reflected. James did want a child and *would* love it. And he'd been willing to accept a child who was neither his nor hers, even one with a physical handicap or who had suffered neglect or abuse. The child came first, as Linda said. So why condemn her own child to a miserable existence without a father or a proper home or loving relatives? 'Oh, Linda,' she said, squeezing her hand in gratitude, 'I'm beginning to feel better. You've helped me see things in a different light.'

'Thank God for that! Actually, I ought to be getting back. Want to walk to the office with me?'

'Yes, 'course. And then I'll go to Oxford Street and buy something for the baby – just to prove it's real.'

'When will you tell James?' asked Linda, as they left the park. 'Tonight?'

'Heavens no! He's going to the hospital and he's always terribly gloomy when he gets home.'

'I know she's his grandma, but isn't he rather overreacting? After all, she *is* eighty-five, so she's had a damned good innings.'

'I don't think it's just Cecilia. She isn't dying, anyway – far from it. She should be discharged in the next few days.'

'What's wrong with her?'

'She had pneumonia. And that *was* serious: James was worried sick. But they put her on a drip and drugs and what-have-you, and she responded surprisingly well. And now she's having physio to get her on her feet again – literally. Mind you, it's a private hospital, so they're probably keeping her in longer than strictly necessary.'

'Ever the cynic, Alison!'

'Look who's talking! Anyway, what I'm trying to say is that Cecilia's health, or lack of it, isn't the reason James is so on edge. No, there's more to it – there must be. I've never known him like this. In fact I can't help wondering if he somehow knows what I've done.'

'How could he? Jim wouldn't tell him, and you said Craig promised not to. Actually, I doubt if Craig meant to carry out those threats. I'm sure it was just macho talk, to frighten you.'

'James does have grounds for suspicion, though. You see, the night I met Jim I arrived home fearfully late *and* in a cab, which must have seemed peculiar. James was beside himself with worry – he thought I'd been mugged or something. I told him this cock-and-bull story about Jim offering to run me home because of the rain, and that his car conked out miles from anywhere and we had to wait hours for the AA. Well, the rain bit was true, at least. And of course I didn't say that Jim was divorced or living on his own – I just went on about his three lovely children and his promotion and his car and stuff. At the time, James didn't question anything. I suppose he was just relieved that I was safe. But afterwards he might have thought it sounded rather fishy.'

'Oh, I shouldn't think so, Al. Paragons of virtue like James never imagine that their nearest and dearest would lie. I bet if someone told him they'd seen you and Jim *in flagrante* he wouldn't believe it. He's so trusting, the poor innocent.' Linda suddenly stopped and clutched Alison's arm. 'Wait a minute, though – what if he's *not* so innocent? You did say he's often home late and he's always banging on about this woman Elaine. Well, perhaps he's having an affair himself.'

'Oh, he wouldn't, Linda, no way. It's completely out of character. In any case he can't stand Elaine. She's the one that's being such a pain at work.'

'Ah, maybe he's just saying that to put you off the scent. Or if he *is* suspicious of you, he could be doing it to retaliate.'

'No,' she said tersely. 'It's against all his principles.'

'*You* had principles too, remember. Yet you still went off the rails and did things you don't believe in. He's only human, after all.'

'No,' she repeated, desperate to suppress the suspicions that had actually crept into her mind some time ago. She mustn't let them take hold or everything would fall apart. James was loyal. And virtuous – that was written in stone.

'I mean, most people see *you* as good. Take Cecilia. It would never occur to her in a thousand years that you'd betray her darling James. Well, maybe he's doing the same – fooling the whole damned lot of us.'

Alison walked on, making a final (hopeless) effort to cling to her faith in James. Of *course* he was obsessed with Elaine: it was blindingly obvious, wasn't it? The countless times they stayed on at the office after everyone else had gone home; the long phone-calls at weekends. She had told herself doggedly that it was nothing more than work, but Linda's words had swept away the last remnant of her deliberate self-deception. All the discordant notes which had been sounding singly day by day now roared and jangled in her head in a shattering cacophony: James's inconsistency in Oxfordshire, veering between affection and impatience; his neglect of the garden and loss of interest in music, even in reading the paper; his bouts of irritability and intense preoccupation. And the fact he was off his food. Admittedly it was Lent – indeed, coming up for Holy Week, when he was always more abstemious – but this year it could be due to guilt rather than spiritual mortification. She had tried to explain the change in him by assuming that he suspected *her*. Which he almost certainly did. Whatever else, he wasn't a fool. In fact she was the fool to imagine she could hoodwink him so easily, sneaking home at four in the morning without him smelling a rat. And the times she'd come back from Craig's, twitchy and defensive and probably looking flushed. Fixated on her own guilt, she had ignored the signs of his; refused to confront her fears. But yes, as Linda said, he might have decided to get even. And getting even for James would mean a terrifying struggle with his conscience. No wonder he couldn't sleep – like her. Like her, he was mired in a crisis.

They turned into South Audley Street. 'Monogamy's not natural anyway,' Linda said, as she pressed the button for the pedestrian lights. 'Any more in humans than in sparrows. You must have heard those theories about people being genetically predisposed to have affairs. Maybe poor old James is just following his genes for once. And, if so, you should be grateful, Al. It lets you off the hook. You're quits!'

Alison crossed the road unseeingly. However hypocritical, she was sickened at the thought of him being involved in some squalid entanglement. James's ideals were so much part of him, part of what she loved – the fact that he *wasn't* just a slave to his brute instincts.

Linda squeezed past a woman with a pushchair. 'Perhaps you should have it out with him – ask if you can meet this Elaine. Invite her to dinner or something and see what his reaction is.'

Alison said nothing. She had always pictured Elaine as a rather plain, hard-headed type. According to James, she lived alone, had never married and had few interests outside work. A bit like Christine by the sounds of it (although younger at thirty-seven): a workaholic with neither time nor inclination for affairs of the heart. But that could be quite wrong. She might be devastatingly beautiful and sexy into the bargain. And there was no question that she was a high-flyer. Otherwise a firm like Garrard Ross would never have taken her on, let alone made her a junior partner. Maybe James admired her body *and* her intellect. He might even be in love with her. Horrific images flashed into her mind – Elaine and James away together, in bed together, committed to each other. It was all very well to talk blithely about setting up on her own with a baby. The reality would be unbearable. No husband. No home. No money. Only loneliness and jealousy, as the new wife supplanted her.

They had reached the porticoed entrance of Midas Marketing. 'Give me a ring, won't you?' Linda said as she went in. 'Let me know what James says and how you are and everything. And don't despair, for God's sake. Things probably aren't half as bad as you think.'

No, twice as bad, she muttered to herself as she stood alone on the pavement. The more she thought about James's behaviour, the more incriminating it appeared – his frequent absences, for instance. She had no proof he was at the hospital every evening, except when she went with him. And he was going to confession even more often than usual; a significant point in itself. He was probably confessing adultery each time, trying and failing to give the woman up.

She made herself walk on, her head reeling with speculations. However much she might yearn for a new start it wasn't just Elaine who stood in the way. There was Craig, as well. And Jim. She had to find a publisher for Craig, which meant that she couldn't avoid future contact with him. And Jim seemed as besotted with her as she had once been with James. It would be cruel to refuse to see him again when he was so depressed about his divorce, but he'd soon realize she was pregnant – not a condition that could be concealed for long. And wouldn't he think it odd after all her talk of infertility? He might put two and two together and guess that he was the father . . .

She realized she was walking round in circles. She ought to go home, but that would mean waiting for James to come back from the hospital. Or from Elaine's warm bed, perhaps. The weekend loomed ahead – Cecilia, Francis, Helen – how could she face any of them? If only there were some bolt-hole where she could think things out in peace.

She remembered passing a phone-box on the corner. Quickly she walked back to it, rummaging in her purse for coins.

'Mum, it's me. How are you? . . . Good. Look, I know it's awfully short notice, but can I come and stay for the weekend?'

24

'It's the biggest one I've ever seen. And Terry's, too! Thank you, Alison, dear.' Her mother removed the Easter egg from its box and peeled back the gold foil. 'Go on – have a piece.'

'Later, Mum, OK? We've only just finished lunch.'

'You should save it for Easter, Connie,' her father muttered, grinding out his cigarette. 'You're always stuffing yourself with sweets.'

'At least sweets don't give you lung cancer. I'd hate to think what my lungs must look like after living with you for thirty-two years. I bet I could claim compensation.'

'Huh! So could I, for putting up with thirty-two years of nagging.'

They hadn't changed, she thought, although in recent years their quarrels had mellowed into bickering and become almost a companionable habit, of little more significance than the ticking of the clock. The room, too, was unchanged; still overstuffed with furniture: battered table and sideboard, shiny three-piece suite. And of course photos of her everywhere – in her pram and her school uniform, in frocks and jeans and cap and gown. How wayward and defiant she looked, outstaring the camera, challenging the world. It couldn't have been easy for her parents, coping with a child who spent her days pretending she was Joan of Arc or Robin Hood, or – later – Lord Byron, transforming sleepy Hunston into the glittering Alps or treacherous Hellespont. She had always kicked against the dreary daily round. How could washing-up and homework compare with writing revolutionary cantos or fighting the infidel?

'You've lost weight,' her mother observed. 'Are you eating properly?'

'Yes, I'm fine.' Although only a few weeks pregnant she felt so extraordinarily different she was astonished they didn't guess.

'You hardly touched your lunch. I made the pasty specially – I know you used to like them.'

'It was lovely. Thanks, Mum.'

'I got the mince from Fletcher's. You can't trust supermarkets these days. I should have made a pudding. Would you have liked an apple tart?'

'No, honestly, I . . .'

'Never mind, we'll have one tomorrow. And a nice shoulder of lamb. I don't like seeing you so peaky.'

'Stop fussing, Connie.' Her father brushed ash from his lap. 'She's barely been here five minutes and you haven't let her get a word in.'

'I'm just concerned about her.'

'Now then, love,' he turned to Alison, 'tell us what you've been up to.'

'Well, I . . . I'm still trying to get a job. But no luck yet, I'm afraid.'

'I can't understand it after all that education we gave you.' Her mother patted her frizz of brittle hair, over-bleached and over-permed. 'And how about the piano lessons? Are you going on with them?'

She nodded, although her practice had been virtually non-existent of late.

'I always wanted to learn, you know.'

'*Did* you, Mum?'

'Oh yes. You wouldn't remember my Uncle Fred – you were only tiny when he died – but he played beautifully. He had a grand piano, a Steinway, and he often let me have a go. He told me I had talent and it shouldn't go to waste. But there wasn't money for lessons in those days.'

'I'll teach you, if you like, Mum. When I've made a bit more progress.'

'What on?' her father asked scornfully. 'There's no grand pianos here. And anyway we never see you, Alison.'

'No, I'm sorry. It's been ages.' It was wrong to have neglected her parents in favour of the Egertons. Her mother looked older than her years, pale and gaunt, with new lines around her eyes. Her hair had thinned and patches of vulnerable pinkish scalp were visible in places. Her father was his usual solid self, although his sandy-coloured thatch had greyed and his complexion, too, was pallid.

'What are you doing for Easter?' her mother asked. 'Why don't you bring James to see us?'

'It's a bit difficult at the moment, Mum. His grandmother's coming out of hospital next week and we ought to be there, to make sure she's all right.' There was so much on her mind: James, Elaine, her pregnancy – yet nothing she could share with them. It wouldn't be fair to tell them about the baby before she had broken the news to James.

'More coffee, dear?'

'No, thanks.'

'I'll have another one. It tastes a darn sight better than the usual stuff you make.'

'That's because it's real coffee. I bought one of those whatsitsnames – caffiteers. Alison's used to things done properly.'

'Not here she isn't. Look at this room. It's full of all your junk.'

'Well, I never seem to get round to tidying up.'

'I don't like things too tidy,' Alison said, surprised to realize it was true.

'I have enough of that with James's family.' Curiously, one of Craig's attractions was the very squalor of his existence. There had been an exhilarating freedom about his shambolic bedsit compared with the Egertons' stifling discipline and her own well-organized house. With Craig she had revelled in being a slut – in all senses.

'You must have time on your hands, without a job,' her father remarked.

'I've been doing a bit of freelance work. On a travel book.'

'Sounds interesting.'

'Yes, it was. A lot of it's set in Mongolia and the Mongolians are the most amazing people, Dad. Very brave and tough, but they drink an awful lot and they can go completely wild and explode at the drop of a hat.' Like me, she thought.

'I expect you miss Shaw Hilliard, don't you?'

'Oh, yes.' However appalling its outcome, the Craig affair had at least reminded her that she had talent, revived her editorial skills, made her feel useful again. And now pregnancy had brought with it a new, gratifying sense of purpose. She might even get more (official) freelance work to do at home while she was waiting for the baby.

'There's chocolate cake for tea,' her mother said, returning with the tray. 'Or would you like a slice now?'

'I'm not hungry, thanks. In fact if you don't mind I'll go up and unpack my things.'

'I'll come too. I've got a little present for you. I bought it in this new shop in the village.'

'Oh, you shouldn't, Mum.' She followed her mother upstairs, noticing how stiff she had become. She was years younger than James's mother, yet moved like an old woman.

'You do like the way I've redone your bedroom, don't you, dear?'

'Yes, it's great.' She had hardly recognized it – new frilled curtains and matching counterpane, even a mock-tortoiseshell brush and comb set on the dressing-table. The rest of the house looked sadder, in comparison; the paintwork dingy, the carpets worn and faded.

'I didn't want James to feel ashamed of us when he comes to stay.'

'Don't be silly, Mum. You know he isn't like that.' She realized with a pang what a thoroughly good man her husband was – or had been until

Elaine appeared on the scene. He never judged people by material things, and treated her parents with such respect and warmth they behaved quite differently in his presence from their normal fractious selves. She was incredibly lucky to have him. If she still did. Perhaps he was spending the weekend with that odious woman while the coast was clear. He'd said that he was going to Helen's but, as Linda had pointed out, if *she* could conceal falsehood behind a smiling mask so, no doubt, could he.

'Gracious! What a fright I look.' Her mother caught sight of her reflection in the mirror. 'I'd better go and make myself respectable. And I'll fetch your present.'

'Thanks, Mum.' As she unpacked her case she was uncomfortably aware of the wedding photo on the chest of drawers. James was gazing at his bride with delighted admiration. Had he broken his vow of fidelity, as she had? And if she told him about the baby would he ditch Elaine? Perhaps she should tell him first about her loss of faith. With Easter fast approaching and the endless succession of services – Maundy Thursday, Good Friday, Easter Day itself – it would be terribly hard to keep up the pretence.

She stared out of the window at the familiar view of poky back gardens strung with washing-lines. So often as a child she had longed to exchange this benighted village for some thrillingly romantic place; to find a handsome prince who would whisk her away from her father's distasteful liaisons: the mysterious women who hovered like briefly glimpsed spectres on the margins of her life. Yet ironically, now that she had found her prince, she felt closer to her father than ever before. As a sanctimonious adolescent she had judged him too harshly, she realized. It was all too easy to lapse into affairs if you were unhappy and confused. And he must often have been lonely as a sales rep, living out of suitcases in anonymous hotels. At least he hadn't abandoned them, like Linda's father, or left them destitute.

'Come in,' she called, hearing a tap on the door – a habit her mother had acquired only since James had been to stay.

Her present was wrapped in pink tissue and topped with a gold rosette. 'It's nothing very much. I'd like to have got you a blouse or something, but that shop's wickedly expensive. Emma Jane, it's called. I ask you! I happen to know her name's Doreen – the girl that owns it.'

Alison opened the package to find a triangle of fuchsia-coloured satin – the last word in fashionable lingerie from Emma Jane, presumably. She held the bikini-pants against her waist. They were so minuscule she doubted if they would fit her now, let alone in a few months' time. 'They're . . . lovely, Mum.'

'Not too bright?'

'No.'

'Unusual colour, isn't it?'

She hugged her mother suddenly. It seemed an infinite sadness that her parents had never given her a present she genuinely liked (apart from the wedding dress, which she had chosen herself). The gulf between them had widened since her marriage, yet she was ashamed of being such a snob, when they'd had so little in the way of money or opportunities. It touched her to the quick that her mother had wanted to learn the piano and never had the chance. She tried to picture her sitting at Uncle Fred's Steinway – young, talented and hopeful. The hopes had vanished when she fell pregnant within months of her wedding and was forced to take soulless jobs – waitressing in a Wimpy Bar, stacking shelves in Tesco's – to make ends meet. Even now she was working as a general factotum in a local insurance office, making tea and stuffing envelopes. And as for her married life, she had endured jealousy and fear of being ousted almost from the start, not (as in her own case) after six secure and happy years.

'Mum,' she said, surprising herself, 'I've got something to tell you. Something exciting. I . . . I'm expecting a baby.'

'Oh, *Alison!* That's wonderful. But I thought you said . . .'

'I know. But it . . . happened. After we'd given up hope. You're the very first to know. I haven't even told James yet.'

Her mother stared at her in silence, tears welling in her eyes.

'What's wrong, Mum?'

'Nothing.'

'You *are* pleased, aren't you?'

'Pleased? I'm over the moon. It's just that I can't believe you told me before . . . before James. I'm so honoured, dear. I always thought I . . . I wasn't that important.'

'Mum, don't say that!'

They clung together awkwardly. Her mother felt thin and bony, and the brooch on her collar dug into Alison's neck. Yet she hugged her tightly, fiercely, wanting to make up for all the stony-hearted years. She had grown inside this scraggy body, cell by cell by cell, and that meant such a lot now.

Finally her mother pulled away and gazed at her with undiluted delight. 'To think, after all you've been through . . . And when we'd more or less given up hope. Oh, I *am* thrilled, Alison! Am I allowed to tell your father?'

'Of course. But can we keep it as our secret for the moment? Just in case anything goes wrong.'

'When's it due?'

'Oh, not till the beginning of December. It's very early days.'

'Still, you mustn't overdo it. I said you were looking peaky. I noticed it the minute you walked in. Have you been feeling sick?'

'No. I haven't any symptoms at all – not yet, anyway.'

'I was terribly sick with you. Right from the word go. I threw up every morning, regular as clockwork.'

'Poor Mum. It sounds awful. I only hope I was worth it.'

'Oh, good gracious, yes!'

She was touched and surprised by this emphatic reply; still more so when her mother continued, 'A child's the greatest gift, you know, even if it's a struggle at times bringing them up. Once you've given birth, you see the world in a completely different way. It gives you a sort of . . . stake in life, something to make it all worth while.'

The words were almost poetic in their intensity, an echo of what Francesca had said. Her mother was actually proud of her – hence the photographs all over the house. It had taken thirty years for that to register, because she too now felt maternal pride (although her child was no more than a tiny embryo).

Her mother picked up the gold rosette and stuck it rakishly in her hair. 'Let's go and tell Dad straight away. He'll be tickled pink!'

'D'you think he really will, Mum? I wasn't sure how he'd react.' Secretly she had wondered whether either of them would welcome the prospect of a grandchild, or view it solely in terms of worry and expense. 'When we told you we couldn't have children he seemed, well, rather relieved.'

'Oh, that's just Dad. You know *him*!'

No, she thought, I don't. There was so much she didn't know about her parents' lives. Nor they about hers.

Her mother was folding the pink tissue with elaborate concentration. 'Actually I always wanted another child myself.'

'Really, Mum?'

'Yes, but . . . it didn't work out.'

Had her parents also argued over that, or might they too have had problems conceiving? Of course money would have been a critical factor. In that respect she was fortunate – her baby would want for nothing with James as its father. The thought of him deserting her filled her with sudden panic. The baby *must* be his; it must be. She would make it so by sheer willpower.

'Bill!' her mother called from the landing. 'Wait till you hear Alison's news!'

He mooched out to the hall, newspaper in hand. 'Well, what is it?'

'Guess!' Connie hurried downstairs with new-found energy, the rosette sailing off in her wake.

'She's moving house.'

'No, silly! Whatever for? They've got a lovely place already.'

'She's going round the world in a balloon.'

'Don't be ridiculous! She's . . . expecting a baby.'

He looked puzzled, then incredulous, and finally produced a sheepish smile. 'Well I never!'

'Is that all you can say, Bill? Aren't you going to give her a hug?'

The embrace was hesitant – like his wife, he had never been one for displays of physical affection. Alison drew him closer, pressing her cheek against his. His nicotine breath was another treacherous reminder of Craig, but Craig was over and done with. There was no question in her parents' mind of this baby being anyone's but James's. From now on it *would* be James's.

'I'll have to start knitting,' her mother said, bustling into the sitting-room.

'Knitting, Connie? Don't make me laugh. The last pullover you made came down to my knees.'

'Well, I'll buy some baby clothes then. I saw these dear little Babygros in the good-as-new shop last week.'

'We can do better than that, for God's sake!' He glanced out of the window, as if seeking inspiration in the sodden lawn and dripping trees. 'I know what – I'll set up a savings account for the baby. That'll be my contribution – something in the bank.'

'Oh, no, Dad. It's sweet of you, but there really is no need.' She knew they could ill afford it, and over the years there were so many things they had gone without themselves. 'Just buy a little thing – a plate or mug or –'

'Now listen to me, Alison, I'm not having you dictate. If I can't put something by for my grandchild . . .' He broke off to light a cigarette, tossing the match in the ashtray with a flourish. 'This calls for a celebration. Have we any booze in the house, Connie?'

'Only your beer.'

'That'll do. Let's drink a toast.'

'We can't, Bill! Not in beer.'

'God, *women*! You do fuss!' He marched out to the kitchen and returned with three cans of Carlsberg and three tumblers patterned with bullfighters. 'Well, what shall we drink to? Another little Alison or another little James?'

'Another little James,' she said fervently. Thank God neither Jim nor Craig was red-headed or black. Her parents had both been fair, so if the baby turned out blond she could say it took after them.

'To the baby.' Her father clinked his glass to hers. 'And if it inherits your mother's brains and my beauty it'll be a champion!'

She laughed to hide her unease. Now that she'd told her parents the baby had become a fact: one she could no longer keep from James. Yet she was still extremely worried about incriminating herself. And tomorrow was Palm Sunday, the start of Holy Week. His mind would be on the Passion – or on his passion for Elaine. Was she becoming obsessed with Elaine; inventing their affair to justify her own? Whatever her suspicions, there was no actual tangible proof. Last Sunday he had gone to Communion as usual, and that would be inconceivable if he were involved in an adulterous relationship. However changed he might be, James would never commit sacrilege (as *she* did every week). Perhaps he was attracted to the woman but hadn't yet slept with her. Or had slept with her and confessed it and was now fighting the temptation to do so again? Clearly something was going on: the evidence was mounting. That book he'd brought home last night – an acclaimed new biography of Brahms, inscribed 'with love, Elaine' – why should a mere business colleague spend £30 on a present? Or, come to that, know his favourite composer was Brahms? And why 'with love' if they were meant to be at daggers drawn, as James implied? And he had definitely been embarrassed about the book . . .

'Anyone mind if I watch the football?' Her father switched on the television and ensconced himself in an armchair with his beer.

'There's no point minding,' her mother said tartly. 'You're going to watch it anyway.'

His only response was to turn up the volume.

Alison stared vacantly at the mêlée of running figures on the screen, her ears assailed by the babble of the commentator and the cheering of the crowd. She remembered endless Saturday evenings watching chat shows with her mother while her father was out 'on business'. Through her teens she had done her feeble best to support her mother, conniving in the pretence that Suzanne or Dawn or Angie were just odd acquaintances. She hadn't had a proper adolescence or a chance to sow wild oats of her own. Even at university, she had continued to live at home as stand-in for her father. And the more irresponsible his behaviour, the more she suppressed her own unruly streak. But now, finally, it had burst out, as if it were part of his legacy, transmitted through his genes. Perhaps Jim and Craig had been her wild oats, ten years late – compensation for a restricted youth. In which case, couldn't she forgive herself?

'And Shearer is nearing the goal. Bergkamp tackles him. But he's got clear – he's going to . . . He's scored!'

The renewed uproar from the crowd left her totally unmoved; her mind was still elsewhere. Craig had brought her no real happiness, any more than the Suzannes or Dawns or Angies had her father. He would return from his flings with his tail between his legs, and more morose than ever. No, her happiness lay with James – and the child. *Their* child.

'That's two–nil and I can't see Arsenal coming back now – the referee's looking at his watch . . .'

'The stupid buggers!' Her father gave a bellow of disgust and thumped the arm of his chair.

'Watch that beer, Bill! You'll have it all over the floor.'

During the relative lull of the commercials, Alison stood up. She was supposed to be here to think things out, but this was getting her nowhere. 'I'm going for a walk,' she announced.

'I thought it was raining.'

'It's stopped. I've got a bit of a headache and I could do with some fresh air.'

'I don't wonder, with your father's infernal smoking. You'll have to pack it in, Bill, when the baby comes along.'

'It won't come along *here* very often,' her father muttered, 'judging by past performance.' He banged his glass on the table. 'How many times have we seen them since they married, Connie? It can't be more than half a dozen at the outside.'

Alison looked at him aghast. Surely he must be mistaken. Yet wasn't she constantly making excuses not to go? – they were busy, James was tired, Helen needed her to babysit . . . 'Oh, Dad, I'm sorry. Honestly. Look, we'll come and visit every couple of months, if you like.'

'I'll believe that when I see it.'

'No, I'm serious, Dad. And you must come and stay with *us*.' Her parents would be an antidote to the baby's other grandparents: wealthy, bourgeois, ultra-Catholic Anthony and Evelyn. She wanted her child to be exposed to different points of view. The irony wasn't lost on her that, after years of championing his 'bloody bigoted papists', she had ended up as sceptical as he.

'Well, if you're going, go, for heaven's sake! I can't see a thing with you standing in the way.'

She would be glad to escape – and not just from her father's disconcerting change of mood (owing, she hoped, to Arsenal's poor performance). The potent cocktail of guilt, fear, pity and love had left her feeling hung-over.

'And while you're out, get me twenty Silk Cut, will you?' He fumbled in his pocket. 'Here, take the money.'

'Dad, if I can't buy you a few cigarettes . . .'

'I believe in paying my way, Alison. I always have and I always will.' He pressed a ten-pound note into her hand. 'Keep the change. Buy yourself some daffs.'

'Gosh, thanks, Dad. Anything *you* want, Mum?'

'Only peace and quiet.' She grimaced as the sport came back on and the volume was turned up full-blast again. 'You'd better borrow my mac, dear. They forecast showers all day and you need to be careful in your condition.'

Alison grinned. It was hardly a condition – yet. But she took the mac to avoid argument. ''Bye. Won't be long.'

Outside, the sun had broken through at last. She strode up the hill and branched left towards Elm Farm. The cigarettes could wait – she needed wider horizons after the confines of the house. The fields stretched either side, vibrantly green with new spring wheat. She had walked (or rather run) up here so often as a child, imagining she owned a glorious white horse who would gallop her away, away. Noisy rooks chattered overhead, and in the distance a grey church spire poked out above a clump of trees: a spire without a church.

As she breasted the hill it began to rain once more, although the sun was still shining brightly. The weather, like herself, seemed to be both weeping and rejoicing: puddles underfoot, gold-tinged clouds above. And all at once a rainbow appeared, a magical, shimmering vision hovering overhead. Spellbound, she stood gazing at it, heedless of the rain. The scale of it was awe-inspiring, a huge arc of coloured light spanning the whole skyline. Yet it looked so uncannily close, she felt she could swing herself up in an instant and climb this bridge to another world. For all her scepticism, the notion of a heaven still appealed, along with the angels, wonders and miracles beloved of Father Gregory. The reality of religion had turned out rather differently: petty squabbles and tuneless singing in an ugly suburban church. But life was undoubtedly easier with certainties and rituals. If only there were a secular form of confession, some way of being absolved, even in the absence of a God. She had sinned extremely gravely – against James and against her marriage vows.

Her eyes remained fixed on the colours, which were changing as she watched: the violet on the inside deepening in intensity while the outer band of red paled to a rose-pink. Wasn't it significant that it should appear at the very moment she had to make her decision? No – more than a decision: in the Church's words, a firm purpose of amendment. She could create her own sacrament here, on this lonely hill with the signs of spring all around and the sky soaring, vast, above. She knew what she must do, without instruction from a priest – forswear Jim, however much he pestered, and devote her life to her husband and child, banishing the threat of Elaine by the sheer strength of her love. And her penance would be the fear and guilt about the baby's paternity; a burden she must bear alone, for ever.

She knelt on the damp grass, moved by a deep inner need to make this moment sacred. There would be no more indecision. She had made up her mind and, if it involved deception, so be it. As Linda said, there was more than one morality. She would tell James about the baby as soon as she got home tomorrow night. And then she would confess her lost faith – one deception was enough. Somehow they would work it out, together. And as for Craig, she would honour her promise to try to find him a publisher. But after that, all contact between them would cease.

The rainbow was beginning to fade, merging with the grey of the sky until only part of it remained. Would she settle for only part of James? *No.* She refused to share him with Elaine, not now that she was pregnant. The child must be a catalyst to save and heal the marriage. She and James had each reached a crisis point, and to continue down the path of betrayal would replicate her parents' miserable state: non-communication and mistrust. Whatever his recent lapses, James was innately good. His goodness must redeem them both. Today was a fresh start and the rainbow her heavenly witness. Although it had dwindled to a fragment, its once bright colours were imprinted on her mind; violet, indigo, blue, green, triumphant gold, festive red. A baby was growing inside her, and that was the most fantastic, marvellous, stupendous fact in the world.

She ran back towards the village, wishing she could share the news with the people in the shops, especially Mrs Foster, who owned the general store and who greeted her with pleasure and inquired fondly after James.

'He's fine,' she smiled. He would be – soon. Elaine didn't want children; he'd said she had told him that. And *he* most definitely did.

Having bought the cigarettes and, on impulse, a bottle of champagne for a more appropriate toast, she remembered her father's mention of daffodils. A frothy yellow mass of them was standing in a bucket outside the shop. 'Could I take all these?' she asked. She wanted to celebrate the baby, celebrate her parents, fill every room in their house with hope and spring.

'Certainly, pet. But how are you going to carry them?'

'I'll manage.' That must be her motto from now on. Her precious baby had been swaddled in negativity thus far; Linda suggesting abortion, she single parenthood. Yet this pregnancy was miraculously right, for James as much as her. James might indeed regard it as a miracle, knowing how long and hard his grandmother had prayed. And in spite of her own loss of faith she, too, could just about accept that Cecilia might have some extraordinary power inexplicable to science. In fact pregnancy itself had made her more aware of different kinds of realities; even different criteria for right and wrong. If, for instance, James *had* succumbed to Elaine, perhaps it was only a subconscious bid to prove his virility, since the fertility treatment had rather sapped his confidence. The baby would be his vindication and therefore hers as well.

Mrs Foster had both arms full of daffodils, their stems dripping water down her skirt.

'You'll never cope with this lot! I'll get Bob to run you home in the van. No, it isn't any trouble. He's just going out on a delivery.'

Bob stowed the forest of flowers in the back and helped her climb into the passenger seat. 'Having a party, are you?' he asked, eyeing the champagne.

'Yes, sort of.'

'Mum! Dad!' she called, on opening the front door. 'I've brought you some flowers.'

'Some?' her father grinned. 'You look as if you've bought the bloody shop! You're a strange one and no mistake.'

'Like *you*, Dad.'

'Oh I *say*!' her mother flustered. 'It's ever so generous of you, dear, but what do we do for vases?'

The phone shrilled an interruption. 'I'll just get that. I expect it's Gwen about the jumble sale.' She returned a minute later. 'It's James.'

'You didn't mention the baby, I hope?'

'Of course not. But he does sound rather peculiar. As if he's upset about something.'

She froze. He had found out about Jim. Or Craig. He couldn't take it. He'd rushed straight to Elaine for comfort . . .

'Well, go on, love,' her father urged. 'Don't just stand there like a ninny. It's long-distance – it'll be costing him a bomb.'

She picked up the receiver. 'James?'

'Darling, I . . . I don't know how to tell you this. I'm afraid . . .'

A cold hand clutched her heart. She felt her knees give under her. *No*, she prayed, don't say it.

There was a pause. She sensed he was weeping silently. 'What *is* it, James? What's wrong?'

Another silence. The longest of her life.

'It's Grandma,' he whispered. 'She died an hour ago.'

25

'We have every hope and confidence,' Father Edmund affirmed, 'that our sister Cecilia is now in heaven, walking hand in hand with her parents, reunited with her brother, and waiting to greet her beloved husband Francis when his time comes.'

Francis was sitting in the front pew, flanked by Anthony and Evelyn, his back ramrod straight, as always. How calm he'd been, Alison reflected, through the traumas of the past ten days, fortified, presumably, by his belief that death was a beginning, not an end. Strange that James, the grandson, should be so much more upset than Francis, the spouse. Of course, like everyone else in the family they'd been devastated by Cecilia's massive heart attack, the day before she was due to be discharged, but while Francis had accepted it with stoic resignation James's reaction seemed excessive.

'Sad though we may be at Cecilia's loss,' Father Edmund continued, 'remember it is only temporary. She has passed on to another stage, a happier stage, where she rejoices in the company of the saints.'

Alison fidgeted in her seat, impatient with the Church's denial of death. There stood the coffin in front of the altar, containing Cecilia's corpse. But despite being certified dead by the hospital she was now, apparently, hobnobbing with her deceased relatives in some paradisaical realm.

Next the priest paid tribute to Cecilia's life on earth – her shining faith, her service to the parish, her long and happy marriage, blessed with four fine sons. Alison felt ashamed that her own sadness was tempered by a measure of relief that now Cecilia would never know about her loss of faith.

His homily over, Father Edmund paused a moment to survey the congregation, an unusually large one for the small Esher church. Every seat was taken and many people were standing at the back. Then he stepped down from the pulpit and rejoined the other three concelebrating priests. Alison watched them bow to each other solemnly at the altar. Two of them, James's Uncle John and cousin Adrian, had also officiated at their wedding. How long ago that seemed now; another era altogether, an age of innocence.

The service dragged on interminably, although there was so much else on her mind (Elaine's last phone-call, in particular) most of it passed her by. Why had the vile woman phoned on Easter Sunday of all times; a holiday, a family day? And why had James been so chary about the call? He had taken it in his study with the door firmly shut and, despite her questions, refused to discuss it afterwards.

Surreptitiously she touched her breasts, which had become fuller and firmer of late. She was now six weeks pregnant and each day brought increasing excitement – and increasing apprehension because James still didn't know. Many times she had been on the verge of telling him, but his grief formed a barrier between them; made the news of a birth seem an insensitive intrusion amid the trappings of death. And the guilt and deceit associated with her pregnancy only added to the difficulty. She had waited in vain for a moment when he was more relaxed and approachable but, as executor of Cecilia's will, he was busier even than usual. This last week she'd seen very little of him, and when he *was* at home he was so distant and distracted they might as well have inhabited different worlds. In fact looking at his sisters and their husbands, sitting with their children in the pew directly in front, she couldn't help envying their intimacy – an intimacy and closeness she and James had once enjoyed.

Mechanically she knelt for the Consecration, her mind still far away, until Fiona suddenly hiccupped and brought her back to the proceedings. The twins broke into giggles and were sternly hushed by their mother. Up to now Cecilia's great-grandchildren had been the model of devotion: their hands joined, their heads bowed, their responses to the prayers word-perfect. But of course as cradle Catholics they had imbibed the faith with their mothers' milk, whereas for her it had been an alien graft with, finally, no root-stock to sustain it. However, on an occasion such as this there was no way she could avoid going up for Communion. Indeed the four priests were just descending the altar steps, each holding a ciborium.

She and James shuffled out of the pew and proceeded slowly up the aisle behind the rest of the family. How blasé she had become these days about receiving the Sacrament in a state of sin, committing sacrilege after sacrilege with little compunction. It was unthinkable, though, that James was doing the same. Indeed, as far as she could judge he had been praying throughout the Mass with something of his old fervour. It suddenly occurred to her that the shock of Cecilia's death might have jolted him back to his innate sense of morality. After all, Cecilia had meant so much to him and her own standards were so high that he must have felt appalling guilt at being involved in a liaison at the very time of her death. If he *had* decided to end the affair, and Elaine's reaction was similar to Craig's – pleas, threats, or even blackmail – it might explain the Easter Sunday phone-call. And also explain James's anguished state.

'The Body of Christ.'

'Amen,' she mumbled as Monsignor John placed the Host in her hand. She kept her eyes cast down, shuddering to think what this imposing priest, Cecilia's second son, might say if he could see into her mind. How horrified he'd be if he knew that the radiant bride of six years ago was an adulteress and an unbeliever.

Returning to the pew she was struck yet again by James's air of desolation. He had aged in the last week, going about his duties like a robot. Unobtrusively she took his hand, wishing she could console him. If Elaine *was* being difficult, he must be suffering terribly, having to cope with her threats as well as the pain of bereavement. And the awareness that he'd sinned would increase the burden further – the fact he had to answer to God as well as to those he'd hurt. She squeezed his hand in sympathy, but he seemed lost in a dark reverie. Or was he simply praying again – for forgiveness?

People were still trooping up for Communion, pew after pew after pew – not just family and friends but half the Esher parish by the looks of it. A stark contrast to *her* grandmother's death, remembered vividly from childhood: the dour, half-empty crematorium and no flowers except a bunch of plastic poppies. The church today was awash in flowers, all tasteful white and gold – Easter lilies on the altar, narcissi along the window-sills, the coffin itself crowned with yellow roses.

The organist was playing a doleful tune, the same monotonous phrases repeated over and over in different keys. They had sung all Cecilia's favourite hymns, and there was only one more to come, thank goodness. The Mass was nearly at an end, although the burial still loomed ahead.

With practised grace the pall-bearers lifted the coffin on to their shoulders and followed the four priests down the aisle. Next came Francis, tired and gaunt; Anthony on his left, Evelyn on his right. Then Francis and Cecilia's two other sons and, behind them, Helen, Pauline and their families. Alison took James's arm and they joined the slow procession past the blurred mass of faces, to the solemn strains of the funeral march.

The four priests stood in the porch to greet each member of the family as they came out of the church. Nervously Alison shook hands with them in turn, then moved away to watch the coffin being put into the hearse. It still seemed unbelievable that Cecilia, the matriarch, should be shut up in that box, extinguished, silenced, never more to preside as stern but gracious hostess at White Lodge. She shivered. Although the day was bright, a vicious wind was whipping the blossom off the cherry trees and scattering inappropriate confetti-showers along the path. She linked her arm through James's and went to talk to the twins, hoping they might cheer him up.

'Look at that lady's hat, Uncle James! It's going to blow away.' Emma dashed off to retrieve it.

'Great-Granny's in Heaven now,' Charlotte announced, picking up some fallen blossom and strewing it in her hair.

'Yes, that's right,' Alison murmured dutifully. What would she tell her own child about death?

Not everyone was going on to the cemetery and, as people began to disperse, a figure emerged from the crowd and walked purposefully towards them. She heard James draw in his breath; saw his expression change from frozen grief to alarm.

'Elaine!' he said.

Elaine? What in God's name was *she* doing here?

'I hope you didn't mind me coming, James, but . . .' She spoke rapidly, uncertainly, her fingers plucking at the sleeve of her coat.

James's tone gave nothing away as he introduced them. 'Alison, this is Elaine, the new partner at Garrard Ross. Elaine, my wife, Alison.'

Having exchanged terse greetings, each scrutinized the other – and with reason. There was an uncanny likeness between them: both were dark-eyed and dark-haired and of similar height, although Elaine seemed taller, strangely, in her loose, flowing navy coat and with her hair swept up on top. When James had first talked about Elaine she had pictured a spinsterish type, assuming that anyone who worked in VAT would either be plain and drab or a bit of a battleaxe. But, once her suspicions were aroused, the image had veered to the other extreme: a femme fatale, a goddess. The reality was more troubling altogether. Elaine was a creature of flesh and blood, sensual yet vulnerable, and looking younger than her thirty-seven years. She wore a cloying scent, more suited to the bedroom than a funeral.

'I know how close James was to his grandmother,' the woman said to her.

Yes, I'm sure you do, she thought, poised between rage and apprehension. Why should a business acquaintance attend a family funeral? Either she and James were still seriously involved or the bitch had come to make more trouble for him.

'So I felt I should pay my respects. I just crept in at the back. I didn't want to disturb you.'

Disturb? She was speechless with shock, not just at Elaine's presence here but the fact that she was attractive, and so . . . *real.*

'I live very close, you see,' Elaine went on, sounding almost defensive. 'It only took me a few minutes in the car.'

Where did she live? In some cosy little bachelor flat, convenient for James? Yet, attractive or no, Elaine looked anything but happy. There were dark circles under her eyes as if, like James, she were sleeping badly. No wonder, if they were both suffering from guilt.

At that moment a gust of wind blew Elaine's loose coat open. Immediately she clutched it round her again but not before Alison had glimpsed the hint of a curve swelling out the dress beneath. She froze. Surely Elaine couldn't be . . .? She didn't *want* children. She wasn't married, lived alone . . .

'Are you coming to the cemetery?' James asked guardedly.

'Oh no. I wouldn't dream of it. I don't want to intrude on the family.'

But you *are* intruding, Alison muttered through clenched teeth.

'I'll see you tomorrow, James. In the office.' Elaine gave him a brief smile, then said to Alison, 'It was nice to meet you. Although I'm sorry it was . . . well, in such sad . . .' She spoke in nervous little bursts and, despite her farewell noises, appeared reluctant to leave James. Putting her hand on his arm for an instant, she said in a low voice, 'Could I possibly have a private word?'

He was visibly embarrassed, as if her hand had scorched him. 'Er, yes, of course. Will you excuse me, darling?' he said to Alison.

She stood rooted to the spot as he and Elaine moved a few paces away. How dare she touch him like that and drag him off to whisper secrets like a conspirator. What on earth was going on between them?

They went into a huddle and talked urgently for two or three minutes, each minute seeming to last an hour. When they returned, James, at least, had the grace to look self-conscious, but Elaine fixed her with an ingratiating smile. 'Do please accept my sympathy,' she said.

Sympathy for what? Cecilia's death, or . . .? Alison couldn't take her eyes off the coat, although Elaine clasped it firmly round herself as she finally turned to go; a waft of her musky perfume lingering in the air. So that was James's 'partner' . . .

'James . . .' Evelyn bustled up. 'Can you give the Carters a lift? Oh, and Mrs Barnes if possible?'

'Yes, of course.'

She should be helping Evelyn to organize the cars, but she could only gaze dumbly after Elaine. Why had James not *told* her she was pregnant? Unless . . . No. Impossible. Yet wouldn't it explain the extraordinary change in him – his mounting grief and agitation? It would also mean that, far from giving Elaine up, he was inextricably bound to her.

'Francis was wonderful, wasn't he?' Mrs Carter said, as James helped her into the car. 'So brave.'

Perhaps she was mistaken and Elaine was just broad around the waist. Hardly likely at her age, though, and with an otherwise slender build. Being pregnant made you intensely aware of other women's bodies, and that telltale curve was instantly recognizable. Elaine had it.

'Such a beautiful Mass!' Mrs Barnes enthused. 'I know Cecilia would have loved it.'

If he *had* made Elaine pregnant he must be living in a private hell. Never in a hundred years would he suggest a termination – the first recourse of many men. Indeed, he would *want* the child, despite the dilemma of being caught between two women. What he didn't know was that he had two babies. Involuntarily she put a hand on her own stomach: still completely flat. Elaine's child would be his first-born. Hers was threatened – might even be rejected. But that was her punishment for planning to deceive him. As he was deceiving her.

'Is the cemetery far?' Mrs Carter inquired, as they drove off from the church.

'Oh, no,' said James. 'Only a couple of miles.'

Yet the drive seemed endless, as they crept along behind the hearse, the silence broken only by stilted pleasantries. She *had* to speak to him, alone – ask him outright about Elaine – yet it might be hours before she had a chance. After the burial, everyone was going back to Francis's for tea, then there was the clearing up and . . .

'Who was the younger priest, the fair one?' Mrs Carter asked.

'My cousin Adrian,' James said. 'I'm afraid we lost him to the Jesuits,' he added with a laugh.

The laugh startled her. James hadn't laughed in weeks.

'All our family were educated by the Benedictines,' he explained to Mrs Carter, 'but Adrian had other ideas. He's always been something of a maverick, and he's making waves at Cambridge, so I understand. He was appointed professor of theology there a couple of years ago.'

'How wonderful! And what a privilege to have so many priests in the family.'

'Well, Father Cecil's not family. He's a very old friend of my grandfather. They were at Ampleforth together. He used to come and preach sometimes when I was there as a boy.'

Alison heard little of the ensuing conversation. She was trying to

244

work out why Elaine had come at all. Deliberately to flaunt herself – to show the barren wife she had a better claim on James? Or might she be angry with him for staying in his marriage? Perhaps he thought he could live a double life, with an official childless wife, plus another woman and child on the side. Except that Elaine had scotched any such plan by turning up today. James had clearly been shaken. Maybe the 'private word' was some sort of ultimatum, too urgent to wait for tomorrow.

'Does Francis plan to stay on at White Lodge?'

James continued to answer Mrs Carter's questions with his usual courtesy. 'No, it's too big for him to manage on his own. He'll probably live with Helen. Four children in the house will help to keep his mind off things.'

Mr Carter glanced out of the window. 'Well, at least we've been spared the rain.'

'The wind's bitter, though,' his wife put in. 'You'd think by now we'd have a bit of sunshine.'

Alison, too, looked out, although all she could see was Elaine's navy coat blowing open again. About fourteen weeks, she'd guess, which would mean that the baby was conceived in late December or early January – party time. What a fool she was to have believed that James was slaving in the office every evening. The fact that he hadn't mentioned her pregnancy was highly suspicious in itself. Normally he told her about his colleagues' personal lives, especially as the Reigate branch of Garrard Ross was much smaller and friendlier than the two-hundred-strong head office. Although friendly wasn't quite the word for James's relationship with his 'partner'. How ironical that Elaine, like her, had reason to feel guilt about her baby. Yet, far from creating a bond of empathy, it made her detest the woman still more.

'Right, here we are.' He turned in at the cemetery gates and nosed into a parking space.

Politely he held the door for Mrs Barnes, then helped the Carters out. Watching his impassive face Alison felt an even greater gulf opening up between them – indeed separating her from the throng of other mourners. They all seemed solid and substantial, rooted in the normal world, while she floundered in shifting sands.

Unsteadily she walked towards the grave, staring down into its cavernous hole. Helen whispered something to her; Emma tugged at her hand and pointed to one of the wreaths, but she was unable to respond. Even when Father Edmund began chanting a psalm, little of it registered, until he reached the words:

> *'Give thanks to the Lord for He is good,*
> *His love has no end.'*

'His love has no end,' the mourners repeated, she alone staying silent.

Once, she too had believed that God's love had no end. And James's love likewise. Now both had been proved false. James had withdrawn his love; made another woman pregnant.

> *'It is better to take refuge in the Lord*
> *than to trust in men . . .'*

Each word seemed to hammer at her skull. As her mother said so often, you couldn't trust men.

> *'It is better to take refuge in the Lord*
> *than to trust in princes . . .'*

Her shining prince was enmeshed in a web of deceit, no more virtuous than she was. And now she had no God either, to take refuge in; no hope of rest, or of sleep tonight – or any night.

The priest stepped forward to bless the grave.

'Eternal light,' she heard, but all she could feel was darkness – choking, blinding darkness, as if she, and not Cecilia, were being lowered into the ground. Francis sprinkled a handful of earth on the coffin.

Earth. Soil. Sin.

Someone threw a single rose. No flower, however beautiful, could mask the taint of her life, or James's. Lives, in the plural. Never would they be one flesh again.

Tears coursed down her face. She let them fall unchecked. Who cared if people saw? They would assume that she was crying for Cecilia.

But she was mourning the death of her marriage, the death of love.

26

'What about supper, James?' Alison had hung her black skirt in the wardrobe and was putting on her jeans. 'Would you like an omelette or something?'

'I'm not hungry, thanks.'

Nor she. She had never felt less like eating in her life. Her head throbbed, her back ached and she was ragged with exhaustion. Somehow she had managed to keep going at White Lodge: helping to serve the funeral tea, washing up afterwards, keeping an eye on the children. Now, though, she longed to creep into bed and simply blank things out. But that was not an option. She had resolved to speak to James before the day was over, break the cycle of mutual deception.

'Anyway,' he said, pulling off his tie, 'I think we ought to talk.'

'Talk?' She tensed. So he had got in first.

'I know you're tired, darling, and maybe this isn't the best time, but there's something I have to tell you.' Nervously he rolled up the tie, then unrolled it again, his brow creased in a frown. 'I've been postponing it and postponing it, saying I'd wait till after the funeral. Well, now it *is* after the funeral . . .'

She took a hasty step towards the door. Suddenly she didn't want the discussion after all; couldn't bear to hear the sordid details from his lips. 'I'll just go and make some tea.'

'No, Alison, please don't go. This is . . . difficult.'

Yes, she thought, painful beyond belief. She had been hoping he would deny it; hoping she'd been wrong. Now their entire future was at stake. She went over to the window, keeping her back to him. The curtains were still open and the garden looked murky-black. The wind was a hostile presence, angrily pestering the bushes, shredding the dark clouds. She heard James clear his throat.

'I just can't deceive you any longer,' he said.

'You're not deceiving me.'

'What d'you mean?'

'Well, if you think I haven't guessed . . .'

'Guessed? But how . . .?'

'I'm not a fool.' She blinked frantically to stop the tears.

'Oh, Alison, don't cry.' He came up behind her and put a hand on her shoulder. 'I knew it would be a shock, but I just couldn't go on lying.'

Furiously she shook his hand off. 'Lying's kinder sometimes.'

'Maybe, but I hate it. I'll continue deceiving the family, if I have to, but not you.'

The pause which followed seemed endless. In the fraught silence one part of her was screaming at him, 'Get on with it, get *on* with it!' while the other part entreated, 'No, don't say, don't say.' His words could sound the death-knell of their marriage.

'I do feel dreadful about it . . .'

'Stop prevaricating, James,' she snapped, finally losing patience and turning round to face him. 'Either speak or shut up.'

'It's . . . it's not easy.'

No easier for her. She was still tempted to escape downstairs, slam the door on him.

Again he made a move to touch her, reaching for her hand. 'It seems, well, unforgivable, getting you so deeply involved in the faith and then abandoning it myself.'

Perplexed, she pulled away. 'James, what are you talking about?'

'What I've just said. I can't in all conscience remain a member of the Church.'

'Because of Elaine, you mean?'

'Elaine? What's she got to do with it?'

'Well, everything, I should have thought.'

'But I've never mentioned it to Elaine. Why on earth should I? I haven't spoken to anyone, except the priests I went to see. And they were no help. They just told me to keep praying and carrying out my religious duties, and eventually my faith would come back. But they're wrong, I know – it won't.'

'You've . . . lost your *faith*?' she asked.

He too looked bewildered now. 'But you said you knew. You'd guessed.'

She pressed her hand against her forehead, trying to clear the pain and confusion. Was he deliberately misleading her, putting up a smoke-screen to divert attention from Elaine?

'Don't imagine for a moment that it wasn't a terrible struggle. I've been agonizing about it for ages. I even made an appointment to see the Abbot of Ampleforth when he was down in London last month. And I've talked to Father Gregory dozens of times.'

He sounded burningly sincere. Even so, she still couldn't grasp it. They should be discussing Elaine, not priests. Her nerves were so raw, perhaps she'd misunderstood. 'James, have I got this right? You don't believe any more?'

'No.' He took off his jacket and stood holding it, his shoulders hunched. 'It seems blasphemous to say so, but' – he shrugged – 'the whole thing's sort of . . . gone.'

'Gone?' she repeated, bemused. James without his faith was almost inconceivable. And what about his family? If *she* had feared their censure, how much worse for him: the once-monk, the Eucharistic minister, bulwark of the local church. 'But how? When? What happened?'

He put the jacket on a hanger, his movements slow and disjointed, as if he were moving in a dream. 'Well,' he said at last, 'it's actually been going on for months. But it was Grandma's death which brought things to a head. When I saw her in the hospital on the Saturday afternoon she looked so utterly . . . dead. And I realized that was the end. Not the start of a new life and all those platitudes at the funeral. But I just couldn't tell you, darling. I mean, I was the one who'd brought you into the Church, and I know how important it is to you and how close you are to Father Peter –'

'Fuck Father Peter!' She almost spat the words out.

'Alison!'

All at once, she began to laugh – great hurting laughs which racked her body. He must think her hysterical. She *was* hysterical. Not just with shock, with overwhelming relief that her own loss of faith would not now cause him pain. Words tumbled out incoherently as she explained her identical position.

He stared at her in astonishment. 'You mean, all this time you've been – ?'

'Yes.'

'But you never said a thing.'

'Nor did you.'

'I didn't want to upset you.'

249

She looked at him uncertainly. 'James, are you sure you're telling me the truth?' She still had deep suspicions about Elaine, although he hadn't actually mentioned her. Was she behind this in some way; she the one who had turned him against his religion?

'Alison' – he took her hand – 'you know I would never lie to you, let alone about something as important as this. I've been absolutely distraught, trying to work out how to break it to you. I've lain awake practically every night . . .'

'I know,' she said feelingly.

'You mean, you were awake too?'

She nodded.

'But why on earth didn't you say?'

'I didn't want to worry you either. So I just shut my eyes and pretended to be asleep.'

'And pretended to pray, I suppose? Like me.'

'Yes.'

'And Father Peter doesn't know? You just went on working for the church?'

'That's right. What are we going to *do*, James? How can we extricate ourselves?'

He shook his head. 'It doesn't bear thinking about. But tell me more about your side of things. I still can't take it in.'

She sank down on the bed. Despite the relief, she also felt annoyance, however irrational or unfair. Why couldn't James have told her long ago; saved her the heartache about telling *him*; spared her all those Masses and hypocritical prayer sessions? But of course he might be thinking the same. She was suddenly sick of religion and everything to do with it and wanted to crawl under the duvet and forget the subject altogether. But she could see James was desperate to talk.

Wearily she got to her feet. 'I need a drink,' she said. 'And you look as if you could do with one.'

Downstairs, she poured them each a Scotch, and sat in silence, her hands cupped around her glass. She ought to be rejoicing that one enormous burden was lifted, but there were too many other imponderables . . .

James took a reflective sip of whisky. 'It's extraordinary that we should both be in the same boat. What went wrong, I wonder?'

'I was about to ask you the same thing. It's a much greater upheaval for *you* to lose your faith.' She made an effort to sound less hostile. For James this was a cataclysmic event, a complete and utter reversal of all he had once held dear. 'When did you first have doubts?'

'Probably at the age of twelve.'

'*What?* But I thought . . .'

'Yes, so did everyone – James the steadfast Catholic, James the plaster saint. I swallowed it all myself. I didn't have much choice, the way I was brought up. Doubts were sinful and had to be suppressed. I was so well drilled in the party line it became second nature very early on. Christ is with His Church to the end of time, so it's divinely inspired, invariably right . . .'

'Yes, but that makes it all the more unlikely that you'd simply throw it off.'

'I didn't simply throw it off. It's been going for years at some subconscious level. And latterly the doubts became more and more insistent. But I did my best to see them as just weakness and temptation, and tried to convince myself that prayer would get me through. While Grandma was alive I couldn't face the possibility that it was more than just a passing stage. It's only now she's . . . gone that I can see how totally she controlled me, right from the beginning. Let's face it, darling, I'm only *here* because of her, as I've never been allowed to forget. Her prayers saved my life. It was a miracle, her miracle, and a debt I knew I had to repay. Even when I was tiny, she impressed on me that she – and God – had great ambitions for me. She always wanted me to be a priest or, even better, a saint. That's very heady stuff for a boy. I *did* feel special, it's true, but also I was scared stiff of letting her down. I saw so much of her as a child – too much, I realize now. She regarded me as her life's work, you see, a soul to be groomed for God. I was her only grandson and, as *she*'d had four sons, she considered herself an authority. And of course sons were special anyway, because only they could become priests. Sometimes I longed to break out and do something really wicked, just to rebel against what she saw as a divine plan.'

'James, it sounds appalling.'

'Yes, I suppose it was. Although it's taken me a heck of a time to face up to it.' He began prowling about the room, restless like the wind outside. 'I understand now, darling – it's all about control. Our family are control freaks. Everything has to be organized and tidy. No loose ends, no uncertainties. Religion included. An authoritarian Church suited us down to the ground. Free thinking's far too dangerous. And doubts and voids are terrifying. But, you know, once I started questioning, the whole fabric fell apart. All those proofs of the existence of God, they're . . .'

She slumped back on the sofa, feeling increasingly resentful. For her, the crucial issue was Elaine, whereas he was still in full flow, discoursing on the proofs of the existence of God. It was as if he were making up for the weeks of torpid grief – perhaps even for the years of childhood submission. Yet everything he'd said could in fact relate back to Elaine. Perhaps he had only considered an affair with her when (and because) he was free of religious restraints – as had happened in her own case.

'You're forbidden to question anything,' he continued, pacing to the window and back. 'I had plenty of questions, even as a child, but Grandma had the answers – the *only* answers, naturally. And how could I defy the family saint? I was tied to Mother Church – Grandmother Church, I should say – by an umbilical cord.'

'James, you sound so bitter.'

'I'm not. I'm really not. I must admit I did feel awful at first – very much at sea and terribly guilty, of course. But now there's this fantastic sense of freedom, as if an immense weight's been lifted from me. I know that must seem disloyal, especially so soon after Grandma's death. And there were lots of good things anyway. She showered me with love and took me to wonderful churches all over the world. And we lit candles and said novenas together, and I revelled in the ritual and drama and the gratifying idea that God had singled me out as His Elect. In my teens it was more difficult. Sex reared its ugly head. And it wasn't just sex, either. Every strong emotion was a sin – pride, anger, envy . . . My role in life was to be good, and that was it.'

'James, you *are* good. Truly. At least I've always assumed so. But there's something I need to ask you – '

'You know, I'm not so sure I *am* good.'

'What do you mean?' Fear prickled down her spine again.

'Well, obviously I submitted out of fear, and there's no virtue in that, is there? The same way as the medieval Church controlled the population with horrific tales of the Last Judgement, and carvings in the churches showing the damned souls writhing in hell. Grandma made me so terrified of hell I didn't dare put a foot wrong.' He gave a sudden laugh. 'They're supposed to have worked out the temperature of hell from descriptions in the Bible: it's four hundred and forty-five degrees Celsius. Just imagine burning in *that* for all eternity!'

He picked up a card on the mantlepiece – from Francesca in São Paulo – and stood looking at it briefly. 'When I was little, Grandma used to bring me back postcards of all the devils in the cathedrals she visited: Chartres, Reims, Albi – you name it. I collected devils like other boys collect stamps. Oh, I realize it sounds funny, but even in the seminary, as grown men, we discussed hell and sin and all the rest of it. And although the official line in this day and age is that hell is simply the absence of God, there was one old chap who loved piling on the agony. He used to preach ghoulish sermons about worms crawling through your eyes when you were dead. And his sadistic accounts of the eternal torments in store for us made Dante's *Inferno* seem positively cosy.' He laughed again, although mirthlessly. 'And, talking of the seminary, Grandma was absolutely devastated when I left. Her reaction so upset me I vowed never to let her down again as long as she lived. I based the whole of my life on *her* standards, until the weekend before last, when she, well . . . set me free. That's an appalling admission, isn't it? I'm ashamed to hear myself say it.'

'No, James. I understand. But I think we need to –'

'It beats me why I never saw it before. It wasn't until I actually looked at her corpse that I realized she was just . . . an old woman. A very dear old woman, who'd given me a great deal throughout my life, but certainly not a saint, or a seer, or a miracle-worker, or all those things I'd been led to believe. In fact,' he said, tossing the card back on the mantlepiece, 'you could almost say it was an abuse of power.'

'James, calm down. You're beginning to shout.'

'I'm sorry, darling. Forgive me. I'm being awfully selfish, ranting on like this, when it must all be a tremendous shock. I've been living with it for weeks, but for you it's a bolt out of the blue.' He sat down heavily and drained his whisky in a couple of swift gulps. 'I don't know what's got into

253

me. I suppose it's such a relief to have told you at last. I feel as if I've just emerged from a long, dark tunnel and the light has gone to my head. This, too,' he said, indicating the empty glass. 'I loathed all the deception, but I didn't want to rock the boat and cause you scandal, as the Church says. So I carried on praying and obeying the priests. And I'm very good at obeying,' he laughed, leaning across to kiss her. 'Oh, darling, thank heavens I've finally got it off my chest! But now it's your turn. I'm still rather mystified about how it happened with you.'

'Just a minute, James. There's something important you *haven't* told me yet.'

'What do you mean?'

'Well, Elaine . . .'

'Elaine!' He held his head in his hands and let out a muffled groan. 'Oh Lord,' he said. 'That's another huge problem in itself.'

'Yes, so I gathered,' she said tersely.

'You can't have guessed that too. Unless you're psychic.'

'All I know is that something's going on between you. And you'd better tell me exactly what.'

'Let's leave it till the morning, shall we? It's such a business and we're both shattered after the funeral.'

'For God's sake, James, you can't fob me off any longer. I'm not a fool, you know. I mean, the way the woman keeps pestering you, and then turning up today of all days . . . Why doesn't she just come out with it and admit she's having an affair with you?'

'An *affair*? Are you out of your mind? I don't even like her much, let alone –'

'Come off it, James. She's damned attractive.'

'Not to me. And anyway I don't believe in affairs. I may have lost my faith, Alison, but not my ideals. And fidelity is one of them, even if it's old-fashioned.'

'I happen to know she's pregnant. Or are you going to deny that too?'

'Hardly. It's her pregnancy that's the problem.'

'I'm sure it is,' she said icily. 'James, I want the truth. Our marriage is on the line. Look me straight in the eye and tell me whether the baby's yours.'

'*Mine?*' His face expressed total incredulity. 'How could you even think such a thing?'

She had her answer. It was patently clear he was telling the truth. Her own child was saved. 'Oh, I'm so relieved, I just can't tell you! I've been in a terrible state about it.'

'Sweetheart, I'm *sorry*. It never crossed my mind you'd –'

'James, you're such an innocent. Can't you see how suspicious it looked, spending all that time with another woman and being so secretive?'

'I did really hate the secrecy, believe me. But Elaine made me promise not to tell a soul. I said I never had secrets from you, but she got so frantic I was forced to agree. She's normally a pretty tough customer, but being pregnant seems to have thrown her off balance. I've never seen such a change in anyone. And I do feel partly to blame. You see, one day when we were working late she asked me, sort of casually, what I thought about abortion. It was in the news at the time, so I never dreamed she was talking personally. Well, I didn't mince my words. After what *we*'ve been through, and you especially, darling, it's hard to be dispassionate. I said thousands of women would give their right arm for a baby and how wrong it was to take a life when someone else could give that baby a chance – people who've moved heaven and earth trying to have their own. To my horror, Alison, she burst into tears and admitted *she* was pregnant but she didn't want the child.'

'Whose child is it?' Alison tried to shut out treacherous memories of beer cellars, Watford flats.

'Well, apparently she's been involved with a chap for years. He's married with two daughters, but as she likes her independence and never wanted children herself she doesn't mind the set-up. In fact the pregnancy was the most awful shock, and she just can't understand how it happened when she's always been so careful. I didn't like to go into details ... To be honest, I was surprised she confided in me at all, but she said she didn't trust anyone else, not even her closest friend.'

'And she must realize you're the most trustworthy person there is.' Alison took his hand and traced the curve of his wedding ring – solid, reassuring. How could she have doubted him? It seemed unforgivable now.

'Actually I wasn't all that sympathetic at first. I felt jealous, I have to say, and even angry. It seems so unfair, when we've tried everything and still haven't got a child.'

But we have, we *have*, she was on the brink of saying. This surely was the moment. Yet still she hesitated. Paradoxically it needed rehearsal to sound spontaneous, and being so overwrought, she might blurt it out all wrong and ruin everything.

'Anyway, when I realized how upset she was I did my best to help. You see, at that stage she hadn't even told her chap. She knew he'd probably want her to get rid of it, and I think *she* felt rather torn. Although in theory she's never wanted children, now that she's pregnant things seem less clear cut. And she's thirty-eight in August, so this might be her only chance – you know, the whole biological time-clock thing.'

Suddenly a branch outside the window tapped against the pane, shaken by the wind. He broke off, startled, looking round for the source of the noise. In the brief silence, she tried to think up words and phrases that would sound natural and impromptu. But as she drew in her breath to speak James pre-empted her.

'Well, as you can imagine, I advised her to keep the baby, or at least not rush into something she'd regret. I assumed she hadn't taken any notice, because the very next day she booked into a clinic to have a termination. But for some reason she didn't go through with it. Of course I was concerned that I'd influenced her unduly, and she's become worryingly dependent on me since. I suggested she get professional help and perhaps find out about having the child adopted. But she couldn't stand the idea of busybody social workers snooping into her private life. Then, one evening when we were working late again, I had a flash of inspiration.' Slowly he got up and took the glasses to the sideboard to refill them. For some moments he stood motionless, the bottle in his hand. 'This may shock you, darling. It shocked me at the time – I mean, the fact that it should even occur to me. But now I think it could just be the answer. If you agree, that is. Oh, Alison,' he said, handing her the glass, 'all this time I've been dying to discuss it with you, but it was only today that Elaine said I could. She sent me an e-mail this morning.'

'An e-mail?'

'Don't worry, darling. Strictly coded. Just saying she agreed to my plan and to go ahead and tell you.'

Alison was too incensed to speak. How dare they send e-mails to each other about her, plot behind her back.

'Of course when she turned up at the funeral I thought she must have changed her mind. But she just wanted to know what you'd said. That's what the "private word" was all about. And to think you suspected we were . . . Oh Lord, I'm sorry to have put you through all that. I was so busy working out the plan it never struck me that our behaviour might seem odd.'

'Very odd.' She smiled, which took an effort. She had already guessed his plan, and it was no longer appropriate. 'So you suggested we adopt her child,' she said tonelessly.

'Well, it's more complicated than that. The idea is that as soon as she has the baby I register the birth in the name of Egerton, with me as the baby's father and you as its mother.'

She stared at him, aghast. 'But, James, that . . . that's illegal, surely?'

He nodded. 'Yes, perjury. But better than killing a child, which was still on the cards until she e-mailed me today. I've already made some inquiries, and surprisingly the plan is feasible – just about. Of course, it would involve us all in lying, but –'

'James, I can't believe I'm hearing this. Are you out of your mind?' This couldn't be the man she'd married, the law-abiding, moral citizen.

'Desperate situations require desperate measures, Alison. And there's another problem, too. When the baby's born Elaine might change her mind. It's very common, apparently, for the mother–baby bond to be so strong that it overrides everything else.'

'Yes, I know.' Even before it's born, she thought, picturing the embryo curled up snugly inside her. She *had* to tell him – now. Yet how could she drop such a bombshell at the very moment he was offering her a baby via a different route? And when she was so outraged at the thought of Elaine turning them into criminals? He obviously expected her to be overjoyed, despite the dubious methods he was proposing. In any case she didn't want Elaine's child – she wanted hers, theirs. 'James, it's not just a matter of her changing her mind. She . . . she might tell people we'd lied, and then we'd really be in trouble. Surely you wouldn't take a risk like that?'

'I'd go to virtually any lengths for a child. And I thought you'd feel the same. I know how depressed you've been since Prescott more or less wrote us off.'

She tilted her glass this way and that, watching the liquid swirl dangerously near the brim. She, too, had reached danger-point and had to fight to keep control. James had talked about control as a bad thing. But worse to lose it and blow everything apart.

'I'm not saying it's simple, Alison. In fact it's the most dreadful dilemma I've ever been in. And even if we succeed there's still the possibility that Elaine could claim the child back at any time, unless we adopted it legally. That's a different procedure altogether – I'd declare myself as father, with Elaine as mother, then you'd apply for what's called step-parent adoption.'

'Step-parent?' This was becoming surreal. *Tell* him, she urged herself. Go on. The longer you put it off, the harder it will be. It had already assumed such ridiculous proportions that just thinking about it induced panic.

She banged her glass down on the coffee-table. Whisky on an empty stomach had made her headache worse. She shouldn't be drinking alcohol at all, but she'd succumbed to the temptation of a taste of golden oblivion. It was James who was oblivious, though – churning out all this rigmarole, with no regard for her feelings.

'It'd have to go through the courts, of course, and I'm no keener on red tape than Elaine is, especially if we're lying through our teeth. But the adoption people I spoke to seemed to think we stood a reasonably good chance, since Elaine doesn't want the child and I'm its legal father . . .'

'You mean you lied to them too?'

'Yes, I had to, to find out what the situation was. Don't look so horrified. I didn't do it lightly.'

'I *am* horrified. You just said you never lied.'

'Not to you.'

'That's splitting hairs, James – and a sort of lie itself. The whole thing's a lie, can't you see?'

He let out a strangled noise, part sigh, part groan. 'Yes, I know. It's been hell, these last few weeks. I wondered if I was losing my sense of morality – deceiving you, deceiving the authorities. I've been lying awake night after night struggling with my conscience. The Church lays everything down in such meticulous detail, if you lose that framework you're thrown on to your own devices. You have to re-examine all you took for granted and decide for yourself what's right or wrong. And it can be very difficult,' he said, his voice tense, as if he were re-experiencing the conflict, 'because Catholicism tends to suppress the moral subtleties; the important grey area between dogmatic black and white. I still need principles, Alison, but *new* ones, including my duty to you. I feel I almost . . . *owe* you a child. After all, it was my religion that wouldn't allow you IVF. And you were the one who had to suffer the ghastly side-effects of the drugs.'

'Forget me. That's all over anyway. It's you I'm concerned about – your so-called principles. They sound downright immoral. Hasn't it occurred to you that the baby has some rights in all this? Or are you prepared to let it grow up without a clue about its true identity? I suppose you think ignorance is bliss. Well, it's not, James! It's a recipe for disaster.' How two-faced she was. Her own child would also be deceived, at least about its father.

'Of course there are problems – hideous ones. I'm not denying that for a second. And of course the child should come first. But isn't the right to life the most basic right of all? Church or no Church, you and I oppose abortion. And the main point is, Elaine's not going through with the abortion now. She's willing to hand the baby over the day it's born – if you agree, that is. Everything depends on you – that stands to reason. But I mentioned what you said about being so desperate for a child that you could understand why people stole them from prams. And d'you know what Elaine –?'

Alison sprang to her feet in fury. 'How dare you discuss me with that . . . that woman! And tell her things I said to you in private.'

'But, darling, I only meant to –'

'James, you've had your say. It's *my* turn. The thought of you being in cahoots with some stranger, arranging my life without even consulting me. It's outrageous!'

'But, Alison, I wasn't free to –'

'Saddling me with babies I don't want . . . Working out your ludicrous little schemes together. I can't think what's got into you. I've never known you like this.'

'And I've never known *you* like this.' He too stood up, to confront her. 'You've been unbearable the last couple of months, if you really want to know. I've tried to make allowances. I thought you were in despair about not being able to conceive. But now you turn round and say you don't want a child.'

'I do want a child. I want *our* child.'

'That's impossible. You know it is. I love you, Alison, and I'd do anything to make you happy. I was fool enough to think you'd jump at this chance. But obviously I've got it wrong.'

'No!' she shouted. 'You don't understand.'

'How can I understand if you shout and scream like a fishwife? Can't we sit down calmly and discuss it?'

'I'm sick of discussing Elaine! She's ruined everything. Why not go and live with her if you want her child so much!'

'Alison, for heaven's sake, I've told you, you're the one who makes the decision. If you don't want her baby – OK, that's the end of it. But she happens to be in trouble and we should at least try to be compassionate.'

'Compassionate? You must be joking! You're a hypocrite, James, can't you see? – forever preaching at people when you're worse than any of them. Look at you, sticking your nose into everyone else's business and giving irresponsible advice. And prepared to deceive an innocent child about who its parents are. And involving me as well, dragging me into court cases just because you've set yourself up as some great Defender of Life. You're playing God – which is pretty rich when you don't even believe in God any more. And that's another thing. You refused to let me have IVF because of your precious Pope. And of course he's the world authority on babies, isn't he? And now you suddenly change tack and decide he's talking rot. But it's too late. You don't care what you put me through.'

'I do care, Alison. I feel guilty as hell.'

'Fuck your guilt!' she yelled. 'I don't want it. I've had enough. I'm going. If you need a wife, send a bloody e-mail to Elaine.' She blundered into the hall and slammed out of the front door.

She heard him coming after her and broke into a run; stumbling, tripping, tears streaming down her face. His footsteps pounded nearer, advancing on her, closing in. He finally caught up and clasped her in his arms.

'I do need a wife,' he said gently, stroking the hair back from her face.

'I'm sorry, darling. I'm terribly terribly sorry. I've been an insensitive fool. You're right. Let's forget about babies, and –'

'We can't,' she sobbed. 'We can't. *We're* going to have a baby. I'm pregnant, James. I couldn't tell you before. I . . . I wanted to be sure. Absolutely certain. So as not to dash your hopes if it wasn't . . . isn't . . . You see, I've only missed one period and –'

'You're . . . pregnant?' His words were drowned by a passing car: a flash of headlights, a roar fading to a drone. Then silence.

'Yes, I'm pregnant,' she repeated, louder. An old man walking his dog looked at her in surprise. She didn't care. All that mattered was James's reaction. He seemed stunned; his body rigid, his face a mask. The wind was flapping at his shirt, untidying his hair, waiting to pounce on his words and snatch them maliciously away.

But there *were* no words. He simply gripped her arm, so tight it hurt, and led her back towards the house, saying nothing.

Nothing.

27

James came up behind her and slipped his arms around her waist. Then he moved one hand to her stomach, tentatively, as if it were made of glass. 'Darling, are you sure it's . . . safe?'

She nodded. Everything was safe now. Her child, her husband, a family house, at last, secure against the wind.

'I mean, it won't harm the baby if we – ?'

'The baby'll be fine.' She could feel his erection pressing against her bare back. She would re-conceive her child tonight and make James its undisputed father. The depth of his longing for a child had staggered her. He was prepared to commit a criminal offence for a baby that wasn't biologically his, conceived by a woman he didn't like and a man he didn't know. Her own pregnancy had come at the perfect time to release him from a whole tangle of lies.

'Kneel, darling,' he whispered, gently pushing her down on the bed.

'N . . . no, James.' That was Craig's position, and Craig must never,

ever, enter this room or impinge on her and James again. 'I'd like you just to hold me a while.' Lying back, she drew him down towards her; kissing his eyes, nose, brow, the top of his head and finally his lips – a restrained but sensuous kiss, just brushing mouth with mouth.

'Your breasts feel wonderful.' He cupped them in his hands. 'So full and sort of taut. I can't think how I didn't notice.'

Because I tried to hide them from you, she thought. Now she could flaunt her body, revel in his approval. He was gazing at her with awe, as if a miracle had happened. It *was* a miracle.

'I still can't quite believe it. I'm frightened of waking up and finding it's just a dream.'

She kissed him again to dispel his doubts. He had been brusque at first, suspecting she might be playing a cruel joke on him, then dumbfounded, and only after she had managed to convince him had he taken her in his arms and told her she was the most brilliant, amazing, clever wife in the world.

Now, though, he seemed nervous of making love, perhaps fearing it might dislodge their precious child. She ran her hand across his chest, then slowly down his stomach, using the lightest teasing pressure; down further to the tight-sprung coils of hair. Grazing her nails through the hair, she built up a slow, caressing rhythm – to and fro, to and fro – then continued with soft feathering strokes along the length of his penis.

She was touched to see that despite his increasing excitement he entered her with the utmost care, as if still worried about hurting the baby. She thrust herself against him, wanting to show him they could both let go; no more need for caution or deception.

He responded instantly, moving faster, picking up her rhythm; all the tension of the last few weeks unlocking from their bodies. The presence of the baby seemed to add a new dimension, as if it, too, rejoiced in this release.

'Darling, no, I'm coming!' James tried to hold back, but she deliberately rocked under him, and suddenly all his pent-up feelings poured into her and into her, fusing in their child.

'I'm sorry,' he said, laying his head on her breasts. 'I couldn't stop myself. I haven't done that since our honeymoon. Remember?'

'Mm. It was wonderful. And tonight was even better.'

'Really? For you too?'

'Oh, yes.' She lay in the silence, lazily stroking his hair. Her body felt exquisite; doing what it was born to do. She imagined the baby growing cell by cell – now established as a real entity, and welcomed by its father.

'Happy?' he murmured.

'Yes, blissful.'

'Think we'll sleep tonight?'

'For a hundred years! Oh, James.' She kissed him. 'I do love you.'

'And I love you. And the baby. What shall we call it?'

'How about Francis, if it's a boy? I thought that might please poor Francis, now he's lost Cecilia.'

'Oh yes, he'd be thrilled.'

'And do you like Francesca for a girl?'

'Mm. It's pretty. And actually it's another family name. My great grandmother was called Francesca. In fact Grandpa was named after her, so we'll be continuing the tradition.'

'That's nice. But I'd also like it for Francesca de Romero. If it hadn't been for her, you know, I'd never have met you.'

'I hope you don't regret it. Just recently I seem to have caused you nothing but trouble.'

'James,' she said, 'I owe Francesca everything. I couldn't have a better husband.' Abruptly she sat up, knelt astride his body and swept her long curtain of hair back and forth across his chest. Gratified to see his penis stir, she wound one tress around it, binding it gently tighter.

Watching in fascination, he gripped her hips to lever himself up and took first one nipple, then the other, into his mouth. 'Imagine the baby doing this,' he whispered.

'D'you think you might be jealous?'

'Possibly. But excited too. Oh, darling, your hair's pulling me stiff!' Urgently he uncoiled it, so that she was free to lie on top of him. 'Let's not sleep quite yet. I want to make it a real honeymoon.'

Alison winced at the strident wail of the alarm clock. 'Quick, James, turn it off. Pretend we didn't hear it.'

'I can't.' He reached out a naked arm and fumbled for the clock. 'I've got that wretched meeting with Brian Webster.'

'Say you're not well.'

'Well, actually, I have got a raging headache. Too much Scotch last night.'

'Too much sex last night!' Her own headache had vanished magically as soon as James had expressed delight about the baby. She tried to coax him back under the covers. 'We're on honeymoon, remember, so we stay in bed all day.'

'Sweetheart, I'd love to, but –'

'D'you realize, James, all the years we've been married, you've never ever phoned in sick. Would it really hurt just once?'

'I don't like lying to them.'

'If you have a headache, you *are* sick.'

'Hardly. A couple of aspirin will take care of that.'

'But you're exhausted. We both are. This is the first night we've slept in ages.'

He yawned hugely, as if to prove her right. 'I must go in. I promised Elaine.'

'James,' she said, more harshly than she'd intended, 'I don't want you to speak to Elaine until we've decided what to do. From now on, there's to be no plotting behind my back.'

'OK. That's only fair. And anyway I don't know what to say to her. It's all become so complicated. But I hate to let her down.'

'Look, we must be clear in our own minds before you commit yourself to anything. Otherwise you may make things worse. Honestly, darling, we could do with a day off, just to work it all out. For once in your life can't you tell the tiniest of white lies and say you think you're going down with flu? After all, it's not quite in the same league as perjury!'

He had the grace to smile. 'All right, I'll see what I can do. I'm sure Elaine can deal with Brian on her own.'

'Now you're talking sense. We do desperately need some time to ourselves. No, don't get up – I'm going to make some tea.'

'Tea in bed. Bliss!'

'And don't fret about the office. Nobody'll be in for another couple of hours.'

She came back with a glass of water and the aspirin. 'By the way, if it makes it easier *I* can phone Garrard Ross for you and tell them you're in bed. Which I hope will be true!'

He laughed. 'No, I'd better do it. I'll need to speak to Elaine.'

'You're worried about her, aren't you?'

'Yes, Alison, I am. She did seem so relieved, you see, not to have to get rid of the baby, especially at this late stage.'

'How far is she?'

'Sixteen weeks. And yesterday she felt it move for the first time. A faint sort of flutter, she said, but enough to convince her it was – well, *real* was how she put it.'

Awesomely real, Alison thought, as she unscrewed the aspirin bottle and tipped two into James's palm. At sixteen weeks the embryo became a foetus and had toes, fingers, eyelids, nails . . .

'Of course I've influenced her in that respect. I told her all along that even a day-old embryo was a human being with a right to life.' James swallowed the aspirin with two swift gulps of water. 'I'm beginning to see I shouldn't have interfered, let alone put pressure on her. And it was definitely wrong to keep labouring the point that you and I would make the perfect parents for her child. I was so concerned with *our* needs, I didn't allow her any space to decide for herself. In fact, reflecting on it now, I suspect I drew her into something which wasn't really in her interests at all.'

'But, James, you meant well. You were doing it for me too, remember, not just for yourself.'

'Maybe. But it was still selfish and high-handed. And I'm afraid having good intentions is no excuse. No, it's a mess, I have to say, and a lot of it's my fault.'

Miserably, she went downstairs to put the kettle on. Whatever her feelings about Elaine, the woman was in a terrible predicament. And she hated to see James blame himself. If anyone should feel guilt, it was *her* – the way she had shouted and even sworn at him last night. 'Fuck' was a legacy from Craig, which made her all the more ashamed. There was not the slightest justification for such an outburst. She had saddled James with her own crimes. He was innocent.

She peered out at the garden, still wreathed in early morning mist. Leaves and broken twigs were littered on the lawn, casualties of the wind last night. The swing was wet with dew; the Wendy house looked garish against the sober greens and browns. Her child would be playing there in a couple of years, and perhaps its namesake, Francesca, would come over to visit with Zach, and they could talk babies as well as novels. Her problems were solved, whereas Elaine's were worse than ever. Elaine had no husband, no father for her baby, no one to confide in except James. And when she discovered he was to have a child of his own, she would probably feel the same jealousy and resentment as *she* had felt towards Elaine's unborn child. Didn't she have a duty to help – for James's sake? She had treated him so badly: lied to him, betrayed him, foisted a child on him which might not even be his. And yet she knew instinctively that she wanted nothing to do with Elaine; wanted to escape the whole imbroglio and never hear her name again.

The kettle clicked itself off, summoning her attention. Lovingly she spread a cloth on the best silver tray, got out the bone-china cups; even went barefoot into the garden to pick an early rose which she propped against the milk jug. She must make things special for James.

She took the tray upstairs and found him sitting up in bed with a book on his lap. He wasn't reading, though, just staring into space, running his fingers distractedly along the edge of the page – a habit that had become increasingly familiar during the past few weeks. Only now did she recognize what appalling strain he'd been under: struggling to keep his faith; going to desperate lengths to obtain a child. And she had been no help – indeed had added to his problems.

Having poured his tea, she sat beside him on the bed. 'Darling, I've been thinking. Couldn't Elaine just get the baby adopted in the normal way? Hundreds of couples are dying for a child. I know you said she doesn't want all the red tape, but –'

'It's not as simple as that. Adoption agencies always press for information about the father, so the child has something to go on when it's older and can build up a picture of both its parents. Elaine's terrified he'll get drawn in.'

'But surely he must know by now?'

'Yes, he does, and he's none too pleased. As far as I can gather, he's in some high-profile job – she's very cagey about what he does exactly, but it's obvious that she dreads the thought of scandal. He and his wife are supposed to be happily married, and he keeps Elaine in a separate compartment – you know, no demands, no ties.'

'It beats me why women allow themselves to be treated like that.'

'Actually, she doesn't seem to mind. I assume it suits her purposes. And anyway she loves him – or so she says.' James got up and put on his dressing-gown. 'I'll ring her now, before she leaves for work. It'll be easier to talk then.'

'Well don't say too much, you promise?'

'No, I won't. I'll blame the headache, tell her I can't think straight. I *can't*!'

After a few minutes he came back, looking wretched. 'She kept asking what you'd decided. I told her we needed more time to discuss it, but she got rather agitated.'

'Poor woman' Alison muttered, still torn between compassion and annoyance. 'And what about your meeting?'

He gave a puzzled frown. 'Oh, of course – Brian Webster. Mm, yes, she agreed to handle that. I suppose that's one good thing.'

'Well, drink your tea, James. It's getting cold.' The 'blissful' tea in bed seemed to have degenerated into yet another worry session.

James picked up his cup and put it down again. 'Darling,' he said, biting his lip, 'I know this is the most fearful cheek, but would you even consider . . .? No, it isn't fair to ask you.'

No, she thought, it isn't. She drank her tea in a single draught, if only to hide her face.

James tried another tack. 'Do you remember when Prescott said we might have twins as a result of the fertility drugs? We were delighted, weren't we?'

She said nothing. One's own biological twins were a different matter entirely.

'And we always planned a big family.'

'James, for heaven's sake, say what you mean! If you want us to take on Elaine's child, why not come straight out with it instead of dropping all these hints?'

'Because I realize what a lot it is to ask.'

'I'm not sure you do actually. It would change our lives for ever. And as for perjuring yourself, it's complete and utter madness. You could lose your job, land up in prison. It's not fair to me, or Elaine, or either child. When you come to your senses, James, I'm sure you'll see it. I think you're suffering from shock. I do sympathize, honestly. You've had so much on your plate – losing your faith, Cecilia dying, Elaine . . .'

'So you want me to tell her we can't help?' he said listlessly.

She stared at the tea tray: the cloth, the rose, the dainty cups. Trifling things, mere window-dressing. It was so easy to throw words about – words like love, commitment – and so heart-wrenchingly difficult to turn them into action. Yet even without a religion she felt a compulsion to atone; to make reparation to James.

The sun had broken through and a ribbon of light fell across his face. This was the man she loved, the man she could have lost.

She walked to the window, where the glistening roof of the Wendy house caught her eye again. Like their home itself, it was plenty big enough for two children. She drew in her breath, determined to say she would have the two, but the words didn't seem to come. 'James, if I feel I . . . can't do it, would it be so terrible for you? How much does Elaine mean?'

'It's not Elaine. It's her child. Ever since I came up with this plan I've been thinking of it as ours, and now I find it hard to be dispassionate. I almost feel bonded with the baby, just by wanting it so much. That was wrong, too – unfair to you and unrealistic. If there's any excuse at all, I suppose I could say I was so excited by the prospect of a child that it clouded my judgement.' He shifted on the bed, dislodging the book from his lap. 'It seemed . . . well, heaven-sent – a perfect, new-born baby, ours for the taking, more or less. I knew you didn't really want an older child, or one who was handicapped or disturbed. And that appeared to be the only option. Until suddenly we're presented with a ready-made solution – as I saw it, anyway.' He gave an embarrassed laugh. 'You're right – I prob-ably *am* a bit shell-shocked at the moment.'

She felt a twinge of fear. In all the years she'd known him, James had been stable and well balanced and, although he was now confessing to a lapse of judgement, there was no guarantee he had dropped his crackpot schemes. 'James,' she said, 'whatever happens I draw the line at doing anything criminal. Or allowing you to, either. I've told you that already and no way am I going to budge. There must be other methods, surely.

Can't people make private arrangements and bypass the authorities?'

'No. Private placements are illegal.'

'Well, what about legal adoption?'

'I very much doubt they'd let us adopt, unless I say I'm the father. It'd be jumping the queue, you see. Hundreds of other couples have already been assessed, which is a long, expensive process. Well, I hardly need to tell you that. We dreaded it ourselves. And imagine how we'd feel if we'd been waiting years and someone else just muscled in.'

'But if Elaine specifically said she wanted us as the parents?'

'I've gone into that and it won't cut any ice. If they think I'm the father, that's different, but otherwise . . .' He shrugged. 'Besides, if we're going to have a baby of our own it's most unlikely they'll agree. And there's another thing I haven't even mentioned. If we did take on Elaine's baby, either she or I would have to leave Garrard Ross. Otherwise the situation at work would be intolerable.'

'But, James, your whole career . . .?'

'I know.' He rubbed his aching head. 'Still, maybe we ought to move, to solve the other problems.'

'What other problems?' The blood rushed to her face. Could he read her mind – the pressing need to escape both Jim and Craig?

'Well, the Church and Father Peter. I can't go on much longer acting as a Eucharistic minister. I feel the most dreadful hypocrite. And then there's the parish council. We've another meeting tomorrow evening.'

'You'd better still have flu, then.'

He laughed. 'I can't have flu for the rest of my life! Oh, is that the postman?'

'You stay there. I'll go.'

She collected the pile of letters from the mat, opening the one from HarperCollins first. Her friend Joanna, the travel editor, had agreed to read Craig's book, or at least a synopsis and two sample chapters which she had sent off a while ago, pleading for a prompt reply. If Joanna's reaction was favourable and (more important) the book was judged a commercial proposition, she could put the two of them in touch and that would be the end of it. She need never see Craig again.

The opening words – 'I'm sorry' – dashed her hopes. Although Joanna tried to soften the blow by saying she found Craig's idea intriguing and his prose style refreshingly direct, the book, alas, didn't suit the Harper-Collins list.

Alison stuffed the letter back into its envelope. Well, she must send the chapters to the next person she'd lined up – Liz Robertson at Viking. And there was no time like the present. The sooner she could get shot of Craig, the better. He was just too dangerous.

She prepared another envelope and left it on the hall table to post, wishing she could oust him from her mind as well as her life. His crude, aggressive rutting was a world away from the closeness she had felt with James last night; the miraculous sense of safety and belonging, of knowing him through and through, loving every cell and pore. Yet love meant generosity and putting the other person first. Couldn't she go straight back upstairs and say she'd do as he wanted? If only there weren't so many stumbling blocks. Her parents, for example, would think it most peculiar for her to have two babies only a few weeks apart in age. And other people might talk. And she couldn't help resenting the fact that Elaine's baby would be born before hers and spoil all the excitement. Petty considerations, but . . .

The phone rang, intruding into her thoughts. She went to pick it up.

'Oh, hello, Anne. No, you didn't disturb us – we've been up a while . . . Oh, I see. I'm sorry, I really am. I'd like to help, but I'm afraid today's impossible.'

'Who was that?' asked James, coming downstairs with the tea tray. The rose was wilting already, she noticed.

'Anne Tidmarsh. She can't do her stint in the crèche today and asked if I could fill in. I suppose I should have said yes, but I don't think I can cope with any more babies just now!'

He pushed aside her dressing-gown and gave her stomach a proprietorial pat. 'Let's make the most of this one. I'm absolutely tickled pink that I'm going to be a father.'

'You *are* a father. Francis-Francesca is nearly an inch long.'

'Oh, sweetheart!' He kissed her. 'When shall we tell my parents, and Helen and everyone? They'll be thrilled to bits.'

'Well, not today, I beg you, otherwise they'll probably all descend on us. Anyway, we've got to decide on what we say or don't say about . . . you know, not believing any more.'

'Oh Lord, they'll expect us to have the baby baptized. I hadn't thought of that.'

'We'll *have* to move.'

'But where?'

'Scotland? Timbuktu? Actually, we *could* go abroad. Hasn't Garrard Ross got offices overseas? How about Brussels? Linda says it's very civilized there. Or we could go to America, even. How does California grab you? Imagine living in Hollywood!' And thousands of miles away from Craig, she didn't add.

He shook his head. 'I haven't the necessary knowledge. All my experience is in UK tax, and the American system's quite different. Anyway, it really is too far. It wouldn't be fair on Grandpa – another upheaval so soon after Grandma's death.'

'Yes, but if he's going to move in with Helen and Philip . . .'

He hardly seemed to hear her interruption. 'Alison, we can't leave Elaine in the lurch. Whatever we agree about her baby, it would be heartless to waltz off when her life is so unsettled and she's so involved with us.'

'But you just said that you'd *have* to leave the firm.'

'If we take her child, yes. Working with her would cause all sorts of difficulties. But not until it's born.'

Alison poured the cold, stewed tea down the sink. So they were back to Elaine again. Like Rome, all roads led to her. And the more James went into details, the more complicated it became. For the next year or two they would be invaded by social workers and embroiled in endless legal quibbling. All the red tape James had tried to spare Elaine would descend on them instead. Yet James had warned that Elaine might change her mind. So any decision, however high its emotional cost, might fall apart in any case, bringing still more turmoil. But despite feeling worn down by the conflict, she found her conscience nagging her to do the decent thing.

James flicked through his letters and put the bills aside. 'No, I think a transfer back to the London office would be much more realistic. Although actually, it doesn't have to be Garrard Ross at all. I could move into industry – maybe a film company, as you're so keen on Hollywood! Funnily enough, that client of mine at Gryphon Films was saying only the other day that they're looking for a UK tax manager. He more or less offered me the job. I laughed it off, of course, but I could always reconsider.'

She stared at him in surprise. 'Darling, this is very unlike you.' Garrard Ross had been another kind of Church for James – secure, hallowed, patriarchal. It had its rules and hierarchy, its dress code, its traditions. And he had been there ever since he qualified, with no doubts, no criticisms.

He nodded. 'Yes, I'm beginning to realize that I've clung to security, not only in religion but in work. It's time I was a bit more adventurous. Gryphon is based in Soho, which would certainly be a change from Reigate! And we could look for a house in north London, or . . . Blast! There's the phone again.'

'I'll get it. Let's hope it's not Father Peter.'

As she picked up the receiver she heard distant chords on the piano. It was ages since James had played – or she either for that matter. The call over, she walked slowly towards the study, listening to the music: an impassioned, joyful piece which instantly lifted her mood.

James broke off as she came in. 'Well, was it Father Peter?'

'No. Pauline.' She squinted at the music. Brahms, as so often, but *molto vivace* this time. Presumably a celebration of the baby – babies.

'Is she OK?' James asked.

'Yes, fine. She suggested she and Helen and I take Francis out to lunch. I managed to cry off.' She perched beside him on the piano stool. 'Honestly, James, two phone-calls already, and it's not even half past eight. It's a good thing we weren't making love! And Father Peter probably *will* ring later. He's having problems with his database and he uses me as technical support. Look, why don't we go out for the day? There's so much we ought to talk about – Elaine, the Church, the family, whether to move and where – and we'll never do it with these constant interruptions. Besides, it's such a waste to be stuck inside when the sun's shining. Tell you what, let's go down to the coast and treat ourselves to lunch at that place in Pevensey Bay – you know, the hotel on the beach where the Cliffords took us last year. We could be there in just over an hour.'

'Oh, Alison, we can't. I'm meant to be off sick. What if someone spotted us?'

'In Pevensey? It's hardly likely. The sea air will do us good. Blow away the cobwebs. Help us sort things out.'

'But Prue might ring. You know how conscientious she is. She'll probably expect me to sign my letters over the phone!'

'Too bad. We'll put it on answer and she'll assume you're sleeping off your flu.'

'I wouldn't be very happy about . . .'

'James, for goodness' sake! You've just said it was time to be more adventurous. Well, a day-trip to the coast isn't exactly kicking over the traces. Anyway, we're about to make one of the most important decisions of our lives, and it's stupid to do it in a rush, without any chance of peace and quiet. Come on – get dressed and let's get the hell out of here before Father Peter's disk drive packs up or Mrs boring Smith wants a hand with the church flowers!'

28

'Oh, James, aren't you glad we came? It's so peaceful.'

'Mm. Being at the seaside takes me back to my childhood.'

'Well, in that case, we'd better have a paddle after lunch!'

'I doubt if I'll be able to move after lunch. Just look at that dessert trolley. What are you going to have?'

'It's a toss-up between the trifle and the lemony thing.'

'Have both. I intend to ask for apple pie with trifle on top.'

'James, for someone with a bad dose of flu there's nothing wrong with your appetite.'

'Nor yours, my darling. Although *you're* eating for two.'

'Actually you're not meant to do that these days. I've been reading up on pregnancy and the baby. D'you know, Francis-Francesca is still only minuscule, with tiny, tiny arms about the size of an exclamation mark, yet they already have hands with the beginnings of fingers and thumbs.'

He glanced at her stomach with an expression close to wonder, an expression she had noticed several times today. She squeezed his hand in gratitude – and guilt.

'Being pregnant makes me feel sort of . . . serious – grown-up at last, I suppose, and doing something important. Don't you feel the same? Someone else's life depending on yours and being affected by who you are and what you think?'

'Oh, absolutely. It gives you a new sense of purpose. When I realized I'd lost my faith and I assumed we couldn't have children, everything seemed empty.' He broke off as the waiter glided up to collect the plates – a fastidious-looking man in an impeccable black coat and trousers.

'I've been thinking,' James went on, once they were alone again, 'that you can redefine a lot of religious concepts and find new meaning in them. Take heaven, for example. It doesn't have to be a realm in the clouds but a chance here, on earth, to let go of the past and start again with fresh hope and a different goal. And if there *isn't* any other life, this one's all the more precious, especially with a child on the way. Francis or Francesca will be our immortality.'

'It's such a mouthful, Francis or Francesca. Couldn't we just shorten it to Fran?'

'Grandma would turn in her grave!'

'How sad, James, that she'll never see her great-grandchild.'

'Well, she had seven already. And a long and happy life. I do miss her terribly, but I'm coming to terms with it. Yesterday, the more Father Edmund insisted she wasn't dead, the more uneasy I felt. It was so galling that we all had to sit in silence, accepting his version of things. At times I was tempted to jump up and object.'

'Thank goodness you didn't. The others would have had a fit! Anyway, aren't you being rather hypocritical? *You* believed all that until only a short while ago. In fact you were the arch-conservative, condemning any objections out of hand.'

'Alison, that makes me feel really guilty – the way I dragged you into my system of belief.'

'You didn't drag me. It was my own decision.'

'Even so . . .' James paused to eat his last mouthful of bread.

'It's only now I realize that by clinging on so obsessively to one narrow point of view I was lying to myself – which is probably the worst type of lie there is.'

No, she thought, there are worse kinds. She smiled at the little boy at the next table, working his way through a large banana split and smearing ice-cream on his clothes.

James was still talking about religion, his hands cupped around his glass. 'I wanted everything in life to be certain and clear cut. Yet that's impossible. No one really understands time or space or nature, not even scientists. Despite the enormous advances in science, it's still a fact that at least ninety per cent of the universe is dark matter – maybe as much as ninety-nine per cent. Which means we can't even see it, let alone comprehend it. And as for a concept as amorphous as God . . .' He frowned, took a sip of wine. 'You mentioned being grown-up. Well, I realize I've been a child all my life, continually needing someone in authority to spell out what's right and what's wrong. My parents are the same. Although they're both in high-powered jobs and tell other people what to do, they have to have a structure which keeps them secure – fossilized, you could say. They've always hated change. Even Vatican II was anathema to them because it threatened their certainties. Truth for them is tradition and conformity and what the Powers That Be have laid down for all time. But truth evolves. So-called facts are proved false. History is rewritten. Nothing's fixed. I mean, moving from the sublime to the ridiculous, people in the seventeenth century thought fresh fruit was bad for you and nicotine was good.'

'So – who knows? – maybe apple pie with trifle on top will do wonders for your cholesterol level!'

He laughed, but immediately returned to the subject. 'Since I first began to question the faith, it's as if I've made a quantum leap from the Middle Ages to postmodernism in the space of a few weeks. It affects everything I do and am, the entire way I see the world.' Neat as always, he brushed a few crumbs from the tablecloth and put them on his side-plate. 'But I keep wondering how *you* must feel. After all, it's a big upheaval for you as well, to throw the whole thing over.'

'Not so much as you think. I was only really worried about admitting it to you.'

'Oh dear! Am I such an ogre?'

'Of course not.' She gave him a wry smile. 'But religion was your life. For me it never went that deep. Even now, I can see your brain working overtime, like a computer-programmer installing a new software package, busily adjusting and readjusting, tweaking it all into place. *I* don't need to do that. It may sound dreadfully superficial, but I can just shrug and let it go.'

'You know, as you say that, I can almost hear my father's cry of reproach! He was always so intense – dotting every *i*, crossing every *t*, feeling compelled to work out exactly what his views were on every single subject and then to label each compartment in his mind. No wonder I'm like I am.'

A discreet cough interrupted him and the waiter's plummy tones: 'Dessert for you, madame?'

'Er, yes. I'll have the lemon mousse.'

'And for monsieur?'

'Could I be really greedy and have trifle *and* apple pie?'

'Certainly, sir. Separately or together?'

They caught each other's eye and stifled a laugh at his patent disapproval. Their casual clothes seemed all the more remiss in the face of his starched perfection, his pale, disdainful face.

'And coffee to follow?'

'Yes, please.'

Simultaneously, they turned to look at the window as the sun suddenly sailed out again, transforming the whole view; the once drab sea and sky now shimmering silver-blue. Only a pane of glass and a short stretch of springy turf separated them from the shingly beach outside. It was as if they were sitting in a ship, rather than a restaurant, with seagulls drifting past and the clouds so low they seemed close enough to touch.

'See Beachy Head?' James pointed with his spoon. 'We could walk there, if you like.'

'I thought you were too full to move?'

'I could amble, just about!'

'OK. But let's skip coffee and set off straight away. We ought to make the most of the sun.'

However, by the time they'd paid the bill, the sky was overcast again, and when they ventured on to the beach the wind pounced on them with unexpected ferocity, clawing at their clothes, their words.

'Wow!' James shouted against the gust. 'Exhilarating!'

'Lovely!' she shouted back. 'A beach to ourselves.'

'Except for the gulls.'

A flock of terns was sitting on one of the battered wooden groynes which led down to the sea. At their approach the birds lifted off and soared lazily inland. Alison envied them their wings as she crunched along the shingle, the stones dragging at her feet. This part of the coast was basic – no golden sands, no amenities for trippers, just a steeply shelving beach and the constant flurry of the waves chafing against the groynes, throwing up cannonades of spray.

James gazed out to sea. 'It's odd, you know,' he said, 'I've had the occasional twinge of panic at the vastness of it all. I realize that's a cliché, but without a God things do seem chaotic. It's like another sort of bereavement.'

She glanced at him anxiously. 'You feel adrift, you mean?'

'More *open*, I think I'd say – open to everything. I've no intention of calling myself an atheist. Or a mere materialist. Just looking at the sea makes you aware of . . .' He shook his head in frustration. 'It's so hard to find the words. One advantage of religion is that the mysteries have names: the Holy Spirit, the Trinity, the Eucharist. Secular mysteries, if you can call them that, are much more tricky to define.'

'I think you'll always be religious, James. With a small r, anyway.'

'Yes, you're right,' he said, as they tramped on again across the unforgiving stones.

'I need a sense of vision. And majesty and ritual, and all those things religion provides. But they're not exclusive to God. There's art and music, to start with, and nature, of course – wonderful places like this, full of atmosphere and history. Imagine the Normans landing on this very strip of coast!'

'And the Saxons before them. And . . . *Ouch*!' She slipped on a piece of driftwood, almost losing her balance.

'Careful, darling. Don't hurt yourself. This is harder-going than I thought. We'll never make it to Eastbourne. Why don't we turn the other way and walk inland to the castle. I seem to remember a footpath.'

'Yes, we went with the Cliffords, didn't we? And it'd certainly be warmer out of the wind. We haven't had our paddle, though.'

'Don't worry. There'll be plenty of time for paddling when we have a family.'

'A family', he had said, not 'the baby'. In less than eight months' time they could be four, not two. All very well for him – he would be at work while she struggled to show equal love to Elaine's child and her own. Would she be able to cope with two at once? Suppose one was difficult – smaller, frailer, more demanding?

'We ought to discuss it,' James said, as if tuning in to her thoughts. 'That's why I took the day off, after all.'

She remained silent as they left the beach and made their way to the footpath. However selfish it might sound she wanted James to herself, if only for a few hours. Of late he had seemed to belong to Elaine – she, the wife, shut out.

He helped her over the stile. 'I was thinking about it while we were driving down, and I very much doubt if they'll let us adopt if I can't say I'm the father.'

'Well you *can't*, and that's that.' She kept her eye on the solid, grey-stone ruins of the castle, lowering in the distance beneath a stone-grey sky.

'Yes, I appreciate your feelings, but there is an alternative plan. There's no law against us looking after Elaine's baby when it's born, just unofficially, helping out a friend. Then, when it's been living with us a while we can apply for a residence order.'

'What's that?' she asked, trying not to feel bitter that he had made all these detailed inquiries behind her back – for *her* sake, she had to remind herself. The irony was, she couldn't rejoice in her pregnancy because of the implications of Elaine's.

'It gives us parental responsibility. We'd need Elaine's consent, of course, and it would involve a court hearing and probably a court welfare report. But, you see, we're more likely to be allowed to adopt in the end if the child's been with us for a year or so and it's obviously working well.'

'Likely, but not certain, you mean?'

'Nothing's certain, darling. That's the story of my life at the moment!'

And mine, she thought, glancing at the lambs in the fields. Mother-hood was no easier for sheep, who also had their offspring snatched away. If you looked after a child for a year or more, wouldn't it be a terrible wrench to give it up? If only she knew what it would be like to take on someone else's baby. Speculation was all she had to go on. James had mentioned dark matter – amorphous stuff you couldn't even see. Her future was like that: hazy, undefined and full of fear. The idea of court proceedings was terrifying in itself, in case the truth about Craig and Jim somehow came to light. Inevitably, there would be talk of paternity – not a subject she welcomed. And later, when Elaine's child asked about its father, it might prompt similar questions in her own child. Did she lie to both of them?

In single file, they ventured on to the narrow bridge which crossed a drainage ditch, and stood looking down at the water, quilted with green lily leaves.

'It's strange to think all this land was sea once,' James reflected. 'Ships sailing right up to the castle. They say that when it was stormy, spray splashed over the south wall.'

It put things into perspective, she thought, as did the Roman walls, standing massive and forbidding for nearly seventeen hundred years. On such a time-scale her own problems dwindled to pin-pricks – in theory, anyway.

'So how does the plan strike you?'

'I'm . . . not sure.' She could feel the bridge trembling under their weight as she gazed into the murky water: evil-smelling, deep.

In uncomfortable silence they trudged on towards the castle, following the line of another drainage ditch, fringed with tall grasses rustling in the wind. Beyond, stretched a freshly ploughed field, combed in gleaming furrows. Everything was tranquil, except her mind.

'Look, James, I'm sorry. I need more time.'

'I understand. And if you feel it's all too much, then I'll respect your decision – that goes without saying. It's just that we ought to tell Elaine as soon as possible.'

'Yes, I know. But can you give me to the end of the day?'

'Of course.'

'And do you mind if we don't talk about it?'

'But wouldn't it be better if I explained more of the ins and outs?'

She hesitated. As he had said, they were here for that purpose, yet she longed simply to relax. If it weren't for Elaine she could actually *enjoy* life, now that her loss of faith was no longer a problem, nor her failure to find a job. How unfeeling and self-centred, though, to see it in that light.

Elaine herself had no chance of enjoying anything in her wretched situation. 'I'm still so fagged, I can't take much in at the moment. Why don't we look round the castle and discuss it a bit later?'

'OK.'

'Remember that weird old chap we met there last year?' She tried to lighten the mood, lighten James's expression.

'Yes. Descended from William the Conqueror, he said.'

'Well, I suppose he might have been. So might you or I, come to that!'

They entered by the East Gate and followed the path between the ruined walls, a bleak and windswept site, capped by threatening clouds.

James glanced up at the sky. 'It looks a bit ominous. We'd better do the church before the castle. There'll be more shelter there.'

They jogged along the path to the massive West Gate and down the lane to St Mary's, arriving in the porch just as the first drops of rain spattered on the ground.

'That was lucky,' James said, catching his breath. 'We were crazy not to bring coats.'

'Today we *are* crazy. And greedy. Let's treat ourselves to a cream tea before we go home.'

'Good idea.' James scanned a notice in the porch. 'They've had an Easter flower festival. I wonder if it's still on.'

'Yes,' she said, pushing the heavy door of the church. 'You can smell it!' The heady scent of flowers swirled like incense through the nave – swathes of narcissi, lilies, carnations, winter jasmine, softening the sombre grey-green stone. She remembered the church from last year, although then the sun had been shining, which made it look much lighter. Today it seemed rather gloomy, if not cavernous, with its massive rafters and dark oak beams. A muted howling noise was coming from the tower: an effect of the wind, presumably.

James, however, was clearly in his element, gazing up appreciatively at the Norman windows in the south wall of the nave. 'Imagine how cold it must have been in those days, with no glass to keep the draughts out! No wonder they set the windows so high.' He continued along the aisle, stopping halfway to examine the roof. 'Those timbers look incredibly strong. Just think of all they've seen in their time – rebuilding, fires, restoration.' He walked as far as the chancel, turning back to take in the view as a whole. 'I love the atmosphere. You can't beat sanctity and antiquity.'

'You're going to miss churches, James, you know.'

'Yes, especially at Christmas. I can't imagine Christmas Day without Mass. Mind you, we could go to St Etheldreda's, just to hear the choir.'

'Oh, yes, and bring the baby. They say babies respond to music, even in the womb. There's no reason why we shouldn't enjoy the ritual, whether we believe or not.'

'*And* pray. When Grandma was dying I prayed for her, despite the fact that I was already losing my faith. I suppose now I see prayer as a form of energy we direct at people we love, to wish them well and show we care. Who knows – it might even work. Like spiritual microwaves.'

'I'm glad Cecilia can't hear you, James. She'd be horrified.'

'And I know what she'd say about this church.'

'What?'

'The same as she said about all old Anglican churches. "It was ours before they stole it." Henry the Eighth was top of her hate list.'

'Yes, I remember how she had it in for the poor old C of E.'

'It was abhorrent to our whole family,' James laughed. 'Far too woolly and forever changing its mind. And the clergy bending over backwards to accommodate all comers. Only the other day Father was beside himself with fury because he'd heard some homosexual vicar say that theism was dead and the Resurrection was a myth.'

'Maybe *my* father was right after all. Except he went too far the other way. There was no spiritual sense at home, no feeling that some issues were important. And no books or art or music. I want our child to have those things.' Children, she should have said.

'I suppose everything we do could be seen as sacred,' James observed. 'Making love, bringing up a child, eating a cream tea, even. It just needs a shift of emphasis.' He paused to scrutinize the Latin words carved elaborately on the pulpit. 'Whatever we happen to believe, it is amazing how long Christianity's lasted. And you can't argue with its ideals – compassion, social justice, all that stuff in the Sermon on the Mount. And as for loving thy neighbour as thyself, frankly it's inspired. I only wish it were incorporated into every country's constitution! I don't want to go overboard and lose God altogether, but to see Him – *it* – as a force for good within us, rather than a despotic Judge sitting on high.'

She peered into the scarlet mouth of a tulip, its petals black-stippled at the base. James would always be moral, always an idealist. Already he seemed to be constructing a new secular religion.

'I'm sure I wanted to be a priest for completely the wrong reasons. It wasn't just Grandma's chivvying, but vanity on my part; a desire to be up here' – he indicated the worn stone steps leading up to the pulpit – 'with an admiring audience hanging on my every word. There's tremendous theatricality in Catholicism: saying Mass dressed up in all the finery, with a retinue of servers bowing and scraping. It's not that far from show business, which rather appealed to me in my teens, much to Grandma's dismay. She was afraid I'd go off the rails and succumb to the perils of sex. She saw it as her duty to castrate me, symbolically, at least, cut me off from my highly dangerous maleness and make me powerful in a different way. And of course that's what the priesthood does. It's funny, darling, when I first met you, I recognized a . . . a wildness in you, which attracted me enormously.'

'Wildness? But I remember being awfully shy.'

'Maybe. But it was there underneath. And all the more compelling because it had been suppressed in *me* for so long. By the way, talking of priests, Father Gregory asked after you and sent his love. I forgot to tell you before.'

'And what did he have to say about your doubts?'

'Oh, he told me to read Julian of Norwich – you know: "All shall be well, and all shall be well, and all manner of things shall be well." It annoyed me rather. I felt he wasn't taking me seriously. But since then I *have* re-read her, and it struck me again how positive she was. When you think she was a child during the Black Death and saw a third of the population die . . .'

Alison's mind was elsewhere. His previous words had stirred up troubling ripples: wildness, sex, going off the rails.

'When I was younger I felt a great affinity with her.' James leaned back against a pew, gesturing like the priest he almost was. 'She spent so much time battling with the problem of evil – how a God who's both all-powerful and all-good could ever allow suffering and sin. And I did much the same, of course.'

'And did she come up with an answer?' Alison asked, a shade

impatiently. They had enough headaches as it was, without adding those of a fourteenth-century anchoress.

'You have to give her marks for trying! She goes back and forth, worrying at the question like a dog with a bone. And eventually she concludes that sin has no substance.'

'What's *that* supposed to mean?'

'It's part of her mystical insight, arrived at after a pretty arduous quest – God is substance, and sin is the opposite of God, so sin is nothing, in a sense.'

'Isn't that rather a cop-out?'

'Well, actually, St Augustine said the same: evil cannot be substance because all substances flow from God. I suppose another way of putting it is to say that evil is parasitic upon good. The host can exist without the parasite but not the other way round. So there can't be evil without good, and therefore evil has no independent existence.'

'It sounds frightfully complicated.'

He nodded. 'Yes, but it gives her cause for great optimism, because it means that sin can be obliterated without destroying anything that's good.'

If only that were so, she thought: Craig and Jim obliterated, her bond with James unscathed.

'And of course it allows her to hold on to God's promise that all shall be well. Which is precisely the point. The sin and misery of this world will be turned to good account, with none of it wasted or unnecessary. Anyway' – he took her hand, drew her close – 'enough of dear Dame Julian. Now that you're expecting our baby, all isn't just well, it's perfect.'

She found it hard to respond. It would have been unthinkable for the old James to embrace her in a church. 'I'd . . . like to look at the flowers,' she said – an excuse to pull away. 'There's Joseph in his Coat of Many Colours, all done in carnations. Ingenious, isn't it?'

'Mm. A work of art.'

'And here's Moses in the bulrushes.' Babies again. If sin really did have no substance, she too would have cause for great optimism. Both her child and Elaine's had been conceived in sin.

'And look, Noah's Ark,' said James, 'with the rainbow overhead. The flowers are fading a bit, but it's beautifully done.'

She stooped to touch the wobbly ark, recalling the rainbow she had seen in Hunston. Noah's rainbow was a sign of hope. And forgiveness. Perhaps all *would* be well.

'Listen!' James held up a finger. 'The rain's stopped. Shall we have a walk round the graveyard?'

They wandered hand in hand among the headstones. The inscriptions were chastening: so many people cut down in their prime.

'Are you still afraid of death?' she asked, aware of his long-standing terror of hell.

'No. That's another turn-around. All my life I've seen myself as a sinner, in imminent danger of damnation. It's a relief to know I'm actually OK as I am and don't need rescuing or saving.' He plucked a leaf from a shrub and studied its delicate tracery of veins. 'I feel I've achieved a sort of personal resurrection, now that I have the freedom to work out my own values and morality.'

Such freedom was terribly demanding, though, she thought. Much easier to be moral within a set framework of rules and penalties, as James was saying last night.

'Oh, look – a baby's grave.' She deciphered the worn Gothic script: '"Flora May, died 26th September, 1872, aged one year and four months."'

'There's another here, with *three* children – the oldest two and the youngest just six weeks.'

Appalled, she stared at the headstone. Babies were so vulnerable. Her own child might die, or she might miscarry in the next few months and fail to conceive again. She was being foolishly shortsighted in not accepting a second baby. *And* mean-spirited in allowing Elaine to suffer. She had none of James's selflessness. Wild she might be; altruistic not.

'If we're going to see the castle,' he said, 'we ought to get a move on. I don't want to be back too late.'

'Oh, James, let's not rush. Please. It's the first time in ages we've been away from things.' She thought with distaste of what awaited them at home: Francis desolate, Helen pious, more lies and prevarications. 'Couldn't we stay the night? I'd love a room overlooking the sea. That hotel even had four-posters, it said.'

'Darling, it's impossible. I can't take any more time off.'

'Why not? We haven't had a holiday for well over a year. We're both in need of one – and more than just a night. This is a lovely part of the country. We could visit Rye and Hastings and –'

'But we haven't any night things.'

'That's OK. We can buy a toothbrush.'

'Yes, but clothes . . .'

'We'll have a root around the charity shops, like Mum does.'

'I don't want germy second-hand stuff.'

'James, don't be such a fuddy-duddy! This is a chance to prove you mean what you say, about being spontaneous and free.'

'It's not that simple, darling. Elaine's expecting me in tomorrow and I really can't let her down. She's waiting for our decision.'

'We haven't made it yet. Taking on a second baby is a terrific responsibility, and I want it to be a free choice, not because you're pressuring me. Right now, I'm knackered, to tell the truth, but give me a week away and –'

'A *week*? But what about Grandpa?'

'He's got the rest of the family. And half the Esher parish. James, you're not indispensable, you know.'

'I *do* know, but –'

She stopped his mouth with her hand. 'Sweetheart, it's not unreasonable to have one short holiday a year. Let's be undutiful for once in our lives and do something we haven't planned. I'm sure Francis will survive without you. And the office. And Elaine.' She took his hand and tugged him to the lych-gate, stepping over a huge puddle on the path. 'Look, the sun's coming out. Like Noah after the flood. Come on, darling, think of the evening ahead – a tour of the castle, a gluttonous cream tea, then a four-poster bed in the Pevensey Beach Hotel!'

29

'Gosh, look at all this post! We've only been away a week and it's halfway up the front door.'

'Leave it. Let's have a drink.'

'James, you're a reformed character! As a rule you rush to answer the letters before the cases are even unpacked.'

'There isn't a case to unpack this time,' he grinned, dumping two bulging plastic bags in the hall. 'And this lot can jolly well wait. What do you fancy, a whisky?'

'No, orange juice. Booze won't do the baby any good. Actually, I feel a bit of a fraud. I'm supposed to be at the stage when I'm sick even at the sight of food, and instead I'm eating like a horse.'

He put his arms around her. 'You deserve an easy time, after all we've been through trying to get pregnant.'

'I'll miss that four-poster,' she murmured as he slipped his hand inside her blouse and under her breasts.

'Don't worry. It's not the bed that counts.' He placed the lightest of teasing kisses on each eyelid. 'More later,' he promised. 'Sit down and I'll get the drinks.'

'Talking of beds, I've just remembered a dream I had last night. Well, it was the baby's dream, really.'

'What on earth do you mean?'

'I can't quite explain, but the baby seemed to be dreaming through me – I was just the vehicle.'

'What was it about? Milk? Or teddy bears?'

'Oh, no. It was serious. A sort of . . . meditation on being born – the challenge and –'

'It sounds like *your* dream, darling.'

'No, it wasn't. I'm certain of that. I woke up feeling rather strange but with the knowledge that the baby was a distinct person, with its own thought processes and fears, even at this stage. It seemed to be saying I have to respect it, and . . . and listen to it – if you can understand what I mean.'

'Only vaguely, I'm afraid. I envy you, in a way. Being pregnant is such a powerful experience, and men can only guess at what it's like.'

'Well, you're going to be part of it, James. You're coming with me for the twelve-week scan, and you'll be there at the birth of course.' As he handed her a glass of juice she couldn't help smiling at his shirt. 'Honestly, they'd die if they could see you in the office! That pink's even more garish here than it was at the seaside.'

'You bought it, darling.'

'Yes, but who could resist it at only a pound . . . And actually, it rather suits your tan. You've caught the sun, you know.'

'More the wind, I think. I was nearly blown off the cliff at Beachy Head!'

The brief holiday had done them both a power of good. James was more relaxed altogether, and her own worries had diminished. This weekend they had lain in bed instead of going to church – the first time he had ever missed Sunday Mass. A milestone they had celebrated by making passionate love.

'Let's see who's rung,' he said, switching the answerphone to play.

'I expect they're mostly for you.'

They were. He grimaced as Brian Webster's disembodied voice launched into a tirade about some new crisis with the Revenue. Calls from two other clients followed; then Father Peter, reporting a losing battle with his database.

'Back to the fray,' she groaned.

'Don't worry – not for long. When I get a new job I'll make sure it doesn't follow me home. And we'll keep well away from priests!'

'Al, where the fuck have you been?'

They both jumped at Linda's peremptory tone.

'You promised to phone after the funeral. I need advice – pronto. Brace yourself for a shock. Derek's asked me to marry him, for God's sake! Well, should I? Or do I say yes, then change my mind once I've got the ring?'

'I can't believe it,' Alison exclaimed. 'Linda getting *married*! I've simply got to find out what she said. I'll phone her right away – I may just catch her at work. You don't mind, do you, darling?'

''Course not. Go ahead. I'll watch the news.'

She went into the hall, dialling Linda's number with a flicker of apprehension. Friends could change when they got married – as Linda had accused *her* of doing.

'Alison, where've you been? I must have rung half-a-dozen times. Are you all right? I was worried. You were in such a state when I saw you last. And then the funeral, and . . .'

'I'm fine. But never mind me. Tell me about you and Derek. *Are* you getting married?'

'Yes. I must be out of my mind! I can't sleep a wink, although I'm not sure if it's terror or excitement.'

'Both, I expect. Oh, Linda, I'm thrilled! Congratulations.'

'Look, I'm flashing the ring at you down the phone. A diamond not *quite* as big as the Ritz!'

'I can't wait to see it. And when's the wedding?'

'We're talking about mid-June at the moment.'

'But that's less than two months away. You're not exactly hanging about.'

'No. Deliberately. I don't want to get cold feet.'

'Linda, are you sure you –?'

'It's OK – only kidding. Derek's the one for me. At least I hope he is. And if we find it's all a hideous mistake, well, there's always divorce.'

'But, Linda, d'you think it's wise to –'

'Stop fussing! Life's too short. And, listen, we've decided to go the whole hog – morning suits, top hats, three-tier cake, the lot. So naturally we'll be needing you as chief bridesmaid – all dolled up in pink frills, of course.'

'Pink frills on top of a bulge? I'll ruin the photographs.'

Linda lowered her voice. 'Al, can you talk?'

'Mm, sort of.'

'I take it you managed to tell James about the baby?'

'Yes.'

'And . . .?'

'Everything's all right.' Alison was also speaking *sotto voce*. 'But there is a slight complication. It's . . . two babies now, not one.'

'Two? Good God, not twins?'

Alison paused before replying. She would have to get used to explaining the situation, so she might as well start with Linda. It wasn't easy – any more than the decision itself had been. Yet she knew it was the right decision. James's delight was proof enough, and she was happy because *he* was.

Linda, though, seemed uncharacteristically subdued. After a garbled attempt at congratulations, and then commiserations, she finally blurted out, 'Alison, I'm gobsmacked. I . . . I don't know what to say.'

Alison bit her lip. Other people would probably react in the same ambivalent way. Secretly she, too, felt somewhat daunted – before the year was out they would go from being a couple to a family of four. But she was trying to view things positively. The future was full of promise: a new job for James, new home, new lifestyle. All she needed was time to adjust.

'Al, I don't want to speak out of turn, but isn't it an incredible cheek, James expecting you to take on someone else's child?'

'He didn't expect me to do anything. I made up my own mind. And, as he says, we're actually very lucky to have two babies, after all that time assuming we'd never even have one.'

'Look, are you free tomorrow, Al?'

'Yes. Why?'

'I think we ought to talk. Why don't you come up here and I'll take you out to lunch.'

'Great! But please don't try to change my mind. I know I'm doing the right thing.'

'Hm. All I can say is rather you than me. Two at once, for Pete's sake! But let's discuss it over lunch. I'm afraid I have to go now. I'm meeting Derek's family tonight and I'm horribly late already. See you tomorrow. Is half past twelve OK?'

'Fine. But it's *my* treat – I insist. To celebrate your engagement. Congratulations again!'

Alison walked slowly back to the sitting-room, one hand across her stomach. *She* might change as much as Linda. With motherhood, step-motherhood. But she must face the challenge head-on. She owed it to James.

'Well?' he said, turning off the television.

'They *are* engaged and the wedding's in June.'

'Good Lord! That's quick. And to think of all the times I've heard Linda say that wild horses wouldn't drag her to the altar.'

'I'm not sure about an altar, darling. I imagine Chelsea Registry Office would be more her line.'

'Even so . . .' He shook his head in bemusement. 'She'll be having babies next!'

'Never. Not Linda. But she can be a kind of un-godmother to ours. I have a feeling she'll be good at it. She'll say they're loathsome little brats and then spoil them rotten.' She sat next to James on the sofa. 'I'm so pleased for her. Her previous men have always been such shits, and Derek seems a really decent sort. I'm sure you'll like him, darling. Shall we have them over for dinner?'

'Yes, why not? How about the weekend after next? Just a minute, I'll get my diary.' The phone rang as he stood up.

'Francis, I bet,' she said. 'On the dot, as usual. You asked him to ring at half past six, didn't you? Do you want to take it, darling?'

'No, you. I had a long chat with him last night.'

But it was a woman, not a man – a curt voice she didn't recognize. 'I'm sorry, who's that? . . . Oh, *Elaine*. Thank goodness. We've been trying to get hold of you.'

'I wanted James, actually, but you'll do, I suppose.'

Alison was stung by the unexpected rudeness.

'Just give him a message, will you? Tell him not to trouble himself about his stupid fucking plan.'

'What do you mean? We've –'

'Could you kindly let me finish? Thank you. Tell your precious James I've done what I should have done at the outset and –'

'Elaine!' Alison's voice rose in alarm. 'We've made the decision. We *do* want your baby. We tried to phone you several times, yesterday and this morning, but –'

'Well, I'm sorry, you're too late. There *isn't* any baby. I've got rid of it. And in case you're wondering – no, it wasn't very pleasant. I was so far gone they had to induce labour, which meant excruciating pain for hours and hours. And if that wasn't enough, I haemorrhaged badly, and I'm still bleeding like a stuck pig.'

30

'*The accident on the Edgware Road has been cleared, but the traffic's still stop-start, backing up towards Marble Arch . . . On the tube, Central Line delays after an incident at Tottenham Court Road . . . Still no service on the Docklands Light Railway between . . .*'

James switched off the travel news, relieved there were no delays on *his* line. He checked his briefcase one last time, surprised how nervous he felt. Still, it was reassuring to have been called for a second interview and, frankly, with Elaine now back from sick leave, the situation at Garrard Ross was becoming all but intolerable. She had been extremely hostile, and no wonder, after the haemorrhage, which had necessitated another operation within hours of the abortion.

He finished his tepid coffee and rinsed the cup and saucer. He should have gone to see her in person, not phoned from Pevensey. But Alison hadn't wanted him to go; hadn't even wanted him to phone until she'd decided about the baby. In doing so behind her back he had bungled the whole thing.

Standing at the sink, he stared out at the waterlogged back garden. The rain had been relentless this last week. May had started wild and blustery; continued cold and wet. Elaine appeared to blame him even for the weather, on top of everything else. With hindsight he realized how insensitive it had been to tell her Alison was pregnant (especially over the phone), although he'd only done it to explain why it was taking them so long to make up their mind. He should have known she'd jump to the conclusion that they wouldn't want a second baby and that their sudden disappearance for a week's unplanned 'holiday' was callous proof of the fact.

Mac and briefcase in hand, he was on his way out when the phone rang. He was tempted to ignore it – at this hour of the morning it was bound to be for Alison. Although of course it might *be* Alison.

He picked it up and said hello, but there was silence the other end. 'Hello?' he repeated. 'Hello?'

Still nothing.

He was about to hang up when a hesitant voice said, 'You're James, I take it.'

'Who's speaking?'

'Craig Hughes. You won't know me.'

'Well, I do know your name. My wife's been helping with your book. I believe she was very impressed with it.'

'Are you taking the piss?'

'No, of course not. Whatever makes you say that?'

'Because it doesn't look as if there'll *be* a book. Alison says no one wants to publish the sodding thing. Put her on, will you.'

'I'm sorry, Craig, she isn't here.'

'Where is she?'

'She's out for the day.'

'Where?'

'Does it matter?' James was beginning to be annoyed by the man's insistence.

'Yes, it bloody well does. I need to speak to her. *Now!* Is there a number where I can reach her?'

James hesitated. He knew Alison had worked hard on the book, but recently, he gathered, things had ground to a halt and she seemed unwilling to do any more. Understandable, if Craig was always this uncouth. In any case she would be busy enough today showing prospective buyers round White Lodge. 'No, I'm afraid it isn't convenient. She's with my grandfather, and he's in bed, unwell.'

'So what? A quick phone-call won't kill him, will it?'

James bristled. 'It's not just that,' he said coldly. 'She has several people coming to view the house.'

'For heaven's sake, if she can't spare me a couple of minutes, after all I've –'

'Craig, I'm on my way out. I suggest you ring this evening.'

'That's no bloody good – I'll be at work. Listen, I've just had this letter from her. She says the book's been rejected by three publishers, so she thinks I should cut my losses and –'

'I'm sorry if you've been let down. It must be an awful blow. But I'm afraid I haven't time to discuss it now.'

'You *were* taking the piss – that's obvious. You think the book's a load of crap. Just like *she* does. Well, what I want to know is –'

'Look, if I don't leave right away I'll miss my train.'

'Hang on. If you won't give me her number, can't you phone her for me and ask her to give me a ring?'

'No, I can't.'

'Fuck!'

James gritted his teeth as more expletives followed. The fellow was quite appalling. Strange that Alison hadn't said. 'I'll tell her you rang, all right? And now I really must go.'

He was about to put the phone down when Craig's manner changed completely: the aggression disappeared and his voice became almost ingratiating.

James listened in growing bewilderment. 'Craig, *what* did you say?' He must have misunderstood.

'Oh, nothing . . .' There was a pause, and then a brief unnerving laugh. 'I was just wondering if Alison really *is* at your granddad's. I wouldn't count on it. You see, she's got this habit of being – well, shall we say, economical with the truth. She's not always where she says she is. And actually I happen to know . . .'

'Thank you, Mr Egerton. We appreciate your time. And the general consensus here is that you'd be eminently suitable for the job. We do have one other candidate to see, but you'll certainly be hearing from us within the week.'

'Thank *you*.' James forced a smile. 'From what I've seen of the company I think I could fit in very well.' He shook hands with the three men in turn, then was ushered out by the secretary, who accompanied him downstairs.

'Do you know your way?' she asked.

'Yes, thanks. I used to work not far from here.' Long ago. In the days of innocence.

She peered out at the rain. 'It's coming down in stair-rods! You'll get soaked.'

He shrugged. He had left his mac behind in the mad dash to the station. And missed the train, of course.

'I could probably find you an old umbrella, if you like.'

'Don't worry.' What did *she* care if he got wet? It was only feigned concern. How could you trust anyone? Even that bastard Craig was probably lying. Stirring up trouble because he was upset about his precious book. There was no proof, was there? Nothing in black and white. Although insinuations were almost worse. A friend of his, he'd said – a young chap who shared his house who'd taken a shine to Alison.

He blundered out into the street, Craig's soft, snide voice injecting venom like a drip-feed into his head. 'She used to go upstairs to see him . . . stay up there for hours . . . seemed to forget all about my book . . . I'm surprised you didn't realize . . .'

Craig had made his contempt quite clear: the pathetic husband, too stupid to suspect.

Although in fact he *had* been suspicious . . . That night she came home in the early hours with some story about bumping into Jim. And many other times, as well, she had acted out of character. But mistrust between man and wife was wrong, so he had given her the benefit of the doubt, praying for strength, ironically.

He walked blindly on, oblivious to the rain and to the sprays of dirty water thrown up by passing cars. The noise of the traffic seemed to hammer through his skull: Craig's voice again, taunting and insidious. Why should he believe the little creep when he was so obviously a nasty piece of work, malicious and foul-mouthed and obsessed with his damned book? Yet wasn't it peculiar the way Alison had stopped talking about the book? At one time she'd been full of it, regaling him with snippets about Mongolian camel auctions or the precarious life of the Reindeer People, then – silence.

All the misgivings he had suppressed until today began to surface like scum on a fetid pond. Those evenings she'd returned from Craig's, talking too much, unnaturally bright, fussing around with over-elaborate meals – he'd attributed it to her elation at working with an author again, but it was nothing to do with books. And those mysterious pains and headaches she'd developed, which even he could recognize as an excuse to avoid making love. Although hurt at the time, he hadn't made an issue of it – indeed had blamed himself. Yet it was infinitely more hurtful to learn the reason for her rejection: she would hardly want the attentions of a tame, insipid husband when she'd been rutting away with some fly-by-night in Kennington.

He turned on his heel, prepared to go straight home and confront her. No – she wouldn't be there. She was at White Lodge, the dutiful grand-daughter-in-law. Or was she? *She's not always where she says she is.*

Mortified, he stopped, trying to recall how often she'd gone to Craig's bedsit. Bedsit – how convenient. Presumably that loathsome friend also had a bedsit. More repellent images heaved up in his mind: naked sweaty bodies grappling on stained sheets . . .

'Oh, I'm sorry,' he said, realizing he was blocking the way of a woman with a push-chair. He moved aside, but stood rooted to the spot, staring at the baby. Was *that* why she had done it – to get a young man's sperm? According to Mr Prescott, there was nothing wrong with *his* sperm. But it was odd that she should suddenly conceive when Craig appeared on the scene, after they had been trying for years. And also very odd that she hadn't mentioned missing a period. After the disappointment at Christmas, she had promised to tell him if she was even one day late. So if there was nothing to hide, why *hadn't* she told him, instead of waiting all those weeks? Weeks when she'd been working on Craig's book. Or so he'd thought.

He leaned against a shop-front, feeling sick and burning hot, in spite of the pelting rain. A young guy, Craig had said. *How* young, he'd like to know? He remembered Alison saying once that Craig was twenty-two, so if the friend was a similar age he was young enough to be his son, for God's sake. A boy. A stud. Overflowing with testosterone.

His head hurt where it was pressing against the window. Stepping back, he noticed his reflection: transparent, insubstantial, only half a man, wavering and shillying in the glass. Good, Alison often called him. Right now he was capable of murder. If he tracked the little shit down he would throttle him with his bare hands. And murder her, as well. She had let him rejoice in their baby when it might not even be his.

He made himself walk on, suddenly recognizing the building opposite. He was in Charterhouse Street, less than half a mile from St Etheldreda's. He stumbled across the road, ignoring the angry hooting of the traffic. The church would be a refuge, if only from the rain.

By the time he reached Ely Place, the wet seemed to have seeped through to his bones. The close was deserted, thank God: he didn't want to see anyone, nor anyone to see him in this state. He crept into the empty church, closing his eyes and joining his hands, partly from desperation, partly from force of habit. Prayer was still a natural instinct. 'Dear Lord,' he begged, 'make it not true.'

But there wasn't any dear Lord. No one to comfort him, to make things better. How he longed for a God now, an utterly truthful Being, incapable of deception. Unlike humans, whose currency was lies. Even a beloved wife. Beloved . . . For all he knew, their whole marriage had been a lie. She could have had other men right from the beginning. He saw her in her wedding gown, standing in this same church, reciting her marriage vows. More lies.

The door banged and an old man shuffled in, wearing a filthy coat and clutching a bottle. He slumped down in the back pew, grumbling to himself. Perfect company, James thought: another broken man.

He buried his face in his hands. If only he could go back to the time when everything was simple: when he'd been sure of his God. Of his wife.

There was a sound of footsteps at the other end of the church: Brother Paul emerging from the sacristy to prepare the altar for the lunchtime Mass. Could it be one o'clock already? He must get away before the service started. But, as he stood up, the sacristan spotted him and smiled, then hobbled down the aisle towards him.

'Hello, James. How are you? Good gracious, you look drenched!'

'I'm fine,' he muttered irritably. There were worse things than getting wet.

'Well, anyway, this *is* a nice surprise. We don't often see you here these days.'

'I know. It's been ages, hasn't it?' He made a conscious effort to be civil. He had known the old fellow for years – they had even served Mass together occasionally – so the least he could do was exchange a few words. 'I had an appointment in the City this morning. An interview. I'm looking for a new job.'

'Oh, really? I hope it went well.'

'Yes,' he said tonelessly. He had already been offered the job at Gryphon Films, so it might be a question of deciding between the two. A happy position in any other circumstances . . .

'And how's Alison?'

'She's . . . all right.' Probably chatting at this very moment about her pregnancy. The whole family were overjoyed at the news. So what now? Did he tell them the child might not be his? That his wife had slept with . . . *Who?* Not knowing made it worse still. A stranger. A cheap pick-up. Some layabout who was free in the afternoons. Perhaps another barman. Had he got her drunk . . .?

'Well, do give her my regards, James.'

'Yes, of course.'

'And it's good to see you at Mass again.'

He swore under his breath. It would be difficult to leave now; Brother Paul would trot back to Father Gregory and tell him he was here. Well, what was one more Mass, added to the thousands he had attended in his time? Besides, where else could he go? Safer to stay put than storm out in a rage and do something he'd regret.

The church was filling up. People were furling umbrellas and shaking out wet coats. One or two gave him sidelong glances. He must look dreadfully dishevelled: his shirt clinging to his skin, his trousers saturated, water dripping from his hair. But it was Alison's hair he could see, dangling over a stranger's stomach or wound around some stiff, young, thrusting cock.

'In the name of the Father, and of the Son, and of the Holy Spirit . . .'

He started. He hadn't noticed Father Gregory come in. His red vestments meant it was the feast-day of a martyr, although he couldn't recall which one. He had lost all track of dates except in so far as they affected Alison's pregnancy. Last night they had sat side by side looking at the photographs in her book: the foetus at ten weeks – a tiny but recognizable human being, with a perfectly formed body, arms and legs, even fingers and toes. It could turn its head, open its mouth, curl its feet, make a fist. He had gazed at the pictures, entranced. Their child. It *had* been theirs last night.

'The grace and peace of God our Father and the Lord Jesus Christ be with you.'

Despite his agitation, the familiar words of the liturgy enfolded him like the embrace of an old friend. How could he live without a God? Without a wife?

'Brothers and sisters, to prepare ourselves to celebrate the sacred mysteries, let us call to mind our sins.'

'I confess . . .'

He *had* sinned. His lack of sensitivity in dealing with Elaine had led directly to the abortion. And the fact it had been a late abortion was due to his meddling in the first place and trying to change her views. Far from saving a baby, he had put its mother through a terrible ordeal which had left her not just physically weak but bitter and depressed.

'I have sinned in what I have done and what I have failed to do . . .'

True. And not only Elaine. His murderous fury was also a sin, the desire to lash out at his wife. He had been brought up not to judge; to look for extenuating circumstances. Which there were. After all, he had

imposed his faith on her, a faith over-burdened with rules and restraints –
forbidding IVF, indeed striving to control the highly complex reproduc-
tive process with hair-splitting caveats. He, too, had found it frustrating,
but whereas he had grown up in the faith (accepting without question the
concept of an infallible Pope), she had grown up with none, and under
the influence of a father who regarded affairs as a normal part of marriage. Had he expected too much of her, his wild and sensuous Alison?

'*May Almighty God have mercy on us, forgive us our sins . . .*'

Couldn't he forgive her, even if she had let some louse run his filthy
paws all over her? No, he could not. She had promised to be faithful, then
apparently betrayed him. Apparently. Apparently. Suppose it *wasn't* true?
There would be nothing to forgive then. But how would he ever know? If
he asked her outright what had been going on at Craig's place she might
only lie again. Perhaps she had never told him the truth in all their seven
years together, and he'd been fool enough to believe everything she said.

'*Lord have mercy. Christ have mercy . . .*'

Mercy. One of those words seldom heard outside church. Words like
redemption, salvation, forgiveness, which still held such power for him.
What were the alternatives? Hatred, vengeance, an eye for an eye?

A woman went up to the lectern – dark-haired like Alison. In the
seminary, he had studied St Jerome, who condemned women as weak and
corrupt, sources of temptation. He had found such views repugnant. But
now . . .

'*A Reading from the first letter of St John. "My children, our love is not to be
just words or mere talk, but something real and active; only by this can we be
certain that we are the children of the truth."*'

Love and truth were virtues he supported. In principle. In theory. He
remembered all the guff he'd talked in Pevensey about forging a new
morality, and what an inspired ideal it was to love one's neighbour as one-
self. He too was a hypocrite. Except it was sometimes a million times
harder to love a wife than love a neighbour. Yet, if there was no divine
love, human love became all the more important. Flawed it might be, but
it was all they had, both of them.

The Gospel passed him by as he wrestled with his conscience. One
baby had died, wastefully and hideously. Shouldn't the remaining one be
cherished? If he walked out on Alison he would be abandoning her child

as well. But that was the dilemma: *her* child, not his. Possibly, probably. In a fortnight's time he would see it on the scan, listen to its heartbeat. He had planned to have the day off and take Alison out to lunch, to celebrate the first glimpse of their baby.

The Mass continued without him, only the word 'forgiveness' jolting his attention back.

'Do not consider what we truly deserve, but grant us Your forgiveness . . .'

'Forgive us our trespasses, as we forgive . . .'

Could he forgive? Did he have the strength?

People were going up to Communion, mostly men – office workers, City types. He followed in a daze, only hesitating as he approached the altar rails. Without a faith he had no right to receive the sacrament. And yet . . .

Father Gregory gave him a brief smile of recognition as he placed the Host in his hand. 'The body of Christ.'

'Amen,' he responded. Amen – so be it; an assent. Could he assent to betrayal and uncertainty, or did he get the hell out and leave the baby fatherless? He couldn't see an idle lout of twenty-odd providing for a child he didn't know existed. And if he was anything like Craig, what a deplorable father he would make.

'May the blessing of Almighty God, the Father, the Son and the Holy Spirit, come upon you and remain with you for ever.'

He crossed himself, moved by the beauty of the words, the power of the blessing – a power and beauty now lost to him.

'The Mass is ended. Go in peace.'

Fat chance of peace, feeling as he did. The Mass had calmed the worst of his fury, but a deep bitterness remained – perhaps would never leave him.

People were filing out of the church, returning to their offices. He could go too; back to Garrard Ross for the afternoon and evening. Workaholism was in his genes, but it was time for change; a terrifying concept that certainly *wasn't* in his genes. Change meant entering the unknown. The future couldn't be controlled. He would never know if his wife had been unfaithful (with Craig's friend or even other men) or if the child was his. Was it possible to live with that?

He stayed in his pew, alone again with the poor wretch across the aisle, who was slurping from his bottle and seemingly unaware that a religious service had even taken place. Looking at the man's ravaged face, he felt ashamed of his own self-pity. Were she still alive, his grandmother would have told him sternly to count his blessings. And she was right. He was lucky to have money, a home, a job; and yes, a wife and child if he so wished. It was up to him. He could go home and say nothing – kiss his wife, bless his child. But he was frightened of losing control when he saw her, perhaps hitting out in anger and revulsion.

He felt a hand on his shoulder. Father Gregory had returned to switch off the lights. 'Ah, James, I hoped you'd still be here. How are you?'

'I'm . . . OK, Father.'

'Well, if you need to come and see me again, don't hesitate.'

About his doubts, that meant. But he had acquired altogether different doubts today and would never again be free of them.

'You look tired, James. Are things all right at home?'

'Yes. In fact, I . . . I meant to tell you, Alison's expecting a baby.'

'But that's wonderful!' Father Gregory embraced him in delight. 'So you're going to be a father at last!'

He nodded.

'Do tell Alison how pleased I am. Congratulations to you both.'

'Thank you, Father.'

'Well, I'd better be off. Someone's coming to see me in ten minutes. All the best.'

'Thank you,' James repeated, reflecting on his words: 'So you're going to be a father at last.' He had longed for fatherhood, and this might be his only chance. If he left Alison, he'd be alone, like Father Gregory: no love, no sex, no child. For five years he had prayed for a child, and now his prayers had been answered in the most perverse, ironic fashion. Yet answered, none the less. There was still a baby in need of a father, a child which might be his. And it *would* be his, if he brought it up, cared for it and cherished it, as he had planned to do with Elaine's child. Recently he had pondered on what faith might mean without a God. A commitment to love, he had concluded, a search for meaning, a determination to shape the future rather than simply letting it happen, to contribute something positive to the world. What would his contribution be? Acceptance of a poor defenceless baby, who hadn't asked to be conceived and who had a right to two responsible parents? Or a broken marriage? A broken child?

The tramp had started coughing – a dry, irritating cough, hacking on and on, violating the silence of the church. James moved further forward. With such a crucial decision to make he wanted no distractions.

Slipping into a pew near the front, he sat down, feeling drained. Above him stood the statue of St John Houghton, whose feast-day, he remembered now, it was. He and his fellow Carthusian priors had endured vastly more than the betrayal of love: hanged on Tyburn Tree after being dragged through the streets on hurdles, yet going to their death, it was said, as joyously as bridegrooms to their wedding.

'Lord, give me their courage,' he prayed, and this time it was a genuine prayer, although still one of desperation. 'Help me to do right.'

Next month he would be forty, and maturity meant acknowledging pain and uncertainty as facts of life. He was faced with a stark choice: peace or war, love or hate. If he wanted peace he must make it for himself. If he wanted love he must salvage it. Despite everything, he couldn't stop loving Alison. And she had suffered more than he during the years of infertility, through the drugs and treatments, the loss of her job and her confidence. And suffered acutely these last weeks, blaming herself for Elaine's abortion. But that was *his* fault, not hers. By interfering and trying to play God, he had done enormous harm. And now he was behaving like a Pharisee, condemning deception in his wife when he had himself contemplated perjury. What arrogance. Yet in Pevensey he'd told her blithely that he was no longer a sinner in need of saving. Wrong again. The anger inside him was threatening to explode into violence, and violence was a sin in any scheme of things.

'Forgive me,' he murmured, not sure if he was addressing God, Alison, Elaine – or even Craig's unspeakable friend, whom he had wanted to consign to hellfire. How could he trust himself to do right when he was in the grip of such emotions? It was no good being grudging or half-hearted. If he accepted the child as his, then he must love it – and its mother – without reservation; create a harmonious home and a happy marriage by giving Alison the benefit of the doubt again, this time for as long as he should live.

'Help me, Lord,' he repeated, 'help me find the strength.'

'You *have* the strength.'

Startled, he looked around the church. No one had spoken. No one was there but the drunken tramp, and even his coughing had subsided. His imagination must be playing tricks.

'The Mass is ended. Go in peace.'

The voice again. He stumbled up to the altar-rails and knelt there in confusion. Hearing voices was a sign of madness. Yet he did suddenly feel a singular peace, as if his rage had been excised from him like a tumour. He sat listening to the silence. The hubbub of the City never penetrated these walls. It was a true sanctuary, a haven. Even the fury of the rain was transmuted to a gentle murmur, lulling to his soul. Could he be wrong about his lost faith – as he'd been wrong about so many things – and there was a God after all, a God who had answered his prayer?

He gazed up at the great east window with its angels and saints, its Christ in Glory. Alison would probably never understand how deep was his hunger for religion. St Etheldreda's embodied all he craved: beauty, ritual, symbolism, tradition, immortality. Whatever his belief, it was a place of holiness – wholeness; a place where good could triumph, evil be overcome. There was no proof of the existence of God, nor any proof against it – nothing conclusive either way. Yet even in the Pevensey church (on the very day he'd been holding forth about his new agnostic stance) he had experienced a sense of the divine. And their discussion then about Julian of Norwich – how sin and suffering could be turned to good account – had now become extraordinarily apt, and imbued with a deep personal significance. Could those words, returning at this critical moment, have come to him from God?

He shook his head impatiently. The Almighty (if He were there) would have more pressing concerns than this sordid little crisis. Yet why else should he feel so different – transformed, he might almost say? It was impossible to explain. All he knew was that somehow he'd been healed, and that pain and sin were an essential part of the healing – built into it and, in Dame Julian's word, 'behovely'.

Rising from his knees, he paused in front of the statue of St Anne Line, a seamstress, executed for sheltering a priest. Had her torments been in vain, or was she even now rejoicing? She looked anything but joyful – instead anxious and irresolute with solemn face and haunted eyes.

Indeed it struck him for the first time that *all* the statues had a pre-occupied expression, as if even saints and martyrs were aware of the myriad uncertainties in death as well as life.

Honouring their courage with a respectful nod, he continued down the aisle, his bewildered shadow preceding him. Mystery was the key: acceptance of the unknowable, of doubt, conjecture, paradox.

He was so lost in thought as he left the church that he nearly collided with Brother Paul coming the other way along the passage.

'I've just heard your news,' the sacristan beamed, clasping James's hand. 'Well I never! So you're going to be a father, James.'

'I *am* a father,' he said, slowly and deliberately, requiring the statement to be witnessed. A committed father, devoted to their child. *His* child, his future, his immortality.

Outside, the sky remained overcast, but there were a few glints of light to the east. He stood looking up, looking up; willing the light to intensify and banish any last remaining darkness from his soul.

Then, walking slowly on, he picked his way between the puddles to the end of Ely Place and crossed the busy junction at Holborn Circus. He stopped at the next set of lights, wincing as the yowl of a siren rose above the general roar of traffic. Yet, even amidst the din, he could still hear the faintest echo of the voice – the voice he'd heard in the church, or thought he'd heard, or deluded himself he'd heard. A reassuring voice; indeed a promise:

> *'All shall be well, and all shall be well, and all manner of things shall be well.'*

Acknowledgements

I am profoundly grateful to the many people who helped me on various aspects of this book.

On church and religious matters, Father Kit Cunningham, Rector of St Etheldreda's, Ely Place, London, and his Sacristan, Linda Helm, both of whom answered my queries with unfailing generosity and good humour – as did my ever-patient brother-in-law Father Bobbie Gates, and James Cross, Brother of the Little Oratory. Also Father Philip Jebb, Prior of Downside, and Father Michael Hopley of Ealing Abbey, for their insight into the Benedictine way of life; Jim Byrne, Head of Theology and Religious Studies at St Mary's University College, Strawberry Hill, who gave up much of his valuable time reading my first draft, and Dr Robin Gibbons, also of St Mary's; Margot and Terry Durkin and their fellow parishioners in Merrow, and Gay and Nick Woodward-Smith and family.

On publishing matters, my agent Jonathan Lloyd, and editors Patricia Parkin, Elspeth Taylor, Mary-Rose Doherty and Georgina Hawtrey-Woore.

On accountancy and taxation, Tony Austin, Michael Collins and Andrew Hayes – the first accountants I've met who didn't charge me a penny!

On medical matters, gynaecologists Andrew Riddle, John Kelly and Alan Gillespie; my GP, Dr Gabriel Steer, for advice beyond the call of duty, and Michael Jarmulowicz of the Guild of Catholic Doctors.

On Mongolia, Humphrey Hawksley, the BBC foreign correspondent.

A debt of gratitude is also due to Mary Gandy of the Catholic Child Welfare Council; Jenny Lord, Child Placement Officer at BAAF; Ather Mirza, Director of Press Relations at Leicester University; and Michael and Kay Nash, Church Watch at St Mary's, Westham.

And last but very much not least, heartfelt thanks to Keith New, Judith Clifford and Dr Christine McAuley.